Pride, Prejudice & Pleasure

JANE AUSTEN

and

EM BROWN

BOOK ONE

CHAPTER ONE

Lizzy woke with a start, her body flushed, her heart beating in her ears, and that intimate space between her legs tingling. To her consternation, instead of the privacy of her own bedchamber at Longbourn House, she found herself bumping along inside a chaise, seated opposite Sir William Lucas and his second daughter, Maria. To Lizzy's relief, her travelling companions were fast asleep, with Maria snoring away as loudly as her father. Had they been awake, they could not have seen into her mind, but she blushed nonetheless to think they might have witnessed her in the throes of a most unladylike dream. Winter had yet to give way to spring, but she unbuttoned her pelisse to release the warmth she felt.

Of all men to infiltrate her dreams, especially one of a most prurient nature, why *him*? She could not have been more rattled and vexed had she dreamt of her cousin, Mr. Collins. Nay, that would have been appalling. She chided herself for summoning such a revulsion to mind. Shuddering, she looked out the window of the chaise, desperately seeking some visual fodder—an interesting formation of rocks, a remarkably tall tree, or a shapely cloud—to replace the vision in her head.

Why could she not have dreamt of George Wickham? That would have been comprehensible. Though he presently pursued another, and her own attachment had subsided, she found him no less amiable or handsome. Their farewell had been perfectly friendly.

Instead, she had dreamt of the one man whom she disliked above all others; the one man she could do without and who, despite his intelligence and articulation, offered nothing, not even the value of amusement afforded by Mr. Collins, when she was able to put aside her exasperation of his personality and observe him with the calm *à la* her father; this so-called gentleman, whose absence she had enjoyed through winter and whom she was not likely to ever see again, if Caroline Bingley was to be believed that they were never to return to Netherfield; and the last individual on earth to waste her thoughts upon now that she had, at least in her mind, bid good riddance to the lot of them.

Mr. Fitzwilliam Darcy.

Perhaps the stress of the journey had seeped into her subconscious, though she had been in good spirits since leaving London, where they had stopped to see her aunt and uncle, the Gardiners, and her sister, Jane, who was staying with them. Jane had looked well enough as to banish all fear for her health, and Mrs. Gardiner had invited Lizzy to tour the northern lakes later in the year. Lizzy was all excitement and good cheer until her dream.

The reverie had begun pleasantly enough. She was lying upon a bed in a luxurious room, a nameless young man seducing her with soft kisses upon her neck. She could feel the ache in her nether region blooming into the most beautiful of sensations. He began untying the top of her stays, then lowered his head to address his lips to the swell of her bosom. What delightful shivers attended this caress! But when he lifted his head to meet her gaze, the face of Mr. Darcy flashed before her.

It was awful. Like finding a spider in one's pudding. Her state of arousal coupled with his physiognomy was an unnerving pairing. Like instruments playing in discordant keys, the two should never simultaneously occupy the same space. She would sooner listen to Sir William recount the *wonders* of his presentation and knighthood for the hundredth time or suffer the many laments of her mother for having turned down the marriage proposal of Mr. Collins, thereby sending him into the arms of Charlotte Lucas, than to have that dream reoccur.

She disdained Mr. Darcy, and she was not alone in her sentiments toward him. Though many a gentlemen had pronounced Mr. Darcy a fine figure of a man and the ladies declared him much more handsome than even Mr. Bingley, and both sexes had initially looked at him with great admiration for his fine, tall person, handsome features, noble mien and the report of his having ten thousand a year, his manners had quickly turned the tide of his popularity. He had been discovered to be proud, to be above his company and above being pleased. Not all his large estate in Derbyshire could then save him from having a most forbidding, disagreeable countenance and being unworthy to be compared to his friend Bingley. Charlotte had been the only person to express his right to be proud as he was "so very fine a young man, with family, fortune, and everything in his favour."

Mr. Darcy's initial affront to Lizzy had engendered no cordial feelings toward him, but her lively, playful disposition, which delighted in the ridiculous, had compelled her to tell the story with great spirit among her friends:

Due to the scarcity of gentlemen at a ball, Lizzy had been obliged to sit down for two dances, and during part of that time, Mr. Darcy had been standing near enough for her to hear a conversation between him and Mr. Bingley, who had come from the dance for a few minutes to press his friend to join it. In contrast to Darcy, Bingley was all affability and politesse.

"Come, Darcy," he had said, "I must have you dance. I hate to see you standing about by yourself in this stupid manner. You had much better dance."

"I certainly shall not. You know how I detest it, unless I am particularly acquainted with my partner. At such an assembly as this it would be insupportable. Your sisters are engaged, and there is not another woman in the room whom it would not be a punishment to me to stand up with."

"I would not be so fastidious as you are for a kingdom! Upon my honour, I never met with so many pleasant girls in my life as I have this evening, and there are several of them you see uncommonly pretty."

"*You* are dancing with the only handsome girl in the room," Mr. Darcy had said, looking at the eldest Miss Bennet, Jane.

"Oh! She is the most beautiful creature I ever beheld! But there is one of her sisters sitting down just behind you, who is very pretty, and I dare say very agreeable. Do let me ask my partner to introduce you."

"Which do you mean?"

Turning round he had looked for a moment at Lizzy, till catching her eye, he withdrew his own and coldly said, "She is tolerable, but not handsome enough to tempt *me*. I am in no humor at present to give consequence to young ladies who are slighted by other men. You had better return to your partner and enjoy her smiles, for you are wasting your time with me."

His very *real* slight of her had produced only the briefest and most inconsequential anguish, but her most *unreal* dream disturbed her greatly. She shivered as if doing so could discard the awkwardness of it all before settling back into her seat. Though she had parted London wistfully, having much enjoyed the company of the Gardiners and Jane, and though it was unlikely Mr. Darcy would have ever ventured as far from Grosvenor Square as Gracechurch Street, she was glad she had not stayed in the city long enough for their paths to cross. If she did not see that man for another ten years, it would be a day too soon.

CHAPTER TWO

When they left the high road for the lane to Hunsford, every eye was in search of the Parsonage, expecting it come into view at every turn. The palings of Rosings Park was their boundary on one side, and once more Mr. Darcy flitted unwanted through Lizzy's thoughts for it was his aunt, Lady Catherine de Bourgh, who resided at Rosings. Wickham had had little in the way of compliments for her ladyship and daughter, who was said to be as good as betrothed to Mr. Darcy. For a moment, Lizzy was struck with a premonition that she had not seen the last of that proud and disagreeable man, but Mr. Darcy was in London, and it would be too much the coincidence for him to visit Hunsford during her time.

At length they discerned the Parsonage, standing between green pales and laurel hedges. Mr. Collins and Charlotte appeared at the door, and the carriage stopped at the small gate which led by a short gravel walk to the house. In a moment they were all out of the chaise, rejoicing at the sight of each other. Mrs. Collins welcomed her friend with the liveliest pleasure, and Lizzy was more and more satisfied with coming when she found herself so affectionately received. She saw instantly that her cousin's manners were not altered by his marriage; his formal civility was just what it had been, and he detained her some minutes at the gate to hear and satisfy his inquiries after all her family. After pointing out the neatness of the entrance, Mr. Collins took them into the house. As soon as they were in the parlour, he welcomed them a second time, with ostentatious formality to his humble abode, and punctually repeated all his wife's offers of refreshment.

Lizzy was prepared to see him in his glory, and she could not help in fancying that in displaying the good proportion of the room, its aspect and its furniture, he addressed himself particularly to her, as if wishing to make her feel what she had lost in having refused his hand. But though everything seemed neat and comfortable, she was not able to gratify him by any sigh of repentance, and rather looked with wonder at her friend that she could have so cheerful an air with such a companion. When Mr. Collins said anything of which his wife might reasonably be ashamed, which certainly was not unseldom, Lizzy involuntarily turned her eye on Charlotte. Once or twice she could discern a faint blush, but in general Charlotte wisely did not hear. After sitting long enough to admire every article of furniture in the room, from the sideboard to the fender, to give an account of their journey, and of all that had happened in London, Mr. Collins invited them to take a stroll in the garden, which was large and well laid out, and to the cultivation of which he attended himself. To work in this garden was one of his most respectable pleasure, and Lizzy admired the command of countenance with which Charlotte talked of the healthfulness of the exercise, and owned she encouraged it as much as possible. Mr. Collins led the way through every walk and cross walk and scarcely allowed them an interval to utter the praises he asked for. Every view was pointed out with a minuteness which left beauty entirely behind. He could number the fields in every direction and could tell how many trees there were in the most distant clump. But of all the views which his garden, or which the country or kingdom could boast, none were to be compared with the prospect of Rosings. They could see the house, a handsome modern building well situated on rising ground, through an opening in the trees that bordered the park opposite the front of the Parsonage.

Lizzy learned that Mr. Collins' patroness, Lady Catherine, was still in the country. It was spoken of again while they were at dinner, when Mr. Collins joining in, observed,

"Yes, Miss Elizabeth, you will have the honour of seeing Lady Catherine de Bourgh on the ensuing Sunday at church, and I need not say you will be delighted with her. She is all affability and condescension, and I doubt not but you will be honoured with some portion of her notice when service is over. I have scarcely any hesitation in saying she will include you and my sister Maria in every invitation with which she honours us during your stay here. Her behaviour to my dear Charlotte is charming. We dine at Rosings twice every week, and are never allowed to walk home. Her ladyship's carriage is regularly ordered for us. I *should* say, one of her ladyship's carriages, for she has several."

"Lady Catherine is a very respectable, sensible woman indeed," added Charlotte, "and a most attentive neighbor."

"Very true, my dear, that is exactly what I say. She is the sort of woman whom one cannot regard with too much deference."

The evening was spent chiefly in talking over Hertfordshire news, and telling again what had already been written. Afterwards, in the solitude of her chamber, Lizzy reflected upon Charlotte's degree of contentment and had to acknowledge she bore her husband very well. Lizzy climbed into bed with hopes for a deep and dreamless slumber, but her contrary and perverse mind *would* dwell on questions best left unasked. Though she had no desire to know the particulars of what Mr. and Mrs. Collins did behind closed doors, she could not help but wonder if matters of the bedchamber were as consonant with what she was able to observe? She wondered that any woman could be excited by Mr. Collins, but perhaps the wifely duty of submitting to a husband's attentions was no more unbearable than the other chores one was expected to perform on a regular basis. Lizzy could not help but be saddened by such a prospect. If the corporal harmony between a man and wife should ever find easy allowance as a topic of discussion, her mother would doubtlessly dismiss with a snort the need to inquire into such a useless subject and Jane would dampen its importance beneath other qualities, such as the moral character of a husband or his level of affection for wife and family. But Lizzy had not Jane's virtues nor Charlotte's practical nature. Perhaps she was alone in the force of her corporal passions. For herself, she could not reconcile to a marriage that did not fulfill in all the important qualities, including what must transpire in the bedchamber.

Her hand crept beneath the hem of her nightshift, and without thought, she grazed her fingers along the softness of her inner thigh. With a sigh, she gave into the concupiscence that had taken a hold of her of late. The first stirrings of desire had come upon her at a tender age, and she had on occasion allowed the passions to overcome her better judgment—twice with a rugged young footman named Francis and once with a barrister and friend of the Lucas family. Both men, fortunately, had not stayed in Hertfordshire. She dreaded that her indiscretions should somehow come to light, not for its impact upon her but the damage it would do to her family. Thus, for the better part of recent years, she had suppressed these inauspicious cravings until coming across *Memoirs of a Woman of Pleasure* a few months ago.

She had found the illicit edition at the home of Sir William on a night when the Lucases were hosting a dinner for a number of officers from the regiment stationed at Meryton. Having a vague notion of the banned novel, she had at first been tempted to leave the book where it had fallen upon the ground in the corridor, but she could not leave it to be found by one of the Lucases' younger children. Inquiring among the guests to see who would claim ownership would have proved too awkward, so she had picked up the story of Fanny Hill.

Compelled by curiosity and a fondness for reading, she had taken the book into the nearest room, Sir William's library. Most of the party had gathered in the drawing-room for cards, and in the library, she was assured of solitude. Beside a lone lamp, she opened the book with every expectation of reading no further than the first few pages to confirm the worthlessness of the work and justification for the prosecution of its author, John Cleland. Instead, she found, much like Fanny Hill in her first licentious experience, that the obscenity intrigued more than disgusted her. She flushed reading the passage of that first encounter between Fanny and Phoebe, and her own body responded in the most unsettling way with that warm aggravation in her loins and moistness between her legs.

"There you are!"

Startled, Lizzy dropped the book and hastily retrieved it to set it, face-down, upon the table beside her, regretting that she had not checked to see that the library doors had been tightly shut.

"I fear you must find the company of my regiment disappointing," Wickham remarked.

The sparkle in his eyes made her cognizant of the weakness of her sex, and she once more admired how dashing he appeared in his bright red coat and white trousers encasing his legs in a tight fit.

"Not at all! I am sorry to give that impression," Lizzy replied. "I was merely replacing a book that I had found in the corridor."

"Ah, that is some relief," he said, advancing toward her. "There is talk of dancing. I think Sir William cannot long refuse your sisters."

"For Lydia and Kitty, no party is complete without dancing."

Wickham gave a gracious smile. "You are not opposed to the activity…I hope?"

Her breath caught. Did he have an interest in dancing with her? He had often shown a preference for her company, and she had accepted his attentions with much agreement.

"Not at all," she found herself repeating. She was happy to join Wickham but wanted a moment to calm the lust her reading had provoked. "I will be in attendance shortly."

She wondered what she would do with the book. Should she leave it in the library and retrieve it later?

"Allow me to replace the book for you," Wickham offered and picked up the book before she could stop him.

"That won't be necessary," she said quickly and tried to pluck the book from his hand. Their fingers brushed, and a palpitation went through her.

He did not relinquish the book but dropped his gaze to her hand, which half-covered his. In doing so, he saw the title. The surprise on his face was evident, and Lizzy felt the flush in her cheeks deepen.

"This is...Sir William's?" he asked.

"I think not," she confessed. "I found it and—and meant to—"

"Read it."

"No!"

"You appeared to be reading it when I walked in."

She dropped her hand and took a step away from him.

He took a step toward her. "Please, I did not mean to offend. I find it remarkable that one of the delicate sex would dare consume the contents of such a book."

This unexpected compliment and the sincerity of his tone thawed her guard, and she was prepared to be amenable to him once more.

"We are not so delicate as your sex would believe or wish, but I am not familiar with the work of Mr. Cleland, so I cannot know if courage is required to read it. I found the book in the corridor and suspect it belongs to one of your brother-in-arms?"

He glanced from the book back to her and, taking her hand, placed it in her grasp. They stood with mere inches separating them. Her breath became uneven, and it seemed his did, too.

"I confess I am intrigued to know your thoughts on what you have read," he said, lowering his head for his voice had become husky and lower in quality.

She hesitated for she worried her voice would waver too much. "Mr. Cleland clearly intends to titillate the reader."

"And do you find he is successful in his aim?"

He had lowered his head to such a degree that she could not comfortably focus upon the whole of his countenance, so she fixed her gaze upon his mouth. His nearness had scattered her thoughts, and she replied, without advanced contemplation, "Perhaps."

The word emerged as a whisper and appeared to undo him. The pupils of his eyes melted, and she was quite certain he would move to touch her, wrap his arm about her waist and perhaps even attempt to kiss her. And she would not deny him if he did. She hoped he would.

"Wickham! Wickham, where have you gone off to?"

Above the deep thudding of her heart, Lizzy heard the giggling of her younger sisters in the corridor.

"Such an exasperating man!" Lydia grumbled.

"We must not be found," Lizzy whispered, pushing her skirts down as she sat up. She was no less disappointed than he, but perhaps it was all for the best.

"Go," Lizzy urged him after taking a breath to cool her ardor. "I think Lydia and Kitty will not rest till they have found you."

He straightened and his disappointment seemed to match hers.

"Will you join us then? Or do intend more reading?" he asked.

She gave him a stern look, but she could not be angry when his eyes glimmered so bewitchingly. "I must properly dispose of this book first."

"Have you no wish to further discuss its merits?"

She made no reply, but her lips curled faintly in a smile. She watched him take a deep breath before facing the library doors and exiting. A minute later, she heard Lydia exclaim, followed by much prattling before the voices faded down the corridor.

The naughty novel found its way back home with Lizzy later that night. In the end, she had finished the book faster than she had read any other. Though she had often thought to dispose of the book and worried that it might be accidentally discovered, she had retrieved it as many times to read certain passages a second or third time. Her body had reacted at every reading. The ribald and bawdy scenes had left her breath heavy and induced a lively pressure between her legs. The author had composed all manner of lechery: orgies in which couples bore witness to one another in the act of congress, a man aroused by the deflowering of virgins, and one in which the act of flogging aided titillation. The more she dwelt upon the contents, the more her curiosity grew.

Her mind turned frequently also to that evening in the library with Wickham. Her pulse quickened whenever she relived the moment.

Alas, they would not get to reprise the scene. The following day brought a devastating letter from Mr. Bingley's sister, Caroline, and Lizzy felt it necessary to attend her heartbroken sister.

The whole Netherfield party—Charles Bingley, his sisters, and Mr. Darcy—had quit Hertfordshire rather suddenly a few weeks prior. The very first sentence of Miss Bingley's subsequent letter to Jane conveyed the assurance of their being all settled in London for the winter, and concluded with her brother's regret at not having had time to pay his respects to his friends in Hertfordshire before he left the country.

Hope was over, entirely over. When Jane could bear to read the rest of the letter, she found the contents chiefly comprised of praise for Mr. Darcy's younger sister and Caroline boasting joyfully of her brother's increasing intimacy with Miss Darcy. Lizzy heard it all in silent indignation. Her heart was divided between concern for her sister and resentment against all others. To Caroline's assertion of her brother's being partial to Miss Darcy she paid no credit. That Bingley was really fond of Jane, she doubted no more than she had ever done; and much as she had always been disposed to like him, she could not think without anger, hardly without contempt, on that easiness of temper, that want of proper resolution, which now made him the slave of his designing friends, and led him to sacrifice of his own happiness to the caprice of their inclination. Had his own happiness, however, been the only sacrifice, he might have been allowed to sport with it in whatever manner he thought best, but her sister's was involved in it. Whether Bingley's regard for Jane had really died away, or were suppressed by his friends' interference; whether he had been aware of Jane's attachment, or whether it had escaped his observation; whatever were the case, her sister's situation remained the same, her peace equally wounded.

Jane's grief was not helped by her mother, who still continued to wonder and repine at his returning no more, and though a day seldom passed in which Lizzy did not account for it clearly, there was little chance of Mrs. Bennet ever considering it with less perplexity. Her daughter endeavoured to convince her of what she did not believe herself, that his attentions to Jane had been merely the effect of a common and transient liking, which ceased when he saw her no more; but Mrs. Bennet's best comfort was that Mr. Bingley must be down again in the summer.

Mr. Bennet treated the matter differently. "So, Lizzy," said her father one day, "your sister is crossed in love, I find. I congratulate her. Next to being married, a girl likes to be crossed a little in love now and then. It is something to think of, and it gives her a sort of distinction among her companions. When is your turn to come? You will hardly bear to be long outdone by Jane. Now is your time. Here are officers enough in Meryton to disappoint all the young ladies in the country. Let Wickham be your man. He is a pleasant fellow, and would jilt you creditably."

Lizzy coloured. "Thank you, sir, but a less agreeable man would satisfy me. We must not all expect Jane's good fortune."

"True," said Mr. Bennet, "but it is a comfort to think that whatever of that kind may befall you, you have an affectionate mother who will make the most of it."

In Mr. Darcy's absence, the whole of his crimes against Mr. Wickham was made publicly known. Wickham had in his first meeting with Lizzy recounted how he and Mr. Darcy had grown up together, how Wickham's father had provided an invaluable service to the late Mr. Darcy in caring for the family's property, and how the late Mr. Darcy had promised to provide for young Wickham by bequeathing to him the position of pastor and its valuable living. The present Mr. Darcy had chosen not to honour the intentions of his father and presented the position to another man.

Shocking. Dishonest. Abominable.

Lizzy had uttered these words and remarked that Mr. Darcy deserved to be publicly disgraced for such a malicious and inhumane act.

Everybody was pleased to know how much they had always disliked Mr. Darcy before they had known anything of the matter.

Jane was the only creature who could suppose there might be any extenuating circumstances in the case, unknown to the society of Hertfordshire. Her mild and steady candour always pleaded for allowances, and urged the possibility of mistakes—but by everybody else Mr. Darcy was condemned as the worst of men.

CHAPTER THREE

About the middle of the next day, as Lizzy was in her room getting ready for a walk, a sudden noise below seemed to set the whole house in confusion. After listening for a moment, she heard somebody running upstairs in a violent hurry, and calling loudly after her. She opened the door and met Maria in the landing place, who, breathless with agitation, cried out,

"Oh, my dear Eliza! Pray make haste and come into the dining-room, for there is such a sight to be seen! I will not tell you what it is. Make haste, and come down this moment."

Lizzy asked questions in vain. Maria would tell her nothing more, and down they ran into the dining-room, which fronted the lane, in quest of this wonder; it was two ladies stopping in a low phaeton at the garden gate.

"And is this all?" cried Lizzy. "I expected at least that the pigs were got into the garden, and here is nothing but Lady Catherine and her daughter."

"La, my dear!" said Maria, quite shocked at the mistake. "It is not Lady Catherine. The old lady is Mrs. Jenkinson, who lives with them. The other is Miss de Bourgh. Only look at her. She is quite a little creature. Who would have thought that she could be so thin and small?"

"She is abominably rude to keep Charlotte out of doors in all this wind. Why does she not come in?"

"Oh, Charlotte says she hardly ever does. It is the greatest of favours when Miss de Bourgh comes in."

"I like her appearance," said Lizzy, struck with other ideas. "She looks sickly and cross. Yes, she will do for him very well. She will make him a very proper wife."

The thought of Mr. Darcy, alas, brought back the strangeness of her dream in full force, and to combat the disconcertion that ensued,

Lizzy recounted all the reasons she disliked the man: chief among them, his transgressions upon Wickham and his part in crushing her sister's happiness. She had no evidence of the latter, but she did not doubt but that he and the Bingley sisters must have had a hand in separating Bingley from Jane

At length, Miss de Bourgh and Mrs. Jenkinson drove on, and the others returned into the house. Mr. Collins no sooner saw Lizzy and Maria than he began to congratulate them on their good fortune, which Charlotte explained by letting them know that the whole party was asked to dine at Rosings the next day.

Mr. Collins's triumph, in consequence of this invitation, was complete. The power of displaying the grandeur of his patroness to his wondering visitors, and of letting them see her civility towards himself and his wife, was exactly what he had wished for. He could not admire enough this prompt instance of Lady Catherine's condescension.

"I confess," said he, "that I should not have been at all surprised by her ladyship's asking us on Sunday to drink tea and spend the evening at Rosings. I rather expected, from my knowledge of her affability, that it would happen. But who could have foreseen such an attention as this? Who could have imagined that we should receive an invitation to dine there—an invitation, moreover, including the whole party—so immediately after your arrival!"

"I am the less surprised at what has happened," replied Sir William. "My situation in life has allowed me to acquire much knowledge of what the manners of the great really are. About the court, such instances of elegant breeding are not uncommon."

Scarcely anything was talked of the whole day or next morning but their visit to Rosings. Mr. Collins carefully instructed them in what they were to expect, that the sight of such rooms, so many servants, and so splendid a dinner, might not wholly overpower them.

When the ladies were separating for the toilette, he said to Lizzy, "Do not make yourself uneasy, my dear cousin, about your apparel. Lady Catherine is far from requiring that elegance of dress in us which becomes herself and her daughter. I would advise you merely to put on whatever of your clothes is superior to the rest—there is no occasion for anything more. Lady Catherine will not think the worse of you for being simply dressed. She likes to have the distinction of rank preserved."

While they were dressing, he came two or three times to their different doors, to recommend their being quick, as Lady Catherine very much objected to be kept waiting for her dinner.

As the weather was fine, they had a pleasant walk of about half a mile across the park. Every park has its beauty and its prospects; and Lizzy saw much to be pleased with, though she could not be in such raptures as Mr. Collins expected the scene to inspire, and was but slightly affected by his enumeration of the windows in front of the house, and his relation of what the glazing altogether had originally cost Sir Lewis de Bourgh.

When they ascended the steps to the hall, Maria's alarm was every moment increasing, and even Sir William did not look perfectly calm. Lizzy's courage did not fail her. She had heard nothing of Lady Catherine that spoke her awful from any extraordinary talents or miraculous virtue, and the mere stateliness of money or rank she thought she could witness without trepidation.

From the entrance-hall, of which Mr. Collins pointed out, with a rapturous air, the fine proportion and the finished ornaments, they followed the servants through an ante-chamber, to the room where Lady Catherine, her daughter, and Mrs. Jenkinson were sitting. Her ladyship, with great condescension, arose to receive them. Mrs. Collins had settled it with her husband that the office of introduction should be hers, and it was performed in a proper manner, without any of those apologies and thanks which he would have thought necessary.

In spite of having been at St. James's, Sir William was so completely awed by the grandeur surrounding him, that he had but just courage enough to make a very low bow, and take his seat without saying a word. His daughter, frightened almost out of her senses, sat on the edge of her chair, not knowing which way to look. Lizzy found herself quite equal to the scene and could observe the three ladies before her with full composure. Lady Catherine was a tall, large woman, with strongly-marked features, which might once have been handsome. Her air was not conciliating, nor was her manner of receiving them such as to make her visitors forget their inferior rank. She was not rendered formidable by silence, but she spoke with authoritative tones that marked her self-importance. Lizzy recalled how Mr. Wickham had described her ladyship and believed the woman to be exactly what he had represented.

When, after examining the mother, in whose countenance and deportment she soon found some resemblance of Mr. Darcy, she turned her eyes on the daughter, a thin and small young woman. There was neither in figure nor face any likeness between the ladies. Miss de Bourgh was pale and sickly. Her features, though not plain, were insignificant, and she spoke very little, except in a low voice, to Mrs. Jenkinson, in whose appearance there was nothing remarkable, and who was entirely engaged in listening to what she said, and placing a screen in the proper direction before her eyes.

After sitting a few minutes, they were all sent to one of the windows to admire the view, Mr. Collins attending them to point out its beauties, and Lady Catherine kindly informing them that it was much better worth looking at in the summer.

The dinner was exceedingly handsome, and there were all the servants and all the articles of plate which Mr. Collins had promised. He took his seat at the bottom of the table, by her ladyship's desire, and looked as if he felt that life could furnish nothing greater. He carved, and ate, and praised with delighted alacrity, and every dish was commended, first by him and then by Sir William, who was now enough recovered to echo whatever his son-in-law said, in a manner which Lizzy wondered Lady Catherine could bear.

But Lady Catherine seemed gratified by their excessive admiration and gave most gracious smiles, especially when any dish on the table proved a novelty to them. The party did not supply much conversation. Lizzy was ready to speak whenever there was an opening, but she was seated between Charlotte and Miss de Bourgh— the former of whom was engaged in listening to Lady Catherine, and the latter said not a word to her all dinner-time. Mrs. Jenkinson was chiefly employed in watching how little Miss de Bourgh ate, pressing her to try some other dish, and fearing she was indisposed. Maria thought speaking out of the question, and the gentlemen did nothing but eat and admire.

When the ladies returned to the drawing-room, there was little to be done but to hear Lady Catherine talk, which she did without any intermission till coffee came in, delivering her opinion on every subject in so decisive a manner, as proved that she was not used to having her judgment controverted. She inquired into Charlotte's domestic concerns familiarly and minutely, gave her a great deal of advice as to the management of them all, told her how everything ought to be regulated in so small a family as hers, and instructed her as to the care of her cows and her poultry. Lizzy found that nothing was beneath this great lady's attention. In the intervals of her discourse with Mrs. Collins, she addressed a variety of questions to Maria and Lizzy, but especially to the latter, of whose connections she knew the least, and who she observed to Mrs. Collins was a very genteel, pretty kind of girl. She asked her, at different times, how many sisters she had, whether they were older or younger than herself, whether any of them were likely to be married, whether they were handsome, where they had been educated, what carriage her father kept, and what had been her mother's maiden name? Lizzy felt all the impertinence of her questions but answered them very composedly. Lady Catherine then observed,

"Your father's estate is entailed on Mr. Collins, I think. For your sake," turning to Charlotte, "I am glad of it, but otherwise I see no occasion for entailing estates from the female line. It was not thought necessary in Sir Lewis de Bourgh's family. Do you play and sing, Miss Bennet?"

"A little."

"Oh! Then—some time or other we shall be happy to hear you. Our instrument is a capital one, probably superior to—You shall try it someday. Do your sisters play and sing?"

"One of them does."

"Why did not you all learn? You ought all to have learned. The Miss Webbs all play, and their father has not so good an income as yours. Do you draw?"

"No, not at all."

"What, none of you?"

"Not one."

"That is very strange. But I suppose you had no opportunity. Your mother should have taken you to town every spring for the benefit of masters."

"My mother would have had no objection, but my father hates London."

"Has your governess left you?"

"We never had any governess."

"No governess! How was that possible? Five daughters brought up at home without a governess! I never heard of such a thing. Your mother must have been quite a slave to your education."

Lizzy could hardly help smiling as she assured her that had not been the case.

"Then, who taught you? Who attended to you? Without a governess, you must have been neglected."

"Compared with some families, I believe we were. But we were always encouraged to read, and had all the masters that were necessary. Those who chose to be idle, certainly might."

"Aye, no doubt, but that is what a governess will prevent, and if I had known your mother, I should have advised her most strenuously to engage one. I always say that nothing is to be done in education without steady and regular instruction, and nobody but a governess can give it. It is wonderful how many families I have been the means of supplying in that way. I am always glad to get a young person well placed out. Four nieces of Mrs. Jenkinson are most delightfully situated through my means; and it was but the other day that I recommended another young person, who was merely accidentally mentioned to me, and the family are quite delighted with her. Mrs. Collins, did I tell you of Lady Metcalf's calling yesterday to thank me? She finds Miss Pope a treasure. 'Lady Catherine,' said she, 'you have given me a treasure.' Are any of your younger sisters out, Miss Bennet?"

"Yes, ma'am, all."

"All! What, all five out at once? Very odd! And you only the second. The younger ones out before the elder ones are married! Your younger sisters must be very young?"

"Yes, my youngest is not sixteen. Perhaps *she* is full young to be much in company. But really, ma'am, I think it would be very hard upon younger sisters, that they should not have their share of society and amusement, because the elder may not have the means or inclination to marry early. The last-born has as good a right to the pleasures of youth as the first. And to be kept back on *such* a motive! I think it would not be very likely to promote sisterly affection or delicacy of mind."

"Upon my word," said her ladyship, "you give your opinion very decidedly for so young a person. Pray, what is your age?"

"With three younger sisters grown up," replied Lizzy, smiling, "your ladyship can hardly expect me to own it."

Lady Catherine seemed quite astonished at not receiving a direct answer, and Lizzy suspected herself to be the first creature who had ever dared to trifle with so much dignified impertinence.

"You cannot be more than twenty, I am sure, therefore you need not conceal your age."

"I am not one-and-twenty."

When the gentlemen had joined them, and tea was over, the card-tables were placed. Lady Catherine, Sir William, and Mr. and Mrs. Collins sat down to quadrille. The remaining were obliged to play at cassino, Miss de Bourgh's chosen game. Their table was superlatively stupid. Scarcely a syllable was uttered that did not relate to the game, except when Mrs. Jenkinson expressed her fears of Miss de Bourgh's being too hot or too cold, or having too much or too little light. A great deal more passed at the other table. Lady Catherine was generally speaking—stating the mistakes of the three others, or relating some anecdote of herself. Mr. Collins was employed in agreeing to everything her ladyship said, thanking her for every fish he won, and apologising if he thought he won too many. Sir William did not say much. He was storing his memory with anecdotes and noble names.

When Lady Catherine and her daughter had played as long as they chose, the tables were broken up, the carriage was offered to Mrs. Collins, gratefully accepted and immediately ordered. The party then gathered round the fire to hear Lady Catherine determine what weather they were to have on the morrow. From these instructions they were summoned by the arrival of the coach. After many speeches of thankfulness on Mr. Collins's side and as many bows on Sir William's, they departed. As soon as they had driven from the door, Lizzy was called on by her cousin to give her opinion of all that she had seen at Rosings, which, for Charlotte's sake, she made more favourable than it really was. But her commendation, though costing her some trouble, could by no means satisfy Mr. Collins, and he was very soon obliged to take her ladyship's praise into his own hands.

Lizzy did not expect to greet future visits at Rosings with exceptional enthusiasm, but she was satisfied that her fear of having Mr. Darcy constantly in her thoughts while in the company of his relations had not come to much fruition, and she anticipated that perhaps she might not think of him at all in a few days.

But such hopes, alas, were to be shortly dashed.

* * * * *

Lizzy woke with a start, sitting up in bed to find her breath shallow and her heart racing. She could not have been more startled had a flock of birds suddenly swarmed through her room. More disconcerting than finding fauna in the house, however, was the degree of wetness between her legs and the knowledge that it had been brought about by yet another prurient dream.

When her senses had calmed, she lay back in bed, for dawn had yet to break, and stared at the ceiling. A part of her would return to the dream in which she had returned to Herfordshire to find Wickham's regiment still in Meryton. After finding a moment alone, Wickham had professed that he had been unable to turn his thoughts from her, even whilst he pursued the hand of women whose fortunes he must depend upon if he was to have the life he sought.

"But I wonder if, in the end, it is worth the loss of one whom I truly admire?" he had asked as he brought her hand to his lips.

His words had satisfied her vanity and the touch of his mouth upon her skin had ignited all sorts of flutters throughout her body.

"I think I would risk it all for one night with you," he had said before circling an arm about her waist and pulling her into him.

His hips had pressed into hers, banishing all chagrin of her weakness, at how easily she could and would succumb to the heat flaring inside her. He had kissed her then, and though it did not sweep her away as much as she had hoped, she was content to melt against him and surrender to the urgency of the moment. No further caresses of affection were required.

But they were interrupted once more. This time, instead of her sisters, the voices of Mr. Bingley and Mr. Darcy stayed them.

Though it was silly to fault a man for the fictional accounts of a dream, Lizzy could not help but think ruefully that Mr. Darcy *would* be the unhappy disruption of so fine a moment. She could find no redeeming quality in him, and his disposition only marred the countenance and figure he had been blessed to have.

That he had once asked her to dance during a ball at Netherfield puzzled her still. Surprised, she had accepted his request, much to her own disconcertion. Taking their place upon the dance floor, they had stood for some time without speaking a word. At long last, she had made some slight observation on the dance. He had replied, and all was silent again. How trying of the man to leave all attempts at conversation to her!

After a pause of some minutes, she had addressed him a second time. "It is *your* turn to say something now, Mr. Darcy. I talked about the dance, and *you* ought to make some sort of remark on the size of the room, or the number of couples."

He had assured her that whatever she wished him to say should be said.

"Very well. That reply will do for the present. Perhaps by and by I may observe that private balls are much pleasanter than public ones. But *now* we may be silent."

"Do you talk by rule, then, while you are dancing?"

"Sometimes. One must speak a little, you know. It would look odd to be entirely silent for half an hour together, and yet for the advantage of *some*, conversation ought to be so arranged, as that they may have the trouble of saying as little as possible."

"Are you consulting your own feelings in the present case, or do you imagine that you are gratifying mine?"

"Both," she had replied archly, "for I have always seen a great similarity in the turn of our minds. We are each of an unsocial, taciturn disposition, unwilling to speak unless we expect to say something that will amaze the whole room, and be handed down to posterity with all the éclat of a proverb."

"This is no very striking resemblance of your own character, I am sure. How near it may be to *mine*, I cannot pretend to say. *You* think it a faithful portrait undoubtedly."

"I must not decide on my own performance."

He had made no answer, and they were again silent till they had gone down the dance, when he had asked her if she and her sisters did not very often walk to Meryton. She had answered in the affirmative, and added, "When you met us there the other day, we had just been forming a new acquaintance."

He had stiffened. "Mr. Wickham is blessed with such happy manners as may ensure his making friends. Whether he may be equally capable of retaining them is less certain."

"He has been so unlucky as to lose *your* friendship," she had replied with emphasis, "and in a manner which he is likely to suffer from all his life."

He had made no answer. At that moment, Sir William Lucas had appeared close to them, meaning to pass through the set to the other side of the room, but on perceiving Mr. Darcy, he had stopped with a bow of superior courtesy to compliment him on his dancing and his partner.

"I have been most highly gratified indeed, my dear sir. Such very superior dancing is not often seen. It is evident that you belong to the first circles. Allow me to say, however, that your fair partner does not disgrace you, and that I must hope to have this pleasure often repeated, especially when a certain desirable event, my dear Eliza—"

And here Sir William had glanced at Jane and Bingley.

"—shall take place. What congratulations will then flow in! I appeal to Mr. Darcy—but let me not interrupt you, sir. You will not thank me for detaining you from the bewitching converse of that young lady, whose bright eyes are also upbraiding me."

Darcy had appeared engrossed in thought. Recovering, he had turned back to her. "Sir William's interruption has made me forget what we were talking of."

"I do not think we were speaking at all. Sir William could not have interrupted two people in the room who had less to say for themselves. We have tried two or three subjects already without success, and what we are to talk of next I cannot imagine."

"What think you of books?" he had said with a rare smile.

"Books—oh! No. I am sure we never read the same, or not with the same feelings."

"I am sorry you think so, but if that be the case, there can at least be no want of subject. We may compare our different opinions."

"No. I cannot talk of books in a ball-room; my head is always full of something else."

"The *present* always occupies you in such scenes, does it?" he had asked.

"Yes, always," she had replied, then exclaimed, "I remember hearing you once say, Mr. Darcy, that you hardly ever forgave, that your resentment once created was unappeasable. You are very cautious, I suppose, as to its *being created*?"

"I am," he had said with a firm voice.

"And never allow yourself to be blinded by prejudice?"

"I hope not."

"It is particularly incumbent on those who never change their opinion, to be secure of judging properly at first."

"May I ask to what these questions tend?"

"Merely to the illustration of *your* character. I am trying to make it out."

"And what is your success?"

She shook her head. "I do not get on at all. I hear such different accounts of you as to puzzle me exceedingly."

"I can readily believe," answered he gravely, "that reports may vary greatly with respect to me, and I could wish, Miss Bennet, that you were not to sketch my character at the present moment, as there is reason to fear that the performance would reflect no credit on either."

"But if I do not take your likeness now, I may never have another opportunity."

"I would by no means suspend any pleasure of yours," he had replied, more coldly than he intended.

She had said no more, and they went down the other dance and parted in silence.

CHAPTER FOUR

The party at the Parsonage had diminished by one for Sir William had stayed only a week at Hunsford, assured that his daughter was most comfortably settled and possessed of such a husband and such a neighbour as were not often met with. While Sir William was with them, Mr. Collins devoted his morning to driving him out in his gig, and showing him the country. After his departure, the whole family returned to their usual employments, and Lizzy was thankful to find that they did not see more of her cousin by the alteration. He spent most of the time between breakfast and dinner at work in the garden, reading and writing, and looking out of the window in his own book-room, which fronted the road. The room in which the ladies sat was backwards. Lizzy had at first rather wondered that Charlotte should not prefer the dining-parlour for common use. It was a better sized room, and had a more pleasant aspect, but she soon saw that her friend had an excellent reason for what she did, for Mr. Collins would undoubtedly have been much less in his own apartment, had they sat in one equally lively, and she gave Charlotte credit for the arrangement.

From the drawing-room they could distinguish nothing in the lane, and were indebted to Mr. Collins for the knowledge of what carriages went along, and how often especially Miss de Bourgh drove by in her phaeton, which he never failed coming to inform them of, though it happened almost every day. She not unfrequently stopped at the Parsonage and had a few minutes' conversation with Charlotte, but was scarcely ever prevailed upon to get out.

Now and then they were honoured with a call from her ladyship, and nothing escaped her observation during these visits. She examined into their employments, looked at their work, and advised them to do it differently, found fault with the arrangement of the furniture, detected the housemaid in negligence; and if she accepted any refreshment, seemed to do it only for the sake of finding out that Mrs. Collins's joints of meat were too large for her family.

Lizzy soon perceived, that though this great lady was not in commission of the peace of the county, she was a most active magistrate in her own parish, the minutest concerns of which were carried to her by Mr. Collins. Whenever any of the cottagers were disposed to be quarrelsome, discontented, or too poor, she sallied forth into the village to settle their differences, silence their complaints, and scold them into harmony and plenty.

With the dream still clinging to her, Lizzy was glad to hear that Mr. Collins and Charlotte were to visit Lady Catherine. Maria opted to stay at the parsonage and tend to her embroidery, leaving Lizzy the option to go for a walk for as long as needed, and she expected she would require a very lengthy stroll to dispel the disquiet in her body.

The weather, being uncommonly warm for early spring, complied. Lizzy took her favourite walk along an open grove that edged that side of the park where there was a nice sheltered path, which no one seemed to value but herself, and where she felt beyond the reach of Lady Catherine's curiosity.

She had walked a good two hours, at a brisk pace so as to discourage her from dwelling upon unwanted thoughts, and found herself on the far side of the parish before contemplating that she ought to head back. The path she had taken wound through a small woodland and down a rocky knoll, concluding at a dirt road. A hill rose on the other side of the road, and, desiring to see what sort of vista could be availed from its crown, she decided to make her way down the knoll toward the road. Her slippers, comfortable but worn, made for a precarious descent. One foot slipped along a level rock, causing her to lose her balance and tumble the rest of the way to the road. Though jarred, she picked herself up and was grateful that she had sustained no serious injury, only a few scrapes against her arms and legs, and a bruise upon her buttock where she had struck a rock.

She was brushing the dirt from her muslin when a curricle came along. It stopped beside her.

"Are you all right, my dear?" the driver asked.

Lizzy turned her attention from the smart-looking vehicle and near identical bays to the driver, a handsome woman with a wide-brimmed hat, beneath which her golden locks framed her countenance in romantic wisps. The tone of her skin and the set of her bones suggested a woman of at least five and thirty in years, but her eyes radiated with youthful energy. She wore a stylish pin-striped gown and cashmere shawl.

"I lost my footing and took a tumble, but my pride sustained the greater injury," Lizzy replied.

"I think it no minor fall. You've torn your sleeve."

Lizzy looked and found the rip beneath one of her arms, along with an abrasion.

"Come," the driver said, "I live but a short ride from here. You may attend yourself there."

"You are very kind, but I can make it back to Hunsford Parsonage without difficulty."

"Hunsford Parsonage?" The woman looked Lizzy over. "On foot?"

"I am accustomed to walking long distances. In fact, I greatly enjoy it."

The woman shook her head. "That is all well and good, but I would rather you did not upset me by refusing my offer."

Lizzy was ready to insist but the woman had spoken so firmly that Lizzy believed she really would have taken offense to any objection. She offered Lizzy her hand, which, after a moment's pause, Lizzy took and climbed into the curricle. With practiced hands, the woman urged her bays into a canter. Lizzy admired the lightness and speed of the vehicle. Any fashionable young man would have welcomed the opportunity to drive it.

"I've not seen you in these parts before," the driver commented, turning a curious eye upon Lizzy, her tone light and interested. "Are you staying at Hunsford Parsonage?"

"I am, with my cousin, Mr. Collins, and his wife, a dear friend of mine."

"Ah, yes, he is newly married. I have had occasion to meet Mrs. Collins once or twice. He is a fortunate man to have found such a partner."

As the woman's assessment matched her own, Lizzy allowed the driver, in all likelihood, to be an observant and intelligent creature.

"Do you reside here in Hunsford?" Lizzy asked.

"I do. My proper name is Abigail Trenwith, but most people address me as Abby. And may I ask whom I have the pleasure of driving?"

"Elizabeth Bennet."

"And you came by foot all this way from the Parsonage?"

"Walking is a favourite pastime of mine."

"How delightful. I think young ladies should not shun such exertions. I know mothers who keep their daughters from any form of exercise, and I think it can cause the young women to look rather weak and sickly."

Lizzy thought instantly of Anne de Bourgh. "I am of the same persuasion, Mrs. Trenwith."

"Do call me Abby. You've no need for formalities with me."

Surprised at the quick familiarity, Lizzy looked closer upon Abigail Trenwith, whose enviable beauty was dampened only by a darkened complexion, but Lizzy felt an instant kinship in that regard, for Mrs. Trenwith must share in her own enjoyment of being out of doors.

"Are you enjoying your stay?"

Lizzy must have hesitated one second too long, for Mrs. Trenwith continued, "You've no need to answer if you find me prying. My friends tell me I am far too inquisitive."

Lizzy owned she might have found the questioning a bit intrusive, but there was such a lighthearted quality to the speech, and with no intimation of judgment, that she could not fault Mrs. Trenwith for attempting a conversation to pass the time.

"I enjoy the adventure of foreign places," Lizzy supplied.

Mrs. Trenwith raised a brow. "Ah, then I fear your enjoyment will be limited in duration. I do not mean to cast a shadow, but there is not much more to see of Hunsford."

"The landscape is pleasant, and the weather fine."

They pulled up before a house as stately as that of Rosings, though Mr. Collins would surely note not as grand and with far fewer windows in the front of the house. A footman greeted and assisted them from the curricle. Once inside, Mrs. Trenwith installed Lizzy in the care of her housekeeper, Mrs. Singh, a short Indian woman with a cherub face, who cleansed her wound and offered to patch the tear in her sleeve. Lizzy refused to be an imposition, replying that her shawl would cover the tear nicely until she was home and able to put needle to thread herself. She was then led into the parlour, a room she found nicely appointed with balanced restraint compared to the ostentatious ornaments preferred by Lady Catherine. After settling upon a settee,

Lizzy continued her study of the room, trying to discern if the décor might provide some insight into her hostess. The tidiness and cleanliness of the room only signified the presence of good house servants. The judicious spacing of the furniture might reflect a person who valued order. The decorative artifacts, by their form and design, revealed a partiality for the Orient.

In the end, however, Lizzy had to conclude her scrutiny a useless exercise. The room told her nothing for certain.

Minutes later, Mrs. Trenwith bustled in, glowing with good spirits. Mrs. Trenwith had such an easy manner about her that her disposition could not be contrived. Lizzy wondered if the woman's temperament resulted more from nature or situation? She would have thought one's quality of wealth to contribute positively to a person's good humor, but that was certainly not the case with the Bingley sisters or Mr. Darcy.

"What, have you not been served any tea while you were waiting?" Mrs. Trenwith asked after motioning for Lizzy to stay seated. She went to ring for a servant.

"I have trespassed upon your time sufficiently, I think," Lizzy said.

"You are not to concern yourself with that. I confess I am quite interested in your company, you are a well-mannered young woman, and I mean to subject you to further interrogation."

Lizzy could not help but smile and like Mrs. Trenwith *more* for the impudence.

"Now, Mr. Singh, we are better hosts than that," she reproached the butler but with an air of such kindness that he could not take offense. She took a seat opposite Lizzy. "Now tell me of yourself."

"There is little to tell, Mrs. Trenwith. I am not that interesting."

"Abby. *Every* person is interesting to begin with. Tell me of your family. Have you brothers, sisters?"

"I have four sisters in all, the youngest at sixteen years of age."

"Five daughters! Your mother must be under such pressure to have the future of so many secured. I have but one daughter. She is married to a barrister and living in London. One was sufficient for me to fret about. I cannot imagine five! But it is unkind of me to despair of your circumstances."

Lizzy thought immediately of Jane and Mr. Bingley with anguish. If anyone deserved to be happy in matrimony, it was Jane. Lizzy had thought the two a perfect match in temperament and style, and had been convinced of their mutual attraction. All of Hertfordshire had. But Jane had been some time in London, and still Bingley had not called upon her. Only his sister, Caroline, had returned Jane's numerous visits, and was even then such an altered creature, by Jane's own account, that Jane resolved to continue the acquaintance no longer. As for the younger Bennet sisters, Kitty and Lydia were silly creatures and Mary too irritable. It was quite possible that none of the Bennet young women would see themselves in satisfactory marriages. The thought made Lizzy more sympathetic to her mother's frequent laments.

"If your sisters are as lovely as you, husbands will come easily enough," Mrs. Trenwith added.

"That is a kindly statement, but, in truth, we have not much in the way of dowries or breeding to recommend us, though my sister Jane has the kindest heart and the most gentle disposition. She certainly *deserves* a good husband, but I am reconciled that providence is an essential ingredient. I have sometimes wished myself a man, that I could do more for my family, but neither sex is immune from necessity. There are men for whom matrimony is as much a means of security as for women."

"It still hardly seems fair," Mrs. Trenwith said with what seemed as much conviction as genuine empathy. "La, but it is easy for me to say! I am one of the fortunate ones to have married a man of income, though it was not always thus. Some would regard us differently for while we have wealth, we lack breeding. We are of the bourgeoisie, you know. But as you will find upon being better acquainted with me, I care little for the opinions of others, and though I dispense mine own freely, I have no expectation that you will favour them any more than I would yours."

"That is most evenhanded!" Lizzy praised, liking Mrs. Trenwith more with each passing moment.

Tea was served, and Lizzy took it gladly. She had worked up a good thirst, as well as an appetite.

"Have you traveled from far?"

"My family live in Hertfordshire, some fifty miles from here."

"I know someone who was in the area of Hertfordshire recently." Mrs. Trenwith appeared to comb her memory. "Ah, yes, Fitzwilliam Darcy."

Lizzy choked on her tea. She covered her mouth with her handkerchief, but it was some time before the coughing fit subsided.

"My dear, are you quite all right?"

Lizzy nodded, sure that she was blue in the face.

"Was there something amiss with the tea? Perhaps a leaf had got past the strainer?"

"No, the tea was fine. The name startled me is all."

"What? Mr. Darcy? Do you know him?"

Regrettably, Lizzy answered in her mind. Aloud she said, "A close friend of his, Mr. Bingley, took up residence at a place called Netherfield Park, not far from Longbourn. My family had the pleasure of being acquainted with Mr. Bingley, and he was rarely without the company of Mr. Darcy."

Mrs. Trenwith took a rare pause and appeared almost amused, though Lizzy could not guess what Mrs. Trenwith could find droll with her statement, which she had purposefully made as mundane as possible, not knowing the nature of the relationship between Mrs. Trenwith and Mr. Darcy.

"I gather you find Mr. Darcy unpleasant."

Lizzy cleared her throat. Had her opinion of Mr. Darcy been that obviously writ upon her face? "I did not say he was or wasn't," she protested.

"Ah, but you did, by what you did *not* say. You could have said that your family had the pleasure of being acquainted with both gentlemen, but you singled out Mr. Bingley alone. And if he was constantly with Mr. Darcy, you could not claim to be *unacquainted* with the latter."

Lizzy looked down at her tea, half-pleased and half-dismayed to be in the company of a clever woman. Mrs. Trenwith overlooked little.

"You've no need to worry. Mr. Darcy rarely makes a good first impression," Mrs. Trenwith said with a sympathetic smile before taking a sip of her tea.

Eager to be off the subject of Mr. Darcy, Lizzy asked, "Would you mind a few questions of mine own?"

"Not at all. It is only fair. Ask away."

"Have you resided in Hunsford long?"

"For several years, yes. My husband had lived in Hunsford as a boy and had always admired this house. That is his portrait on that wall."

Lizzy studied the painting of a man in his fifties with gentle features, though not as striking as his wife.

"Mr. Trenwith passed away two years ago."

"I am sorry to hear it. He could not have been very old."

"He was twelve years my senior and had contracted malaria some years ago on a trip to the Malay Kingdoms. He had accounts with the British East India Company and travelled often for his business. I accompanied him once when he took a tour of India and China."

Lizzy could not help but gape. "I spoke of Hunsford as 'foreign,' but my use of the word is overstated. India *and* China? I can scarce imagine such an experience."

"The travelling was very difficult and rough. Though Mr. Trenwith made the journey a number of times, once was sufficient for me. But the sights were, without a doubt, incredible."

Mrs. Trenwith had Lizzy enraptured with her descriptions of the varied and dissimilar landscapes, the strange smells, the flavourful and sometimes revolting foods, the dramatic colours, the eccentric and at times scandalous clothing, the fascinating customs, and remarkable people. Lizzy did not mark the time till the miniature clock tower on the fireplace mantel struck the hour.

Lizzy gasped. "Oh my! I am to dine at Rosings tonight!"

"With the Lady Catherine de Bourgh?"

Lizzy nodded, calculating that she would be hard pressed to walk the length back to the Parsonage and be dressed in time to stroll the half mile to Rosings.

"My chaise is at your disposal, and I will brook no protest. I feel responsible for your lost time, having insisted upon your company and then regaling you with descriptions of my travels."

"If you bear any culpability, it is only because you have been exceedingly kind and allowed my fascination of your travels to encourage the *tête-à-tête*. I accept your offer as I am certain to be tardy without the convenience of a horse and wheels."

Mrs. Trenwith rose and rang once more for a servant. "I have both a carriage and the curricle. You seemed to enjoy the ride in the latter."

"I did."

"I would drive you myself, but…you will have an easier ride with my man Lee."

Lizzy wondered at the pause and what Mrs. Trenwith had intended to say. She replied, "Your skills with the ribbons seem more than adequate, Mrs. Trenwith—Abby."

"I like driving myself whenever possible. It seems a waste of effort for someone to drive me so that I can have the luxury of boredom while I sit."

Impressed by Mrs. Trenwith's show of independence, Lizzy was sure she could have stayed hours at tea with the woman.

"It has been a delight meeting you, Miss Elizabeth," Mrs. Trenwith said as she walked Lizzy out. "If you are to be in Hunsford for some time, you are welcome to pay me a visit anytime. Indeed, I hope you will."

Lizzy secured her bonnet. "Thank you for your hospitality. My fall, it would seem, has turned into a fortunate incident."

"I hope the sentiment to remain."

The statement struck Lizzy a little odd, but Mrs. Trenwith had turned from her to stroke one of the horses.

The ride back to the Parsonage passed almost too quickly, for Lizzy had much to reflect upon her new acquaintance. After arriving, however, she better understood what Abby might have meant by her cryptic words.

Mr. Collins had been standing in the front of the house engaged in his frequent pastime of watching the road.

"Miss Elizabeth, this is a surprise," he noted of her transportation and the slender Chinese driver.

"I took a long walk and had a fall upon some rocks at the end of it," Lizzy explained as Lee assisted her from the curricle.

Instead of being impressed by the vehicle, Mr. Collins eyed the whole of it with a certain amount of vexation. "I do not recognize this chaise and did not think Lady Catherine to possess a curricle."

Lizzy thanked Lee, who tipped his hat before taking the ribbons. She turned to Mr. Collins. "Perhaps because it belongs to Mrs. Abigail Trenwith. She happened by me after I had fallen. It was quite the lucky coincidence. She is a most interesting and cordial person."

The distress increased upon her cousin's features. When the curricle had left the Parsonage, he said hastily, "That may be, upon first impression, but there is more to Mrs. Trenwith than meets the eye."

This only served to intrigue Lizzy more. "Do you mean to warn me against her?"

"I have not heard Lady Catherine speak well of her, and Lady Catherine is most discerning. Her assessment of a person has never been wrong. Indeed, she can ferret the true worth of an individual within minutes of meeting them, no matter how obliging or honest they may appear. I do not think she would approve of any association with Mrs. Trenwith."

Mr. Collins did not know it, but the disdain of Lady Catherine only improved Mrs. Trenwith in Lizzy's eyes. "And what qualities or activities of Mrs. Trenwith fail to meet the approval of Lady Catherine?"

When Mr. Collins could only respond by looking further vexed, Lizzy determined she would indeed attempt to pay another visit to Mrs. Trenwith. Lady Catherine was as proud and impertinent as her nephew, Darcy, and Lizzy placed little stock in what her ladyship thought.

"I know not the particulars," Mr. Collins said at last, "but know that you may utilize Lady Catherine's sound and learned intelligence without fear. Indeed, Lady Catherine would be greatly satisfied that her opinions were adopted by others to good effect."

I am sure she would, Lizzy said to herself as she turned from the road. Aloud, she said, "Nonetheless, I prefer to render mine own judgment and not shirk from the labor of it."

He followed her inside the house, still vexed. "You do not mean to see her again? She lives on the far side of the parish—fortunately."

Lizzy toyed with the idea of teasing her cousin with the notion, but as she anticipated a long evening at Rosings, she wanted only to go to her chamber for some peace and quiet.

"I will take what you have told me under advisement."

Mr. Collins looked relieved for the moment, then brightened. "The topic had so disturbed me that I nearly forgot to report that Mr. Darcy is expected at Rosings."

CHAPTER FIVE

Despite the clouds in the sky the following morning, Lizzy determined that she would still attempt a walk to escape her cousin, who, having yet to receive from her agreement or a manner of assurance that satisfied him, had often revisited the subject of Mrs. Trenwith.

"Those that would feign goodness are often accomplished at hiding their immorality," Mr. Collins had said.

"That is a strong statement! What crime has this woman committed?" Lizzy had asked.

Mr. Collins had bristled but could not, or would not, say.

"None that we are aware of," Charlotte had supplied, "but a strange mystery hovers about her and Trenwith House. Her servants are never known to gossip."

"That only speaks to their loyalty and integrity—and the good judgment of Mrs. Trenwith in employing them."

"She attends church sparingly," Mr. Collins said. "I suspect her a heretic."

That Mrs. Trenwith's absence from church should offend Mr. Collins surprised Lizzy none at all. Perhaps that was the source of the 'strange mystery.'

"We would all do well to stay our distance," Mr. Collins had affirmed.

Lizzy had little time to reflect upon her cousin's cautions for the dreaded person herself now appeared before the Parsonage.

Mrs. Trenwith, wearing her usual radiance, drew up in her curricle. Though Lizzy was certain Mr. Collins was aware of the visitor, as he made it a point to know of every arrival before anyone else, he did not come out of the house.

"I was making a delivery of pamphlets and thought to come and see how you fared," Mrs. Trenwith explained.

Abby was dressed fashionably in a calico *en neglige*, a bonnet trimmed with green ribbon and a large ostrich plume, and a long string of beads, but the item that caught Lizzy's eye was a medallion with an image of a black slave upon bended knee and the inscription *Am I not a Man and a Brother?*

Seeing the direction of her gaze, Abby said, "Yes, I am a firm believer of abolitionism. Slavery is a dreadful institution that ought to be rejected throughout the British Empire."

That Abby would offer her views so readily on such a polemical topic surprised Lizzy, whose social circles shied away from political discourse, especially in the presence of the fair sex.

Abby peered at the house. Lizzy thought she saw a movement in the window.

"I would call upon the parson and Mrs. Collins, but trust me when I say I am doing them a favor by making my stay as short as possible. Are you about to take a walk?"

Lizzy nodded. Abby looked up at the cloudy sky.

"It is certain to rain."

"I intended a short walk before the weather turned."

"Do you enjoying reading, Miss Elizabeth?"

"Exceedingly."

"I have in my library a large collection of books from a bookstore that had shuttered its business, and mean to sort through the inventory and make a donation to the orphan asylum for girls. Could I impose upon you to assist in the task?"

"It would be no imposition."

Lizzy went back inside the house to inform Charlotte and Mr. Collins. "Surely neither you nor Lady Catherine would object to this act of goodwill?"

"Lady Catherine is a benefactress of the orphan asylum as well," Mr. Collins replied. "As her ladyship exemplifies philanthropy, she would have taken action if she saw a great need for additional charity."

"The books would do no good sitting in the Trenwith library."

"I think it rather ill of Mrs. Trenwith to engage your assistance in her housecleaning."

"I, too, am a good judge of character. If there is anything nefarious in the way of Mrs. Trenwith, I shall discern it soon enough."

"What if you are not returned when Miss de Bourgh passes by?"

Maria asked.

"I do not think she would venture out in such questionable weather, and she would hardly notice my absence as she clearly prefers the conversation of Charlotte or yourself."

Nothing could be said to deter Lizzy. Mr. Collins, looking more displeased than the moment when he had finally realized Lizzy was never going to accept his hand in marriage, declared a need to work in the garden, but not before saying,

"You will only confirm Lady Catherine's appraisal and find you have wasted a good many hours in the effort. I hope in the future you will see the efficiency of using her judgment for your own."

Returning outside, Lizzy eagerly climbed into the curricle.

"You may think it rude of me not to have alighted," Abby said, "but perhaps Mr. Collins has shared with you that he does not welcome my presence."

With such knowledge, it was brazen of her to call at the Parsonage, Lizzy thought. Then she remembered that Mrs. Trenwith did not concern herself much with the opinions of others.

"As he knows me little, his sentiments toward me are more a reflection of the attitude of Catherine de Bourgh," Abby continued.

Lizzy perfectly understood why Lady Catherine would disapprove of the free and outspoken Mrs. Trenwith.

"I have not heard her to mention you, but Mr. Collins did note your absenteeism from church," Lizzy replied.

"No doubt he considers me a great heretic."

The idea amused them both, and they shared a smile.

"You must be aware, my dear Elizabeth that you risk censure in your association with me."

"Yes," Lizzy contemplated, "and perhaps it is selfish of me to seek your company for I have certainly upset Mr. Collins and perhaps Charlotte, too. I hope that Lady Catherine is dispassionate enough not to fault Mr. and Mrs. Collins for my errant ways. I have no fear of her wrath and would prefer it to fall upon my shoulders alone."

"I should not have placed you in such a difficult position and will call upon you at the Parsonage no more, though I admit that, on occasion, as with this morning, I am given to the whims of mischief such that I cannot refrain from perturbing Mr. Collins or even Lady de Bourgh. Mistake me not, she is to be respected in her right, but we are cut from different cloths."

"I think you would get on very well with my father," Lizzy remarked.

"Would I? Well, if he is half as agreeable as you, my dear, I should think you correct."

Back at Trenwith House, Abby showed Lizzy into the library, a splendid room stuffed to the brim with books on every wall, save for the one with the large bay window. Lizzy could see herself spending hours engrossed in a book while curled before the hearth or among the cushions at the window or lounging on the long sofa. The inventory Mrs. Trenwith had acquired, stacked upon the tables and in boxes upon the floor, consisted of diverse genres. Lizzy and Abby combed through everything from John Milton to Adam Smith to find books appropriate for young girls. Lizzy found there were few works of great literature that Abby could not comment upon. Mrs. Trenwith was certainly the most well-read woman she had ever come across.

Lizzy had just finished setting aside copies of *The Fables of Aesop* when Mr. Singh entered to inform Mrs. Trenwith that a Mrs. White had come to call and was most anxious to speak with Mrs. Trenwith.

"This may take some time," Abby informed Lizzy, "but I think a respite is required. You have been most industrious."

"I would have gone at a faster pace had I not been drawn to read a bit for myself," Lizzy admitted.

After Abby had left, Lizzy decided to stretch her legs by walking about the room and perusing what books the Trenwiths kept. She found a section of literature devoted to the abolition of slavery, with the writings of Olaudah Equiano and Granville Sharp, and a section on philosophy, with the works of John Locke and Mary Wollstonecraft, among others. The wall on the far side of the room began with rows of poetry at the bottom, followed by the dramas of Ben Johnson and Christopher Marlow, and on the top shelves, inaccessible without aid, were the writings of the Comte de Mirabeau, Rétif de la Bretonne, and the Marquis de Sade.

Lizzy narrowed her eyes, unsure that she had seen correctly. She pulled a chair from the writing table and used it as a stepstool. She had not been mistaken. Reaching for one of the books, she pulled out a copy of *Justine ou Les Malheurs de la vertu*. Why did the Trenwith library have a work Napoleon deemed "the most abominable book ever engendered by the most depraved imagination?" Was Abby aware of the book? If so, did she know its contents?

Like Pandora holding a *pithos*, Lizzy weighed the book in her hands. What little she knew of the book and its author suggested the substance to be far more offensive than anything found in *Fanny Hill*. Did she dare open the cover?

After a moment of hesitation, she opened the book to an arbitrary page and glanced at a passage:

The third bade me mount upon and straddle two somewhat separated chairs and, seating himself betwixt them, excited by Dubois, lying in his arms, he had me bend until his mouth was directly below the temple of nature; never will you imagine, Mme., what this obscene mortal took it into his head to do; willy-nilly, I was obliged to satisfy his every need... Just Heaven! what man, no matter how depraved, can taste an instant of pleasure in such things... I did what he wished, inundated him, and my complete submission procured this vile man an intoxication of which he was incapable without this infamy.

"That were no gentle reading."

Nearly falling off the chair, Lizzy turned to see Mrs. Trenwith at the threshold. Though her hostess ought to have been the more embarrassed party for being in possession of such a wicked article, Lizzy felt as if she were the child caught pilfering from the jar of biscuits. Her cheeks coloured.

"Are you mortified, my dear?"

The question confirmed to Lizzy that Abby was fully aware of the book's presence in her house. Lizzy knew not what to make of the affirmation.

"I cannot deny my surprise, but having no direct knowledge of this novel, my response need be deferred."

Mrs. Trenwith approached and verified the book that Lizzy held. "I would not recommend it to a novice."

"You have read it?"

"Setting aside the outrageous events, it is a tale that exposes certain institutions—the aristocracy and the church—and doctrines that the author finds suspect. It is told with remarkable rhetoric."

"There is intellectual value in this work?" Lizzy asked in disbelief.

"Indeed, though it is no easy matter to stomach the sordid violence, especially as the story begins with a maiden but twelve years of age. My first attempt to read de Sade resulted in such disgust that my sleep was disturbed for several days thereafter."

Lizzy stared at the book, still attempting to come to some estimation of it all. Was this the 'strange mystery to which Charlotte had alluded? Perhaps she should have appreciated the warnings of her cousin. His objection was not unwarranted. And yet, the frank admittance of Mrs. Trenwith, as if reading *Justine* was no more scandalous than perusing a copy of the *Lady's Magazine*, confused Lizzy.

"I have no designs to debase your reputation through my association," Abby said with a careful gaze upon Lizzy. "I should take no offense if you wished to take your leave of me. Lee can return you to the Parsonage, and I promise never to disturb you again."

Torn, Lizzy said nothing. She had never met anyone like Abby Trenwith before and was still intrigued with the woman, to a greater degree in light of the current discovery. Her instincts told her that Mrs. Trenwith was sincere and without artifice, but was it possible for such a commendable quality to reside in an immoral bosom?

"You referred to me earlier as a 'novice,'" Lizzy said, buying time to sort through her thoughts, "Though I have never read the likes of Mirabeau or de Sade, I consider myself well read."

"I did not mean a novice in reading but a novice in the contemplation or pursuit of the libidinous."

Lizzy caught her breath, and her pulse quickened. *Fanny Hill* weighed heavily upon her mind. Having been completely alone in her experience, she had a sudden desire to confess. Surely Abby could be that perfect confidante without castigation?

"I have read John Cleland," Lizzy blurted.

Abby paused, then her eyes took on a sparkle. "How wonderful!"

Lizzy released her breath.

"Provided you enjoyed it," Abby added. "Did you?"

Blushing, Lizzy nodded. She had never thought she would find herself conversing of *Fanny Hill*, and with someone practically a stranger.

"My dear, do not be abashed in *my* presence! The forces of lust reside in us all. No animal is without it, or we would see a quick end to our species."

"Yes, but…it is a failing, if not a sin, to allow the corporeal to govern us."

"I will be the libertine in your eyes, but I see more harm in the suppression of our natural urges. Whom have you harmed by reading *Fanny Hill?*"

"My soul might prove the ultimate victim."

"A belief I find quite antediluvian compared to the canons of other civilizations far older than ours."

Was this why Mrs. Trenwith failed to attend Church? She was both a heretic and a libertine. Lizzy now fully comprehended the reservations Mr. Collins had of the woman.

"I have said too much," Abby noted of Lizzy's pensiveness. "I have known you but a day, Miss Elizabeth, but am struck by your manners and intelligence. It would be deceitful of me to allow you to develop a friendship with me without knowing the entire truth."

Lizzy raised her brows. There was more?

Abby took *Justine* from her hands and placed it upon a table. "Come. I have something to show you."

CHAPTER SIX

A bby led lizzy down a hall to a gallery. Well lighted by large, dual south-facing windows, the room was a veritable museum of erotic art: paintings, sculptures, engravings and pottery of all cultures. From ancient Greek kylixes to contemporary Italian paintings, the art varied from subtly libidinous to graphic depictions of coition. Lizzy wondered that she could witness it all, but she was to find the articles of the room paled in comparison to that which Mrs. Trenwith would later reveal.

The nearest wall was lined with rather benign paintings, including replicas of Annibale Carracci's *Loves of the Gods*, Raphael's *La Fornarina*, Francisco José de Goya's *The Nude Maja*, and Reuben's *The Three Graces*.

"The carnal is celebrated in other parts of the world," Abby said. "In some, copulation is even a means to spiritual fulfillment. In China, the act of mating is an exchange of *yin-yang*, or the forces of life. The pleasure of a woman is encouraged to increase the essence of *yin*."

Lizzy looked upon a porcelain figurine of a man and woman, both naked, lying together. He had a hand between her legs.

"From the Ming Dynasty," Abby said.

They walked to a series of scrolls, each depicting a couple in a different position. Though the couples were often partially clothed, the private areas of the bodies were graphically drawn.

"Japan draws much of its influences from ancient China. These are called *shunga*, which I believe means 'picture of spring.'"

Lizzy looked at the scrolls, incredulous that such contortions of the body were possible or desired. They walked to a tapestry of an Indian prince crouching between the spread legs of a woman. Lizzy liked the setting of the terrace with the moon above the couple, who lay upon multicoloured fabrics surrounded by ornaments. The man and woman were gazing at each other with small smiles upon their faces.

"There is an ancient Hindu text that describes *kama,* or sensual pleasure, as one of four goals to a full and virtuous life."

"Such perspectives are certainly appealing, seductive even, but also convenient," Lizzy commented.

"Would you define morality as abstention from temptation?"

"It is not *I* who defines morality."

"There are men and women who possess the inclination to sin, be it gluttony, adultery or murder. There are those who possess the tendency to be noble and virtuous. But in all of us, whether we sin or strive to be all that is good, there resides desire. Were we endowed with this quality merely to prove our will and ability to overcome? Are we the more honourable if we denied our thirst or other bodily urges?"

Lizzy put a hand to her temple. These were questions of a philosophical nature and required greater thought than she was capable of at the moment. Her mind was still reeling from the information and the visuals before her. She could not stem the feelings stirring within her from the provocative art. Try as she might, she could not view the art before her dispassionately.

They proceeded to a display of Grecian and Roman ceramics and marble statues. One marble statue was the god Pan with an extremely large phallus. Beside it, upon a pedestal, lay a Roman oil lamp depicting a woman between two men. Lizzy paused in front of a bronze figure of a woman, her legs spread, her hand at her crotch with what appeared to be a cock between her fingers. Lizzy gazed upon it more closely.

"I do not think it a penis," Abby noted of Lizzy's scrutiny, "but an exaggeration of the female clitoris, a most gifted organ."

Clitoris. It was a new word for her and one that sounded rather mundane.

"This collection is the work of many years between my husband and I," Abby continued, appraising the contents of the gallery with genuine gratification and even affection. "But you are overwhelmed, I think. Perhaps I had best return you to the Parsonage."

Lizzy nodded, her thoughts and feelings still in disarray. Abby thanked her for her assistance with the books and determined that Lee would take her home in the carriage.

"If you wish, you may return the morrow to continue with the books, but if you elect, after contemplation, that you have no wish to continue your acquaintance with me, I shall think you no less for it," Abby said. "I shall continue to regard you as a delightful and intelligent young woman, Miss Elizabeth."

Only when the carriage had pulled away from Trenwith House did Lizzy begin sorting through her astonishing afternoon. The exhibitions of art had stimulated an uncomfortable warmth within her, much as the Cleland novel had. She would require many more walks of great length to dispel the visions in her head. But perhaps it was fruitless to attempt to dismiss what naturally resided in every animal, from the least evolved insect to the most intelligent of mankind? Instead of fleeing her desires, might she find it less taxing to accept them, or embrace them even, as Mrs. Trenwith had done?

And what was she to think of Abby Trenwith? The woman's prurient interests were most unexpected, but did they diminish her intellectual and charitable qualities, her pleasing disposition, and her refreshing candor? Lizzy reflected back upon the art. The intercourse between a man and a woman was natural. But what of the other representations—of a man placing his erection in a woman's mouth, of men and women reveling in orgy, of Greek pederasty? And those images might prove paltry compared to the text of the Marquis de Sade, though Mrs. Trenwith, while finding value in the work, had not specifically stated that she approved of the lascivious novel.

The dinner at Hunsford Parsonage was a quiet one. No one questioned Lizzy on her visit with Mrs. Trenwith. Despite his confidence in Lady de Bourgh's assessment of Mrs. Trenwith, Mr. Collins did not seek corroboration of his earlier counsel. Lizzy was glad not to have to answer to any inquiries. As much as she might disdain being in agreement with Mr. Collins and Lady de Bourgh, she could not wholeheartedly disagree with them. Was Mrs. Trenwith to be trusted? Were her noble qualities genuine? Was it fair to question them simply because of one fault—if it could be deemed a fault? Mrs. Trenwith had certainly been under no obligation to reveal all that she had. She could have denied knowledge of the Marquis de Sade novel. Instead, she had been forthcoming, unabashed, even brave—for what she had shared with Lizzy, she risked criticism and scorn—but for her avowed disregard for the opinions of others.

Lizzy crawled into bed that night but was unable to sleep, her mind still whirling. She shuffled through each image and repeatedly recalled the Indian tapestry. Desire, already simmering since the afternoon, flared with a strength she could not ignore. Her hand crept between her thighs and found its way to that little bud of flesh at the apex of her womanhood.

Lizzy crawled into bed that night but was unable to sleep, her mind still whirling. She shuffled through each image and repeatedly recalled the Indian tapestry. Desire, already simmering since the afternoon, flared with a strength she could not ignore. Her hand crept between her thighs and found its way to that little bud of flesh at the apex of her womanhood. She had discovered the existence and sensitive nature of the nubbin when she was sixteen years of age and wondered as to its purpose. Could it be what Abby had termed the *clitoris*?

Languidly, Lizzy stroked the nub with her forefinger. The application generated an agitation throughout her lower body, but worse was the absence of it, for when she stopped her petting, she felt bereft. Her body wanted the return of that agitation. Resuming her ministration, she stroked, pulled, and pressed herself there till the sensations sweetened, the indulgence richer than the most decadent trifle or the ripest sweetmeat. She felt as if she were scratching an itch, only the source did not remain in the same spot, and the satisfaction spread far beyond the point of contact. Closing her eyes, she allowed herself to bathe in the pleasant aggravation. For half an hour or more she plied that little rosebud. The sensitivity grew and intensified to a level that persuaded her she should stop, but she—

Merciful heavens! Small but potent paroxysms rippled through her body. She nearly cried aloud as her limbs jerked of their own accord. Though her caresses now became uncomfortable, the satiation she felt was nothing short of wondrous, a true reward for her efforts. She could think of no corporal event that could engender the exhilaration equal to what she had experienced. She lay in the pleasant glow of fulfillment and knew then that desire, rather than dissipating, had come nearer to full bloom, and left her wanting of more.

* * * * *

The carriage of Lady Catherine approached the Parsonage around the following midday. Lizzy, Charlotte, and Maria were engaged in light conversation and heard the thump of a piece of furniture being overturned in the study where Mr. Collins was engaged in reading. A moment later, Mr. Collins had thrown open the door and stood breathless upon the threshold.

"Quick, Charlotte!" he called. "It is Lady de Bourgh herself!"

Charlotte leaped to her feet and joined her husband in exiting the house to greet the carriage before it came to a stop. Maria and Lizzy joined them outside.

Mr. Collins attended her ladyship like a moth to a flame, assisting her from the carriage, escorting her inside, and installing her in the best seat in the drawing-room, that she may enjoy the view out the window but not have to contend too much with the sun's rays.

"We were to take tea at the top of the hour, if your ladyship would care to join us?" Mr. Collins offered.

Lady Catherine regarded the room with the air of a schoolmaster reviewing a composition for errors of spelling or grammar. As her countenance was naturally a dour one, it was difficult to ascertain her thoughts. The room must have met with her approval, however, for she made no recommendations to Charlotte and instead replied to Mr. Collins,

"I think tea would be in order."

The delight of Mr. Collins was writ plainly upon his face as he motioned at Mrs. Collins.

Lady Catherine addressed herself mostly to Mr. Collins on matters of the parish, inquiring after his intentions for Easter service and endorsing certain passages she deemed most appropriate for the occasion, all of which Mr. Collins absorbed with the greatest rapture and repeated nodding of the head. When tea was served, Lady Catherine at last turned her attention to the other persons in her company.

"Miss Elizabeth, I heard you had a visit with Mrs. Abby Trenwith."

From the sides of her eyes, Lizzy could see Mr. Collins with a satisfied expression.

Without waiting for confirmation, Lady Catherine proceeded, "You should know that the company of Mrs. Trenwith is not one that will serve you well."

"Indeed?" Lizzy replied.

The lightness of her tone seemed to rattle Lady Catherine a little. "I speak in earnest. All good society shun the woman."

"What has she done to merit such malignancy, I wonder?"

"You need not wonder, but her grievances are not paltry."

"In my experience, she has been nothing but amiable."

"A simple young woman like yourself would not be wise to her arts."

Lizzy was unsure if the adjective applied to herself was intended as a compliment, but then, she did not think she would necessarily welcome praise from Lady Catherine.

"When Mr. Collins told me that Mrs. Trenwith had stopped at the Parsonage, I had to intervene," her ladyship continued.

"And we are fortunate to be the recipients of Lady Catherine's time and benevolence," Mr. Collins supported.

"Mrs. Trenwith had invited me to assist her in cataloging some books for an orphan asylum," Lizzy explained.

Lady Catherine appeared as if she had sniffed a disagreeable odor. "Beware, child, she engages in a variety of inappropriate activities."

Lizzy wanted to inquire how a charitable donation qualified as an inappropriate activity, but she suspected nothing Mrs. Trenwith did would earn the approval of Lady Catherine. But perhaps her ladyship was aware of the candor and exultation Abby treated the pleasures of the flesh? Lizzy suspected, however, that Lady Catherine had never been in the Trenwith art gallery. Her statement following confirmed this.

"Last month she was distributing leaflets advocating the abolition of slavery."

"Do you not think slavery an institution that ought be questioned?"

Mr. Collins paled and even Charlotte, who was more accustomed to Lizzy's attitudes, splashed the tea she had been pouring.

"If it is," Lady Catherine said with narrowed eyes, "it is not the business of women to address such a solemn subject. It is quite unbecoming in a woman of her station and wholly improper of her to rouse the masses to attend a matter that has nothing to do with them and is above their comprehension."

Lizzy flushed. She almost knew not which of Lady Catherine's insults to confront first.

"Surely my lady does not think the mind of the fair sex inferior to that of a man?"

Or you would not instruct Mr. Collins half as often as you do, Lizzy added silently.

"On the whole, no," Lady Catherine replied, "but women do have more delicate constitutions, and it is not our duty to comment on matters that are the responsibility of Parliament. Out of compassion, I did approach Mrs. Trenwith and advised her as much, but she clearly has not taken heed of what I had to say."

Lizzy wondered if that was not Abby's greatest offense.

"I must say she keeps an odd assortment of servants," Mr. Collins offered.

The Indian housekeeper and butler, as well as the Chinese driver, were certainly not what Lizzy was accustomed to seeing, but their performance differed not at all from what was to be expected of a domestic.

"Yes, her late husband was known to bring settlers from China and attempt to secure employment for them with English shipping companies," Lady Catherine added. "He was a friend of a man named John Anthony and promoted his naturalization. Imagine! A Chinaman with all the rights and privileges of a British citizen. I find it all rather shady business."

"Aside from her offenses of a political nature, of what other crimes is she guilty?" Lizzy asked.

The stumped look of disconcertion upon Lady Catherine convinced Lizzy that her ladyship was not aware of Mrs. Trenwith's erotic proclivities.

"Suffice it to say that Mrs. Trenwith is a vulgar and suspect person. Only a fool or crook would seek her company."

Mr. Collins gave an emphatic nod and echoed, "It behooves us all to discourage her association."

Feeling the discussion to be at an end, Lady Catherine then proceeded to commend Charlotte on serving a brew that was similar to the one that she herself was partial to serving at Rosings.

CHAPTER SEVEN

Though lady catherine had inspired more compassion than antipathy for Mrs. Trenwith, Lizzy resolved that, for the sake of her cousin and Charlotte, she would be a poor guest if she did not take their recommendation under advisement, which she expressed upon the following morning. Mr. Collins, though visibly disappointed that Lizzy had not capitulated beneath the impressive persuasion of her ladyship, nonetheless applauded the progress and again touted the wisdom of deferring to Lady Catherine's good opinions.

"But I should like to offer to finish the project with the books before reaching any final decisions," Lizzy said as she tied the ribbons of her bonnet.

"Dark clouds have gathered in the skies," Charlotte noted. "You might get caught in a rain."

Lizzy looked out the window. "They are a distance yet, and I can walk at a brisk pace. If need be, Mrs. Trenwith has never hesitated to offer the use of her carriage."

Not eager to have anything of Mrs. Trenwith at the Parsonage, Mr. Collins added, "If you make haste, you may well stay ahead of the clouds."

But the clouds moved faster than anyone would have hoped, and a little more than halfway to Trenwith House, a drizzle began. Lizzy contemplated turning around, but she had brought an umbrella and, as the rain was light, determined that she would prefer to fulfill her intentions rather than dwell upon them another day. She even teased herself with the possibility that if she put an end to her association with Mrs. Trenwith, she might also put an end to the ardor that persisted to flame in her body. Cultivating further friendship with Abby could only antagonize her situation.

By the time she arrived at the house, the light shower had become a steady pour. Her skirt and petticoats were wet to the knees as the rain would sometimes come at an angle when the wind blew. Mrs. Singh ushered her into the drawing-room, fussed about Miss Elizabeth catching a cold, set her before the hearth, and insisted on bringing a tray of hot tea. Lizzy was meditating on the comfort—or lack thereof—of working in sodden stockings and slippers when the doors opened. Expecting Abby to sail into the room with her customary vivacity, Lizzy was surprised to find a tall and slender gentlemen instead. Dressed in trousers that accentuated his long legs and boasting a finely tied cravat, he reminded her a little of Wickham, but, judging by his fine fashion, in possession of greater pecuniary assets. He seemed equally surprised to see Lizzy.

"Forgive the intrusion. I had thought to find Abby here."

By his familiar use of her name, Lizzy wondered if he might not be a lover of Abby's, despite his looking years younger. But then she recalled how Abby preferred the informal.

"I expected her, too," Lizzy replied, "for I think Mrs. Singh to have informed her of my presence."

They each performed a quick survey of the other. It seemed he was not disappointed to find Lizzy in place of Abby. With no information, Lizzy could only judge him to be handsome in countenance with an easy smile.

"Where are my manners?" he asked, striding toward her. He bowed. "Nicholas Trenwith."

Lizzy took in his hair, a dusty flaxen colour, worn in a modish carefree style, his eyes of muted blue, his slim nose, and rakish grin, but detected nothing that reminded her of Abby. Perhaps he was a distant relation. She bobbed a short curtsy.

"Elizabeth Bennet."

"Are you a houseguest here?"

She wondered why he made that assumption. Given her appearance, it was not likely.

"I was assisting Mrs. Trenwith yesterday with some books and returned to finish the work."

"Capital. Mother is never short of projects but rarely has assistance. You must be new to Hunsford. I have never seen you before."

"Do you know everyone in Hunsford, then?" Lizzy could not resist, for he seemed rather delighted with his assertion.

Her reply had him taken aback, but only momentarily, and his smile broadened. "I think I see why Mother invited you here."

Lizzy raised her brows.

"Please take it as a compliment for it was meant only as such. Mother likes women of wit."

"Then I fear I shall disappoint. I do not consider myself witty or clever."

"Perhaps you are being too modest—a noble quality but unnecessary for the likes of me."

"I am confident in my sincerity and have no interest in feigning attributes I do not possess."

Her statement gave him pause as he wondered if she had taken offense at what he had said, while Lizzy wondered that Abby had made no mention of a son.

"Nicholas! I knew it would not take you long to sniff out the presence of a pretty lady," remarked Abby from the entry. She approached the two and spoke to Lizzy. "I take it my stepson has introduced himself already?"

"We had the pleasure," Nicholas answered.

"Nicholas arrived yesterday from London and will be staying awhile, but my dear Lizzy, I would not have expected you to come in this weather! Mrs. Singh has laid out some clothes for you to change into. Fortunately, you are similar in height to my daughter, and she only a bit more slim. Once you are dry, you will take some tea."

Lizzy noticed that a dark-skinned maid awaited at the door. Protest would have been futile, and she welcomed a pair of dry stockings. But the prospect of Nicholas taking tea with them was disappointing for she had hoped to speak to Abby in private. Upstairs in a guest chamber, the maid assisted her out of every article. The replacement garments were much more elegant, the weave of the fabric being more fine and the cut more flattering.

To her relief, when she returned to the drawing-room, she found only Abby, though it was possible Nicholas might join them at any point.

"You look lovely, my dear," Abby said. "That spring muslin becomes you well."

"The print of faint yellow flowers is exquisite," Lizzy acknowledged as she sat across from Abby.

Abby poured the tea and wasted little time before stating, "I am not one to beat about the bush as it were, but I think for your sake, and that of your cousin and friend, that it is best you make this visit your last. It would not do for you and the Collinses to have Lady Catherine's displeasure. Pray, do not take this gesture as a form of rejection, for you know I hold you in good esteem, but I will not have it upon my conscience if you or the Collinses should lose her ladyship's respect."

Lizzy marveled at Abby's prescience and could not decide if she were disappointed or relieved that the decision to continue their acquaintance was no longer her burden.

"Mr. Collins has been most earnest in earning her approbation," Lizzy said.

"No doubt, and I have no reason to put all that good effort to waste."

"But I do not come to this end of this gladly. Meeting you will surely be one of the most a memorable occasions of my stay here ."

"I did not horrify you yesterday with my collection of art and literature?"

"It was…intriguing," Lizzy replied with a blush.

"I am glad, though I surely would not have faulted you for being shocked and appalled. Too many of us shun that which is most natural in man and beast. The lack of understanding is astonishing and makes what ought be beautiful something to fear or scorn. I can recall all too well the wedding night of my first marriage. I was so overcome with fright, for my mother had impressed upon me nothing but that it would be painful and something I had to suffer as a good wife, that death would have been easier to face."

Despite the delicacy of the topic, Lizzy felt just comfortable enough to ask, "Was it…painful?"

"Extremely. The first time is the worst. I felt as if my body would break in twain. But while the pain subsided in subsequent encounters, there was no pleasure in the act for me. It was not until I had met and married dear Mr. Trenwith that I learned that *great* pleasure can be derived. It is the most marvelous of things, the enjoyment of which does not fade with time or frequency of use."

Lizzy noted how Abby's eyes shined even brighter as she spoke. She continued,

"I was astounded and even dismayed that I once suffered through nights dreading when my husband would come into my bed. I do not blame my first husband. We neither had the knowledge nor the belief that it could be different, but I determined that as many women as possible should not have to endure what I had to. You may have heard that activities of a suspect nature occur here, and that is because I invite any woman who wishes to become informed to experience that which I had not till later in my life. I am certain the prospect of matrimonial bliss can be enhanced when women are armed with improved intelligence."

Lizzy could hardly believe her ears. The gallery and views of Mrs. Trenwith were scandalous enough, but she had made a public practice of her beliefs?

"Make no mistake, Trenwith House is *not* a brothel. It is a sanctuary where men and women can embrace the natural urges of their bodies. I am quite selective with my guests. As you can imagine, exposure would only earn them contempt and derision, thus my guests are beyond discreet, and their appreciation enforces their confidentiality."

This was a charitable endeavour of sorts? Lizzy wondered.

"I have also been blessed with the most loyal of servants. None better can be found."

As Lizzy tried to absorb the intelligence that Abby had revealed, she stayed upon a safer topic. "I imagine such loyalty is earned."

"I am not so humble to claim otherwise, but their situations prior to being at Trenwith House did lend an opportunity to win their devotion. Sally, the maid who assisted you, had worked in a brothel in the parish of St. Giles in London. She had been a slave to a brutal man who often beat her, but he had taken her with him to England, unaware that she would be free upon setting foot on English soil. She fled from him but had neither any funds nor skills to improve her situation. I came upon her in a gutter where she had fainted after subsisting on bread and water for a fortnight."

Abby told the story without the slightest hint of pride or satisfaction and with a sternness that suggested any compliment would be most unwelcome. Lizzy was convinced that the profane and the glorious could reside in one bosom. She believed Abby acted from a genuine concern for her fellow man. That her good deeds earned her contempt rather than praise among people like Lady Catherine only reinforced Lizzy's belief of Abby's altruism; and even that which others would dub profane or lewd possessed qualities of compassion and humanity.

A flash of lightning followed by the roar of thunder turned both their attentions.

"Goodness! You cannot walk back in this storm," Abby said.

"I should dearly like to finish the task we had begun yesterday," Lizzy said, knowing that Abby would offer the carriage. "That was my intention irrespective of the present weather, and perhaps by the time we are done, the storm will have abated."

"You are a dear! Well, I would be a fool to decline such able assistance and am delighted to have your company a little while longer."

They finished their tea and returned to the library, where everything was just as it was. They worked in relative silence for a length, but Lizzy could not dampen her curiosity and gradually amassed the courage to ask after the particulars.

"How do you invite women—or, what is it they expect to learn or experience?"

"I invite members of both sexes," Abby clarified, "as men can be as nonplussed as women when it comes to carnal matters. Has your mother provided you any inkling?"

Lizzy shook her head. "I might not have known to expect the menses were it not for Jane preceding me, and she was quite bewildered when her menses came for the first time."

"The first 'lesson' in a Trenwith education is to foster an understanding of your own body."

"Are you the 'instructor'?"

"Are you thinking of Phoebe from Fanny Hill?"

"I suppose a woman might know the body of another woman better than a man would."

"A man, if he be a good student, patient, and above all, observant and responsive, can be taught to become as skilled as any woman. I am seldom the instructor and prefer to match couples when possible."

Lizzy tried to imagine being with a stranger but found more comfort with the thought of Abby as 'instructor.'

"I have never had a dissatisfied student. For some, the revelation is so great that it is not unlike a spiritual awakening of sorts, and I am regarded as some sort of angel, which I find amusing given that others would say I am surely damned to hell."

"And you have had women willing...to be with someone they are unacquainted with?"

"Lest they are lovers already, it is better that way, though there is always the danger of falling in love with one's instructor or pupil, especially by the fair sex. You look skeptical, my dear."

"If all that is shared is of a carnal nature, there does not seem to be enough substance for the foundations of *love*."

"Do not underestimate the influence of the physical, but you are right, it is the *impression* of love with most. When powered by true affection, however, the result is even more wondrous."

Lizzy stared at the book she held in her hands, but her focus was blurred by the reeling of her mind.

"Do you recommend this sort of education to many?"

Abby shook her head. "By no means. Only persons of a certain character. They cannot be silly, dishonest, or have weak constitutions, and I will not disavow it takes fortitude to expose oneself to such vulnerability and intimacy. From what I discern, *you*, Miss Elizabeth, have the necessary qualities."

Wordless, Lizzy knew only that her pulse surged.

"If you were to place your trust in me, I would assure you a gentleman who had not only the skills to be a proper instructor but whose manners were beyond the pale, gentle and considerate."

Lizzy's heart beat with the rapidity of a rabbit's hind legs. Was this an invitation?

She placed her book in the stack to be donated. They continued in a busy silence. The storm outside showed no signs of abating.

When they had completed their inventory, Abby indicated she would ring for Lee to prepare the carriage.

"Though I hesitate to have you journey into such gruesome weather."

Looking out the window at the darkness and pelting rain, Lizzy concurred.

Minutes later, Lee appeared to inform them the roads were too muddy for travel by carriage.

"I fear you will have to be my guest for a while longer," Abby pronounced to Lizzy, "for venturing out on horseback in this weather, you will catch your death of cold."

"My friends will worry," Lizzy protested.

"When the worst of the storm has subsided, Lee can attempt the Parsonage on horseback. He is an experienced rider with poor conditions."

Lizzy assented and retired to the chamber she had used earlier. Abby had insisted her guest take an early supper with her. Sally attended to Lizzy, who, with closer examination, confirmed the maid no longer appeared to subsist on bread and water alone. At supper the women were joined by Nicholas, who reminded Lizzy once again of Wickham. With his pleasant countenance and affable demeanor, Nicholas would easily have been as popular among the ladies as Wickham. Nicholas asked a great many questions of Lizzy until Abby insisted that their guest be allowed to consume more than a spoonful of her soup. Having understood that Lizzy had been recently in town but that her stay was short, he regaled her with descriptions of the best sights London had to offer. As he professed a great preference for staying in town, Lizzy gathered he did not call Trenwith House home.

After supper, Nicholas recommended a game of cards, but Abby intervened by noting that Miss Elizabeth had had a long day and that a quiet or solitary activity would be more fitting. Lizzy did not feel as tired as Abby allowed—quite the contrary, she felt enervated, as she often was in the company of Mrs. Trenwith—and would have sustained a few rounds of piquet easily. She almost suspected Abby of deliberately separating Nicholas from her, though the reason eluded her. Perhaps the attention Nicholas was paying her concerned Abby, though she ought not have worried that Lizzy would have pretensions above her station. And as jovial as Nicholas was, Lizzy preferred to be alone with her thoughts at the moment, especially when, as the rain had not abated, it was determined that Lizzy would stay the night at Trenwith House.

* * * * *

Lizzy tossed and turned much of the night and was little surprised to wake up in the morning with a cough. She had thought long and hard of all that Abby had said and, in the middle of the night, had attempted to render her thoughts coherent by writing to Jane. By candlelight, she went through several drafts, and in the end, tore them all in twain. She had no intention of sharing her shocking decision to avail herself of an 'education' at Trenwith House. Jane would only worry herself ill.

Abby received the news as if Lizzy had told her nothing more significant than that she desired more butter for her bread.

"As the roads are still poor, you will worsen your cold if you travel on horseback through this rain," Abby noted after their breakfast. "I will have Lee deliver a letter to the Collinses to that effect."

Lizzy was reminded of the time when her mother had sent Jane to Netherfield on horseback in poor weather, with the hopes that Jane would be required to spend the night due to rain. The plan had succeeded beyond Mrs. Bennet's wishes, for Jane had fallen ill and was obliged to stay with the Bingleys at Netherfield for several more days. Now, under different intentions and circumstances, a similar fate had befallen Lizzy, but perceiving that her own illness was no more than a trifling cold, she refused to be confined to rest in bed and inquired if Abby had another project that required assistance?

"If you will not rest, then I insist on only docile activities," Abby replied. "A healthy pupil is an attentive one. I have matters of business to attend with my steward, but you are to be as familiar here as a member of the family."

The weather prevented a walk in the garden, and Lizzy took herself to the library instead. Without thinking, she made her way to the far shelf and retrieved a collection of poems titled *An Essay on Woman*, which she promptly dropped when she heard a voice behind her.

"You've an interesting taste in poetry, Miss Elizabeth," Nicholas noted, retrieving the work and placing it back in her hands. His eyes glimmered.

Lizzy flushed. "I've not read anything by Mr. Wilkes before."

His smile widened. "These are poems of a most bawdy nature."

She flushed deeper and began to cough, her disconcertion furthered by his proximity and the obvious appreciation in his eyes as he observed her attire. She had to admit the simple gown of cambric fit her figure well. The wide neckline dipped a little low for a morning dress but exposed to fine effect the work of her stays in lifting and separating her breasts.

Withdrawing a step from him as if to spare him from her cough, she asked, "You have read them?"

He waved a hand. "I have read most of the works on this shelf."

"Are you an avid reader then?"

"Of sorts. Are you?"

"Reading is a favourite pastime of mine."

"Have you a favourite work or author?"

"Too many to name. And you?"

"For poetry, I favour *Venus and Adonis* by William Shakespeare."

"Ah."

Somehow she had not expected that answer but one more along the lines of *A Ramble in St. James's Park.*

"Did you come across this shelf by chance or did my mother direct you?"

"The opportunity to peruse such an extensive collection of books is too great a temptation," she replied, wondering at his motive for asking.

"And have you seen her collection of art as well?"

She held her breath. Did he know of the erotic art? As the son, it was likely he would have knowledge of its presence.

"Few have seen it, admittedly," he continued. "If you have not, and possess an interest, I should be honoured to have the role of curator."

Though she was curious to look once more upon the art, viewing the salacious objects with a man she hardly knew was not to be entertained. She was surprised enough to be discussing literature of an erotic nature with him.

"I have been to the gallery with your mother," she replied.

His eyebrows rose, but her answer clearly pleased him. "May I inquire into your opinions on the collection?"

Despite her unease, she spoke as if the topic of discussion was as dull as water. "The art is scandalous."

He blinked several times, then laughed. "I like your manners, Miss Elizabeth. Do you find the art indecent?"

"Many an upright citizen would."

"Are you among the few who would not? Or perhaps you do not consider yourself *upright* at all?"

"Do you often badger your mother's guests with impertinent questions?"

"The lady is sharp of wit and tongue," replied Nicholas, amused rather than unruffled. "I beg your pardon if I offended."

"You may find it easy to discuss the, er, collections here at Trenwith House, but the nature of them are entirely new to me."

He bowed. "I made a precipitate assumption. Forgive me."

As he sounded sincere, Lizzy chose not be angry with him. "As we are barely acquainted, perhaps we should keep to tamer subjects?"

"Agreed, but I would offer a parting advice."

He removed the collection of poetry she held and replaced it with Ovid's *Ars Amatoria*.

"More tame," he explained, standing once more at a proximity within reason but dangerously unsettling.

She met his gaze. Though roguishly handsome, he did not fit her inclinations for any profound attachment, but perhaps he would do for a partner within physical limitations. Surprised by the wantonness of her own wonderings, she started to cough once more, causing Nicholas to retreat a step.

"Pardon me. I think I had best return to my chambers to rest and not worsen this cold," she said. She looked at the book in her hands. "Thank you for the recommendation."

"If you are inclined to discuss its merits, I would welcome the thoughts of a female reader on his teachings."

She nodded, relieved to be taking her leave of his company. He reminded her a little of Casanova and imagined he could—or did—seduce a fair number of women. She would have to be on her most vigilant guard with him.

CHAPTER EIGHT

Despite the light shower of rain, Darcy allowed his horse to amble along the road to Hunsford. The unfavourable conditions meant the journey would take more than half the day, but, ignoring the incredulous look of his butler and insisting he would not require his valet in advance, he had set out early in the morning. Time had failed to wipe Miss Elizabeth Bennet from his mind, and he would try any means at his disposal.

While in town he had filled every waking hour with matters of business, letters to his sister Georgiana, and calling upon acquaintances and friends. For a moment it seemed as if his application to industry had the desired effect. He knew there was little chance of returning to his initial indifference of Miss Elizabeth, but he wanted some relief from the frequency with which her bright eyes haunted his reverie. He had at first scarcely allowed her to be pretty, had looked at her without admiration at that first ball, and when they next met, had looked at her only to criticise. But no sooner had he made it clear to himself and his friends that she hardly had a good feature in her face, than he began to find it was rendered uncommonly intelligent by the beautiful expression of her dark eyes. To this discovery succeeded some others, equally mortifying. Though he had detected with a critical eye more than one failure of perfect symmetry in her form, he was forced to acknowledge her figure to be light and pleasing; and in spite of his assertion that her manners were not those of the fashionable world, he was caught by their easy playfulness.

She, however, did not seem to reflect the same level of interest in him. At a party assembled at the Lucas home, wishing to know more of her, he had moved toward her. His doing so had drawn her notice, and she turned unhappily to her friend, Miss Charlotte Lucas.

"What does Mr. Darcy mean," said she to Miss Lucas, "by listening to my conversation with Colonel Forster?"

"That is a question which Mr. Darcy only can answer."

"But if he does it any more I shall certainly let him know that I see what he is about. He has a very satirical eye, and if I do not begin by being impertinent myself, I shall soon grow afraid of him."

Taken aback by her remarks, Darcy stood awkwardly where he was. He had not intended to be caught eavesdropping and could not now invite himself into their conversation.

Miss Lucas defied her friend to speak, which immediately provoking Elizabeth to do it, she turned to him and said:

"Did you not think, Mr. Darcy, that I expressed myself uncommonly well just now, when I was teasing Colonel Forster to give us a ball at Meryton?"

"With great energy," he replied, "but it is always a subject which makes a lady energetic."

"You are severe on us."

"It will be her turn soon to be teased," said Miss Lucas. "I am going to open the instrument, Eliza, and you know what follows."

"You are a very strange creature by way of a friend, always wanting me to play and sing before anybody and everybody! If my vanity had taken a musical turn, you would have been invaluable, but as it is, I would really rather not sit down before those who must be in the habit of hearing the very best performers." On Miss Lucas's persevering, however, she added, "Very well, if it must be so, it must." And gravely glancing at him, "There is a fine old saying, which everybody here is of course familiar with: 'Keep your breath to cool your porridge'; and I shall keep mine to swell my song."

Her performance was pleasing, though by no means capital. After a song or two, and before she could reply to the entreaties of several that she would sing again, she was eagerly succeeded at the instrument by her sister Mary, who having, in consequence of being the only plain one in the family, seemed impatient to display her accomplishments.

Miss Mary had neither genius nor taste, but possessed a pedantic air and conceited manner. Miss Elizabeth, easy and unaffected, had been listened to with much more pleasure, though not playing half so well; and Mary, at the end of a long concerto, was glad to purchase praise and gratitude by Scotch and Irish airs, at the request of her younger sisters, who, with some of the Lucases, and two or three officers, joined eagerly in dancing at one end of the room.

Darcy stood near them in silent indignation at such a mode of passing the evening, to the exclusion of all conversation, and was too much engrossed by his thoughts to perceive that Sir William Lucas was his neighbour, till Sir William began:

"What a charming amusement for young people this is, Mr. Darcy! There is nothing like dancing after all. I consider it as one of the first refinements of polished society."

"Certainly, sir; and it has the advantage also of being in vogue amongst the less polished societies of the world. Every savage can dance."

Sir William only smiled. "Your friend performs delightfully," he continued after a pause, on seeing Bingley join the group, "and I doubt not that you are an adept in the science yourself, Mr. Darcy."

"You saw me dance at Meryton, I believe, sir."

"Yes, indeed, and received no inconsiderable pleasure from the sight. Do you often dance at St. James's?"

"Never, sir."

"Do you not think it would be a proper compliment to the place?"

"It is a compliment which I never pay to any place if I can avoid it."

"You have a house in town, I conclude?"

Darcy bowed.

"I had once had some thought of fixing in town myself—for I am fond of superior society; but I did not feel quite certain that the air of London would agree with Lady Lucas."

He paused in hopes of an answer, but Darcy was not disposed to make any for Miss Elizabeth at that instant was moving towards them.

"My dear Miss Eliza, why are you not dancing?" Sir William called out to her. "Mr. Darcy, you must allow me to present this young lady to you as a very desirable partner. You cannot refuse to dance, I am sure, when so much beauty is before you."

And, taking her hand, Sir William would have given it to Darcy, who was not unwilling to receive it, when she instantly drew back.

With some discomposure, she replied, "Indeed, sir, I have not the least intention of dancing. I entreat you not to suppose that I moved this way in order to beg for a partner."

Darcy, with grave propriety, requested to be allowed the honour of her hand, but in vain. Miss Elizabeth was determined, nor did Sir

William at all shake her purpose by his attempt at persuasion.

"You excel so much in the dance, Miss Eliza, that it is cruel to deny me the happiness of seeing you, and though this gentleman dislikes the amusement in general, he can have no objection, I am sure, to oblige us for one half-hour."

"Mr. Darcy is all politeness," she said.

"He is, indeed, but, considering the inducement, my dear Miss Eliza, we cannot wonder at his complaisance—for who would object to such a partner?"

Miss Elizabeth looked archly, and turned away. Her resistance did not injure her, however, with him, and he was thinking of her with some complacency when accosted by Miss Caroline Bingley.

"I can guess the subject of your reverie."

"I should imagine not."

"You are considering how insupportable it would be to pass many evenings in this manner—in such society, and indeed I am quite of your opinion. I was never more annoyed! The insipidity, and yet the noise—the nothingness, and yet the self-importance of all those people! What would I give to hear your strictures on them!"

"Your conjecture is totally wrong, I assure you. My mind was more agreeably engaged. I have been meditating on the very great pleasure which a pair of fine eyes in the face of a pretty woman can bestow."

"Indeed? What lady has the credit of inspiring such reflections?"

"Miss Elizabeth Bennet."

"Miss Elizabeth Bennet!" repeated Miss Bingley. "I am all astonishment. How long has she been such a favourite? And pray, when am I to wish you joy?"

"That is exactly the question which I expected you to ask. A lady's imagination is very rapid; it jumps from admiration to love, from love to matrimony, in a moment. I knew you would be wishing me joy."

"Nay, if you are serious about it, I shall consider the matter is absolutely settled. You will be having a charming mother-in-law, indeed, and, of course, she will always be at Pemberley with you."

He listened to her with perfect indifference while she chose to entertain herself in this manner, and as his composure convinced her that all was safe, her wit flowed long.

* * * * *

"Darcy!" Abby greeted him upon entering the parlor. Her radiance and joy warmed him in an instant and set him at ease, making him believe that she welcomed his appearance though he had sent no word of his coming. He had written her that he was to visit his aunt for Easter and intended to call upon her after he had arrived at Rosings.

"Pray forgive the unexpected intrusion," he said after he had kissed her hand.

She pressed his hand with affection, her smile never failing to make him feel adored. She looked to be in good health, her cheeks rosier than he last remembered. He fancied she flushed in delight at his presence for she had often told him that he was a favourite of hers.

"Nonsense!" she chided before taking a seat facing the hearth. "You know that you are welcome any time here at Trenwith House."

His riding breeches still damp from the rain, Darcy remained standing in front of the fire.

"But how reckless of you to ride through this weather," she admonished. "Mr. Singh informed me that you came on horseback."

"I met with rain only when I neared Hunsford."

"Do you mean to ride on to Rosings? Lee tells me the roads are quite wretched."

"That is my intention," he replied, though his aunt did not expect him till the following day and he much preferred the company of Abby to Lady de Bourgh.

She appraised him from head to toe and seemed a little pensive. "You ought to dry yourself here before venturing back into the deluge."

"Your reasoning eludes me. How am I benefitted by being dry before I become wet again?"

"Perhaps that was my awkward attempt to get you to stay for supper."

If she had demanded he stay for supper—and he had expected her to be forthcoming with such a request for he had never known Abby to be demure—he would have done it. Abby always brimmed with élan, but this evening he sensed an edge to her verve.

"If that is your invitation, I accept," he said.

"Wonderful! Mr. Singh can prepare a room for you in the West Wing."

He raised his brows. On all past occasions, he had always had the same room in the East Wing.

She waved a dismissive hand. "Nicholas is here."

It was an adequate but not entirely convincing pretext, but as he had never been partial to the company of Nicholas Trenwith, he made no objections.

Mrs. Singh entered with a tray of tea and coffee. Abby prepared his coffee as she knew he preferred it, with a modicum of milk and no sugar.

"I thought Colonel Fitzwilliam was to come as well," she remarked, handing him his coffee.

"He had another matter to attend. We were to travel to Rosings together tomorrow, but I will meet him at the nearest posting inn instead."

She eyed him keenly, and the cup of coffee he held afforded him no place to hide. "And what urgency compelled you to ride out on your own such that you could not wait a day for your cousin?"

He sipped his coffee. A part of him wanted to divulge the entire truth to her, but he had come here to forget about Miss Elizabeth Bennet, not perpetuate her memory by speaking of her.

"Pray, do not *insult* me by *flattering* me that you could hardly wait to be in my company," she warned.

"I felt myself restless," he admitted, "and will not tire you with the details at this time."

She knew him well enough not to goad him when he was not in the mood and obliged him by making more mundane conversation. "How is Georgiana?"

"In good health and spirits. I am having a new pianoforte delivered to Pemberley. I am told the quality of sound is extraordinary and the keys particularly sensitive to the touch."

"I'm sure she will be quite delighted. And how is your friend, Charles Bingley? When does he return to Netherfield?"

Darcy stiffened. "I do not think he will return."

"What? Had he not just leased the property recently?"

"He did."

"Does Hertfordshire not agree with him?"

"There were circumstances there that…his sisters and I believe he is better situated elsewhere."

She stared at him, and he knew his cryptic answer did not satisfy her, but, again, she refrained from pressing; nonetheless, Abby did not forget small details and could often find a way to unearth the information she sought before one was even aware that anything had been divulged.

"I will have Mrs. Singh bring supper to your room. If you are not expected at Rosings till the morrow, you ought to stay the night here. Pierre can serve as your valet."

He breathed in relief, for he had hoped she would extend just such an invitation. "If it is not too much an imposition—"

"Darcy, you are never an imposition. Quite the contrary. Your arrival is most timely."

She took in a deep breath, and he wondered if she was unsure of herself. He had never known Abby to be uncertain.

"I have as a guest a young woman in need of an *introduction*. Of all those who have served as instructor, I have determined your manners to be the most tender and most suitable to her naïveté."

Though she had never before been reticent to address him, she refrained from looking at him directly.

He hesitated. "It has been some time since…"

She smiled to reassure him. "You were far too good a student to forget your art."

"Nonetheless, I am out of practice."

"She will not know it. She is a complete virgin. You spoke of being restless. Perhaps a lesson would calm whatever ails you."

He weighed her words. The responsibility—and pleasure—of awakening a woman to the capabilities of her own body would surely divert his attention from Miss Elizabeth. Abby waited in silence for his response, and he knew then there was no refusing her. She would wait an eternity without word lest he gave her the answer she wanted.

"I should be honoured."

"Her family is of a good sort, I believe. In all honesty, I know very little of her or her background, but I am quite taken by her. Her decision to seek an education caught me by surprise, and I wonder that she may suffer buyer's remorse at any time. We must take every care to guard her identity."

He almost protested the need for such reminders for he had never been indiscreet.

"I have formed quite a fondness for her and wish her to have the best experience possible."

"I will endeavour to do my best."

Abby beamed. "Of course you will, and I trust you above anyone."

"I doubt I merit such a compliment."

Her eyes gleamed. "I can say unequivocally you were my best student."

"And I am forever indebted to you that you were willing to take on the mantle of teacher with me."

"The pleasure was mine."

Their exchange thereafter was the warm and easy affection he remembered till Mr. Singh came to inform them that the guestroom was ready. After Abby promised to join him for supper, they parted ways.

In his room, while Pierre assisted him from his riding clothes, Darcy reconsidered his decision not to share the events at Hertfordshire with Abby. His conscience weighed on him. It was his persistent persuasion, as well as the efforts of Bingley's sisters, Caroline and Louisa, that had compelled Charles to quit Netherfield.

While in London, Miss Jane Bennet had called upon Miss Bingley. Between him and Caroline, they had kept the knowledge of Miss Bennet's presence to themselves. He was not pleased with his duplicity in not informing Charles, and as if by way of punishing himself, he did not pass a single day without thinking of Miss Elizabeth. After she had refused his hand in dance at the Lucas assembly, he had considered it just as well that she took no interest in him. Perhaps her response would cool his own. But shortly thereafter Nature and the Bennets had, unknowingly, conspired otherwise.

After the Lucas ball, at the request of her brother, Caroline had invited Miss Bennet to dine with her and Louisa at Netherfield. Despite the dreary weather, Jane had arrived on horseback rather than by carriage. Darcy had thought it rather suspect and would not have been surprised if Mrs. Bennet had sent her daughter through the rain on purpose. As a consequence, intended or not, Miss Bennet had fallen ill and was obliged to remain at Netherfield.

But Darcy could not be vexed with the situation for the following morning brought Miss Elizabeth to Netherfield to inquire after her sister. He remembered the surprise her appearance, with her dirty stockings and her face glowing from the warmth of exercise, had engendered among those gathered in the breakfast-parlor.

That she should have walked three miles so early in the day, in such dirty weather, and by herself, was almost incredible to Louisa and Caroline. They could not hide all their contempt but received her politely. Bingley was good humour and kindness. Darcy said little, being divided between admiration of the brilliancy which exercise had given to her complexion and doubt as to the occasion's justifying her coming so far alone.

Her inquiries after her sister were not very favourably answered. Miss Bennet had slept ill, and though up, was very feverish, and not well enough to leave her room. Miss Elizabeth seemed glad to be taken to her immediately. The apothecary came and pronounced his patient to suffer from a violent cold. Miss Elizabeth stayed by her sister's side for the day, and when it seemed her departure would cause Miss Bennet much concern, Bingley was obliged to convert his offer of his chaise to an invitation to remain at Netherfield for the present.

Dinner with Miss Elizabeth had passed with some awkwardness. Bingley, quite anxious for Miss Bennet's health, bestowed his attentions upon her most amply. Caroline and Louisa said but a few words to her; and Mr. Hurst, Louisa's husband, an indolent man, who lived only to eat, drink, and play at cards, had nothing to say to her when he found her to prefer a plain dish to a ragout.

When dinner was over, Miss Elizabeth returned directly to her sister, and Caroline began abusing her as soon as she was out of the room. Her manners were pronounced to be very bad indeed, a mixture of pride and impertinence. She had no conversation, no style, no beauty.

Louisa thought the same, and added, "She has nothing, in short, to recommend her, but being an excellent walker. I shall never forget her appearance this morning. She really looked almost wild."

"She did, indeed, Louisa. I could hardly keep my countenance. Very nonsensical to come at all! Why must she be scampering about the country, because her sister had a cold? Her hair, so untidy, so blowsy!"

"Yes, and her petticoat; I hope you saw her petticoat, six inches deep in mud, I am absolutely certain; and the gown which had been let down to hide it not doing its office."

"Your picture may be very exact, Louisa," said Bingley; "but this was all lost upon me. I thought Miss Elizabeth Bennet looked remarkably well when she came into the room this morning. Her dirty petticoat quite escaped my notice."

"You observed it, Mr. Darcy, I am sure," said Miss Bingley; "and I am inclined to think that you would not wish to see your sister make such an exhibition."

"Certainly not," he said.

"To walk three miles, or four miles, or five miles, or whatever it is, above her ankles in dirt, and alone, quite alone! What could she mean by it? It seems to me to show an abominable sort of conceited independence, a most country-town indifference to decorum."

"It shows an affection for her sister that is very pleasing," said Bingley.

"I am afraid, Mr. Darcy," observed Caroline in a half whisper, "that this adventure has rather affected your admiration of her fine eyes."

"Not at all," he replied, "they were brightened by the exercise."

A short pause followed this speech, and Louisa began again, "I have an excessive regard for Miss Jane Bennet, she is really a very sweet girl, and I wish with all my heart she were well settled. But with such a father and mother, and such low connections, I am afraid there is no chance of it."

"I think I have heard you say that their uncle is an attorney in Meryton."

"Yes, and they have another, who lives somewhere near Cheapside."

"That is capital," added her sister, and they both laughed heartily.

"If they had uncles enough to fill all Cheapside," cried Bingley, "it would not make them one jot less agreeable."

"But it must very materially lessen their chance of marrying men of any consideration in the world," replied Darcy.

To this speech Bingley made no answer, but his sisters gave it their hearty assent, and indulged their mirth for some time at the expense of their dear friend's vulgar relations.

With a renewal of tenderness, however, they returned to her room on leaving the dining-parlour, and sat with her till summoned to coffee. Miss Bennet was still very poorly, and Miss Elizabeth would not quit her at all, till late in the evening after she had the comfort of seeing her sleep. The whole party was at loo when she entered the drawing-room and was invited to join them. She declined and, making her sister the excuse, said she would amuse herself for the short time she could stay below, with a book. Mr. Hurst looked at her with astonishment.

"Do you prefer reading to cards?" said he, "that is rather singular."

"Miss Eliza Bennet," said Miss Bingley, "despises cards. She is a great reader, and has no pleasure in anything else."

"I deserve neither such praise nor such censure," cried Miss Elizabeth, "I am not a great reader, and I have pleasure in many things."

"In nursing your sister I am sure you have pleasure," said Bingley; "and I hope it will be soon increased by seeing her quite well."

She thanked him from her heart, and then walked towards the table where a few books were lying. He immediately offered to fetch her others—all that his library afforded.

"And I wish my collection were larger for your benefit and my own credit, but I am an idle fellow, and though I have not many, I have more than I ever looked into."

She assured him that she could suit herself perfectly with those in the room.

"I am astonished," said Caroline, "that my father should have left so small a collection of books. What a delightful library you have at Pemberley, Mr. Darcy!"

"It ought to be good," he replied, "it has been the work of many generations."

"And then you have added so much to it yourself, you are always buying books."

"I cannot comprehend the neglect of a family library in such days as these."

"Neglect! I am sure you neglect nothing that can add to the beauties of that noble place. Charles, when you build your house, I wish it may be half as delightful as Pemberley."

"I wish it may."

"But I would really advise you to make your purchase in that neighbourhood, and take Pemberley for a kind of model. There is not a finer county in England than Derbyshire."

"With all my heart. I will buy Pemberley itself if Darcy will sell it."

"I am talking of possibilities, Charles."

"Upon my word, Caroline, I should think it more possible to get Pemberley by purchase than by imitation."

Miss Elizabeth seemed so much caught with what passed, as to leave her very little attention for her book; and soon laying it wholly aside, she drew near the card-table, and stationed herself between Mr. Bingley and his eldest sister, to observe the game.

"Is Miss Darcy much grown since the spring?" said Caroline; "will she be as tall as I am?"

"I think she will. She is now about Miss Elizabeth Bennet's height, or rather taller," Darcy answered.

"How I long to see her again! I never met with anybody who delighted me so much. Such a countenance, such manners! And so extremely accomplished for her age! Her performance on the pianoforte is exquisite."

"It is amazing to me," said Bingley, "how young ladies can have patience to be so very accomplished as they all are."

"All young ladies accomplished! My dear Charles, what do you mean?"

"Yes, all of them, I think. They all paint tables, cover screens, and net purses. I scarcely know anyone who cannot do all this, and I am sure I never heard a young lady spoken of for the first time, without being informed that she was very accomplished."

"Your list of the common extent of accomplishments," said Darcy, "has too much truth. The word is applied to many a woman who deserves it no otherwise than by netting a purse or covering a screen. But I am very far from agreeing with you in your estimation of ladies in general. I cannot boast of knowing more than half-a-dozen, in the whole range of my acquaintance, that are really accomplished."

"Nor I, I am sure," said Caroline.

"Then," observed Miss Elizabeth, "you must comprehend a great deal in your idea of an accomplished woman."

"Yes, I do comprehend a great deal in it," he replied.

"Oh! certainly," cried Caroline, "no one can be really esteemed accomplished who does not greatly surpass what is usually met with. A woman must have a thorough knowledge of music, singing, drawing, dancing, and the modern languages, to deserve the word; and besides all this, she must possess a certain something in her air and manner of walking, the tone of her voice, her address and expressions, or the word will be but half-deserved."

"All this she must possess," added Darcy, "and to all this she must yet add something more substantial, in the improvement of her mind by extensive reading."

"I am no longer surprised at your knowing *only* six accomplished women. I rather wonder now at your knowing *any*," Miss Elizabeth said

"Are you so severe upon your own sex as to doubt the possibility of all this?"

"I never saw such a woman. I never saw such capacity, and taste, and application, and elegance, as you describe united."

Louisa and Caroline both cried out against the injustice of her implied doubt, and were both protesting that they knew many women who answered this description, when Mr. Hurst called them to order, with bitter complaints of their inattention to what was going forward. As all conversation was thereby at an end, Miss Elizabeth soon afterwards left the room.

"Elizabeth Bennet," said Caroline, when the door was closed on her, "is one of those young ladies who seek to recommend themselves to the other sex by undervaluing their own, and with many men, I dare say, it succeeds. But, in my opinion, it is a paltry device, a very mean art."

"Undoubtedly," replied Darcy, perceiving the remark was chiefly addressed to him, "there is a meanness in all the arts which ladies sometimes condescend to employ for captivation. Whatever bears affinity to cunning is despicable."

Miss Bingley was not so entirely satisfied with this reply as to continue the subject.

CHAPTER NINE

The following morning brought more visitors in the form of Mrs. Bennet and her two youngest daughters. Though finding Miss Bennet improved in health, the mother refused, nevertheless, to hear of Jane being removed Netherfield. Darcy admitted to some gladness at the prospect of having Miss Elizabeth's company a while longer.

"I hope you do not find your daughter worse than expected?" Bingly inquired, attending to his guests in the breakfast parlour.

"Indeed I have, sir," was her answer. "She is a great deal too ill to be moved. Mr. Jones says we must not think of moving her. We must trespass a little longer on your kindness."

"Removed!" cried Bingley. "It must not be thought of. My sister, I am sure, will not hear of her removal."

"You may depend upon it, Madam," said Caroline, with cold civility, "that Miss Bennet will receive every possible attention while she remains with us."

Mrs. Bennet was profuse in her acknowledgements.

"I am sure," she said, "if it was not for such good friends I do not know what would become of Jane, for she is very ill indeed, and suffers a vast deal, though with the greatest patience in the world, which is always the way with her, for she has, without exception, the sweetest temper I have ever met with. I often tell my other girls they are nothing to her. You have a sweet room here, Mr. Bingley, and a charming prospect over the gravel walk. I do not know a place in the country that is equal to Netherfield. You will not think of quitting it in a hurry, I hope, though you have but a short lease."

"Whatever I do is done in a hurry," replied he, "and therefore if I should resolve to quit Netherfield, I should probably be off in five minutes. At present, however, I consider myself as quite fixed here."

"That is exactly what I should have supposed of you," said Miss

Elizabeth.

"You begin to comprehend me, do you?" cried he, turning towards her.

"Oh! yes—I understand you perfectly."

"I wish I might take this for a compliment, but to be so easily seen through I am afraid is pitiful."

"That is as it happens. It does not follow that a deep, intricate character is more or less estimable than such a one as yours."

"Lizzy," cried her mother, "remember where you are, and do not run on in the wild manner that you are suffered to do at home."

"I did not know before," continued Bingley immediately, "that you were a studier of character. It must be an amusing study."

"Yes, but intricate characters are the most amusing. They have at least that advantage."

"The country," said Darcy, "can in general supply but a few subjects for such a study. In a country neighbourhood you move in a very confined and unvarying society."

"But people themselves alter so much, that there is something new to be observed in them for ever."

"Yes, indeed," cried Mrs. Bennet, sounding offended by his manner of mentioning a country neighbourhood. "I assure you there is quite as much of that going on in the country as in town."

Everybody was surprised, and Darcy, after looking at her for a moment, turned silently away. Mrs. Bennet, who fancied she had gained a complete victory over him, continued her triumph.

"I cannot see that London has any great advantage over the country, for my part, except the shops and public places. The country is a vast deal pleasanter, is it not, Mr. Bingley?"

"When I am in the country," he replied, "I never wish to leave it, and when I am in town it is pretty much the same. They have each their advantages, and I can be equally happy in either."

"Aye—that is because you have the right disposition. But that gentleman," looking at Darcy, "seemed to think the country was nothing at all."

"Indeed, Mamma, you are mistaken," said Miss Elizabeth, blushing for her mother. "You quite mistook Mr. Darcy. He only meant that there was not such a variety of people to be met with in the country as in the town, which you must acknowledge to be true."

"Certainly, my dear, nobody said there were, but as to not meeting with many people in this neighbourhood, I believe there are few neighbourhoods larger. I know we dine with four-and-twenty families."

Nothing but concern for Elizabeth could enable Bingley to keep his countenance. His sister was less delicate, and Darcy often found her eyes directed at him with a very expressive smile. Miss Elizabeth, appearing for the sake of saying something that might turn her mother's thoughts, now asked her if Charlotte Lucas had been at Longbourn since her coming away.

"Yes, she called yesterday with her father. What an agreeable man Sir William is, Mr. Bingley, is not he? So much the man of fashion! So genteel and easy! He has always something to say to everybody. That is my idea of good breeding; and those persons who fancy themselves very important, and never open their mouths, quite mistake the matter."

"Did Charlotte dine with you?"

"No, she would go home. I fancy she was wanted about the mince-pies. For my part, Mr. Bingley, I always keep servants that can do their own work; my daughters are brought up very differently. But everybody is to judge for themselves, and the Lucases are a very good sort of girls, I assure you. It is a pity they are not handsome! Not that I think Charlotte so very plain—but then she is our particular friend."

"She seems a very pleasant young woman," Bingley remarked.

"Oh! Dear, yes, but you must own she is very plain. Lady Lucas herself has often said so, and envied me Jane's beauty. I do not like to boast of my own child, but to be sure, Jane—one does not often see anybody better looking. It is what everybody says. I do not trust my own partiality. When she was only fifteen, there was a man at my brother Gardiner's in town so much in love with her that my sister-in-law was sure he would make her an offer before we came away. But, however, he did not. Perhaps he thought her too young. However, he wrote some verses on her, and very pretty they were."

"And so ended his affection," said Miss Elizabeth with impatience. "There has been many a one, I fancy, overcome in the same way. I wonder who first discovered the efficacy of poetry in driving away love!"

"I have been used to consider poetry as the food of love," said Darcy, finding himself a little eager for her attention.

"Of a fine, stout, healthy love it may. Everything nourishes what is strong already. But if it be only a slight, thin sort of inclination, I am convinced that one good sonnet will starve it entirely away."

Mrs. Bennet began repeating her thanks to Mr. Bingley for his kindness to her daughter with an apology for troubling him also with Miss Elizbaeth. Mr. Bingley was unaffectedly civil in his answer, and forced his younger sister to be civil also, and say what the occasion required. She performed her part indeed without much graciousness, but Mrs. Bennet appeared satisfied, and soon afterwards ordered her carriage. Upon this signal, the youngest of her daughters put herself forward. The two girls had been whispering to each other during the whole visit, and the result of it seemed, that the youngest should tax Mr. Bingley with having promised on his first coming into the country to give a ball at Netherfield.

Lydia was a stout, well-grown girl of fifteen, with a fine complexion and good-humoured countenance. She seemed a favourite with her mother and possessed a sort of natural self-consequence and assurance. She was very equal, therefore, to address Mr. Bingley on the subject of the ball, and abruptly reminded him of his promise, adding, that it would be the most shameful thing in the world if he did not keep it. His answer to this sudden attack delighted their mother.

"I am perfectly ready, I assure you, to keep my engagement; and when your sister is recovered, you shall, if you please, name the very day of the ball. But you would not wish to be dancing when she is ill."

Lydia declared herself satisfied. "Oh, yes! It would be much better to wait till Jane was well, and by that time most likely Captain Carter would be at Meryton again. And when you have given your ball, I shall insist on their giving one also. I shall tell Colonel Forster it will be quite a shame if he does not."

Mrs. Bennet and her daughters then departed, and Miss Elizabeth returned instantly to her sister. Bingley's sisters set immediately to remarking upon the departed Bennets, and Darcy had to agree with them. Caroline, however, could not prevail upon him to join in their censure of Miss Elizabeth, in spite of all Caroline's witticisms on fine eyes.

* * * * *

The following day passed much as the day before had done. Bingley's sisters had spent some hours of the morning with the invalid, who continued, though slowly, to mend. In the evening Miss Elizabeth joined their party in the drawing-room and took up some needlework. The loo-table, however, did not appear. Darcy was writing to Georgiana. Caroline, seated near him, rained commendations upon his handwriting, the evenness of his lines, and the length of his letter, all of which he received with unconcern.

"How delighted Miss Darcy will be to receive such a letter!" Caroline said.

He made no answer.

"You write uncommonly fast."

"You are mistaken. I write rather slowly."

"How many letters you must have occasion to write in the course of a year! Letters of business, too! How odious I should think them!"

"It is fortunate, then, that they fall to my lot instead of yours."

"Pray tell your sister that I long to see her."

"I have already told her so once, by your desire."

"I am afraid you do not like your pen. Let me mend it for you. I mend pens remarkably well."

"Thank you—but I always mend my own."

"How can you contrive to write so even?"

He was silent.

"Tell your sister I am delighted to hear of her improvement on the harp; and pray let her know that I am quite in raptures with her beautiful little design for a table, and I think it infinitely superior to Miss Grantley's."

"Will you give me leave to defer your raptures till I write again? At present I have not room to do them justice."

"Oh! it is of no consequence. I shall see her in January. But do you always write such charming long letters to her, Mr. Darcy?"

"They are generally long; but whether always charming it is not for me to determine."

"It is a rule with me, that a person who can write a long letter with ease, cannot write ill."

"That will not do for a compliment to Darcy, Caroline," cried her brother, "because he does *not* write with ease. He studies too much for words of four syllables. Do not you, Darcy?"

"My style of writing is very different from yours."

"Oh!" cried Caroline, "Charles writes in the most careless way imaginable. He leaves out half his words, and blots the rest."

"My ideas flow so rapidly that I have not time to express them— by which means my letters sometimes convey no ideas at all to my correspondents."

"Your humility, Mr. Bingley," said Miss Elizabeth, "must disarm reproof."

"Nothing is more deceitful," said Darcy, surprised to find himself a little jealous of his friend, "than the appearance of humility. It is often only carelessness of opinion, and sometimes an indirect boast."

"And which of the two do you call *my* little recent piece of modesty?"

"The indirect boast; for you are really proud of your defects in writing, because you consider them as proceeding from a rapidity of thought and carelessness of execution, which, if not estimable, you think at least highly interesting. The power of doing anything with quickness is always prized much by the possessor, and often without any attention to the imperfection of the performance. When you told Mrs. Bennet this morning that if you ever resolved upon quitting Netherfield you should be gone in five minutes, you meant it to be a sort of panegyric, of compliment to yourself—and yet what is there so very laudable in a precipitance which must leave very necessary business undone, and can be of no real advantage to yourself or anyone else?"

"Nay," cried Bingley, "this is too much, to remember at night all the foolish things that were said in the morning. And yet, upon my honour, I believe what I said of myself to be true, and I believe it at this moment. At least, therefore, I did not assume the character of needless precipitance merely to show off before the ladies."

"I dare say you believed it, but I am by no means convinced that you would be gone with such celerity. Your conduct would be quite as dependent on chance as that of any man I know; and if, as you were mounting your horse, a friend were to say, 'Bingley, you had better stay till next week,' you would probably do it, you would probably not go—and at another word, might stay a month."

"You have only proved by this," cried Miss Elizabeth, "that Mr. Bingley did not do justice to his own disposition. You have shown him off now much more than he did himself."

"I am exceedingly gratified," said Bingley, "by your converting what my friend says into a compliment on the sweetness of my temper. But I am afraid you are giving it a turn which that gentleman did by no means intend; for he would certainly think better of me, if under such a circumstance I were to give a flat denial, and ride off as fast as I could."

"Would Mr. Darcy then consider the rashness of your original intentions as atoned for by your obstinacy in adhering to it?"

"Upon my word, I cannot exactly explain the matter; Darcy must speak for himself."

"You expect me to account for opinions which you choose to call mine, but which I have never acknowledged. Allowing the case, however, to stand according to your representation, you must remember, Miss Bennet, that the friend who is supposed to desire his return to the house, and the delay of his plan, has merely desired it, asked it without offering one argument in favour of its propriety."

"To yield readily—easily—to the *persuasion* of a friend is no merit with you."

"To yield without conviction is no compliment to the understanding of either."

"You appear to me, Mr. Darcy, to allow nothing for the influence of friendship and affection. A regard for the requester would often make one readily yield to a request, without waiting for arguments to reason one into it. I am not particularly speaking of such a case as you have supposed about Mr. Bingley. We may as well wait, perhaps, till the circumstance occurs before we discuss the discretion of his behaviour thereupon. But in general and ordinary cases between friend and friend, where one of them is desired by the other to change a resolution of no very great moment, should you think ill of that person for complying with the desire, without waiting to be argued into it?"

"Will it not be advisable, before we proceed on this subject, to arrange with rather more precision the degree of importance which is to appertain to this request, as well as the degree of intimacy subsisting between the parties?"

"By all means," cried Bingley; "let us hear all the particulars, not forgetting their comparative height and size; for that will have more weight in the argument, Miss Bennet, than you may be aware of. I assure you, that if Darcy were not such a great tall fellow, in comparison with myself, I should not pay him half so much deference. I declare I do not know a more awful object than Darcy, on particular occasions, and in particular places—at his own house especially, and of a Sunday evening, when he has nothing to do."

Darcy ony smiled. He would not have taken offense but for the fact that the words had been uttered before Miss Elizabeth, who appeared to check her laughter. Caroline warmly resented the indignity Darcy had received, in an expostulation with her brother for talking such nonsense.

"I see your design, Bingley," said Caroline. "You dislike an argument, and want to silence this."

"Perhaps I do. Arguments are too much like disputes. If you and Miss Bennet will defer yours till I am out of the room, I shall be very thankful; and then you may say whatever you like of me."

"What you ask," said Miss Elizabeth, "is no sacrifice on my side, and Mr. Darcy had much better finish his letter."

Darcy took her advice and finished his letter.

When that business was over, he applied to Caroline and Elizabeth for an indulgence of some music. Caroline moved with some alacrity to the pianoforte, and, after a polite request that Miss Elizabeth would lead the way which the other as politely and more earnestly negatived, she seated herself.

Louisa sang with her sister, and while they were thus employed, Darcy took the opportunity to observe Miss Elizabeth, who turned over some music-books that lay on the instrument. She caught his gaze twice, but rather than blush or be disconcerted or offended, she returned to her business. He gathered she did not care enough for his approbation to merit a response of any kind.

He could not resist. While Caroline varied some Italian songs by a lively Scotch air, he drew near Miss Elizabeth and asked, "Do not you feel a great inclination, Miss Bennet, to seize such an opportunity of dancing a reel?"

She smiled, but made no answer. He repeated the question, with some surprise at her silence.

"Oh!" said she, "I heard you before, but I could not immediately determine what to say in reply. You wanted me, I know, to say 'Yes,' that you might have the pleasure of despising my taste, but I always delight in overthrowing those kind of schemes, and cheating a person of their premeditated contempt. I have, therefore, made up my mind to tell you, that I do not want to dance a reel at all—and now despise me if you dare."

"Indeed I do not dare."

Miss Elizabeth seemed surprise at his gallantry, but there was a mixture of sweetness and archness in her manner which made it difficult for her to affront him. She was really quit bewitching. If it were not for the inferiority of her connections, he should be in some danger.

Caroline saw, or suspected enough to be jealous. She often tried to provoke Darcy into disliking her guest, by talking of their supposed marriage, and planning his happiness in such an alliance.

"I hope," said she, as they were walking together in the shrubbery the next day, "you will give your mother-in-law a few hints, when this desirable event takes place, as to the advantage of holding her tongue; and if you can compass it, do cure the younger girls of running after officers. And, if I may mention so delicate a subject, endeavour to check that little something, bordering on conceit and impertinence, which your lady possesses."

"Have you anything else to propose for my domestic felicity?"

"Oh, yes! Do let the portraits of your uncle and aunt Phillips be placed in the gallery at Pemberley. Put them next to your great-uncle the judge. They are in the same profession, you know, only in different lines. As for your Elizabeth's picture, you must not have it taken, for what painter could do justice to those beautiful eyes?"

"It would not be easy, indeed, to catch their expression, but their colour and shape, and the eyelashes, so remarkably fine, might be copied."

At that moment they were met from another walk by Louisa and Miss Elizabeth herself.

"I did not know that you intended to walk," said Caroline, in some confusion, lest they had been overheard.

"You used us abominably ill," answered Louisa, "running away without telling us that you were coming out."

Then taking Darcy's disengaged arm, she left Miss Elizabeth to walk by herself. The path just admitted three. Darcy felt their rudeness, and immediately said, "This walk is not wide enough for our party. We had better go into the avenue."

But Miss Elizabeth laughingly answered, ""No, no. Stay where you are. You are charmingly grouped, and appear to uncommon advantage. The picturesque would be spoilt by admitting a fourth.

Good-bye."

She then ran gaily off. If he were not so vexed with Bingley's sisters, he would have savored the enchantment of her rambling away.

* * * * *

After dinner, Miss Bennet was well enough to come into the drawing-room. Darcy addressed himself to Miss Bennet, with a polite congratulation; Mr. Hurst also made her a slight bow, and said he was "very glad;" but diffuseness and warmth remained for Bingley's salutation. He was full of joy and attention. The first half-hour was spent in piling up the fire, lest she should suffer from the change of room; and was she removed at his desire to the other side of the fireplace, that she might be further from the door. He then sat down by her, and talked scarcely to anyone else.

When tea was over, Mr. Hurst reminded his Caroline of the card-table—but in vain. Perhaps because Darcy had expressed earlier that he had no wish for cards. She assured him that no one intended to play, and the silence of the whole party on the subject seemed to justify her. Mr. Hurst had therefore nothing to do, but to stretch himself on one of the sofas and go to sleep. Darcy took up a book; Caroline did the same; and Louisa, principally occupied in playing with her bracelets and rings, joined now and then in her brother's conversation with Miss Bennet.

Caroline attended to his book as much as her own, perpetually making some inquiry, or looking at his page. She could not win him, however, to any conversation; he merely answered her question, and read on.

At length, quite exhausted by the attempt to be amused with her own book, she gave a great yawn and said, "How pleasant it is to spend an evening in this way! I declare after all there is no enjoyment like reading! How much sooner one tires of anything than of a book! When I have a house of my own, I shall be miserable if I have not an excellent library."

No one made any reply. She then yawned again, threw aside her book, and cast her eyes round the room in quest for some amusement; when hearing her brother mentioning a ball to Miss Bennet, she turned suddenly towards him and said:

"By the bye, Charles, are you really serious in meditating a dance at Netherfield? I would advise you, before you determine on it, to consult the wishes of the present party; I am much mistaken if there are not some among us to whom a ball would be rather a punishment than a pleasure."

"If you mean Darcy," cried her brother, "he may go to bed, if he chooses, before it begins—but as for the ball, it is quite a settled thing; and as soon as Nicholls has made white soup enough, I shall send round my cards."

"I should like balls infinitely better," she replied, "if they were carried on in a different manner; but there is something insufferably tedious in the usual process of such a meeting. It would surely be much more rational if conversation instead of dancing were made the order of the day."

"Much more rational, my dear Caroline, I dare say, but it would not be near so much like a ball."

Caroline made no answer, and soon afterwards she got up and walked about the room. Her figure was elegant, and she walked well. Darcy felt it all aimed at him but remained studious.

"Miss Eliza Bennet," Caroline said, "let me persuade you to follow my example, and take a turn about the room. I assure you it is very refreshing after sitting so long in one attitude."

Darcy looked up and unconsciously closed his book. Miss Elizabeth appeared surprised but agreed. He was directly invited to join their party, but he declined it, observing that he could imagine but two motives for their choosing to walk up and down the room together and his joining them would interfere with either purpose.

"What could he mean? I am dying to know what could be his meaning?" Caroline asked of Miss Elizabeth.. "Can you understand him at all?"

"Not at all," was her answer; "but depend upon it, he means to be severe on us, and our surest way of disappointing him will be to ask nothing about it."

Caroline, however, persevered in requiring an explanation of his two motives.

"I have not the smallest objection to explaining them," he said as soon as she allowed him to speak. "You either choose this method of passing the evening because you are in each other's confidence, and have secret affairs to discuss, or because you are conscious that your figures appear to the greatest advantage in walking; if the first, I would be completely in your way, and if the second, I can admire you much better as I sit by the fire."

"Oh! Shocking!" cried Caroline. "I never heard anything so abominable. How shall we punish him for such a speech?"

"Nothing so easy, if you have but the inclination," said Miss Elizabeth. "We can all plague and punish one another. Tease him— laugh at him. Intimate as you are, you must know how it is to be done."

"But upon my honour, I do *not*. I do assure you that my intimacy has not yet taught me *that*. Tease calmness of manner and presence of mind! No, no. I feel he may defy us there. And as to laughter, we will not expose ourselves, if you please, by attempting to laugh without a subject. Mr. Darcy may hug himself."

"Mr. Darcy is not to be laughed at!" cried Miss Elizabeth. "That is an uncommon advantage, and uncommon I hope it will continue, for it would be a great loss to *me* to have many such acquaintances. I dearly love a laugh."

"Miss Bingley," said Darcy, "has given me more credit than can be. The wisest and the best of men—nay, the wisest and best of their actions—may be rendered ridiculous by a person whose first object in life is a joke."

"Certainly," replied Miss Elizabeth—"there are such people, but I hope I am not one of *them*. I hope I never ridicule what is wise and good. Follies and nonsense, whims and inconsistencies, *do* divert me, I own, and I laugh at them whenever I can. But these, I suppose, are precisely what you are without."

"Perhaps that is not possible for anyone. But it has been the study of my life to avoid those weaknesses which often expose a strong understanding to ridicule."

"Such as vanity and pride."

"Yes, vanity is a weakness indeed. But pride—where there is a real superiority of mind, pride will be always under good regulation."

Miss Elizabeth turned away to hide a smile.

"Your examination of Mr. Darcy is over, I presume," said Caroine, "and pray what is the result?"

"I am perfectly convinced by it that Mr. Darcy has no defect. He owns it himself without disguise."

"No," he said, "I have made no such pretension. I have faults enough, but they are not, I hope, of understanding. My temper I dare not vouch for. It is, I believe, too little yielding—certainly too little for the convenience of the world. I cannot forget the follies and vices of others so soon as I ought, nor their offenses against myself. My feelings are not puffed about with every attempt to move them. My temper would perhaps be called resentful. My good opinion once lost, is lost forever."

"*That* is a failing indeed!" cried Miss Elizabeth. "Implacable resentment *is* a shade in a character. But you have chosen your fault well. I really cannot *laugh* at it. You are safe from me."

"There is, I believe, in every disposition a tendency to some particular evil—a natural defect, which not even the best education can overcome."

"And *your* defect is to hate everybody."

"And yours," he replied with a smile, "is willfully to misunderstand them."

"Do let us have a little music," cried Caroline, tired of a conversation in which she had no share. "Louisa, you will not mind my waking Mr. Hurst?"

Her sister had not the smallest objection, and the pianoforte was opened, and Darcy, after a few moments' recollection, was not sorry for it. He had begun to feel the danger of paying Miss Elizabeth too much attention and decided that she had been at Netherfield long enough. She attracted him more than he liked—and Caroline was uncivil to *her*, and more teasing than usual to himself. He resolved to be particularly careful that no sign of admiration should *now* escape him, nothing that could elevate her with the hope of influencing his felicity.

Steady to his purpose, he scarcely spoke ten words to her through the whole of the following day, and though they were at one time left by themselves for half-an-hour, he adhered most conscientiously to his book, and would not even look at her.

CHAPTER TEN

"You are hardly in the pink," said Abby to Lizzy as the evening drew to a close. The two women had spent the past hour in the drawing-room, the hostess reviewing her correspondence and Lizzy penning a letter that came nowhere near to portraying the disquiet swirling within her. "But we could begin your first lesson tonight if you wished."

The rain had not relented but for a few minutes, and Lizzy was obliged to spend another night at Trenwith House. She comforted her guilt by reasoning that any other person, Maria or Charlotte or Mr. Collins himself, would be hard pressed to do otherwise if caught in a similar situation. Of course they would never have conceded to what she was about to do, but she doubted that they were as afflicted as she with such feelings of craving and impatience.

"You're not to do anything that you do not wish," Abby said. "No one—not I, nor your partner—will be offended. *You* are to command your experience. If it is not to your liking, I urge—nay, I expect—you to voice your concerns. Do you understand?"

Lizzy nodded while trying to calm her pounding heart.

Abby took her hand and pressed it warmly. "Our time together has been short, but you have become like a daughter to me. Are you ready?"

Lizzy took a deep breath. "I am."

"Sally will see to your toilette and take you to the Red Chamber."

As Abby accompanied her back to her chamber, Lizzy noticed her hostess seemed more pensive than loquacious. Did Abby harbor reservations?

But before Lizzy could inquire, Abby turned to her with a bright smile, "I have complete faith and trust that your partner will provide you an exquisite entrée to the fleshly pleasures."

"Am I to know this partner?"

"No!" Abby replied with surprising emphasis. "It is unnecessary and would only prove a distraction. Your focus is to be placed upon your body, its responses, and enjoyment. I promise you a safe and exhilarating experience."

Too nervous to speak much, Lizzy only nodded once more and returned Abby's smile. Her cough had improved, though her throat was still rough, lending her speech a husky quality. She had spent a quiet afternoon resting and reading, finding amusement in the poet's oft times ludicrous counsel to men on how to seduce a woman or to women on how to attract a man, such as his advice to men that when accompanying a lady to the horse-races, "one should gallantly brush the dust from her gown, and if there is not dust there, brush it nonetheless." This agreeable manner of passing the time was followed by a supper that Abby had insisted she consume in the peace and ease of her own room.

After supper and a long soak in a warm bath of scented water, Lizzy sat at the vanity, vacillating between eagerness and misgiving. Had she made a hasty decision? Was she rash to have placed such a high degree of trust in a woman she barely knew? What if the worst were to occur and she were discovered? The shame upon her friends and family would be too great to imagine. But if she did not seize upon this opportunity, it would be gone forever. The rains had proven a fortuitous circumstance, compelling her to stay at Trenwith House without fear of censure. Moreover, the lust in her body might find relief in a forward address and cure her disquiet where long walks had failed.

Sally had dressed her in the garments of several decades ago, with a corset that laced in the back down to the tailbone. The discomfort of the confining corset was partially but not wholly offset by the softness of the remaining undergarments. The chemise and petticoats were short, stopping just below the knees to reveal her stockings and slippers. Instead of a dress, Sally had covered her shoulders with a silk robe not unlike a banyan.

"This will help shield your identity," Sally explained as she held a powdered wig with layers fluffed atop the head and half a dozen coils of hair that fell below the shoulders.

Sally then applied a rouge to the lips and a beauty patch near the bottom corner of her mouth. Looking in the mirror, Lizzy felt she wanted only a satin frock and she could have attended the court of

Louis XVI and Marie Antoinette.

"We are ready, ma'am," Sally said after affixing the final accessory, a crystal Venetian mask accented with blue sapphires.

Lizzy finished a glass of port for additional courage and followed Sally to the room Abby had dubbed the Red Chamber.

* * * * *

The objectionable display of the Bennet family, paired with the powerful feelings he was experiencing toward Miss Elizabeth, had convinced Darcy that an early departure from Netherfield was urgently warranted. Though he felt he had saved his friend from an unsavoury match with a young woman who, in his observation, lacked any passionate feeling toward Bingley and came from a rather intolerable family, he was less assured of his own wellbeing. All attempts to eradicate Miss Elizabeth from his conscience had, thus far, been futile. He yearned, on a visceral level, to be near her.

As Darcy appraised his wardrobe in the mirror, he hoped that his evening at Trenwith House would provide the antidote to his desperate longing. Pierre had laid out his costume of fresh linen, silk coat and breeches, an embroidered waistcoat, stockings, silver-buckled shoes and a peruke. Darcy was glad that the fashion for men had changed considerably since the last century, but he donned the garments willingly. In addition to its assistance in preventing recognition, the costuming added an element of playfulness and freed the participants to assume different identities. After donning a simple black mask that covered the majority of his face, he walked himself to the Red Chamber.

The room was as he remembered, from what he could discern, for most of it was cast in shadow, its only light the glow of the fireplace. The salubrious fire had been burning for some time, warming the intimate confines. The walls were covered with inviting silk paper and adorned with golden candelabras and tall, narrow mirrors that reflected slivers of the four-post bed, draped in a mix of satin and sheer linen, in the middle of the room. The only other furnishings consisted of a chaise lounge upholstered in red velvet, an end table, a sideboard, an armoire stocked with amorous accoutrements, and a pair of wing-chairs. He remembered sitting in one of those chairs with a 'student' astride him. She had called herself Justine and become quite the naughty wanton. He should have paced the lessons to better evaluate the abilities of the young woman to handle her newly awakened ardor. Though Abby's judgments were, for the most part, sound, he knew enough of humankind not to underestimate the unpredictable. The challenge was, of course, that one could not, by definition, prepare well for that which one could not foresee.

He almost did not see the woman of the evening for she sat in the shadow of a curtain upon the edge of the bed without movement or sound. His pulse skipped and he felt all the nerves from his years of abstinence, as if he were being asked to play the pianoforte without having practiced for the same length of time. He hoped he would prove an adequate partner.

"Good evening, *mademoiselle*," he greeted in a whisper as he stepped onto the expansive Persian carpeting, wishing the heels of his shoes weren't quite so high.

The young woman started to cough, and he detected the sounds of a cold.

"Pardon me," she said in a throaty voice when her coughing had subsided.

He offered her a cordial and, when she nodded, was relieved to have the innocuous activity to start the evening. Handing the beverage to her, he had an improved view of her. She had a nice form—the shoulders, collarbone, and bust all decidedly feminine without appearing too meek. He was not partial to small, willowy frames. Though her hands trembled a little when she took the drink, her posture and air hinted at maturity and resolution. And something oddly familiar.

He continued in a low and gentle voice, "Would you care for another glass?"

She shook her head.

He took a deeper breath. "Shall we begin, then?"

"Yes."

From the armoire he retrieved a red satin kerchief. "I will attempt to explain all that I am to do as we proceed. If at any time you wish to desist, you may apply a safety word, and I will cease instantly."

"A safety word? Is a simple protest not sufficient?"

"What may seem as a rebuff can be arbitrary and subject to interpretation. It is necessary to have a specific mechanism that is unambiguous to both parties."

"Very well. And what shall this safety word be?"

Failing to remember what he once used, he recalled the name of his last dance with Miss Elizabeth Bennet. "Montreal."

"Montreal?"

"You will not hesitate to speak it?"

"I think not."

"Repeat it for me."

"I assure you I am capable of uttering a simple word."

"If you cannot speak it in idleness, how am I to be assured you will speak it when we are occupied?"

"Montreal. Montreal. Satisfied?"

He frowned. This was no submissive and unquestioning pupil before him.

"Again."

Taken aback by his directive, she raised her brows.

"Practice makes perfect," he supplied with deliberate condescension, to make the point that he was the teacher and she the student.

She pressed her lips together, but replied with exaggerated enunciation. "Mon-tre-al."

His tactic worked, for perturbation had quickly replaced her nervousness.

"I will now apply this blindfold. The removal of sight will eliminate the most easy distractions and enhance your other senses."

She hesitated but made no objection. He secured the kerchief over the eyes of her mask before stepping back to survey her.

"*Charmante.*"

She almost laughed. "You need not seduce me with false compliments, sir! For in such dim lighting, surely you can discern little. Why, my complexion may be marked by the pox, my eyes set too narrowly apart, and the bridge of my nose adorned with warts!"

"Have you had the pox?"

"Luckily, no."

"Have you warts?"

"No, but—"

"And do you deem your eyes unattractive?"

"That is not my point—"

"Then I stand by my evaluation."

He was tempted but refrained from protesting his aversion of falsehoods or explaining that some element of loveliness could be found in almost any woman, even those most would find homely.

"Forgive me, I divert you from your program. Pray, continue, only know that such praise falls upon skeptical ears."

"Are you often given to provoking your tutors?"

"My tutors were few and of short duration."

Little wonder, he thought to himself. He was too much the gentleman to voice the rejoinder aloud but not so much that he would not *think* it.

"If you will not accept my flattery, perhaps, modesty notwithstanding, you would allow which bodily attributes you consider most attractive in yourself?"

He liked to identify where a woman was most confident and apply his attention there.

"Praise myself? What you ask is unbecoming in a modest lady, but…! You are in luck, sir! For I do not feign modesty where none is to be had and will give you my honest opinion. I like my eyes the best."

Damn. He could not make love to her eyes, especially as they were blindfolded. He could have done much with the neck, the hand, or even the ankle.

"Any others?"

"My other qualities are not noteworthy."

"You are overly critical."

"Perhaps. But I am not so self-absorbed as to have dwelt on each of my features and given them an appraisal."

Darcy held his sigh. He made for a poor Casanova. What had convinced Abby he could fulfill the role?

He knew her answer. She would point to all his successes and argue that the singular young woman before him now was an anomaly. A new supposition came to mind.

"Does your resistance bespeak your reservations in these, er, proceedings?"

She seemed mildly impressed. "A keen observation and perhaps not wholly unwarranted, but if it is the case, it is not done with conscious awareness. I have not forgotten that if I wish to cease and desist, I may avail myself of that safety word: Montreal."

"It is natural to feel uneasy in these circumstances."

"What techniques you employ! Praise, solicitude, empathy, and reassurance."

"Do you make a habit of remarking upon every action before you?" he replied, wondering if he would be able to persevere the evening with her.

"I confess a curiosity and desire to understand how these 'lessons' take place."

"There is no curriculum to speak of."

"Rules?"

"These will be determined by the 'pupil,' as it were."

"How fascinating and extremely vague."

In some cases, he would attempt to put a woman at ease with conversation, but encouraging a *tête-à-tête* with this one might prove hazardous. He walked over to the sideboard to pour himself a glass of sherry.

Sensing his departure, she asked, "How long have you been an instructor for Mrs. Trenwith?"

"Is that relevant?"

"Of course. Your years speak to experience."

"What information I provide will only prejudice you. Judge the results instead."

"Do you employ the same methods with every woman?"

"You have a great many questions."

"I am inquisitive, a quality that makes me an apt pupil."

"An apt pupil also follows directions well."

"Ah! Are we to commence the 'lesson?'"

"If you are done stalling with your chatter."

CHAPTER ELEVEN

Had she irked him? Lizzy wondered, half-amused with her own antics, for she was indeed using discourse as a stalling mechanism and a façade for her own nervousness. She had been on edge for some time and receiving the blindfold had helped matters none at all. While the darkness of the room helped to conceal her, it also obscured his features. She had suspected the mysterious man to be Nicholas at first. She had no aversion to the thought of Nicholas as 'instructor,' but the form of the other occupant was not as sinewy and, unless Nicholas was assuming a different personality, the speech, being more deliberate and less animated, did not match. She then speculated that perhaps it was one of the servants, for she had observed no other person at Trenwith House, but the manners of the stranger did not fit a hireling.

Well, she had asked of her own volition for this, and it would be silly of her not to see it through.

"Is the blindfold truly necessary?"

"Will you talk less without it?"

"Now who is the one doing the provoking?"

"*Touché*. Let us cease the verbal sparring and attend to the purpose of this night."

Lizzy hesitated. Was she truly ready for this?

"We will proceed only as you wish," he reassured.

Not wishing to be one of those flighty women who knew not their own mind, she replied, "I am ready."

She heard his footsteps approach the bed and silently cursed the blindfold. It increased her perturbation. She sat at an angle to the edge of the bed, and she sensed him standing behind her.

"Permit me to loosen the robe about your shoulders."

Realizing she had been clutching the garment tightly about her, she loosened her grip. He slid the rob a few inches off her shoulders.

Her heart stilled.

"I will touch your right shoulder," he said.

Dear God, Lizzy breathed to herself and shut her eyes despite all previous attempts to see through the fabric. Her heart resumed an erratic beat. She had never before been touched by a man there and braced herself. He placed a hand upon her right shoulder. His touch felt warm, steady, and devoid of anything wanton.

After allowing her time to become accustomed to the weight of his hand, he told her, "I will now move toward your neck."

He slid his hand toward her neck. With his thumb, he smoothed the flesh near her shoulder blade. She shivered.

"Much tension is accumulated in this area. I shall attempt to ease it."

He kneaded the shoulder with his thumb and fingers. Lizzy was unsure if she liked being touched in this manner by a stranger. If she could not abide by his attention to her shoulder, surely all other efforts would prove futile?

"The neck is an intimate area, but I will be gentle."

He cupped the base of her neck and rubbed both sides in steady circular motions. At first, she did not like his hand there. She felt disconcertingly vulnerable and began to cough. He removed his hand and waited patiently for her to calm. When she had cleared her throat, he resumed his ministrations.

"I will now tend to the left shoulder as well."

He placed both hands upon her, gripping and rubbing her shoulders in firm but tender grasps. Her breath returned to a normal pace, gradually elongating as her shoulders relaxed. He moved a hand once more to her neck and rubbed away the stiffness. She had not realized the amount of strain in these parts. As his hand moved up her neck, she felt like melting into his grasp, finding the application of his hands now quite pleasant and soothing. With both hands, he pressed his fingers about the area behind her ears, lulling her into a trance-like state.

"Feeling better?"

She murmured an affirmative.

"You may now remove your robe."

Her nerves stood at attention once more. "Already?"

"I would have you lie upon the bed that we may continue in the same manner upon the whole of the back. We are far from any lewd activity, if that is what you fear."

Was lewd activity not her objective? Slowly, she eased her arms from the robe. There. She was naked but for her undergarments before a completely unfamiliar member of the opposite sex. Despite the warmth from the fire, she was conscious of every inch of exposed skin as if she were met with an icy cold. The ensuing silence, though brief, felt of an eternity. She heard the rustle of pillows being moved near her. Then he took her gently by the arms and guided her into position atop a pile of plush pillows along the foot of the bed. She was prone, face-down, blindfolded, defenseless. Was she mad for placing such trust in a stranger? Not only were her legs wholly on the bed, but her ankles were bare before him.

"The purpose of the following activity is for you to relax, *mademoiselle*. Let your limbs calm, and free your mind of all but peaceful thoughts. Take a deep breath and release it slowly."

She did as told, and the comforting effect was immediate. She allowed herself to settle into the luxuriant bed, its linen among the finest and most silken she had ever felt.

"Once more."

He had her take near a dozen such breaths, which had the desired result of softening the edges of her nerves.

"I will now unlace the corset."

Lizzy embraced the pillow beneath her chest. She could not recall a more apprehensive experience. Her first attempt at riding a horse could not compare. The time when, at the age of nine, she had had Lydia placed in her care and thought her sister to have wandered off the estate to be lost forever, only to later discover the toddler hiding beneath a table with a jar of biscuits, generated perhaps equal anxiety.

"Breathe," he reminded her.

The bed sank with his weight. He sat near her hip. She felt his hands upon the laces. When he had them undone, he pried apart the stiff material. The bed rose, and she heard him take his place at the edge of the bed before her head.

"I will now apply a pomade to your back."

She heard him uncork a bottle. The scent of hibiscus wafted through the air. She heard him rub his hands, then felt them gliding upon her shoulders and her upper back. She shivered at where his hands were and considered if they might yet find their way to even more intimate areas. The thought agitated and excited her.

"I will repeat my earlier application to your shoulders."

The tension had collected once more, and she welcomed the kneading of her shoulders and neck.

"Where did you learn such a fine skill?" she murmured.

"From my mentor."

"Is that all?"

"I answered your question."

"You are not a man of many words."

"That is a sweeping statement given upon limited observation."

"Ah, are you quite garrulous in other circumstances?"

"Are you here for conversation?"

"I am not acquainted with the proper etiquette for such a situation and would not wish to appear impolite. But I suppose, as we are defying the greatest of propriety by our actions here, the customary politesse need not apply."

"If you wish."

"I did not mean to imply a preference for abandonment but to comment upon the irony of—*oh!*"

His hands had slid beneath her chemise toward her lower back. In similar manner, his hands grasped and rubbed her along both sides of her spine, at one point perilously close to scraping the sides of her breasts. He had been diligent in providing her advance notice of what he was to do, and the surprise left her bereft of words. She idly wondered if that had been his intention. His hands had been upon her lower back earlier, but now they lingered there, gradually working their charm. Without sight, she was deprived of a major source of stimulation and had mostly the sense of touch to focus upon. She found she rather liked the feel of his hands, masculine in their size and strength but possessing a gentle touch.

Her resistance melting away, she allowed him to continue in silence and herself to enjoy the effect of his efforts. Before she realized it, the steady crackle of the fire and soothing motions of his hands had lulled her to sleep.

CHAPTER TWELVE

It was not possible, but the woman lying in the bed across from where Darcy sat was oddly familiar to him. Even the scent of her, though he would be hard-pressed to describe it, seemed reminiscent. With her asleep, he could have lighted a candle and examined her features more closely to ascertain if he might have met her before, but he would not breach the confidence of darkness. Also, he wanted the reprieve her slumber provided. He felt unsettled and attributed the condition partially to their exchange but mostly to his being out of practice and out of sorts. Alas, this woman had done nothing to recede all thoughts of Elizabeth Bennet.

He went to stoke the fire. She stirred. Awake, she lifted the blindfold and, recouping her bearings, assessed her surroundings. She looked at the robe he had covered her with. All else was as it had been.

"How long have I been asleep?"

"About forty minutes," he replied. "I can lace your corset or ring for Sally to assist you."

She was briefly abashed. "Are we finished?"

"For the evening."

She seemed disappointed.

"It is not unusual for the first appointment to consist purely of establishing a level of comfort," he explained. The fact that she had fallen asleep suggested she had attained a great deal of ease with his person, but he was ready to conclude the night. He was to meet his cousin, Colonel Fitzwilliam, if the weather was sufficiently fine in the morning, and proceed to Rosings together. The sobering company of his aunt might prove the antidote he required.

Pulling her arms from the corset and leaving it upon the bed, she drew the robe around her and sat up. "I had expected…more."

"It is only the first lesson."

"Yes, but, I require an accelerated program, if you will. I do not reside in Hunsford and my duration here is limited."

"You have no qualms to continue?" he asked, though she had spoken with certitude.

"I would not say all reservations have gone, but they are sufficiently diminished."

Again he hesitated. Her desire to proceed with him did bolster his confidence, and she was not unpleasant to the touch. Her skin had felt firm, soft and smooth without the aid of the pomade.

"But if *you* are in doubt," she said, "I will not force your hand."

His sense of obligation took over. "Not at all."

He wandered over to the armoire. where a copy of *Memoirs of a Woman of Pleasure* lay. "I am told you take great pleasure in reading."

"Yes. I would be a guest here for an eternity with such a fine library."

"The collection is singular with rare translations not known to the public. Have you partaken of its offerings?"

"I was given a copy of Ovid's *Ars Amatoria* by Mr. Tr— I was advised the other texts would be, perhaps, too coarse."

Mr. Trenwith, she no doubt intended to say. Darcy could not speak ill of Nicholas, being the stepson of his mentor, but he wondered that Nicholas might have gained admittance into Trenwith House were he not a relation.

"But you have read the story of Fanny Hill?" he inquired, holding up the book.

"I have."

He walked over and handed it to her. "Read a passage that excites you."

"It is rather dark."

He found and lit a candle, which he set on a stand beside the bed. She adjusted her mask and browsed the book till she came to a page of interest. Her gaze moved over the words.

"Aloud," he clarified then went back to the wing-chair he had occupied before.

She cleared her throat with a few coughs and began, "' Nor was it till after a few enjoyments had numbed and blunted the sense of the smart, and given me to feel the titillating inspersion of balsamic sweets, drew from me the delicious return, and brought down all my passion, that I arrived at excess of pleasure through excess of pain.'"

He was struck with the sultry quality her cold had lent her voice. Despite his earlier reticence, his body responded to the imagery expressed.

"Continue. Slower."

"'But, when successive engagements had broke and inured me, I began to enter into the true unalloyed relish of that pleasure of pleasures, when the warm gush darts through all the ravished inwards; what floods of bliss! what melting transports! what agonies of delight! too fierce, too mighty for nature to sustain?... well has she therefore, no doubt provided the relief of a delicious momentary dissolution, the approaches of which are intimated by a dear delirium, a sweet thrill, on the point of emitting those liquid sweets, in which enjoyment itself is drowned, when one gives the languishing stretch out, and die at the discharge.' Cleland writes such colourful prose, I wonder whether his portrayals reflect or embellish a truthful experience. Certainly, being a man, he can only imagine what transpires in the fair sex."

She seemed to flush, though it was hard to discern in the dimness, but the quality of her tone had changed. The hastened, mechanical reading turned slow and breathy, allowing the words time to paint the picture in her mind, to sink into her consciousness and warm her body.

He rose from his chair. "Shall we determine if his accounts are accurate?"

* * * * *

By all means, Lizzy responded, surprised at her own eagerness. The bawdy text had not failed to incite her lust, stirring the warm discomfort in her loins. Pleased he seemed, at last, interested in the lesson beyond the obligations of duty—she knew not what accord, if any, compelled him and if he were compensated for his services. If his position was wholly voluntary and he was not repaying a favour to Abby, he could quit their arrangement at any time, though a man of lesser restraint would hardly forego the opportunity to bed a woman *gratis* when others had to pay for the privilege. But she suspected this man was not a terrible wanton, for he had seemed rather reluctant.

"Shhhh," he whispered as if attempting to quiet her thoughts. He stood but a few inches from her.

"My mind insists on being busy though I would will it be silent," she said. "Perhaps another cordial would help."

"How many have you consumed?"

"Two, the one you provided and another in my bedchamber earlier."

He contemplated, then replied, "While I support a modicum of wine to ease inhibitions, I prefer the participant to be in full of possession of her faculties or she invites remorse the morrow. Wine, moreover, dulls the senses. I would you could fully appreciate the experience you seek."

"That is quite reasonable. Though I do not think the addition of *one* more would put me in such an inebriated state. I am not so light of weight that I can be felled—"

Lowering his head, he cut her off with a kiss. The shock of it rendered her immobile and scattered all thought from her head. Overwhelmed as she was by his lips upon hers, she could but clutch his hand, which cupped her chin and secured her head in place. She could feel the warmth of his breath upon her face. The capacity of the room shrank in an instant with the nearness of his body and the weight of his mouth covering hers. Slowly, his lips parted from hers, and she found herself bereft, longing for a return of the pressure. Its pleasantness surprised her.

When her mind had recovered enough for her to form a sentence, she remarked, "I thought—I thought you were to advise your every step in advance?"

"I required the element of surprise to achieve the desired effect."

"Desired effect?" she echoed, still in a haze from her very first kiss.

"Of incapacitating your inner dialogue."

"My inner dialogue?"

"Women of intellectual abilities are blessed and cursed all at once. Corporal pleasure can by stymied by thinking overmuch."

"I am a woman of intellectual abilities? That is a sweeping statement given upon limited observation."

She thought she saw the corner of his mouth quirk upward. Her heart had never beat so rapidly, and she could not have been more surprised than at her own articulation, given how the world whirled about her with a force as great as any that could result from one too many glasses of cordial. *All that from a mere kiss,* she marveled.

She wanted an encore.

And he seemed prepared to give it. Cupping her face betwixt his hands, he tilted her chin upward as if he meant to drink from it. The lowering of his head provided warning of what he intended. His lips were upon hers at an angle that prevented their masks from rubbing against each other. Once more she felt a surge of warmth flare through her veins, swirling in her abdomen and concentrating about her womanhood. This time his lips parted and moved over her hers, surveying and sampling the terrain of her mouth. She closed her eyes and submitted to the kiss, the intoxication of it making her mind wheel in a sort of delightful merry-go-round.

He released her mouth, once more leaving her wanting, her thirst addressed but not quenched. He seemed to search her face.

"Do you recall the safety word?"

She blinked, having forgotten for a moment, but recovered. "Montreal."

She had no desire to invoke it and was dissatisfied that he chose to rattle her from her lovely stupor to ask it.

"If you would stand, I will remove your robe and caress the parts revealed."

Heart thumping madly, she got to her feet and loosened her hold upon the robe. He swept it off her shoulders and let it pool at her ankles. Instinctively, she crossed her arms about herself. He discarded her petticoats next. Standing in but her shift and stockings, she could not meet his gaze as he stepped back to observe her. It seemed his breath was a little uneven, too.

Standing behind her, he slid the shift from her left shoulder and replaced it with his hand, his movements cautious, as if she were some small critter he dare not frighten. The warmth of his hand upon her bare skin caused her heart to palpitate erratically. His hand upon her was not new, but this time his touch intended not to soothe, but to excite. He placed his other hand upon her right arm and pressed his mouth to the connecting shoulder. She felt a ripple up her spine. If such were the weapons employed by rakehells, she had underestimated their power. She felt fortunate she had never been prey to any such person.

With a pace that thrilled and agitated, he planted kisses along the shoulder, upon the nape of her neck, and between her shoulder blades, then up her neck, beneath her ear, and down the side of her throat, each one a delight gift that produced shivers within her. He pulled her other arm from her chest.

"We must do away with maidenly modesty here," he said, sliding a hand down her arm as if savouring the texture of her skin.

The exposure of her body alarmed and excited her. She could not stop the rise and fall of her bosom. It drew his attention, and he passed a hand delicately over the brim of the shift where the swell began. She watched his movement with dread and desire, yet felt a dampness begin to form between her thighs. His hand slid beneath the flimsy garment and cupped a breast. The nipple hardened beneath his firm grasp, stirring raucous sensations between her legs. He kneaded the supple flesh, and a faint groan escaped her lips as the area beneath her navel grew in warmth and need. She marveled at how acutely the stimulation of one part excited another seemingly unconnected part.

Circling an arm around her waist, he pulled her with him as he sat down upon the bed. He fitted her between his legs. Her rump touched his thigh. The closeness, the indecency—all worried but enflamed her. She had never been of such proximity to a member of the opposite sex, rare as it was with even one of her own. With his chest at her back and his legs on either side of her, she felt surrounded by him. What did he intend by such a position?

"There is nothing to fear," he said. "Your pleasure is the only objective."

She nodded, took a deep breath, and willed her limbs to relax. His hands once more roamed her body. Her neck, shoulders, back and ribs all received notice. And her breasts. This time he palmed them both, pushing the orbs together and pulling them apart, rolling them beneath his hands, squeezing them tenderly, then with demand, his touch graduating from worshipful to wanton. Her breath grew shallow, and the intimate area between her legs throbbed. He pinched and pulled a nipple. A current shot from its tip to that place betwixt her legs. With his digits, he fondled and teased the little rosebuds. Such delicious torment! She knew not whether to recoil or arch her breasts farther into his hands.

Withdrawing one hand while the other continued, he reached for her thigh. This time his touch did not trouble her, for desire, raw and powerful, overwhelmed any lingering hesitation. She wanted for him to complete the lesson and to hopefully sate the heat he had stoked within her. His hand slid to the guarded side of her leg, to the apex of her thighs.

"I will touch you there," he confirmed.

Yes, touch me there, she found herself urging. He drew one thigh aside and she allowed him to insinuate his hand between her legs. The shift proved no effective barrier as he began to rub her. Rather, the friction of the fabric only added to the sweet agony. She moaned, an expression of satisfaction and lament, for she foresaw the loss of control over her own body. It would go its own way, dashing headlong into the dark and mysterious forest of lust.

Delving his hand beneath her shift, he pried open the plump lips that hid the most sensitive little nub, which he stroked with his finger. With a gentle circling, he coaxed delicious ripples from that rosebud. The sensations, far from superficial, penetrated a deeper part of her. He lengthened his strokes and pressed a little harder upon her flesh. Like the scratching of an itch, but of a more refined nature, the action soothed and excited. All the muscles below her waist clenched, even those inside of her.

"Relax," he whispered.

How? she wondered when she wanted more—much more—of the lovely torment flaring through her body. The small, precious area between her thighs had become the world. He quickened his pace. Small gasps and grunts escaped her. She strained against him. Without realizing it, she grasped his arm for support. The nectar of her desire soaked her shift. She began to pant. Her legs tightened and her toes curled. How was it possible such simple caresses could wreak such havoc?

For a while she exalted in the pleasurable torture as he strummed her body without slowing, without pause. The seat of her desire pulsed. She prayed he would not cease until the rightful conclusion had been reached, but as the fire between her legs grew, she feared the imminent loss of control. She wondered that her legs could survive the wave of sensations emanating from her womanhood. Her legs twitched involuntarily. The intensity was too much. Her body felt as if it was coiling within itself. Surely her body would hurl itself against the bedposts when all the tension released?

"No, no," she murmured.

"Do you require the safety word?" he asked, halting.

The absence of torture was worse. She shook her head, panicked, until he resumed agitating his fingers against her once more. Rather than causing a recession of arousal, the unwanted respite lent greater poignancy to the delightful assault upon her.

"Allow yourself to spend," he said as he stroked her with increased ferocity.

Shutting her eyes, she gripped the sheets with one hand and his arm with the other as the concentration of pleasure drilled deeper into her flesh, deeper into her womanhood. She screamed as the paroxysm tore through her body. Her limbs jerked of their own accord. Her body bowed into him as if attempting to escape from the waves of sensations crashing at her with rapid succession. She was aware of nothing save for the beautiful, wondrous, overwhelming ecstasy.

He eased his touch, for, though hitherto desired, it now had an adverse effect. She felt her body at last begin to descend from its climax, shuddering along the way, though she continued to throb between the legs. Her heart had never beat so loudly. She knew not if she breathed. But of one thing she was certain, despite the warm daze still soaking her: She had bitten the forbidden fruit and wanted more.

CHAPTER THIRTEEN

Though overcast the following morning, the skies signified little of the rain that had beset them the past few days. Darcy had woken early and was immediately flooded by memories of the prior evening and the young woman he had held in his arms as she recovered from the fine and pleasurable end of desire fulfilled. He could still hear her groans. How soon they had escalated into hasty cries! Hearing and seeing a woman brought to pleasure was incredibly satisfying. And provocative. But his own gratification was inconsequential in his position and not to be brooked, especially at the first encounter.

"How long is she staying as your guest?" he inquired as he and Abby took breakfast at a small table before a window in a quaint parlor of the West Wing.

"She is visiting family and stayed the night because the roads were poor. Are you travelling on to Rosings to-day?"

He watched her as she poured more coffee into his cup. Though he had not been much in her company of late, he knew her well enough to discern an agitation, albeit minute.

"Yes. My effects are being prepared as we speak."

"And you mean to quit Trenwith House this morning?"

"As early as you wish."

"Pray do not misconstrue my question, Fitzwilliam. You know you are welcome here for as long as *you* wish."

The warmth with which she smiled upon him satisfied him that she was not trying to hasten his departure. But he wondered what might be troubling her. He would not have hesitated to offer his assistance if he could.

"I take it you will not be travelling to Hertfordshire again, if Charles means to quit Netherfield, but he only recently acquired the place did he not?" she inquired with more of her customary gaiety.

"His sisters and I are persuasive."

"Ah, and why can you not allow a grown man his own choice in property?"

He decided to confide the truth. "Charles is in love—again. But I think it shall pass."

He reached for a slice of toast and ham to distract from the grimness he felt, but Abby was too perceptive.

"Indeed? You do not approve of his lady of choice?"

"It is a poor match, and her family objectionable, to term it mildly."

"But that does not trouble your friend?"

"His sisters and I are in full agreement that his attachment to Miss Bennet would only do him harm."

Abby looked up sharply from her coffee. "What has this family done to merit such a harsh assessment?"

"Their offense is not confined to a single egregious act but several instances displaying a want of character. Fortunately, they live in Hertfordshire, and if Charles can be convinced to quit his residence there, they may not cross paths for some time, if ever."

"Your judgment has always been sound, but does it apply to every member of the family? Surely this Miss Bennet cannot be disagreeable if Charles is partial to her?"

Darcy frowned. "Miss Bennet is quite amiable and, from what I can determine, gentle in nature, if not a touch simple. She has also a sister who is…interesting."

"Interesting?"

He realized the error in his choice of adjectives, for women were prone to pouncing on descriptives of other women.

"Intelligent," he corrected, then felt the need to add as many negative qualities to dampen Abby's curiosity. He had come to Trenwith House to forget, not expound upon, Miss Elizabeth. "But far too at ease with her intellect, at the risk of overestimating her own abilities. And rather verbose for my taste."

While drinking his coffee, he felt Abby's bright, keen eyes upon him. He changed the subject, inquiring, "What is to become of your latest pupil?"

"If you are staying at Rosings a while, she can continue with you. If you are up to the task."

He nodded. The distraction he had hoped for at Trenwith House was very promising. For the first time in many days, his first thought in the morning was not of Miss Elizabeth Bennet.

* * * * *

The clock above the fireplace mantel chimed the noon hour, surprising Lizzy awake. She could not remember when last she had slept till such a late hour. Surveying her chamber at Trenwith House from her bed, she flushed in recollection of all that had transpired last night. Had she indeed allowed a man to touch her *intimately*? Had she thrilled to his caresses and abandoned herself to their seductive qualities? And had he elicited the most violent, yet delightful, release?

She clenched her thighs in affirmation. His hand had been *there*, in her most private area. Her own hand wandered to that part. How was it a man, and a stranger at that, produce a result more satisfying than her own hand? She fingered the nub of flesh that he had so skillfully plied. Feeling the carnal craving coming upon her, she stopped. Though a delicious consequence had greeted her surrender yesterday, she wished to confirm she could exert control of herself and her body. Nor could she dawdle in bed longer. What a wanton she had become!

"You are nursing a cold," Abby defended for her when Lizzy decried the lateness of the day. "I can hear it in your voice still."

The two women sat in the dining-room, partaking of a light meal. Having missed breakfast, Lizzy ate heartily of the bread, meat, and cheese.

"And I am pleased you slept well in an unfamiliar bed," Abby continued. "I pray you were not awash in excessive guilt and remorse upon waking."

Lizzy waited till the maidservant had left the room before answering, "I admit to some shock and horror at what I had done. But excessive? No. After all, I had given it sufficient thought prior to committing myself."

"Nonetheless, emotions can and will evade prediction."

"But regret is a rather useless sentiment. For what purpose should I bemoan that which I cannot change and which I knowingly and willfully engaged in?"

"You would not advise, if you could, your past self to desist and take a different course?"

"I would not. The lesson was…quite satisfactory."

A broad smile spread over Abby. "I am relieved and very, very glad to hear it. Forgive my persistence, but I wanted you to be quite certain. I once had a student who had all the appearances of confidence in what she did, only to suffer a severe case of buyer's remorse the following day, lamenting that she had committed some great sin and could never again look her family in the eyes with honesty. Contrary emotions are to be expected, and the first lesson is always the most awkward."

Lizzy blushed. "Your appointed instructor had a reassuring way about him."

"Did he?"

"Yes. Though I think I provoked him at times, he was…a *gentleman*—if one can apply the word in such situations."

"You can and shall! I do not take my role lightly in these affairs and prefer an honest account, good or bad, of the people I have entrusted with such significant responsibilities."

Though they sat alone in the room, Lizzy lowered her voice even more. "I am in wonder that our bodies can produce such rapture."

Abby leaned in, eyes gleaming. "And that was but your first lesson! I take it your experience to be more than 'quite satisfactory' then?"

Lizzy nodded. "For certain it exceeded my expectations."

"Wonderful! And will you take a second lesson with the same instructor?"

"I would."

The words came out quicker than she had planned, but before they could make arrangements, a servant appeared to announce Mr. Collins had arrived. Lizzy could not have been more disappointed, but she rallied herself that some time and distance from Trenwith House could prove beneficial to reflection and ease the giddiness she felt at all that had transpired here. She faced a quandary in that she had as good as promised the Collinses that she would cease her friendship with Mrs. Trenwith, but a continuance of her 'lessons' would not be possible without Abby.

Desperate to depart as soon as possible, Mr. Collins insisted on standing outside while the stable hands tried their best to relieve his gig of the mud clinging to the wheels. Once he and Lizzy were headed back to the Parsonage, he explained his rationale for confronting the poor roads.

"Lady Catherine is expecting her nephews. Although an explanation for your absence could have been provided—it was unfortunate but understandable that the weather forced you to stay at Trenwith House—I would rather eschew any mention of it that we may not place her ladyship or her family in awkwardness of hearing it."

Lizzy readily agreed, for Trenwith House now held too much significance to herself. She applied herself in assisting Charlotte the remainder of the day, but only with much effort could she engage in dialogue with her friend, for her mind persisted in returning to Trenwith House and recalling the many ways in which he had touched and fondled her. How many more lessons remained? As many as desired and required by the student? How many lessons would she wish for? Did she dare abandon the last wall of virtue in pursuit of this 'education?'

"I protest," Charlotte said later that day as they replaced fresh flora in all the vases. "You are unwell and weary. I could not require your assistance at the expense of your health."

"It is a mere cold that sounds worse than it feels," Lizzy replied while suspecting that her appearance of weariness owed itself to a wandering mind.

"I have seen colds worsen into influenza."

"I assure you I feel quite up to task."

Enough time had passed as to remove all distress of the disturbing dream Lizzy had of Mr. Darcy. She could now laugh in recollection of it, for she was sure Mr. Darcy was not a man to be found engaged in such a position. It amused her to wonder what sort of lover he could be. Despite her own limited experience, she nonetheless felt empowered to form judgment, and predicted he would be as stiff and un-engaging as he had always been in the company of others. She fancied he would be awkward, bumbling, flustered, for it would have been beneath him to appreciate and apply himself to pleasuring another human being. Woe to the poor woman who must submit to Mr. Darcy for a lover!

"What thought makes you smile?" Charlotte asked.

Lizzy was saved from having to answer by the entry of Mr. Collins, who, judging from his fast breathing, must have hurried home to deliver intelligence that Mr. Darcy had indeed arrived. On the following morning, he hastened to Rosings to pay his respects. There were two nephews of Lady Catherine to require them, for Mr. Darcy had brought with him a Colonel Fitzwilliam, and, to the great surprise of all the party, when Mr. Collins returned, the gentlemen accompanied him. Charlotte had seen them from her husband's room, crossing the road, and immediately running into the other, told the girls what an honour they might expect, adding,

"I may thank you, Eliza, for this piece of civility. Mr. Darcy would never have come so soon to wait upon me."

Lizzy had scarcely time to disclaim all right to the compliment, before their approach was announced by the door-bell, and shortly afterwards the three gentlemen entered the room. Colonel Fitzwilliam, who led the way, was about thirty, not handsome, but in person and address most truly the gentleman. Mr. Darcy looked just as he had been used to look in Hertfordshire—paid his compliments, with his usual reserve, to Mrs. Collins, and whatever might be his feelings toward her friend, met her with every appearance of composure. Lizzy merely curtseyed to him without saying a word.

Colonel Fitzwilliam entered into conversation directly with the readiness and ease of a well-bred man, and talked very pleasantly; but his cousin, after having addressed a slight observation on the house and garden to Mrs. Collins, sat for some time without speaking to anybody. He seemed more awkward than ever before—troubled even. Lizzy thought he glanced at her with a reaction that appeared very much like dismay. At length, however, his civility was so far awakened as to inquire of Lizzy after the health of her family. She answered him in the usual way, and after a moment's pause, added:

"My eldest sister has been in town these three months. Have you never happened to see her there?"

She was perfectly sensible that he never had, but she wished to see whether he would betray any consciousness of what had passed between the Bingleys and Jane, and she thought he looked a little confused as he answered that he had never been so fortunate as to meet Miss Bennet. The subject was pursued no farther, and the gentlemen soon afterwards went away.

CHAPTER FOURTEEN

Darcy paced the rug of his bedchamber as if intending to wear it into the ground. His valet, a good man in his employ for over ten years, having never seen Mr. Darcy in such a state, seemed torn between letting the man alone or staying in the event his services should be required and could, by chance, alleviate some of the distress his master was clearly experiencing. But the intensity with which Mr. Darcy strode from one end of the room to the other had a silencing effect on the valet, who continued in his indecision by saying and doing nothing at all.

Too engrossed in his own thoughts, Darcy barely noticed the presence of another. Having left Trenwith House the other day with new hope that his interest for Miss Elizabeth had the prospect of diminishing, he had been dealt a set-back upon learning from Mr. Collins that she was staying at the Parsonage. Of course, within such proximity, he could not avoid paying her a visit and had all too keenly agreed to return with Mr. Collins that very morning, attributing part of his eagerness to curiosity whether the sight of her would enflame his feelings or whether they would remain the same. The latter he considered a minor victory, but he was prepared for either.

He was wholly unprepared for the shock of hearing her voice.

It couldn't be her.

Stranger coincidences than two women suffering from a similar cold could occur easily enough, he reasoned to himself. And yet, with every word she spoke, he was thrown back into the Red Chamber. The huskiness of both voices, that of Miss Elizabeth and of the young woman at Trenwith House, would not allow for a perfect match, but there were other qualities of speech to regard: the cadence, the inflection, and the mannerisms. What and how she spoke. Had he not thought the woman in the Red Chamber familiar?

Preferring to leave the ease of conversation to his cousin, Darcy would not have talked much even had he not been in a state of disbelief and took the opportunity to make a comparison of Miss Elizabeth. The Red Chamber had been dark, certainly, but the posture, the breadth of the shoulders, the length of the neck, and general shape of the torso were all too similar. At one point, he had tried to picture Miss Elizabeth sans clothing to assist in his evaluation, but he had quickly ceased, silently berating himself for the impropriety of such an effort. He did not dwell on the irony. His mind had been thrown into a tumult at the notion that, if the two, Miss Elizabeth and the woman of the Red Chamber, were one and the same, then he had...

Good God.

The length of his legs up through his groin ached. He could recall only one other time in his life when he had felt such distress—when he had thought his sister to be eloping with Wickham. His agitation could wait no longer.

"My hat and gloves," he called out without knowing whether his valet had stayed or left.

He could hardly wait for his horse to be saddled and rode to Trenwith House at as fast a gallop as could be had with the roads still wet. Once arrived, he perceived the relaxed pace of Mr. Singh's speech and movements to be agonizingly slow and was tempted to announce himself, were he not in possession of better manners.

Abby was sitting at a writing table in her husband's study, a room she had little altered since his passing as he had spent a great deal of time in it.

"My dear Fitzwilliam, you look positively pale!" she remarked as she looked over a pair of spectacles at him. "Are you unwell?"

"I am fine," he answered of his health. "I came— But forgive my intrusion—if you've no wish to be disturbed, I hope you will send me away. I can call at a more opportune time."

She appraised him more closely. "But why should I send you away now that you are here? Clearly something of an urgent nature brought you here."

At her acceptance of his company, he sat down upon a sofa before the writing table, but, restless, he rose to his feet again. "The young woman—the Red Chamber—"

The air felt thin, and he had to take several breaths before continuing, "Who was she?"

Abby frowned. "Fitzwilliam, you know better than anyone I never reveal an identity."

He took once more to pacing as he weighed the rules of engagement against his own desire for confirmation.

Dabbing her quill in ink, she continued penning the letter before her, asking, "Why such an interest in this young woman?"

He paced a bit more before sitting down. "Because I have reason to believe I know her."

She paused but did not look up. "Perhaps you do. Perhaps you don't. Really, it is inconsequential."

She resumed her writing.

"I fear it is not," he protested, a little surprised at her detachment. "I need to know—I need to know if she is Miss Elizabeth Bennet."

The quill stopped, but as her face was lowered toward her letter, he could not discern her expression. When she did look at him, her countenance was impassive. "And why such a desire to know?"

He met her gaze for but a moment before looking away, but she saw it all despite his not having said a word.

"You fancy her!"

Damnation. How was it she possessed such perception? He recalled a time, albeit of short duration, when he fancied he had been a little in love with Abigail because of her cleverness.

Putting down her pen, she scrutinized him with the purpose of appraising the depths of his affection. "Indeed. I have never seen you this shaken. Are you in love with this Elizabeth Bennet?"

"Do you deny you know her?" he asked, almost hopeful.

"I know of her. She is one of two guests staying with Mr. Collins. But as to the name of your pupil, I will, of course, deny everything."

He tempered his aggravation. He abhorred deceit, but he understood she acted out of discretion and respect for the lives and reputations of her students and teachers.

"But I have every wish to ease your distress," she continued, rising to her feet and approaching him. "If this young woman reminds you of Miss Elizabeth Bennet, and you are not up to task, I can appoint another to continue her lessons."

"No! I meant..."

Darcy knew not which was worse—the knowledge that he had possibly deflowered Miss Elizabeth or the thought of another man touching her.

"You are looking worse, Fitzwilliam." She went to the sideboard and poured him a glass of Madeira. "The pupil you met with the other night wishes to pursue another lesson, andI need to know if you are prepared to give it."

He put a hand to his brow.

"But perhaps it is wisest to relieve you of your position regardless," she contemplated aloud as she handed him the drink.

He surprised her by downing it in one gulp. He took a deep but harried breath. "I am up to the task."

The thought of another man taking his place would drive him mad if the young woman was indeed Miss Elizabeth.

Abby appeared unconvinced. "You must put it out of your head that your pupil reminds you of Miss Elizabeth. I am putting a great deal of faith and trust in you if I allow you to continue."

He nodded. "I have no wish to disappoint you."

She sat down beside him. For several minutes they sat in silence, each in their own thoughts.

"It has been many years since a woman has caught your eye," she commented. "Miss Elizabeth must be an exceptional young lady."

"Love looks not kindly upon me. Twice I have been afflicted and twice with women wholly unsuitable for me."

"The blush of first love is often reckless. You were young when you took a fancy to Delana. I no longer call her a friend after her treatment of you."

"I harbor no resentment toward her. What woman of sophistication and breeding would entertain with seriousness the affections of a callow suitor?"

"I prefer to talk of this Miss Elizabeth."

"And I would not," he replied as he stood.

"You will not satisfy my curiosity?"

He was tempted, for he had confided his feelings for Miss Elizabeth to no one. "Perhaps another time. I am reminded of my duty and will endeavour my best."

"I am confident in your abilities, but I warn all my students—and instructors bear reminding as well—to guard against affection."

The concern in her eyes was evident, and he admitted his own confidence to waver, but prolonging his stay would not produce the results he sought. Preparing to take his leave, he bowed. Though his agitation had not dissipated, he found some calm in the clarity of his newfound goal: to determine for himself if the young woman of the Red Chamber was Miss Elizabeth Bennet.

* * * * *

These clandestine visits will not do, Lizzy admonished herself. And yet, when Mr. Collins and Charlotte had left to attend dinner at the home of a friend in town, and Maria, complaining of having a headache, took to her room early, Lizzy could not resist having a horse saddled and making her way to Trenwith House. Lizzy apologized profusely for the disturbance when she was admitted to see the lady of the house.

"You should never have offered up your hospitality, for I fear I may trespass upon it often," Lizzy told Abby as they sat down in the drawing-room.

"I pray it will be so!" Abby declared with sufficient enthusiasm that Lizzy would not have doubted the sincerity of her words, were she not always inclined to vivacity. "I only wish I could promise you that I will always be here to receive you, though you are to make Trenwith House your home in my absence. Are you here for your second lesson?"

Lizzy coloured. "I would not expect a lesson, as I had provided no prior notice."

"Let us see what can be done, shall we?"

Making her way to a writing table, she found paper and pen. She scrawled a brief note and rang for Mr. Singh. Lizzy waited, knowing she had a chance to put a stop to the effort, as she had considered doing the other day. She had even contemplated confessing to Charlotte but decided against burdening her friend and risking their friendship. In the end, Lizzy came to a partial reconciliation that she was, simply, a selfish being. She craved the knowledge that Abby Trenwith, and *only* Abby Trenwith, offered. Such an opportunity would not avail itself elsewhere in a lifetime.

"I commend you for your bravery," Abby said when Mr. Singh had departed with the note.

"Or reprove me for my depravity."

"There are enough of those who would condemn us for what we do and what we believe. Do not add to their voices with your own.

There may yet come a time when we shall not regard with sanctimony the withholding of that most natural act between all creatures, the concealment and avoidance of which encumbers the fair sex more. In this, I would almost believe that God had punished women for the sins of Eve, for *our* pleasure is not as easily discerned. But to counter the argument for this inequity, we are rewarded with more possibilities."

"I would that I had the conviction of your eloquence."

"Patience, my dear Lizzy. Yours is a bold frontier. It is natural to feel a mix of emotions: fear, excitement, guilt, and shame."

"I have felt all those. Sin that goes unnoticed can only mask itself as virtuous. What are these additional possibilities you speak of?"

Abby smiled. "You will learn soon enough if you continue the lessons. Though I do not think a reminder required of you, I should nonetheless warn you of becoming partial to your instructor. I had once thought to engage a different instructor for each lesson, such is the danger of attachment, but it was impractical, and the trust that builds between instructor and pupil over time is an asset to learning."

"You have no fear with me. I do not fall in love easily."

"Have you ever?"

"Fallen in love? I thought affection to grow once for a certain gentleman in regimentals, but it was too fleeting to approach love. Nay, I wonder that I ever will fall in love. My criteria are far too substantial."

She paused, contemplating another person whose standards might exceed her own. The discussion had occurred, while she was visiting Jane at Netherfield, between her, the Bingleys and Mr. Darcy .

"It is amazing to me," Bingley had said, "how young ladies can have patience to be so very accomplished as they all are."

"All young ladies accomplished!" Miss Bingley had exclaimed. "My dear Charles, what do you mean?"

"Yes, all of them, I think. They all paint tables, cover screens, and net purses. I scarcely know anyone who cannot do all this, and I am sure I never heard a young lady spoken of for the first time, without being informed that she was very accomplished."

"Your list of the common extent of accomplishments," Darcy had said, "has too much truth. The word is applied to many a woman who deserves it no otherwise than by netting a purse or covering a screen. But I am very far from agreeing with you in your estimation of ladies in general. I cannot boast of knowing more than half-a-dozen, in the whole range of my acquaintance, that are really accomplished."

"Then," Lizzy had observed, "you must comprehend a great deal in your idea of an accomplished woman."

"Yes, I do comprehend a great deal in it."

"Oh! certainly," his faithful assistant had cried, "no one can be really esteemed accomplished who does not greatly surpass what is usually met with. A woman must have a thorough knowledge of music, singing, drawing, dancing, and the modern languages, to deserve the word; and besides all this, she must possess a certain something in her air and manner of walking, the tone of her voice, her address and expressions, or the word will be but half-deserved."

"All this she must possess, and to all this she must yet add something more substantial, in the improvement of her mind by extensive reading."

"I am no longer surprised at your knowing *only* six accomplished women," Lizzy had said. "I rather wonder now at your knowing *any*."

"Are you so severe upon your own sex as to doubt the possibility of all this?" Miss Bingley had asked.

"I never saw such a woman. I never saw such capacity, and taste, and application, and elegance, as you describe united."

Lizzy felt she could apply a similar assessment to the other sex. And despite the rarity of any one individual possessing all the traits she desired in a partner, she nonetheless felt she required the presence of them all before she could fall in love.

"I would be content to leave love to my sisters. They take to matters of the heart more readily than I," Lizzy said to Abby.

"Are you more prone to abhor men?"

"I make no special effort to disdain them. On the whole, I find many of them agreeable. I recently made the acquaintance of Colonel Fitzwilliam, who displayed no faults that I am aware of and whose company I would welcome anytime."

"Unlike his cousin?" Abby added with a sly smile.

"Yes, well..." Lizzy bit her tongue before she found herself saying anything too critical.

"I know you are not overly fond of Mr. Darcy, but do you see no redeeming traits in him at all?"

"I understand he has a delightful library," Lizzy replied, in recalling Miss Bingley's praise of Pemberley.

Abby laughed. "Oh dear, is he as bad as that?"

"But you are acquainted with him. You must know better if he possesses more amenable qualities than what he has displayed to us?"

"And if he were in possession of such, would that change your recommendation of him?"

"Of course. *Your* opinion of him, if it be agreeable, would affect my consideration."

"I am flattered by your regard."

Lizzy was only slightly curious to hear what Abby thought of the man, as she suspected that the opinion of the latter could not be too divergent from her own, but their conversation was put to an end with the arrival of Mrs. Singh with the tea. When they resumed talking, it was not of Mr. Darcy. After half an hour had passed, Mr. Singh returned with a note for Mrs. Trenwith.

Abby read it, then looked at Lizzy. "It would seem you can have your second lesson this evening."

CHAPTER FIFTEEN

"I am told you will not be taking dinner here?" asked Lady Catherine as she observed her nephew putting on his cloak in the vestibule.

"Regretfully, no," Darcy replied. Upon receiving the note from Abby, he had brooked no hesitation in replying in the affirmative.

"Anne herself contributed to the menu for the evening. With my guidance, she has recommended an exceptional repast."

"I will convey my apologies to her in person and ensure my stay is of a duration that I may sample many other menus of hers in the days to come."

Never satisfied when her plans were upset, Catherine frowned. "And what matter of business calls you away at this hour?"

As she was his aunt and hostess, Darcy stymied his objection at her prying. "My assistance is required."

"By whom?"

Darcy paused, knowing full well his aunt's regard, or lack thereof, rather, for Abby. "By Mrs. Trenwith."

The shock in Catherine's face was as he had expected, but he continued to put on his gloves and hat.

"Mrs. Trenwith! *Abigail* Trenwith?"

"Yes."

He was spared from further discussion by the announcement that his horse was ready. Still in the haze of disbelief, she ambled behind him as he headed out but stopped at the threshold. She stomped her cane. "This will not do. Have you any idea what that woman is about?"

"Your pardon, but a quick departure will hasten my return," he said as he mounted his bay.

Unable to refute him, and perhaps sensing his determination, she said nothing, but the look of consternation upon her face needed no words.

Darcy urged his horse into a gallop. Perhaps it had been foolish of him to be truthful, though Catherine was unlikely to reveal to anyone his acquaintance with Abby. Under no circumstances would he admit the full truth of what occurred at Trenwith House, but he had no tolerance for prevarication if it could be avoided. He knew he had opened a Pandora's box with Catherine and was sure to hear more from her on the matter.

At Trenwith House, he was shown to his usual chambers and learned that Nicholas had went into town with a friend. To his knowledge, Nicholas had never been indiscreet, but he would have preferred to trust Nicholas with as little as possible. If it *was* Miss Elizabeth, she would do well to be cautious around him.

"I have the same assessment of my stepson," Abby informed Darcy when he expressed his concerns, "and endeavour my best to restrict his access to my students."

"But my pupil—she has already met Nicholas," Darcy said as he donned a powdered wig.

"By happenstance. I cannot guard against all circumstances of chance, but the young woman is aware of the risks she takes in coming here."

Abby stood before him and adjusted his cravat. "Your pupil is ready for her second lesson but not prepared to surrender her maidenhead."

He reviewed himself in the mirror and remarked of the improvement she had made, "You have not lost your skill."

"Having undone many a cravat, I am quite intimate with the tying of linen."

Dressed once more in silk breeches and a satin waistcoat, he looked fully prepared for an evening at Almack's. After fitting a black velvet mask over his eyes, he took a deep breath to quiet his nerves but to no avail. His heart continued to pound. Abby opened her mouth, but decided against what she had intended to say.

"I always did like the look of a man in breeches," she remarked instead, sweeping her gaze over his tight clothing. "If I were years younger, I should be madly in love with you."

"And I thought you to disdain artifice as much as I," he replied.

She shook her head. "My dear Darcy, you are far too solemn. You require, I think, a woman of lighter spirit, who enjoys humor and can laugh at herself. After all, do we not engage in a most covert undertaking?"

He had long seen the irony of his disposition against deception and the pretense required of Trenwith House but was convinced the balance of good tilted toward the latter.

He stood, surveying himself in the mirror. All the eagerness that had driven him to Trenwith House stalled with the possibility that his apprehensions might be confirmed.

"She awaits in the Red Chamber," Abby prodded.

With a nod, he took his leave, the careful gaze of his hostess upon him till he disappeared from her view. Before entering the Red Chamber, he required a moment to steel his nerves. He had spent the better part of the night pondering the ways he might subtly ascertain her identity without revealing his own, and preparing himself if his suspicions should prove themselves. What he would do upon discovery, however, he knew not.

She sat before the fireplace, this time in full dress from the same period, a plumed mask upon her, reading from *Fanny Hill*. As she had not heard his entry, he had the opportunity to observe her unnoticed. Her neck was of no remarkable length, but her shoulders had a nice contour. The arms were of similar thickness to those of Miss Elizabeth. The bust, constrained by a corset and covered by a fichu, could not be assessed. But his heartbeat quickened as his gaze moved up to study her lips. The shape, the suppleness—

She must have felt his scrutiny, for she looked up and in his direction.

"A favourite book of yours?" he inquired, almost forgetting to mask his own voice.

"Hardly, but it is significant in that it is the first bawdy novel I have ever read."

Her cold, though improved, lingered. To encourage her continued speech, he asked, "And how do you esteem the work?"

"I found myself caring enough for the heroine and what was to become of her. And I cannot help but be amused by Cleland's prose. His reference of, well, that *anatomy* as a 'machine' or 'weapon' is too droll. This implement must be quite the wonder, for all the women in his story are drawn to it like moths to a flame and cannot remark enough upon the look and size of it."

"I think our sex is prone to paying that, er, part more attention than warranted."

"I thank you for your admittance, for I had suspected as much, and that the *devotion* Fanny and her peers pay to that 'instrument' is more a reflection of the author than of womankind. But I will match your honesty by saying that I am not without some natural curiosity of that which is concealed from the fair sex. Perhaps if I were to dispel my naiveté by viewing the mysterious 'weapon,' my admiration for it may yet grow."

"I think you are as like to mock it as extol it."

One corner of her mouth quirked into a smile. "Perhaps. Is it truly as awesome as described?"

He started. Never had he been asked such a bold question. She was more impertinent than Miss Elizabeth, but perhaps, protected by her guise and the security of anonymity, she allowed herself more freedom. It would not surprise him to discover in Miss Elizabeth an irreverence to all which others would pay excessive worship. In that, he and Miss Elizabeth might be kindred spirits, for he, too, distrusted exaggeration and sycophants.

He answered, "That would be in the eye of the beholder, *mademoiselle*."

She pursed her lips in thought. With the glow of the fire upon her, she presented a lovely vision. It had been but days since he had undressed her and felt the softness of her skin beneath his hands. The blood coursed stronger through his veins.

Straightening, he took a serious tone. "You are new to Trenwith House. I know Mrs. Trenwith to have advised you on the need for discretion. You ought trust no one but the mistress of the house."

"I have no intention of bringing suspicion upon myself or anyone here."

"Who knows of your presence here?"

She tilted her head at the tension in his voice. "Mrs. Trenwith, naturally. Mr. Singh showed me in. Sally assisted with my toilette. You."

"Anyone else? Members of your family? Friends?"

"No."

Her answer relieved him only a little. "What of your prior visits here?"

"It might be known that I have called upon Trenwith House by others beyond whom I have named, but it is not known what I *do* here. I was assured the confidentiality of our activities will not be breached."

"The past is an imperfect predictor of the future."

He sensed her eyes narrowing at him from behind her mask. "Is this all part of your seduction?"

He stiffened. "Even the most diligent can overlook innocent details. If you should be discovered, you would be ruined."

"I am aware of the consequences," she replied grimly. "The effect upon my family and my sisters weighs upon me more than what I should suffer."

His ears perked. He could not resist asking, "Have you many sisters?"

"Yes. Perhaps it is unfair of me to risk their standing to indulge my own selfish desire for knowledge…and pleasure."

"It is a very dangerous risk. If your sisters are unmarried, their futures might be forever impaired."

She lowered her gaze to her hands and was silent for a moment. "And you? Do you have family?"

"I do."

"Do you not risk your own reputation and theirs?"

"The consequences are graver upon the fair sex, but I am cognizant of how exposure might harm my family."

She looked at him. "Then why do you do it?"

He wanted to ask her the same, but she had beaten him to the query. "I felt fortunate to have, myself, received an 'education.' My instructor did much to ease the anguish and shame I felt of the lust within me. I am indebted to Ab—to Trenwith House."

"And you are fulfilling your obligation as an instructor?"

"Not only did my experience vanquish my torment, I have become privileged to a whole new understanding of humankind."

"That is what I seek, though my sentiments are not as noble as yours."

Remembering he wore a wig, he resisted running a hand through his hair. He was all too tempted to dissuade her from continuing her 'education,' but it would be the height of hypocrisy to deny her the enlightenment that he had been granted and a betrayal of the mission dearest to Abby, whose views were radical in the extreme but had at their heart good and selfless intentions.

"I can tell you are a gentleman. Are there not others who can fulfill your role?"

"I am persuaded by Abby, not many."

"She *is* a very persuasive woman."

They shared a smile.

"Ah, I forgot," the young woman said of a sudden and rose to her feet. From her décolletage, she pulled out a handkerchief for him. "I washed it thoroughly. I imagine it is too fine for you to part with."

He stared at it, soaking in the realization that the cloth had been pressed against her breast. "Keep it."

"Are you quite sure?"

"My mother enjoyed embroidery. It was one of her favourite pastimes. This particular handkerchief she had made only a pair, but I am not short of handkerchiefs."

It was not in the rules to assign tokens of one's stay at Trenwith House, but it gave him some satisfaction to know that she had something of his.

She now stood within arm's reach of him. He felt he could seduce away whatever reservations he had helped stoke, but he was rendered immobile by the war between desire and mortification. How could this woman not be Miss Elizabeth? He wanted to ask her any number of questions to validate his suspicion but would not appear prying. And yet, it was too fantastical, surely too much a coincidence, that he could make love to the very woman he dwelled upon over all others? Perhaps he already had. He had not even dared to dream of her in that manner before. How had Miss Elizabeth come upon Abby Trenwith?

It was enough to drive him mad.

"Are you certain you wish to continue?" he asked.

"You are uncommonly talkative tonight."

"Perhaps I was uncommonly taciturn the night before."

She allowed for that possibility, then decided to answer his question. "I had already embarked upon this path of peril when I agreed to the first lesson. While additional visits may improve opportunities for discovery—"

"*Will* improve."

"I see no increase in jeopardy for the time being, as I am already here. I may as well proceed with the lesson. I can review the decision to prolong the education thereafter."

He groaned silently.

"But I confess—and if I may be forward—that you, sir, appear in some distress. If it would ease your state to delay——"

"No, that is not necessary. I am up to the task."

The last thing he wanted was the opportunity to be replaced as her instructor or compel her to make another trip. With a shaky breath, he prepared himself.

"Do you recall the safety word?"

"Montreal," she supplied with confidence.

The tables had turned. The instructor was now more nervous than the student. He took an uncertain step toward her. Perhaps he could put it out of his mind that this was Miss Elizabeth, that Fate could not be so cruel.

Alas, circumstance would not abet him. He touched a tendril of hair that coiled about her collar. Despite the lighting, he recognized the colour.

"No powdered wig tonight," he commented.

"My evening is limited. I ought return home before my absence becomes noteworthy."

Then he had no time to waste. For her sake. And because he had a duty to fulfill. But he could only stand before her and regard her as if she were a porcelain doll that would break with too much contact. With much exertion, he finally put his hands upon her shoulders.

She waited patiently, then said, "My feelings are not easily hurt. If I am repulsive to you——"

"No!"

To prove it, he wrapped an arm about her waist and pulled her to him. The smell of her, the feel of her body pressed to his, all made his blood heat in an instant. It was his undoing. He lowered his head and captured her mouth.

By God. He was very likely kissing Elizabeth Bennet. The realization that this might be his only occasion to kiss her deepened his embrace a little more forcefully than he intended as he drank in the headiness of her lips. How soft and pliant they were beneath his. How sweet and intoxicating. He took mouthfuls of her, his hunger growing with each bite, the primal urges roaring to life.

But judging her to be a little overwhelmed, he forced a rein upon his desire and trailed lighter kisses down her neck. His lust was bested by a greater desire to satisfy *her*. His own vanity demanded that he provide her an unforgettable experience. Placing a hand at the small of her back, he fitted her closer to him. His cock lengthened in response. He would grind her into his groin but deemed the action too coarse for the second lesson. Wrapping his other hand around the back of her neck, he massaged her there, his fingers rimming the edge of her scalp. She relaxed into his arms, a slight murmur of contentment escaping her lips.

"What do you seek in your lesson tonight, *mademoiselle?*" he whispered in her ear.

"What are my options and what would you recommend?"

The trust she was placing in him was no small responsibility. He answered, "We ought continue the exploration of your body. There are many possible points of pleasure upon a woman's body. Shall we attempt to find them all?"

She inhaled sharply. He himself had found it difficult to speak fluidly of his own suggestion.

"Yes," she pronounced.

God have mercy, he silently blasphemed. Gathering every ounce of restraint, he caressed her ear with his mouth with a gentle tug at the lobe, then flicking his tongue into the opening.

"Ahh," she gasped.

He nuzzled the area behind her ear and planted hot, wet kisses down the side of her neck. She moaned her approval. He cupped her chin with both hands, titled her mouth up to his, and paid homage to her lips with deliberation and tenderness. If he did not desire her more, he would be content to kiss her for an eternity. When he felt her lips moving with his, he slid his tongue at hers. She jumped a little in surprise but quickly acclimated to his intrusion. With more experience, she could participate in the dance of a kiss, but he was content to do the sampling and the leading, careful not to shove his tongue too deep but keeping it light and teasing. When he lifted his head to give her a chance to catch her breath, she seemed almost disappointed that he had stopped.

Dropping his hands down to her shoulders, he ran his thumbs along her collarbone. He pushed aside the fichu to expose the décolletage. With the knuckle of his forefinger, he traced the swell of one breast. Her bosom lifted with her breath.

"I will undress you—completely," he informed her.

She nodded.

How easy she could have made his life if she would refuse! The steadiness of his hand surprised him as he unpinned her fichu.

Turning her away from him, he began to unbutton her bodice with a measure that belied an exhilaration he wished did not exist.

"If at any time you wish me to desist…"

"Is there a purpose to your drawn pace?"

"Prolonging the anticipation can intensify the excitement."

He slid the garment from her, baring her arms. He liked the look of them: healthy and with feminine plumpness. There was substance to her, not like some of the young women who appeared as if they were wasting away before one's eyes or whose thinness made them as a scrawny as a shriveling old woman. He felt it when they kissed, and in the hold of their hands as they danced. He was certainly not partial to the women who felt as if they had as much solidity as porridge or who might melt away if he kissed too ardently. Miss Elizabeth and his student had presence.

He unpinned her skirts next, then untied her petticoats until she was clad similar to the first lesson. His heart began to pound as he saw the colour of her garters through the thin shift. Being a man, he was not always indifferent to the physical charms of his pupils. Nor did any sense of attraction disturb him. But this was different. This was excruciating.

"Is something the matter? Or is this part and parcel of anticipation?" she asked after he had stood too long in awe of what he beheld.

"Merely admiring the sight," he answered hoarsely.

Coercing his mind to task, he reached for her corset and methodically loosened the laces. When he had freed her from its confines and dropped the article atop her other apparel, he paused once more. A last article of clothing and she would be stripped to the buff save for her garters, stockings and mask. Notwithstanding the disquiet he felt, his cock was fully erect and visibly stretching the tightness of his breeches.

He grasped her shoulders and kissed the nape of her neck. He caressed the area with his lips till he heard her soft moan. He grasped a breast in each hand and kneaded the thick, full orbs. Her moan grew louder. He lightly pinched and pulled at the already hardened nipples. She arched herself deeper into his hands. With one hand, he rolled the little nub between his thumb and forefinger, while his other hand dropped down to cup her womanhood.

Though her shift remained between them, there was not a part of her that did not feel exquisite beneath his hands. The blood coursed strongly through his body, causing his erection to throb. He wondered if he had enough control to last the lesson.

CHAPTER SIXTEEN

Lizzy shivered as if from cold despite the warmth from the fire. When she sensed herself growing abashed, she would focus upon the dancing shadows cast by its flames. She was not accustomed to being naked before anyone, and he was still very much a stranger despite their first lesson together. The arousal she felt from his kisses surprised her. Did it prove that the carnal was a force of its own, apart from emotion or reason? Or might she be attracted to this man? Abby had alluded to students commonly forming feelings for their instructors, a natural consequence of the dynamics of the relationship, but Lizzy had thought herself above schoolroom sensibilities.

Then how did this man cause such flutters in her stomach and the warmth to surge in her loins? How was it his touch could persevere through her awkwardness, which had not dissipated, perhaps because she sensed a peculiar difference in him this night.

But the effect of his caresses was unchanged. As his hands roamed her body, she submitted to the pleasure, enjoying the feel of her soft flesh beneath his masculine grip upon her breasts, ribs, waist, abdomen, hips, and thighs. One hand slid between her legs and rubbed her shift against the dampness there. His other arm circled around her and, clasping her to him, reached for the far breast and toyed with the nipple. She writhed in his grasp as the torturous delight built within her.

He pulled her shift down till it fell to her ankles. She barely had time to think of her nakedness, though, for he resumed his fondling. Pleasure shot from the nipple down to her womanhood, where his fingers grazed her clitoris over and over again, her wetness allowing him to glide effortlessly along her flesh. *My God*, she thought to herself as her body succumbed all too easily. He increased his assault. Her legs weakened and just when she thought they might give way, the pressure within her burst into a hundred shards of pleasure, making her convulse as they tore through her body.

He caught her around the waist as she jerked and shuddered. As he eased his stroking, she felt the last waves of her paroxysm move through her before she crumbled to the ground in the wrap of his embrace.

Her head upon his shoulder, she gathered her breath as the echo of her heartbeat receded. If this be one of the joys allowed by matrimony, then perhaps she had underrated that institution. And if she should never marry, she would be forever grateful to Trenwith House for an experience that she would loath never to have discovered.

"Let us finish upon the bed," he said.

"Are we not finished?" she asked after he had scooped her up.

"Are you satisfied to end now?" he asked before laying her upon the bed.

She would have been perfectly content, but now she was curious. "If there is more to the lesson, I am ready."

Now that her lust had been satiated, she was conscious of her nudity. She made a move to pull the bedclothes over her, but he stayed her hand. He moved onto the bed next to her. The bulge at his crotch caught her eye.

"Is there—what—rather, should I return the favour?"

"These lessons are for your benefit, not mine," he replied almost as if he were vexed with her.

"But..."

He closed her mouth with his. She thrilled at the pressure of his lips over hers. Would she ever tire of kissing? No two were alike and held a myriad of possible characteristics and sequences, from short and sweet, slow and gentle, to long and passionate, fast and forceful. When his arm encircled her midsection and pulled her closer, her arms went around his neck. She liked the warmth of his body and the scent of his shaving pomade. What little she had learned of kissing through their exchange, she attempted to return. It seemed to incite him, for his kisses became ardent, hungry. He grasped a buttock. She would have yelped in surprise if his mouth did not muffle hers. He squeezed her arse, and before she could comment or object, he had rolled atop her, pinning her body beneath his as he continued to explore the depths of her mouth.

Her nipples dug into his chest and she could feel his protrusion hard against her thigh. She was suddenly quite curious about the object. Upon instinct, she moved her leg and rubbed against it. He went instantly to his knees. Propping himself up, his body hovering above hers, he moved his attention from her mouth to her breasts. He flicked his tongue at a nipple, then covered it with his mouth. She groaned when he began to suck. The heat between her legs churned. She watched as he teased the sensitive bud till her back arched and she thought she might go mad. He trailed kisses down to her navel and farther to her—

Surely he did not intend...

Heart thudding, she clenched her thighs together. But he parted her knees and settled himself between them. She shut her eyes, embarrassed and hardly able to believe that he was in such an intimate area. At first she felt only his breath there.

"Calm yourself," he instructed. "I mean only to kiss you here."

The force of her dream came rushing back to her. Only it wasn't Darcy between her legs. It was a skilled lover—nay, instructor. His earlier actions had pushed her arousal beyond where she could truly halt herself from seeking that joyful end. But could she enjoy the action when her dream had left her soured of the vision?

"What is amiss, *mademoiselle*?"

Given his location, she could not look him in the eye.

"Nothing. Rather, I simply feel a little uncertain..."

"Do you require the safety word?"

Perhaps, she thought to herself. Aloud, she said, "Proceed first."

He kissed the down at the base of her pelvis. When he flicked his tongue at the wanton little rosebud between her folds, she nearly leaped off the bed.

"Are you all right?"

She let out a haggard breath, then nodded.

He licked her there once more, appraised her reaction, and licked her a third time. She trembled with every touch. How lewd and naughty was the act! How provocative! His tongue tickled at first, but the lapping of the warm, moist, thick and uneven flesh against hers soon ignited that sublime agitation. The strokes of his tongue were a wholly different sensation, and he never seemed to fail at finding the spot that excited her most. Pleasure reverberated through her legs. A few times he allowed his tongue to slide lower, and she found the pressure along her slit produced an ache inside her most sacred place, a desire for more pressure. She had not thought she could be aroused so quickly after spending but a few moments before, but when all resistance had subsided and she could fully glory in his skills, it seemed the swell of her previous tide assisted a new one in lifting her higher and higher till her toes curled and her fingers dug into the sheets.

She cried out as she reached her climax.

He held her in place as he wrung the last of her spasms from her body, till his touch became jarring and uncomfortable. When the final shudders had subsided and she could catch her breath, she stared at the canopy above in amazement of her own body.

"Would you care for a third or is the time now short?" he inquired.

A third time? Was that possible?

She flushed to see the glisten of her wetness about his mouth and chin. She glanced at a clock upon the far wall and sat up quickly in response.

"I ought to return before my absence calls attention," she said.

He went to retrieve her clothing and lent her the assistance of a chambermaid. Oddly, she felt more embarrassed dressing before him than she had felt when he had disrobed her.

"No cosmetic can enhance the loveliness in a woman more effectively than the glow of spending," he said after he had finished buttoning her dress. "Pray, do not dwell in shame. You are entitled to the pleasures of your own body."

"Thank you for your compassion—and the lesson. Perhaps your concern would be lessened if you were not so accomplished an instructor."

He stiffened.

"Ah! Someone who despises compliments as much as I!" She smiled.

He seemed to relax.

"Do not worry of me, sir. I am quite capable of handling myself and do not intend to torture myself with guilt and shame, even if I may not be indifferent to them."

He shifted in awkward silence.

"Your handkerchief," he presented at last.

To relieve him of his unease, she presented him her hand. He held it for a moment longer than necessary before placing a kiss upon it.

"Thank you for the lesson," she said, feeling more herself. "Good night and God bless."

He only nodded.

She took her leave of him, thinking her instructor a rather strange fellow.

* * * * *

"Where have you been, Eliza?" Maria worried when Lizzy had returned to the Parsonage. "That was quite a long ride. I had become a bit frightened being alone, and in a home not my own."

Lizzy apologized and hoped that it would not happen again. Fortune seemed to smile upon her, for Mr. Collins and Charlotte had not arrived before her, and she soon learnt that after Easter, Mr. Collins was to spend two days in the neighboring parish that had recently installed a new rector, and Lady Catherine had recommended Mr. Collins bestow some of his earned knowledge on the good cleric. Ever eager to please his patroness, Mr. Collins could not thank her ladyship enough for the compliment. It was decided that the ladies, moreover, would make a day of perusing the local millinery and haberdashery. Lizzy said nothing, for she had every intention of begging out of the excursion.

With a giddiness uncommon to her, Lizzy wrote of this news to Abby and it was arranged that Lizzy was to have her third lesson in a few days' time. Pleased with the impending opportunity, Lizzy enjoyed with increased fervor the company of those at the Parsonage, agreeing with Charlotte and Maria's admiration of Colonel Fitzwilliam's manners and their sentiment that he must add considerably to the pleasures of their engagements at Rosings. It was some days, however, before they received any invitation thither—for while there were visitors in the house, they could not be necessary; and it was not till Easter day, almost a week after the gentlemen's arrival, that they were honoured by such an attention, and then they were merely asked upon leaving church to come there in the evening. For the last week they had seen very little of Lady Catherine or her daughter. Colonel Fitzwilliam had called at the Parsonage more than once during the time, but Mr. Darcy they had seen only at church.

CHAPTER SEVENTEEN

For some time, Darcy could not bring himself to speak to Miss Elizabeth. He envied his cousin's trips to the Parsonage and had been sorely tempted more than once to join the Colonel. His cousin had looked baffled enough when Darcy declined, no doubt wondering why he was choosing the company of Lady Catherine over the company of a lovely and articulate young woman. Darcy knew it was Miss Elizabeth, and not the virtues of anyone else, who drew his cousin to the Parsonage. Though Lady Catherine would not have objected to the visits, Darcy was disinclined to provoke her after upsetting her with his call to Trenwith House.

As he had predicted, when he had returned that evening, he was summoned to Lady Catherine's anteroom and received her caution and advice in full. Having spent many hours formulating her case, she was more superfluous than ever in her argument. He had listened to her politely and attentively, and had not been moved to speak a word till she had mentioned that she had advised Miss Elizabeth Bennet of the same and was satisfied that the young woman had taken her counsel.

"Miss Bennet?" Darcy echoed, his heart stalling.

Having delivered the bulk of what she had to say, Catherine finally partook of the tea beside her and replied, "Yes, the one staying with Mr. and Mrs. Collins. A bit headstrong, that Elizabeth Bennet, but at least she had the sense to see the effect her continued acquaintance with Abby Trenwith would have upon her friends and family."

Too preoccupied with the intelligence he had just been presented, he made no remark that Mrs. Trenwith was not as highly disregarded as Catherine's own opinion would have her believe. He had held to a small grain of hope that his pupil at Trenwith House was *not* Miss Elizabeth.

"How is Elizabeth Bennet acquainted with Mrs. Trenwith?" he

wondered aloud.

"I know not the particulars, but that Abby Trenwith dared pay a visit to Miss Bennet at the Parsonage. If the woman had a generous bone in her body, she would leave decent folk alone. What matter of business did she require of you?"

"It is a private matter," he said.

Catherine knit her brows together with a frown, but it was not her place to question her nephew further. Instead, she said, "I hope, in the future, that Abby Trenwith would have the civility to request the assistance of another. She is too fortunate that yours is a most giving spirit. You ought not to allow her to trespass upon your benevolence further. That woman knows no bounds. I must warn Mrs. Jenkinson, should Trenwith dare approach Rosings, to keep my daughter at a safe distance. I hope you will assist in protecting your cousin from that woman?"

"I doubt Mrs. Trenwith to have any inclination to come to Rosings, but, if it is within my power to ensure the two never meet, I will endeavour to do so."

Satisfied that his answer bespoke his willingness to assent to all of her counsel, Catherine intended to proceed to happier topics, but, citing the late hour, Darcy excused himself.

In the quiet of his own room, the full weight of the evening sank in. The woman, his pupil, was Elizabeth Bennet.

Elizabeth Bennet.

No oath could do justice to what he felt. The coincidences were far too many. He recalled his conversation with Abby, who had acknowledged knowing Miss Elizabeth but revealed nothing more, her omittance no doubt intended to protect Miss Elizabeth. Nonetheless, it had not occurred to him then that she could have easily relieved him, without jeopardizing the identity of any other party, by rejecting his suspicions had he been in error. But she had not.

He put his head in his hands. The situation was terrible. Given his response during the lesson, he was more deeply attracted to Miss Elizabeth than ever. He knew now he desired her in every way. Every movement of hers, every sound she uttered had ignited his desire. And watching her spend had made his lust surge. He wanted to do more with her, to her—in part because he would not do anything for himself. Not until he had returned to his own room at Trenwith House did he attend to his own needs.

He remembered every inch of her. He had caressed every inch of her. Touched and kissed her most intimate parts. Only her maidenly sanctum remained pristine. What a wretched soul was he! He had seduced a good and decent young woman. Abby would have protested that he had given his pupil a gift, but he felt he had received the greater privilege. Abby would admonish him for his qualms and disparate treatment of Miss Elizabeth, but such was the benefit of anonymity.

"*She* made the choice. Would you condemn her decision?" he could imagine Abby saying.

Of course not. But it was a dangerous journey for a young woman to make. Convinced of the merits of her efforts, Abby weighed the risks a little too lightly for his comfort. Perhaps it was fortunate, and not merely a cruel trick of Fate, that he was the instructor for Miss Elizabeth. He knew not the other instructors Abby employed. They might not take as much care in protecting their pupils.

This conclusion appeased him. Nonetheless, he found it difficult to be in the company of Miss Elizabeth, knowing that he had seen her naked and that she had submitted her body to him.

However, he could not eschew her presence forever. An invitation had been extended and accepted by the Collinses and their guests. Lady Catherine received the party civilly in her drawing-room, but it was plain that their company was by no means so acceptable as when she could get nobody else; and she was, in fact, almost engrossed by her nephews, speaking to them, especially to Darcy, much more than to any other person in the room.

Though her gown was not nearly as stylish as that of Miss de Bourgh, Darcy thought Miss Elizabeth looked absolutely engaging. A few curls of her dark hair framed her round face, and a touch of rouge upon her lips was the perfect adornment to her bright countenance.

Darcy noted the look of genuine pleasure upon his cousin as he greeted the guests. Mrs. Collins's pretty friend had caught the Colone's fancy very much, Darcy thought a bit wryly as he watched the Colonel take a seat beside her. Darcy was not a jealous man, but he envied his cousin. He could not help looking in their direction repeatedly. Miss Elizabeth seemed greatly entertained by what the Colonel was saying. The two conversed with so much spirit and flow as to draw the attention of Catherine, who did not scruple to call out,

"What is that you are saying, Fitzwilliam? What is it you are talking of? What are you telling Miss Bennet? Let me hear what it is."

"We are speaking of music, madam," said he, when no longer able to avoid a reply.

"Of music! Then pray speak aloud. It is of all subjects my delight. I must have my share in the conversation if you are speaking of music. There are few people in England, I suppose, who have more true enjoyment of music than myself, or a better natural taste. If I had ever learnt, I should have been a great proficient. And so would Anne, if her health had allowed her to apply. I am confident that she would have performed delightfully. How does Georgiana get on, Darcy?"

He gave her an affectionate account of his sister's proficiency. Feeling the gaze of Miss Elizabeth upon him as he spoke, he turned in her direction. She looked away and exchanged a smile with his cousin.

"I am very glad to hear such a good account of her," said Catherine, "and pray tell her from me, that she cannot expect to excel if she does not practice a good deal."

"I assure you, madam, that she does not need such advice. She practices very constantly."

"So much the better. It cannot be done too much, and when I next write to her, I shall charge her not to neglect it on any account. I often tell young ladies that no excellence in music is to be acquired without constant practice. I have told Miss Bennet several times, that she will never play really well unless she practcses more; and though Mrs. Collins has no instrument, she is very welcome, as I have often told her, to come to Rosings every day, and play on the pianoforte in Mrs. Jenkinson's room. She would be in nobody's way, you know, in that part of the house."

Uncomfortable with his aunt's ill-breeding, he made no answer. He tried not to make his study of Miss Elizabeth too obvious, but he had little interest in attending to anyone else. Though he was convinced of her attendance at Trenwith House, he wished he could have the whole picture. He wanted to know how and why she had made the decision to become a participant? He had received notice yesterday from Abby confirming a third lesson. Never had excitement been so tortuous and fraught with such turmoil.

When coffee was over, Fitzwilliam reminded Lizzy of having promised to play to him, and she sat down directly to the instrument. He drew a chair near her. Catherine listened to half a song, and then talked, as before. But Darcy had no ear for her. His thoughts had turned to Miss Elizabeth at every free moment the past few days. He had denied himself her presence long enough. With his usual deliberation, he made for the pianoforte and stationed himself so as to command a full view of the fair performer's countenance.

She noted what he was doing, and at the first convenient pause, turned to him with an arch smile, and said, "You mean to frighten me, Mr. Darcy, by coming in all this state to hear me? I will not be alarmed though your sister *does* play so well. There is a stubbornness about me that never can bear to be frightened at the will of others. My courage always rises at every attempt to intimidate me."

"I shall not say you are mistaken," he replied, "because you could not really believe me to entertain any design of alarming you, and I have had the pleasure of your acquaintance long enough to know that you find great enjoyment in occasionally professing opinions which in fact are not your own."

Miss Elizabeth laughed heartily at this picture of herself, and said to Colonel Fitzwilliam, "Your cousin will give you a very pretty notion of me, and teach you not to believe a word I say. I am particularly unlucky in meeting with a person so able to expose my real character, in a part of the world where I had hoped to pass myself off with some degree of credit. Indeed, Mr. Darcy, it is very ungenerous of you to mention all that you knew to my disadvantage in Hertfordshire—and, give me leave to say, very impolitic too—for it is provoking me to retaliate, and such things may come out as will shock your relations to hear."

Shock would only be the half of it, he thought, but aloud he said with a smile, "I am not afraid of you."

"Pray let me hear what you have to accuse him of," cried Fitzwilliam. "I should like to know how he behaves among strangers."

"You shall hear then—but prepare yourself for something very dreadful. The first time of my ever seeing him in Hertfordshire, you must know, was at a ball—and at this ball, what do you think he did? He danced only four dances, though gentlemen were scarce; and, to my certain knowledge, more than one young lady was sitting down in want of a partner. Mr. Darcy, you cannot deny the fact."

"I had not at that time the honour of knowing any lady in the assembly beyond my own party," he defended.

"True, and nobody can ever be introduced in a ball-room. Well, Colonel Fitzwilliam, what do I play next? My fingers wait your orders."

"Perhaps," said Darcy, "I should have judged better, had I sought an introduction, but I am ill-qualified to recommend myself to strangers."

"Shall we ask your cousin the reason of this?" she said, still addressing his cousin. "Shall we ask him why a man of sense and education, and who has lived in the world, is ill qualified to recommend himself to strangers?"

"I can answer your question," said Fitzwilliam, "without applying to him. It is because he will not give himself the trouble."

"I certainly have not the talent which some people possess," said Darcy, "of conversing easily with those I have never seen before. I cannot catch their tone of conversation, or appear interested in their concerns, as I often see done."

"My fingers," said Lizzy, "do not move over this instrument in the masterly manner which I see so many women's do. They have not the same force or rapidity, and do not produce the same expression. But then I have always supposed it to be my own fault—because I will not take the trouble of practising. It is not that I do not believe *my* fingers as capable as any other woman's of superior execution."

He smiled and said, "You are perfectly right. You have employed your time much better. No one admitted to the privilege of hearing you can think anything wanting. We neither of us perform to strangers."

Save at Trenwith House, he told himself. Here they were interrupted by his aunt, who called out to know what they were talking of. Miss Elizabeth immediately began playing again.

Lady Catherine approached, and, after listening for a few minutes, said to Darcy, "Miss Bennet would not play at all amiss if she practised more, and could have the advantage of a London master. She has a very good notion of fingering, though her taste is not equal to Anne's. Anne would have been a delightful performer, had her health allowed her to learn."

Darcy made no reply. He felt Miss Elizabeth's study and met her gaze, admiring the humor and intelligence of her eyes. How was it she was lovelier than when he had seen her last? When she looked down at the keys, he took the opportunity to look upon her neck and the area of her collarbone. How inviting they were. He hoped he was the first and only man to have gained admittance to her charms.

Catherine continued her remarks on the performance, mixing with them many instructions on execution and taste. Miss Elizabeth received them with all the forbearance of civility, and, at the request of the gentlemen, remained at the instrument till her ladyship's carriage was ready to take them all home. By then Darcy was relieved to see Miss Elizabeth go, for she had stirred up a set of greatly inconvenient feelings. To have such lust for a pupil was unprincipled. He would be better served to dampen his sentiments. The honourable thing to do would be to remove himself from his position as her instructor.

CHAPTER EIGHTEEN

Lizzy was sitting by herself the next morning, and writing to Jane while Mrs. Collins and Maria were gone on business into the village, when she was startled by a ring at the door, the certain signal of a visitor. As she had heard no carriage, she thought it not unlikely to be Lady Catherine, and under that apprehension was putting away her half-finished letter that she might escape all impertinent questions, when the door opened, and, to her very great surprise, Mr. Darcy, and Mr. Darcy only, entered the room.

He seemed astonished too on finding her alone, and apologised for his intrusion by letting her know that he had understood all the ladies were to be within.

They then sat down and, after her inquiries after Rosings were made, seemed in danger of sinking into total silence. It was absolutely necessary, therefore, to think of something, and in this emergence recollecting *when* she had seen him last in Hertfordshire, and feeling curious to know what he would say on the subject of their hasty departure, she observed:

"How very suddenly you all quitted Netherfield last November, Mr. Darcy! It must have been a most agreeable surprise to Mr. Bingley to see you all after him so soon; for, if I recollect right, he went but the day before. He and his sisters were well, I hope, when you left London?"

"Perfectly so, I thank you."

She found that she was to receive no other answer, and, after a short pause added, "I think I have understood that Mr. Bingley has not much idea of ever returning to Netherfield again?"

"I have never heard him say so, but it is probable that he may spend very little of his time there in the future. He has many friends, and is at a time of life when friends and engagements are continually increasing."

"If he means to be but little at Netherfield, it would be better for the neighbourhood that he should give up the place entirely, for then we might possibly get a settled family there. But, perhaps, Mr. Bingley did not take the house so much for the convenience of the neighbourhood as for his own, and we must expect him to keep it or quit it on the same principle."

"I should not be surprised," said Darcy, "if he were to give it up as soon as any eligible purchase offers."

Lizzy made no answer. She was afraid of talking longer of his friend, and, having nothing else to say, was now determined to leave the trouble of finding a subject to him.

He took the hint, and soon began with, "This seems a very comfortable house. Lady Catherine, I believe, did a great deal to it when Mr. Collins first came to Hunsford."

"I believe she did—and I am sure she could not have bestowed her kindness on a more grateful object."

"Mr. Collins appears to be very fortunate in his choice of a wife."

"Yes, indeed, his friends may well rejoice in his having met with one of the very few sensible women who would have accepted him, or have made him happy if they had. My friend has an excellent understanding—though I am not certain that I consider her marrying Mr. Collins as the wisest thing she ever did. She seems perfectly happy, however, and in a prudential light it is certainly a very good match for her."

"It must be very agreeable for her to be settled within so easy a distance of her own family and friends."

"An easy distance, do you call it? It is nearly fifty miles."

"And what is fifty miles of good road? Little more than half a day's journey. Yes, I call it a *very* easy distance."

"I should never have considered the distance as one of the *advantages* of the match," cried Lizzy. "I should never have said Mrs. Collins was settled *near* her family."

"It is a proof of your own attachment to Hertfordshire. Anything beyond the very neighbourhood of Longbourn, I suppose, would appear far."

As he spoke there was a sort of smile which Lizzy fancied she understood. He must be supposing her to be thinking of Jane and Netherfield, and she blushed as she answered,

"I do not mean to say that a woman may not be settled too near her family. The far and the near must be relative, and depend on many varying circumstances. Where there is fortune to make the expenses of travelling unimportant, distance becomes no evil. But that is not the case *here*. Mr. and Mrs. Collins have a comfortable income, but not such a one as will allow frequent journeys—and I am persuaded my friend would not call herself *near* her family under less than *half* the present distance."

Mr. Darcy drew his chair a little towards her, and said, "*You* cannot have a right to such very strong local attachment. *You* cannot have been always at Longbourn."

Lizzy looked surprised. The gentleman experienced some change of feeling; he drew back his chair, took a newspaper from the table and, glancing over it, said, in a colder voice, "Are you pleased with Kent?"

A short dialogue on the subject of the country ensued, on either side calm and concise—and soon put an end to by the entrance of Charlotte and her sister, just returned from her walk. The *tete-a-tete* surprised them. Mr. Darcy related the mistake which had occasioned his intruding on Miss Bennet, and after sitting a few minutes longer without saying much to anybody, went away.

"What can be the meaning of this?" said Charlotte, as soon as he was gone. "My dear, Eliza, he must be in love with you, or he would never have called on us in this familiar way."

But when Lizzy told of his silence, it did not seem very likely, even to Charlotte's wishes, to be the case, and after various conjectures, they could at last only suppose his visit to proceed from the difficulty of finding anything to do, which was the more probable from the time of year. All field sports were over. Within doors there was Lady Catherine, books, and a billiard-table, but gentlemen cannot always be within doors; and in the nearness of the Parsonage, or the pleasantness of the walk to it, or of the people who lived in it, the two cousins found a temptation from this period of walking thither almost every day. They called at various times of the morning, sometimes separately, sometimes together, and now and then accompanied by their aunt. It was plain to them all that Colonel Fitzwilliam came because he had pleasure in their society, a persuasion which of course recommended him still more; and Lizzy was reminded by her own satisfaction in being with him, as well as by his evident admiration of her, of her former favourite George Wickham; and though, in comparing them, she saw there was less captivating softness in Colonel Fitzwilliam's manners, she believed he might have the best informed mind.

But why Mr. Darcy came so often to the Parsonage, it was more difficult to understand. It could not be for society, as he frequently sat there ten minutes together without opening his lips; and when he did speak, it seemed the effect of necessity rather than of choice—a sacrifice to propriety, not a pleasure to himself. He seldom appeared really animated.

"I cannot make him out," Charlotte had said to Lizzy once. "He certainly looks at you a great deal, but it is not apparent to me if his expression is one of love."

Lizzy laughed at the idea. "It is more likely that he looks my way to find a quality to criticize. I wonder that it is in his nature to harbor a sentiment such as love?"

"It may be nothing more than absence of mind for when he does gaze upon you, he looks quite steadfast and earnest. Still, I believe it quite possible for him to be partial to you, Eliza. And I think *you* would not be so inclined to dislike him if you supposed him to be in your power."

Lizzy balked. "I would not care in the least to have that man in my power. "

"I suppose Colonel Fitzwilliam, beyond comparison, the most pleasant man, and his admiration is more obvious. His situation in life is most eligible, but then, Mr. Darcy has considerable patronage in the church, and his cousin could have none at all."

* * * * *

Between visits from Colonel Fitzwilliam and reminiscing of her lessons at Trenwith House, Lizzy found much to occupy her time. She counted the days till her third lesson. Her reservations had faded further after the exalting experience of the second lesson. She had not had the opportunity to speak to Abby of her impressions, but the two exchanged letters. Abby congratulated her, for not every pupil could achieve a paroxysm, let alone two, by the second lesson, though such achievements owed themselves more to blessing than skill. At times, mostly at church, Lizzy wondered if she was not headed to purgatory for her deeds, but what she did was no different than what a married man and woman might do. If hers was a crime because it did not occur within the sanctity of marriage, then half the men in England— among them peers, ministers, and princes—were guilty.

She walked daily. More than once, in her ramble within the park, did she unexpectedly meet Mr. Darcy. She felt all the perverseness of the mischance that should bring him where no one else was brought, and, to prevent its ever happening again, took care to inform him at first that it was a favourite haunt of hers. How it could occur a second time, therefore, was very odd! Yet it did, and even a third. It seemed like wilful ill-nature, or a voluntary penance, for on these occasions it was not merely a few formal inquiries and an awkward pause and then away, but he actually thought it necessary to turn back and walk with her. He never said a great deal, nor did she give herself the trouble of talking or of listening much, but it struck her in the course of their third rencontre that he was asking some odd unconnected questions.

"Have you enjoyed being at Hunsford?" he asked after a lengthy silence.

Disappointed to have to cut short her walk due to his company, she gave a curt reply. She had hoped Maria to be done perusing the fashion plates in *The Lady's Magazine* by the time she finished her walk, but now she would be asked to give her opinion on every trim and accessory upon her return.

They walked several more minutes before he spoke again.

"Mr. and Mrs. Collins give the appearance of being satisfied with one another. Marriage has perhaps improved their happiness?"

"Happiness is the aim and hope of marriage, is it not?"

Silence settled once more between them. She suppressed her sigh at the interruption of her walk on a day with the most agreeable weather.

"You seem to take great pleasure in solitary walks," he said.

"I always find the air outside invigorating, and the *solitude* allows me to put some order to the clutter of thoughts in my head."

"Are your thoughts often in a state of disorder?"

"*You* might think it so. My thoughts are more often clear than muddled, but reflection can further clarify their definition."

The turmoil she experienced of late was certainly the result of Trenwith House.

"Sometimes, the lack of confusion denotes nothing more than a simple life or a simple mind."

His reply surprised her, for she had been prepared for him to make a judgment of her. She lowered her guard a little.

"Enlightenment must come from chaos and conflict," she added.

"*Qui onques rien n'enprist riens n'achieva.*"

She raised her brows. Mr. Darcy hardly seemed a man to risk anything. That she should be in a situation resembling agreement with him confounded her into reticence.

"Do you find yourself more inclined to take risks or seek the shelter of security?" he asked after a long pause.

What did he mean by this query? she wondered.

"I am not afraid of risk," she answered blandly, for she had no desire to illuminate her character to him.

"It was not a question intended to assess your courage."

"Indeed, and any attempt by me to classify myself as either one who seeks or one who shuns risk would be an unjust generality, for valuation of risk is unique to circumstance."

He made no reply, and she was satisfied to turn her attention to the flora along their path.

"Do you confine your walks to the park?"

She looked at him. Was he truly so bored at Rosings that he sought conversation with her?

"I have walked some three or four miles before," she said.

"I recall you once walked the distance from Longbourn to Netherfield—through mud."

"Yes, I must have presented quite the wild appearance, especially to Miss Bingley and Mrs. Hurst. I am sure my dirty petticoats and untidy hair did not escape their notice!"

"I find exercise can greatly improve one's complexion."

She was taken aback. It was not quite a compliment but certainly the only kind comment he had ever directed toward her.

"Where is the farthest you have walked here?"

Recalling the day she met Abby Trenwith, Lizzy looked in that direction. "Some four miles, I think."

He followed her gaze. "There is an estate worthy of note down the road there. Trenwith House. Had you come across it or been upon its grounds?"

She paused. "Yes."

"Have you met its proprietress?"

"Yes," she replied, almost daring him to advise as his aunt had. "I had taken a fall and, luckily, Mrs. Trenwith happened upon me. She was exceedingly kind."

"And had you formed any other opinions of her?"

"I was recommended not to."

"But you would otherwise give your opinions freely."

It was more statement than query, and she could not resist being a little irked. "It matters not in this event. I am sure we would not be in agreement."

"I had not offered my opinion."

"You need not have."

"Why? Because you have the ability to read minds? That must be a very convenient talent."

She narrowed her eyes at him. "An educated conjecture."

"Or premise given upon limited information."

She started. Where had she heard a similar remark? They had reached the gates of the pales opposite the Parsonage, and her impending departure from his company lifted her spirits.

"If it is combat you seek, Mr. Darcy," she said merrily, "I fear I cannot oblige you at this time. Perhaps another day."

With a smile and curtsy, she denied him the opportunity to open the gate for her by opening it herself. *What a trying man*, she thought, and promised herself to walk a different path on the morrow.

CHAPTER NINETEEN

As darcy watched Miss Elizabeth disappear into the house, he cursed himself. Her perturbation had been apparent. This was not how he had intended their dialogue to proceed and further substantiated that the less he conversed with her, the better. He might not have been so plain-spoken had he not been confident that she could walk away unscathed, albeit vexed, by any remark from him, but she did not deserve his impertinence, no matter her faults.

For days he had vacillated between continuing her instruction and removing himself from the picture. The thought of another man touching her was unbearable. But he had to ask himself what course of action was objectively best. If he intended to distance himself from Miss Elizabeth—and he had practiced this aim to no avail every time he made a point to encounter her on her walks or paid her a visit at the Parsonage—a third lesson would set him back grievously, perhaps past the point of no return.

He had called upon Abby to inform her of his noble intent to give up his position as Miss Elizabeth's instructor, but was informed that Mrs. Trenwith had taken herself into town for a few days to attend a friend in need. She was expected to return Saturday, the appointed day for Miss Elizabeth's third lesson. He did not receive this news disfavourably, however, for Miss Elizabeth would only suffer a mild disappointment if she came to Trenwith House on Saturday to learn her instructor was indisposed. The delay would provide him the opportunity to speak in greater depth with Abby of his concerns regarding Miss Elizabeth.

Alas, when Saturday had come, Fate did not prove an obliging cohort. He arrived at Trenwith House to learn Abby's return was to be delayed a day. Her presence was not required, as Pierre and Sally were seasoned servants and could ensure the lessons proceeded smoothly without the guidance of their mistress. Darcy determined that he would deliver a letter to Miss Elizabeth expressing his regrets and apologies for the inconvenience his unavailability would cause, but his plans were dashed upon learning that, while Abby was not returned from town, Mr. Nicholas had, and was presently entertaining Miss Elizabeth.

"They have been an hour upon the south portico," Pierre answered when asked.

Disconcerted by the information, Darcy felt empty of recourse. While he could still have a letter delivered to Miss Elizabeth, he was loath to leave her with her present company, yet he could not intrude upon them without revealing himself. Perhaps, upon receiving the letter, she would see no reason to continue at Trenwith House and take her leave. But what if she did not? He needed to remove Miss Elizabeth from Mr. Nicholas.

"Have Sally inform Miss Bennet—discreetly, of course—that she can prepare for her lesson," he instructed Pierre, "and notify me when Miss Bennet has retired to her chambers."

By the time Pierre returned, Darcy had made up his mind that he would risk discovery by seeking out Nicholas. He wanted to ascertain what the young man knew of Miss Elizabeth's presence at Trenwith House and his intentions toward the lady. As Darcy made for the terrace overlooking the garden, he wished Miss Elizabeth were not nearly so engaging nor so pretty. From George Wickham to Colonel Fitzwilliam and himself, she had amassed quite the bevy of admirers in the time he had known her.

Once upon the terrace outside, he was met with only a maidservant attending to the remains upon the table.

"Where is Mr. Trenwith?" he asked, noting the two used wine glasses she placed upon her tray.

"Beggin' your pardon, sir, he left here but a few minutes ago," she replied. "To where, I know not."

Darcy eyed the open bottles upon her tray. One of them was unusually small for a wine bottle.

"Had he and the lady with him been drinking much?" he asked.

"They finished this one, to be certain. Or, rather, she seemed to drink from it more." The maid held up the curious flask. "Mr. Nicholas had this one upon him. I have never seen its like in the cellar a'fore. He preferred the claret."

Darcy took the dark amber-coloured bottle from her and sniffed it.

He poured the last remaining drop onto his finger. Upon tasting the liquid, he turned pale. The brew had been greatly sweetened, but the distinctive flavours of the aphrodisiac could not be entirely masked. He did not favour the use of such tonics, but the Duchess had found them intriguing and had experimented with them extensively. The one that Miss Elizabeth had been imbibing was dubbed Nectar of Rati, one of the more potent agents. If she had consumed the majority of the bottle, and over the course of an hour, she would be in a precarious state at this time.

Biting back an oath, Darcy dispatched the maid to Miss Elizabeth's chamber with the directive that the guest was not to leave the room under any circumstance, nor was anyone to enter. He quickly took himself back to his own chambers, where he found Pierre waiting. With Nicholas prowling about the premises, the first order of business was to remove Miss Elizabeth from his reach, but she would be in no condition to return home until the effect of the aphrodisiac had worn off.

"Have Sally install her in the Temple of Bastet," Darcy said as he threw off his coat.

The Temple of Bastet was a small, enclosed pavilion tucked in the far end of the garden and hidden from view by a thicket of hazel trees. Few knew of its existence, and Nicholas had no affinity for walking about the garden. Miss Elizabeth could be safely ensconced there until the Nectar of Rati ran its course. Someone would have to keep Miss Elizabeth company during that time, and Darcy trusted no one but himself to ensure her safety.

"Shall I assist your wardrobe first?" Pierre asked.

"No!" Darcy answered. "After you have delivered the directions to Sally, find the whereabouts of Mr. Trenwith."

Pierre, too proficient to ask questions, did as he was bid.

In his haste, Darcy opted simply to throw a banyan over his clothes and affix a mask over his eyes.

"I am told Mr. Trenwith was headed to the West Wing," Pierre reported upon his return.

"And Sally?"

"Leading the miss to the Temple as we speak. It is fortunate timing. Before she left for London, Mrs. Trenwith had requested the Temple be prepared for the warmer spring weather."

Darcy had not considered the state of the Temple. He only wanted a place to shelter Miss Elizabeth for an hour or two. His heart pounded as if he had run some distance, and not a moderate walk through the Trenwith garden. He paused before the pavilion, simple in construct with a red cupola, ivory columns, and single marble door. Two stone cats of alabaster guarded the entry. It had been many years since Darcy had set foot within its confines, though Abby preferred it to any other location.

Inside the rotunda, sunken reliefs and carvings of gods and goddesses, in various states of dress and copulation, looked down upon a low platform bed with a canopy of coral-coloured fabric above the headrest. A mountain of pillows decked the new bed clothes, a mix of hand-woven linen and raw silk. Lighting came from small pottery with floating wicks and warmth from a half-dozen torches evenly spaced in the pavilion, which otherwise would have been cold and pitch black.

Miss Elizabeth sat in the room's only chair. His breath left him upon seeing her, dressed in a *kalasiris* with straps. The sheath reached just to the ankle, exposing sandals and feet to view, and its upper edge barely extended above the nipples. He could not help his gaze from lingering a superfluous second upon the gleaming orbs. A pleated shawl covered her shoulders and a turquoise mask concealed the upper half of her countenance. With her dark hair unadorned, and skin tanned from all her walking, she did not appear out of place in the apparel.

Seeing his study, she said, "Sally thought this costume fitting for the location."

Darcy only nodded. She shifted her hips in discomfort, though he did not suspect the furniture to be the cause.

"I must admit to being quite confused at this appointment," she said.

He could see her clenching her thighs together through the thin muslin. He could barely swallow.

She continued, "I had received direction that I am to meet you in the Chamber of the Golden Phoenix in the south wing. Now I have been shown *here*."

He decided against telling her that the note she had received had likely come from Nicholas. She pulled at her neck and released a haggard breath. Her discomfort was contagious, and he found himself wishing he had fortified himself with a stiff drink before he came.

"I fear, *mademoiselle*," he said, "that you have partaken of an aphrodisiac."

She stared at him blankly.

"A substance that arouses sexual desire," he defined.

"I know what an aphrodisiac is," she replied, "but you must be mistaken."

As she spoke, her disbelief seemed to fade. "I *do* feel...*peculiar*. I thought perhaps I had partaken of a little too much claret?"

"Were you not drinking of another beverage whilst in the company of Mr. Trenwith?"

"Yes, it tasted of cloves and cinnamon...you think he...?" She squirmed in her seat and began fanning herself with her hand. "What am I to do?"

"Nothing. We shall wait for the effect to dissipate."

She knit her brow in thought. "But we are to have our third lesson, are we not?"

He pulled at his cravat. "Given your condition, I think it best we forego any lesson."

"I am not incapacitated. I merely feel...*flush*."

"You are under the influence of a drug."

"I am in possession of my faculties."

"I respectfully disagree. You cannot have had much experience with aphrodisiacs."

"But you have?"

"I have seen its effects in others."

"Does it not aid our purpose here?"

"All too readily," he replied drily.

"Then what is your objection?"

He frowned. The next two hours would not be easy.

"It was not without difficulty that I came here," she continued. "The opportunities for these lessons are few, and the window upon them slim. If there is no *good* reason not to proceed—"

He turned from her. The dress molded her body in a fashion as to set his mind on fire. He faced a statue of Bastet, her feline eyes staring at him as if to demand how he dared commit blasphemy in her presence by not engaging in amorous activity.

"Are you ill?" she asked. "But you must have recovered or you would not have sent that second note to me."

"That was not mine." He looked about, but in a rotunda, there was no corner to retreat to.

"That would explain the different handwriting," she mused aloud. "But who then…?"

"I would hazard Mr. Nicholas Trenwith to be the author."

Understanding seemed to dawn for her. "You think he gave me the aphrodisiac intentionally?"

"Did I not warn you to be on your guard?" he responded more angrily than he intended.

"Forgive me if I do not suspect everyone of poisoning me!"

He put a hand to his head in frustration. What was he to do?

"Is the aphrodisiac dangerous?"

"Not that I am aware."

Though she had consumed a fair amount.

Agitated, she rose to her feet but wavered within a few steps, as if about to faint. He was at her side in an instant.

"One would think me inebriated," she said with a hand at her head.

He helped her sit upon the bed. "Perhaps you had best lie a while."

She nodded and allowed him to place her feet upon the bed as she reclined against the pillows. Her gaze roamed the rotunda, eventually falling upon a hieroglyphic of a man penetrating a woman from behind.

"What is this place?" she inquired.

"Abby names it the Temple of Bastet, said to be the goddess of sensual pleasure and defender of the pharaohs. She often takes the form of a cat or lioness."

Miss Elizabeth observed the many appearances of the feline creature around them, including a gold embroidery upon a pillow. She rubbed her thighs together. He attempted to keep from looking anywhere below her neck.

"A fitting place for amorous pursuits," she murmured. "Are you still opposed to the lesson?"

"Yes."

"Why?"

He took a deep breath through his nose as he attempted to conjure a credible explanation, but nothing of satisfaction came to mind.

"You are inebriated, of a sort," he repeated and went to stand against the wall.

She put a hand upon her forehead and crossed one leg over the other. Her breath was uneven. "Still, I fail to comprehend why that is an obstacle?"

"It is simply my principle not to engage if a pupil is intoxicated," he replied brusquely.

Her squirming increased. A hand gripped the sheets. "A noble policy, I am sure, but rather unnecessary. I came here with full and *sober* awareness of what I engage in."

"You will thank me later," he muttered. It was no use. He could refrain from looking upon her directly but could still detect her motions from the periphery of his eyes.

"You mean to deny me then? But how ungenerous of you!"

A muscle rippled along his jaw.

"Then why are we here?"

"You will be safe here till you are returned to normalcy."

"Safe? From what?"

He made no answer.

"I refuse to be imprisoned here," she stated and sat up.

"It would be more prudent to stay," he said quickly.

"For what purpose? To stare at titillating Egyptians?"

"When you are not under the influence of the aphrodisiac—"

"I am perfectly capable of handling myself."

She stood up. He came to her.

"You might come across Nicholas."

She arched an eyebrow at him. "And what if I do? It is none of your affair."

His jaw tightened and his cock tensed. "Given his treatment of you, you dare place yourself in danger of further mischief?"

"Take care, sir, your *tone* is in grave danger of condescension!"

She took a step forward but he grasped her by the arm. She looked down upon his hand.

"Lest you are disabled in some manner," she began, and here her gaze dipped lower to where his hardened cock bulged against his pants, "I appeal to your consideration. A *gentleman* would not keep a lady in distress."

The blood drained from his face and collected in his groin.

"Please."

The small and breathy plea, passing between two supple and exquisite lips, was his undoing. With a devastated groan, he pulled her into his arms and pressed his mouth to hers. Surprised by the force of his movement, she lost her footing and they toppled to the bed. He landed atop her, and the feel of her body beneath his ensured defeat of all forbearance.

CHAPTER TWENTY

Lizzy had little time to revel in her triumph. When his lips seared her neck, all sentiment was lost in a sea of lust. She was not satisfied to have his body cover hers but twisted and pressed against him in an effort to join every inch of her to him. His kisses felt more urgent, more passionate than ever before, but did not match her ardor. She threaded her fingers through his hair and gripped his head in place lest he should disengage for a breath. His kisses would be her air. She assaulted his lips and tongue as if emerging from famine. He matched her aggression and plunged his tongue deep into her mouth, mining the hot, wet orifice for desire's relief.

The hardness at his crotch had grown. She rubbed herself against it. He moaned low in his throat and turned his attention next to her breasts. He pulled down the décolletage and freed her nipples, which he fondled by hand and mouth. When he suckled a teat the ache between her legs swelled. She was past needing efforts to arouse. Her body, already aflame, craved release. She pushed her hips at him. He took the hint and put a hand to her crotch, but the *kalasiris* clung tightly to her body, allowing limited penetration. She grunted in frustration. He took the hem of the dress and managed to pull it up past her knees. He reached beneath the dress and—glory!—his magnificent fingers were at her womanhood. His manipulation of her there was less gentle and precise than her prior experiences, but she welcomed the rougher touch. She wanted to spend, and spend fast.

Though he had found a way to caress her, the dress hampered the range of his access. She pulled at the confounding material, wishing to hoist it past her thighs. Sensing her vexation, he grasped the dress and tore it between his hands. It ripped all the way to her hip. His hand was instantly at the nub of flesh nestled between her folds. He stroked her with his thumb, dipping at times to her perineum. The wetness between her legs grew.

"Faster, harder," she moaned, pushing herself into his hand.

He obliged and intensified his fondling. Lowering his head to her neck, he took whole mouthfuls of her. She threw back her head and arched her back, wanting him to address as much of her body as possible. His caresses fed her desire, but she wanted more. She wanted more of him. Gripping his banyan, she pulled it down past his shoulders. He shrugged out of the garment and barely missed a beat as he resumed his kisses and ministrations. She had an ache deep within her that only he could satiate.

Wrapping her hands around his neck, she returned his kisses with a vigor that seemed to surprise him, but he did not resist and met every thrust of her tongue, every bite and suck of the lips. She reached for his crotch and rubbed the swell there. This was what she needed, what she desired. If all that she had read held true, this hardness between his legs could produce the most wondrous effects. But he pushed her hand away. She looked at him with brows raised. To appease her, he slid a finger into the tight, hot, wet crevice below her clitoris. She gasped at the intrusion. She thought she heard him moan. Slowly, gently, he pulled his finger from her, then gradually reinserted it. She shivered. The pressure felt a little strange at first, but as he grazed the swollen bud with his motions, the sensations became delightful, a perfect pairing. The muscles within her pulsed about his finger.

Studying her reaction, he asked, "Do you require the safety word?"

She was adamant. "No!"

"Do you recall it?"

She did not, but when he paused, she scrambled to find the word. She needed him to continue.

"I shan't need it," she insisted.

"Montreal," he supplied. "Repeat it."

She felt ready to burst and panted, "Montreal, Montreal, Montreal."

He sank another finger into her and seemed to meet a resistance. His breath caught as her molten desire coated him, lubricating a path for his fingers. Sensing his hesitation still, she ground herself into his hand. There was a flare of discomfort as his fingers breached the wall inside. She gasped. He stilled. Then his thumb circled her clitoris, recalling the beautiful sensations.

She groaned her pleasure, but her climax remained at bay. More of him was required. She reached once more for his groin.

"No," he refused harshly.

But she ignored him. If he was not aroused, he would not possess such stiffness there. Thus, he must have some level of desire for her. She rubbed her right hand along the knob. When he pulled her hand away, she used her left, determined to stoke his arousal. Grabbing her wrists, he pinned her arms above her head. Undeterred, she gyrated her hips against him.

"Stop."

She would have protested, but her body spoke more forcefully. Wrapping her legs around him as she had seen done in so much of the artwork in Trenwith House, she pressed herself against him.

He groaned. "You know not what you do."

That she could undo the resistance of a practiced mentor was exhilarating. If she had been in an impassioned state of mind, she might marvel at what little flair was required to seduce a man, and that one as inexperienced as she could yet cultivate the primal urges in the opposite sex. Pulling a hand free from his grasp, she reached for the buttons of his fall. This time he did not brush away her hand. She slid her hand between the fabric and...*oh my*. The appendage really was as hard as intimated. But smooth to the touch.

He pulled away from her. "I cannot. I am ill prepared."

But she grabbed both his arms. Her heart was pounding in her ears. He held the key to quench the burning deep inside of her.

"Perhaps you could simply rub it against me," she suggested and shifted her hips so that her thigh skimmed his erection. Without waiting for his reply, she ground herself against the full length of his desire.

"You must desist," he grunted.

She paid him no heed. The feel of his cock against her, bumping, sliding between her legs, enflamed her craving even more. She wanted it. She wanted to experience the forbidden ecstasy.

"Desist," he repeated.

"Are instructors granted safety words as well?" She could not resist, for she felt the balance of power tilted in her favour.

"You will rue this moment," he warned. "The aphrodisiac, not your will, prompts your actions."

"I wish to have the full extent of this education."

He shook his head. "There will be pain…"

"Equal to the pain of deprivation?"

She bucked her hips against him. Her clitoris struck the head of his cock over and over. It felt delicious. She wanted more. She could feel his resistance ebbing.

"*Please*," he begged.

She grabbed his head between her hands and crushed her lips to his without mercy. "Take me. Take me, please! Now!"

Never had she been so demanding, but she thought she would go mad if she could not be satisfied. With a relenting groan, he pushed his cock at her hot, wet opening. She gasped loudly upon its entry. He stilled.

Sensing he was about to withdraw, she tightened her hold of him. "No."

She took a fortifying breath. He felt much larger than she had expected. Undeterred by the discomfort, her lust throbbed hot and wet about him. He slid a little farther.

Good God.

His cock might as well have been made of flint or steel. The hardness felt almost unnatural. Her body rejected the intrusion at first. Perhaps her folds were not pliant enough, her entry too tight, his cock too thick, or any combination of the aforementioned. But once again, desire prevailed over all opposition. Desire indicated this, above all else, was the path to glory.

"Are you in great pain?" he asked, his voice full of concern.

She shook her head. It was tolerable pain. They kissed for several minutes as she cradled him between her legs. At last, his shaft moved deeper inside of her. Her fingers dug into his shoulders as he entered further into depths that had never been touched before. She understood now Cleland's metaphors of weaponry, for surely this was what it felt like to be speared.

He covered her with kisses, as if they could take away the anguish. Angling his hips, he slowly withdrew, grazing his cock against her most sensitive and arousing spot. She shivered. Gently he pushed himself back into her. The pain began to defer to the delightful stimulation of his motions. Her quim pulsed about him, now welcoming the invader. She, too, angled her hips so that his hardness could better rub against her nub of pleasure. His rhythmic thrusting both satisfied and amplified her craving.

"Oh...yes," she breathed as he plunged deeper.

She clasped him harder as the pressure mounted deep within her womb. Her nipples chafed against his chest, but she adored every sensation. She undulated her hips, wanting to maximize the friction, wanting him to fill her as much as possible. It was all so maddening, thrilling, agitating, and glorious.

"Yes, yes, yes," she encouraged.

He quickened the offensive, making the bed shake with his efforts. Perspiration beaded upon his brow. The sound of flesh smacking against flesh joined their grunts and groans, echoing off the chamber walls. In heated desperation, she impaled herself more forcefully upon his cock, attempting to push herself past the precipice. He responded by shoving himself faster and harder at her. Her release came as an eruption, catapulting her into an overload of blinding magnificence. A loud cry tore from her throat. Her body jerked uncontrollably against him. She thought her teeth to chatter as spasm after spasm rolled through her body.

After the apex of her euphoria had passed, she cringed and shuddered. The sensations, now past their prime, became too much. She was spent. Her heart hammered as if she had sprinted against winged gods. Her quim pulsed wildly about his cock, which remained throbbing inside of her. And in the warmth of his body, the weight of him upon her, she felt a surprising comfort and strangely secure. She took in a long breath and soaked in the brilliance of what she had just experienced.

* * * * *

After rolling off of her, Darcy folded her in his arms as they lay upon the now sodden bedclothes. Her body was warm and damp from perspiration, her cheeks flushed, her breathing audible. He thought she had never appeared more beautiful. He had had every intention, before he spent, of withdrawing from her, though nothing had ever felt more divine than the wet heat that pulsed around his shaft. But the look of her, the sound of her, the feel of her as she succumbed to the throes of lustful passion, had proven too much.

"My God, what have I done?" he groaned silently after his seed had emptied inside of her.

For one brief moment, he had never felt more glorious, his body having shot into the heavens of carnal pleasure, but as he glimpsed the blood upon her thighs, the penitence set in swift and deep. What he had done was irresponsible. Unforgivable. She had trusted him, Abby had trusted him, to do right by his student. And he had failed.

His lust for her had proven the stronger rival to his conscience. Even now, awash in misery over his failing, he reveled in the pleasure of holding her. If only he could have her thus for an eternity. Without guilt. Without shame. His to possess by right.

The simple solution came to him then. He could not undo his error, but he could made amends by preventing the worst of consequences from materializing and, concurrently, satisfy his own, heartfelt wish.

CHAPTER TWENTY-ONE

She was a changed woman. The loss of her maidenhead—no small detail, to be sure—ensured this irreversible alteration. And yet she greeted this new permanence with surprising calm, though she had not given herself the premeditation of the first two lessons, and the aphrodisiac had played no small role in her fate. After the effects of the aphrodisiac had dissipated completely, the knowledge of what Nicholas had done angered her readily. She had felt violated and wished to confront him, but her instructor had forbid any contact with the rogue, promising her that Nicholas would never again cause harm in Trenwith House.

How tender her instructor had been in words and manner yesterday! They had lain for some time in the Temple of Bastet. She had fallen asleep in his arms, as comfortable as a babe in the embrace of its mother. The soreness between her legs recalled the significance of what had happened, and the sight of blood upon her and the linen confirmed it. Gently, he had cleansed the blood from her, wrapped his banyan about her, and escorted her to her bedchamber. As he handed her over to Sally, Lizzy fancied him reluctant to part with her. They had spoken little, and he had seemed preoccupied, but she felt more kindred with him. Afterall, she had allowed him to penetrate her most intimate place.

Remorse, perhaps even panic, would come soon enough in the ensuing days, but for the present, Lizzy wanted only to marvel at her discovery, for such it was and most wondrous! She felt a little sheepish but also exhilarated by her own wantoness. For at least one day, she would revel in the amazing pleasure her body was capable of. The afterglow lent a lightness to her step, more colour to her sight, and a flush to her cheeks whenever she recalled some part of what had transpired for her at Trenwith House. In such good spirits was she, and convinced of nothing that could dampen her outlook, that she dared to come across Mr. Darcy by taking a walk in the park. But it was Colonel Fitzwilliam who surprised her.

"I did not know before that you ever walked this way."

"I have been making the tour of the park," he replied, "as I generally do every year, and intend to close it with a call at the Parsonage. Are you going much farther?"

"No, I should have turned in a moment."

And accordingly she did turn, and they walked towards the Parsonage together.

"Do you certainly leave Kent on Saturday?" said she.

"Yes—if Darcy does not put it off again. But I am at his disposal. He arranges the business just as he pleases."

"And if not able to please himself in the arrangement, he has at least pleasure in the great power of choice. I do not know anybody who seems more to enjoy the power of doing what he likes than Mr. Darcy."

"He likes to have his own way very well," replied Colonel Fitzwilliam. "But so we all do. It is only that he has better means of having it than many others, because he is rich, and many others are poor. I speak feelingly. A younger son, you know, must be inured to self-denial and dependence."

"In my opinion, the younger son of an earl can know very little of either. Now seriously, what have you ever known of self-denial and dependence? When have you been prevented by want of money from going wherever you chose, or procuring anything you had a fancy for?"

"These are honest questions—and perhaps I cannot say that I have experienced many hardships of that nature. But in matters of greater weight, I may suffer from want of money. Younger sons cannot marry where they like."

"Unless where they like women of fortune, which I think they very often do."

"Our habits of expense make us too dependent, and there are not many in my rank of life who can afford to marry without some attention to money."

Is this meant for me, thought Lizzy. She coloured at the idea, but, recovering herself, said in a lively tone, "And pray, what is the usual price of an earl's younger son? Unless the elder brother is very sickly, I suppose you would not ask above fifty thousand pounds."

He answered her in the same style, and the subject dropped. To interrupt a silence which might make him fancy her affected with what had passed, she soon afterwards said:

"I imagine your cousin brought you down with him chiefly for the sake of having someone at his disposal. I wonder he does not marry, to secure a lasting convenience of that kind. But, perhaps, his sister does as well for the present, and, as she is under his sole care, he may do what he likes with her."

"No," said Colonel Fitzwilliam, "that is an advantage which he must divide with me. I am joined with him in the guardianship of Miss Darcy."

"Are you indeed? And pray what sort of guardians do you make? Does your charge give you much trouble? Young ladies of her age are sometimes a little difficult to manage, and if she has the true Darcy spirit, she may like to have her own way."

As she spoke she observed him looking at her earnestly, and the manner in which he immediately asked her why she supposed Miss Darcy likely to give them any uneasiness, convinced her that she had somehow or other got pretty near the truth.

She directly replied, "You need not be frightened. I never heard any harm of her, and I dare say she is one of the most tractable creatures in the world. She is a very great favourite with some ladies of my acquaintance, Mrs. Hurst and Miss Bingley. I think I have heard you say that you know them."

"I know them a little. Their brother is a pleasant gentlemanlike man—he is a great friend of Darcy's."

"Oh! Yes," said Lizzy drily; "Mr. Darcy is uncommonly kind to Mr. Bingley, and takes a prodigious deal of care of him."

"Care of him! Yes, I really believe Darcy *does* take care of him in those points where he most wants care. From something that he told me in our journey hither, I have reason to think Bingley very much indebted to him. But I ought to beg his pardon, for I have no right to suppose that Bingley was the person meant. It was all conjecture."

"What is it you mean?"

"It is a circumstance which Darcy could not wish to be generally known, because if it were to get round to the lady's family, it would be an unpleasant thing."

"You may depend upon my not mentioning it."

"And remember that I have not much reason for supposing it to be

Bingley. What he told me was merely this: that he congratulated himself on having lately saved a friend from the inconveniences of a most imprudent marriage, but without mentioning names or any other particulars, and I only suspected it to be Bingley from believing him the kind of young man to get into a scrape of that sort, and from knowing them to have been together the whole of last summer."

"Did Mr. Darcy give you reasons for this interference?"

"I understood that there were some very strong objections against the lady."

"And what arts did he use to separate them?"

"He did not talk to me of his own arts," said Fitzwilliam, smiling. "He only told me what I have now told you."

Lizzy made no answer, and walked on, her heart swelling with indignation. After watching her a little, Fitzwilliam asked her why she was so thoughtful.

"I am thinking of what you have been telling me," said she. "Your cousin's conduct does not suit my feelings. Why was he to be the judge?"

"You are rather disposed to call his interference officious?"

"I do not see what right Mr. Darcy had to decide on the propriety of his friend's inclination, or why, upon his own judgment alone, he was to determine and direct in what manner his friend was to be happy.

But," she continued, recollecting herself, "as we know none of the particulars, it is not fair to condemn him. It is not to be supposed that there was much affection in the case."

"That is not an unnatural surmise," said Fitzwilliam, "but it is a lessening of the honour of my cousin's triumph very sadly."

This was spoken jestingly, but it appeared to her so just a picture of Mr. Darcy, that she would not trust herself with an answer, and therefore, abruptly changing the conversation, talked on indifferent matters until they reached the Parsonage. There, shut into her own room, as soon as their visitor left them, she could think without interruption of all that she had heard. It was not to be supposed that any other people could be meant than those with whom she was connected. There could not exist in the world *two* men over whom Mr. Darcy could have such boundless influence. That he had been concerned in the measures taken to separate Bingley and Jane she had never doubted, but she had always attributed to Miss Bingley the principal design and arrangement of them. If his own vanity, however, did not mislead him, *he* was the cause, his pride and caprice were the cause, of all that Jane had suffered, and still continued to suffer. He had ruined for a while every hope of happiness for the most affectionate, generous heart in the world; and no one could say how lasting an evil he might have inflicted.

"There were some very strong objections against the lady," were Colonel Fitzwilliam's words; and those strong objections probably were, her having one uncle who was a country attorney, and another who was in business in London.

"To Jane herself," she exclaimed, "there could be no possibility of objection; all loveliness and goodness as she is—her understanding excellent, her mind improved, and her manners captivating. Neither could anything be urged against my father, who, though with some peculiarities, has abilities Mr. Darcy himself need not disdain, and respectability which he will probably never reach." When she thought of her mother, her confidence gave way a little; but she would not allow that any objections *there* had material weight with Mr. Darcy, whose pride, she was convinced, would receive a deeper wound from the want of importance in his friend's connections, than from their want of sense; and she was quite decided, at last, that he had been partly governed by this worst kind of pride, and partly by the wish of retaining Mr. Bingley for his sister.

The agitation and tears which the subject occasioned, brought on a headache; and it grew so much worse towards the evening that, added to her unwillingness to see Mr. Darcy, it determined her not to attend her cousins to Rosings, where they were engaged to drink tea. Mrs. Collins, seeing that she was really unwell, did not press her to go and, as much as possible, prevented her husband from pressing her, but Mr. Collins could not conceal his apprehension of Lady Catherine's being rather displeased by her staying at home. When they were gone, Lizzy, as if intending to exasperate herself as much as possible against Mr. Darcy, chose for her employment the examination of all the letters which Jane had written to her since her being in Kent. They contained no actual complaint, nor was there any revival of past occurrences, or any communication of present suffering. But in all, and in almost every line of each, there was a want of that cheerfulness which had been used to characterise her style, and which, proceeding from the serenity of a mind at ease with itself and kindly disposed towards everyone, had been scarcely ever clouded. Lizzy noticed every sentence conveying the idea of uneasiness, with an attention which it had hardly received on the first perusal. Mr. Darcy's shameful boast of what misery he had been able to inflict, gave her a keener sense of her sister's sufferings. It was some consolation to think that his visit to Rosings was to end on the day after the next—and, a still greater, that in less than a fortnight she should herself be with Jane again, and enabled to contribute to the recovery of her spirits, by all that affection could do. She could not think of Darcy's leaving Kent without remembering that his cousin was to go with him; but Colonel Fitzwilliam had made it clear that he had no intentions at all, and agreeable as he was, she did not mean to be unhappy about him. While settling this point, she was suddenly roused by the sound of the door-bell, and her spirits were a little fluttered by the idea of its being Colonel Fitzwilliam himself, who had once before called late in the evening, and might now come to inquire particularly after her. But this idea was soon banished, and her spirits were very differently affected, when, to her utter amazement, she saw Mr. Darcy walk into the room.

CHAPTER TWENTY-TWO

When he had received the information that Miss Elizabeth was not to be in attendance, Darcy leaped at the opportunity to speak to her alone, startling his aunt with his haste in departing Rosings. He had not slept all night, overcome with shame, regret, and even lust. There was no moment with her that he did not relive—and savour. His conscience could not mar the exquisiteness of how it had felt to hold her, but the full meaning of bittersweet came to bear upon him. He had thought better of himself, expected better, but if ever he had felt the shortcomings of being a mortal man, Miss Elizabeth had proven his weakness beyond the shadow of doubt. How he had wanted to beg her forgiveness, but he had resolved not to alarm her or cause her greater sorrow with his regrets. She would require some time to comprehend the events. If there should be a chance for her to enjoy the moment, however brief, he wanted it for her.

Morning brought with it further clarity as to his obligation. He knew better than to fool himself into thinking he acted out of *noblesse oblige* alone, for he had tried time and again, unsuccessfully, to conquer his feelings for her. That he was the one to have comprised her only added to the urgency. By seeking her hand, he would satisfy his attachment and preserve her honour. He could not appeal to the latter without divulging the confidence of Trenwith House and his own deception. He would be putting her in an embarrassing, even mortifying, situation if he did. But given his circumstance in life vis-à-vis hers, no case need be made. She would be flattered and grateful for his offer.

Though he was not a practiced suitor, he knew he could not begin with the proposal itself, and spent the better part of the day contemplating the preamble. The articulation of feelings had never been his forte. He had expressed his love only once before, and his awkward delivery had proven a source of amusement for the Duchess. Not having the standing of the Duchess, Miss Elizabeth must possess more modesty and gratitude. That she no longer was in possession of her honour must make her further indebted to him. Nonetheless, he hoped for a short duration to the meeting and that she would not seek to prolong the conference, as only a woman would wish to do.

Upon entering and finding Miss Elizabeth, he immediately began, in a hurried manner, an inquiry after her health, imputing his visit to a wish of hearing that she were better. Too agitated to acknowledge the coldness of her answer, he sat down for a few moments, and then getting up, walked about the room.

After a silence of several minutes, he came towards her, and began, "In vain I have struggled. It will not do. My feelings will not be repressed. You must allow me to tell you how ardently I admire and love you."

She stared at him, coloured, and was silent. He was prepared for her possible surprise and continued his avowal of all that he felt.

"You may be astonished to know that I have long had tender feelings for you. At the risk of inflating your vanity, I took quick notice of your intelligence and articulation. Your manners are civil and the compassion you have shown your sister admirable. You may wonder why I made no overt effort to court you, but you are surely aware of the difference in our stations. Despite the intensity of my affection, which has refused to diminish with time or distance, I could not easily surrender to emotion and cast aside all responsibility to my position and family. Your inferior place in society implores opposition. No one in my family has ever lowered themselves in such a manner before. There are few, if any, who would recommend our attachment, but the strength of my feelings persist in the face of such obstacles. In spite of all my endeavours, I have found my feelings for you impossible to conquer. Thus, I find myself in a rare state of apprehension and anxiety but hope that you will reward my devotion with an acceptance of my hand."

Having finished his speech, he leaned against a mantelpiece and awaited her response.

The blush rising in her cheeks, she answered him, "In such cases as this, it is, I believe, the established mode to express a sense of obligation for the sentiments avowed, however unequally they may be returned. It is natural that obligation should be felt, and if I could *feel* gratitude, I would now thank you. But I cannot—I have never desired your good opinion, and you have certainly bestowed it most unwillingly. I am sorry to have occasioned pain to anyone. It has been most unconsciously done, however, and I hope will be of short duration. The feelings which, you tell me, have long prevented the acknowledgment of your regard, can have little difficulty in overcoming it after this explanation."

Darcy felt the blood drain from his face. Her response, wholly unexpected, stunned him. The set of her countenance, the manner in which she returned his steadfast gaze, confirmed the earnestness of her words. *If I could feel gratitude... But I cannot*, she had said. How could she not? Surely she could not have the audacity to think herself equal to him? He was almost tempted to point out to her that, were it discovered she was no longer considered a woman of virtue, she should never expect an offer of marriage. From anyone. Did she not appreciate her compromised state? That she may even, heaven forbid, be with child?

At length, he forced his voice to calm. "And this is all the reply which I am to have the honour of expecting? I might, perhaps, wish to be informed why, with so little *endeavour* at civility, I am thus rejected. But it is of small importance."

"I might as well inquire," replied she, "why with so evident a desire of offending and insulting me, you chose to tell me that you liked me against your will, against your reason, and even against your character? Was not this some excuse for incivility, if I *was* uncivil? But I have other provocations. You know I have. Had not my feelings decided against you—had they been indifferent, or had they even been favourable, do you think that any consideration would tempt me to accept the man who has been the means of ruining, perhaps forever, the happiness of a most beloved sister?"

As she pronounced these words, he flushed but allowed her to continue uninterrupted.

"I have every reason in the world to think ill of you. No motive can excuse the unjust and ungenerous part you acted *there*. You dare not, you cannot deny, that you have been the principal, if not the only means of dividing them from each other—of exposing one to the censure of the world for caprice and instability, and the other to its derision for disappointed hopes, and involving them both in misery of the acutest kind."

She paused, then appeared vexed at his response, or lack thereof.

"Can you deny that you have done it?" she repeated.

He replied, "I have no wish of denying that I did everything in my power to separate my friend from your sister, or that I rejoice in my success. Towards *him* I have been kinder than towards myself."

"But it is not merely this affair," she continued, "on which my dislike is founded. Long before it had taken place my opinion of you was decided. Your character was unfolded in the recital, which I received many months ago from Mr. Wickham. On this subject, what can you have to say? In what imaginary act of friendship can you here defend yourself? Or under what misrepresentation can you here impose upon others?"

His colour heightened. "You take an eager interest in that gentleman's concerns."

"Who that knows what his misfortunes have been, can help feeling an interest in him?"

"His misfortunes!" repeated Darcy, unable to keep the contempt from his voice. "Yes, his misfortunes have been great indeed."

"And of your infliction," she cried with energy. "You have reduced him to his present state of poverty—comparative poverty. You have withheld the advantages which you must know to have been designed for him. You have deprived the best years of his life of that independence, which was no less his due than his desert. You have done all this! And yet you can treat the mention of his misfortune with contempt and ridicule."

"And this," he responded with quick steps across the room, "is your opinion of me! This is the estimation in which you hold me! I thank you for explaining it so fully. My faults, according to this calculation, are heavy indeed!

"But perhaps," added he, stopping in his walk, and turning towards her, "these offenses might have been overlooked, had not your pride been hurt by my honest confession of the scruples that had long prevented my forming any serious design. These bitter accusations might have been suppressed had I, with greater policy, concealed my struggles, and flattered you into the belief of my being impelled by unqualified, unalloyed inclination; by reason, by reflection, by everything. But disguise of every sort is my abhorrence. Nor am I ashamed of the feelings I related. They were natural and just. Could you expect me to rejoice in the inferiority of your connections? To congratulate myself on the hope of relations whose conditions in life are so decidedly beneath my own?"

He could see her struggle between anger and composure. "You are mistaken, Mr. Darcy, if you suppose that the mode of your declaration affected me in any other way, than as it spared me the concern which I might have felt in refusing you, had you behaved in a more gentlemanlike manner."

He started at this rejoinder as if she had slapped him forcefully across the face.

"You could not have made the offer of your hand in any possible way that would have tempted me to accept it."

Too astonished, he could not mask his expression of incredulity and mortification and listened in silence at her continuance.

"From the very beginning—from the first moment, I may almost say—of my acquaintance with you, your manners, impressing me with the fullest belief of your arrogance, your conceit, and your selfish disdain of the feelings of others, were such as to form the groundwork of disapprobation on which succeeding events have built so immovable a dislike; and I had not known you a month before I felt that you were the last man in the world whom I could ever be prevailed on to marry."

Recovering his senses at last, he replied, "You have said quite enough, madam. I perfectly comprehend your feelings, and have now only to be ashamed of what my own have been. Forgive me for having taken up so much of your time, and accept my best wishes for your health and happiness."

And with these words, he hastily left the room.

CHAPTER TWENTY-THREE

The tumult of her mind was now painfully great. She knew not how to support herself and from actual weakness sat down and cried for half-an-hour. Her astonishment, as she reflected on what had passed, was increased by every review of it. That she should receive an offer of marriage from Mr. Darcy! That he should have been in love with her for so many months! So much in love as to wish to marry her in spite of all the objections which had made him prevent his friend's marrying her sister, and which must appear at least with equal force in his own case! It was gratifying to have inspired unconsciously so strong an affection. But his pride, his abominable pride—his shameless avowal of what he had done with respect to Jane—his unpardonable assurance in acknowledging, though he could not justify it, and the unfeeling manner in which he had mentioned Mr. Wickham, his cruelty towards whom he had not attempted to deny, soon overcame the pity which the consideration of his attachment had for a moment excited. She continued in very agitated reflections till the sound of Lady Catherine's carriage made her feel how unequal she was to encounter Charlotte's observation, and she hurried away to her room.

She awoke the next morning to the same thoughts and meditations which had at length closed her eyes. She could not yet recover from the surprise of what had happened; it was impossible to think of anything else; and, totally indisposed for employment, she resolved, soon after breakfast, to indulge herself in air and exercise. She was proceeding directly to her favourite walk, when the recollection of Mr. Darcy's sometimes coming there stopped her, and instead of entering the park, she turned up the lane, which led farther from the turnpike-road. The park paling was still the boundary on one side, and she soon passed one of the gates into the ground.

After walking two or three times along that part of the lane, she was tempted, by the pleasantness of the morning, to stop at the gates and look into the park. The five weeks which she had now passed in Kent had made a great difference in the country, and every day was adding to the verdure of the early trees. She was on the point of continuing her walk, when she caught a glimpse of a gentleman within the sort of grove which edged the park; he was moving that way; and, fearful of its being Mr. Darcy, she was directly retreating. But the person who advanced was now near enough to see her, and stepping forward with eagerness, pronounced her name. She had turned away; but on hearing herself called, though in a voice which proved it to be Mr. Darcy, she moved again towards the gate.

He had by that time reached it also, and, holding out a letter, which she instinctively took, said, with a look of haughty composure, "I have been walking in the grove some time in the hope of meeting you. Will you do me the honour of reading that letter?"

And then, with a slight bow, turned again into the plantation, and was soon out of sight.

With no expectation of pleasure, but with the strongest curiosity, Lizzy opened the letter, and, to her still increasing wonder, perceived an envelope containing two sheets of letter-paper, written quite through, in a very close hand. The envelope itself was likewise full. Pursuing her way along the lane, she then began it. It was dated from Rosings, at eight o'clock in the morning, and was as follows:

"Be not alarmed, madam, on receiving this letter, by the apprehension of its containing any repetition of those sentiments or renewal of those offers which were last night so disgusting to you. I write without any intention of paining you, or humbling myself, by dwelling on wishes which, for the happiness of both, cannot be too soon forgotten; and the effort which the formation and the perusal of this letter must occasion, should have been spared, had not my character required it to be written and read. You must, therefore, pardon the freedom with which I demand your attention; your feelings, I know, will bestow it unwillingly, but I demand it of your justice.

"Two offenses of a very different nature, and by no means of equal magnitude, you last night laid to my charge. The first mentioned was that, regardless of the sentiments of either, I had detached Mr. Bingley from your sister, and the other, that I had, in defiance of various claims, in defiance of honour and humanity, ruined the immediate prosperity and blasted the prospects of Mr. Wickham. Wilfully and wantonly to have thrown off the companion of my youth, the acknowledged favourite of my father, a young man who had scarcely any other dependence than on our patronage, and who had been brought up to expect its exertion, would be a depravity, to which the separation of two young persons, whose affection could be the growth of only a few weeks, could bear no comparison. But from the severity of that blame which was last night so liberally bestowed, respecting each circumstance, I shall hope to be in the future secured, when the following account of my actions and their motives has been read. If, in the explanation of them, which is due to myself, I am under the necessity of relating feelings which may be offensive to yours, I can only say that I am sorry. The necessity must be obeyed, and further apology would be absurd.

"I had not been long in Hertfordshire, before I saw, in common with others, that Bingley preferred your elder sister to any other young woman in the country. But it was not till the evening of the dance at Netherfield that I had any apprehension of his feeling a serious attachment. I had often seen him in love before. At that ball, while I had the honour of dancing with you, I was first made acquainted, by Sir William Lucas's accidental information, that Bingley's attentions to your sister had given rise to a general expectation of their marriage. He spoke of it as a certain event, of which the time alone could be undecided. From that moment I observed my friend's behaviour attentively; and I could then perceive that his partiality for Miss Bennet was beyond what I had ever witnessed in him. Your sister I also watched. Her look and manners were open, cheerful, and engaging as ever, but without any symptom of peculiar regard, and I remained convinced from the evening's scrutiny, that though she received his attentions with pleasure, she did not invite them by any participation of sentiment. If *you* have not been mistaken here, *I* must have been in error. Your superior knowledge of your sister must make the latter probable. If it be so, if I have been misled by such error to inflict pain on her, your resentment has not been unreasonable. But I shall not scruple to assert, that the serenity of your sister's countenance and air was such as might have given the most acute observer a conviction that, however amiable her temper, her heart was not likely to be easily touched. That I was desirous of believing her indifferent is certain—but I will venture to say that my investigation and decisions are not usually influenced by my hopes or fears. I did not believe her to be indifferent because I wished it; I believed it on impartial conviction, as truly as I wished it in reason. My objections to the marriage were not merely those which I last night acknowledged to have the utmost force of passion to put aside, in my own case; the want of connection could not be so great an evil to my friend as to me. But there were other causes of repugnance; causes which, though still existing, and existing to an equal degree in both instances, I had myself endeavoured to forget, because they were not immediately before me. These causes must be stated, though briefly. The situation of your mother's family, though objectionable, was nothing in comparison to that total want of propriety so frequently, so almost uniformly betrayed by herself, by your three younger sisters, and occasionally even by your father. Pardon me. It pains me to offend you. But amidst your concern for the defects of your nearest relations, and your displeasure at this representation of them, let it give you consolation to consider that, to have conducted yourselves so as to avoid any share of the like censure, is praise no less generally bestowed on you and your elder sister, than it is honourable to the sense and disposition of both. I will only say farther that from what passed that evening, my opinion of all parties was confirmed, and every inducement heightened which could have led me before, to preserve my friend from what I esteemed a most unhappy connection. He left Netherfield for London, on the day following, as you, I am certain, remember, with the design of soon returning.

"The part which I acted is now to be explained. His sisters' uneasiness had been equally excited with my own; our coincidence of feeling was soon discovered, and, alike sensible that no time was to be lost in detaching their brother, we shortly resolved on joining him directly in London. We accordingly went—and there I readily engaged in the office of pointing out to my friend the certain evils of such a choice. I described, and enforced them earnestly. But, however this remonstrance might have staggered or delayed his determination, I do not suppose that it would ultimately have prevented the marriage, had it not been seconded by the assurance that I hesitated not in giving, of your sister's indifference. He had before believed her to return his affection with sincere, if not with equal regard. But Bingley has great natural modesty, with a stronger dependence on my judgment than on his own. To convince him, therefore, that he had deceived himself, was no very difficult point. To persuade him against returning into Hertfordshire, when that conviction had been given, was scarcely the work of a moment. I cannot blame myself for having done thus much. There is but one part of my conduct in the whole affair on which I do not reflect with satisfaction; it is that I condescended to adopt the measures of art so far as to conceal from him your sister's being in town. I knew it myself, as it was known to Miss Bingley; but her brother is even yet ignorant of it. That they might have met without ill consequence is perhaps probable; but his regard did not appear to me enough extinguished for him to see her without some danger. Perhaps this concealment, this disguise was beneath me; it is done, however, and it was done for the best. On this subject I have nothing more to say, no other apology to offer. If I have wounded your sister's feelings, it was unknowingly done and though the motives which governed me may to you very naturally appear insufficient, I have not yet learnt to condemn them.

"With respect to that other, more weighty accusation, of having injured Mr. Wickham, I can only refute it by laying before you the whole of his connection with my family. Of what he has *particularly* accused me I am ignorant; but of the truth of what I shall relate, I can summon more than one witness of undoubted veracity.

"Mr. Wickham is the son of a very respectable man, who had for many years the management of all the Pemberley estates, and whose good conduct in the discharge of his trust naturally inclined my father to be of service to him; and on George Wickham, who was his godson, his kindness was therefore liberally bestowed. My father supported him at school, and afterwards at Cambridge—most important assistance, as his own father, always poor from the extravagance of his wife, would have been unable to give him a gentleman's education. My father was not only fond of this young man's society, whose manners were always engaging; he had also the highest opinion of him, and hoping the church would be his profession, intended to provide for him in it. As for myself, it is many, many years since I first began to think of him in a very different manner. The vicious propensities—the want of principle, which he was careful to guard from the knowledge of his best friend, could not escape the observation of a young man of nearly the same age with himself, and who had opportunities of seeing him in

182

unguarded moments, which Mr. Darcy could not have. Here again I shall give you pain—to what degree you only can tell. But whatever may be the sentiments which Mr. Wickham has created, a suspicion of their nature shall not prevent me from unfolding his real character—it adds even another motive.

"My excellent father died about five years ago; and his attachment to Mr. Wickham was to the last so steady, that in his will he particularly recommended it to me, to promote his advancement in the best manner that his profession might allow—and if he took orders, desired that a valuable family living might be his as soon as it became vacant. There was also a legacy of one thousand pounds. His own father did not long survive mine, and within half a year from these events, Mr. Wickham wrote to inform me that, having finally resolved against taking orders, he hoped I should not think it unreasonable for him to expect some more immediate pecuniary advantage, in lieu of the preferment, by which he could not be benefited. He had some intention, he added, of studying law, and I must be aware that the interest of one thousand pounds would be a very insufficient support therein. I rather wished, than believed him to be sincere; but, at any rate, was perfectly ready to accede to his proposal. I knew that Mr. Wickham ought not to be a clergyman; the business was therefore soon settled—he resigned all claim to assistance in the church, were it possible that he could ever be in a situation to receive it, and accepted in return three thousand pounds. All connection between us seemed now dissolved. I thought too ill of him to invite him to Pemberley, or admit his society in town. In town I believe he chiefly lived, but his studying the law was a mere pretence, and being now free from all restraint, his life was a life of idleness and dissipation. For about three years I heard little of him; but on the decease of the incumbent of the living which had been designed for him, he applied to me again by letter for the presentation. His circumstances, he assured me, and I had no difficulty in believing it, were exceedingly bad. He had found the law a most unprofitable study, and was now absolutely resolved on being ordained, if I would present him to the living in question—of which he trusted there could be little doubt, as he was well assured that I had no other person to provide for, and I could not have forgotten my revered father's intentions. You will hardly blame me for refusing to comply with this entreaty, or for resisting every repetition to it. His resentment was in proportion to the distress of his circumstances—and he was doubtless as violent in his abuse of me to others as in his reproaches to myself. After this period every appearance of acquaintance was dropped. How he lived I know not. But last summer he was again most painfully obtruded on my notice.

"I must now mention a circumstance which I would wish to forget myself, and which no obligation less than the present should induce me to unfold to any human being. Having said thus much, I feel no doubt of your secrecy. My sister, who is more than ten years my junior, was left to the guardianship of my mother's nephew, Colonel Fitzwilliam, and myself. About a year ago, she was taken from school, and an establishment formed for her in London; and last summer she went with the lady who presided over it, to Ramsgate; and thither also went Mr. Wickham, undoubtedly by design; for there proved to have been a prior acquaintance between him and Mrs. Younge, in whose character we were most unhappily deceived; and by her connivance and aid, he so far recommended himself to Georgiana, whose affectionate heart retained a strong impression of his kindness to her as a child, that she was persuaded to believe herself in love, and to consent to an elopement. She was then but fifteen, which must be her excuse; and after stating her imprudence, I am happy to add, that I owed the knowledge of it to herself. I joined them unexpectedly a day or two before the intended elopement, and then Georgiana, unable to support the idea of grieving and offending a brother whom she almost looked up to as a father, acknowledged the whole to me. You may imagine what I felt and how I acted. Regard for my sister's credit and feelings prevented any public exposure; but I wrote to Mr. Wickham, who left the place immediately, and Mrs. Younge was of course removed from her charge. Mr. Wickham's chief object was unquestionably my sister's fortune, which is thirty thousand pounds; but I cannot help supposing that the hope of revenging himself on me was a strong inducement. His revenge would have been complete indeed.

"This, madam, is a faithful narrative of every event in which we have been concerned together; and if you do not absolutely reject it as false, you will, I hope, acquit me henceforth of cruelty towards Mr. Wickham. I know not in what manner, under what form of falsehood he had imposed on you; but his success is not perhaps to be wondered at. Ignorant as you previously were of everything concerning either, detection could not be in your power, and suspicion certainly not in your inclination.

"You may possibly wonder why all this was not told you last night; but I was not then master enough of myself to know what could or ought to be revealed. For the truth of everything here related, I can appeal more particularly to the testimony of Colonel Fitzwilliam, who, from our near relationship and constant intimacy, and, still more, as one of the executors of my father's will, has been unavoidably acquainted with every particular of these transactions. If your abhorrence of *me* should make *my* assertions valueless, you cannot be prevented by the same cause from confiding in my cousin; and that there may be the possibility of consulting him, I shall endeavour to find some opportunity of putting this letter in your hands in the course of the morning. I will only add, God bless you.

FITZWILLIAM DARCY

CHAPTER TWENTY-FOUR

For lizzy, the contents of the letter had excited a contrariety of emotion. Her feelings as she read were scarcely to be defined. With amazement did she first understand that he believed any apology to be in his power; and steadfastly was she persuaded that he could have no explanation to give, which a just sense of shame would not conceal. With a strong prejudice against everything he might say, she began his account of what had happened at Netherfield. She read with an eagerness which hardly left her power of comprehension, and from impatience of knowing what the next sentence might bring, was incapable of attending to the sense of the one before her eyes. His belief of her sister's insensibility she instantly resolved to be false; and his account of the real, the worst objections to the match, made her too angry to have any wish of doing him justice. He expressed no regret for what he had done which satisfied her; his style was not penitent, but haughty. It was all pride and insolence.

But when this subject was succeeded by his account of Mr. Wickham—when she read with somewhat clearer attention a relation of events which, if true, must overthrow every cherished opinion of his worth, and which bore so alarming an affinity to his own history of himself—her feelings were yet more acutely painful and more difficult of definition. Astonishment, apprehension, and even horror, oppressed her. She wished to discredit it entirely, repeatedly exclaiming, "This must be false! This cannot be! This must be the grossest falsehood!" When she had gone through the whole letter, though scarcely knowing anything of the last page or two, she put it hastily away, protesting that she would not regard it and that she would never look in it again.

In this perturbed state of mind, with thoughts that could rest on nothing, she walked on; but it would not do. In half a minute, the letter was unfolded again and, collecting herself as well as she could, she again began the mortifying perusal of all that related to Wickham, and commanded herself so far as to examine the meaning of every sentence. The account of his connection with the Pemberley family was exactly what he had related himself; and the kindness of the late Mr. Darcy, though she had not before known its extent, agreed equally well with his own words. So far each recital confirmed the other; but when she came to the will, the difference was great. What Wickham had said of the living was fresh in her memory, and as she recalled his very words, it was impossible not to feel that there was gross duplicity on one side or the other; and, for a few moments, she flattered herself that her wishes did not err. But when she read and re-read with the closest attention, the particulars immediately following of Wickham's resigning all pretensions to the living, of his receiving in lieu so considerable a sum as three thousand pounds, again was she forced to hesitate. She put down the letter, weighed every circumstance with what she meant to be impartiality—deliberated on the probability of each statement—but with little success. On both sides it was only assertion. Again she read on, but every line proved more clearly that the affair, which she had believed it impossible that any contrivance could so represent as to render Mr. Darcy's conduct in it less than infamous, was capable of a turn which must make him entirely blameless throughout the whole.

The extravagance and general profligacy which he scrupled not to lay at Mr. Wickham's charge, exceedingly shocked her; the more so, as she could bring no proof of its injustice. She had never heard of him before his entrance into the militia, in which he had engaged at the persuasion of the young man who, on meeting him accidentally in town, had there renewed a slight acquaintance. Of his former way of life nothing had been known in Hertfordshire but what he told himself. As to his real character, had information been in her power, she had never felt a wish of inquiring. His countenance, voice, and manner had established him at once in the possession of every virtue. She tried to recollect some instance of goodness, some distinguished trait of integrity or benevolence, that might rescue him from the attacks of Mr. Darcy; or at least, by the predominance of virtue, atone for those casual errors under which she would endeavour to class what Mr. Darcy had described as the idleness and vice of many years' continuance. But no such recollection befriended her. She could see him instantly before her, in every charm of air and address; but she could remember no more substantial good than the general approbation of the neighbourhood, and the regard which his social powers had gained him in the mess. After pausing on this point a considerable while, she once more continued to read. But, alas! the story which followed, of his designs on Miss Darcy, received some confirmation from what had passed between Colonel Fitzwilliam and herself only the morning before; and at last she was referred for the truth of every particular to Colonel Fitzwilliam himself—from whom she had previously received the information of his near concern in all his cousin's affairs, and whose character she had no reason to question. At one time she had almost resolved on applying to him, but the idea was checked by the awkwardness of the application, and at length wholly banished by the conviction that Mr. Darcy would never have hazarded such a proposal, if he had not been well assured of his cousin's corroboration.

She perfectly remembered everything that had passed in conversation between Wickham and herself, in their first evening at Mr. Phillips's. Many of his expressions were still fresh in her memory. She was *now* struck with the impropriety of such communications to a stranger, and wondered it had escaped her before. She saw the indelicacy of putting himself forward as he had done, and the inconsistency of his professions with his conduct. She remembered that he had boasted of having no fear of seeing Mr. Darcy—that Mr. Darcy might leave the country, but that *he* should stand his ground; yet he had avoided the Netherfield ball the very next week. She remembered also that, till the Netherfield family had quitted the country, he had told his story to no one but herself; but that after their removal it had been everywhere discussed; that he had then no reserves, no scruples in sinking Mr. Darcy's character, though he had assured her that respect for the father would always prevent his exposing the son.

How differently did everything now appear in which he was concerned! His attentions to Miss King were now the consequence of views solely and hatefully mercenary; and the mediocrity of her fortune proved no longer the moderation of his wishes, but his eagerness to grasp at anything. His behaviour to herself could now have had no tolerable motive; he had either been deceived with regard to her fortune, or had been gratifying his vanity by encouraging the preference which she believed she had most incautiously shown.

Every lingering struggle in his favour grew fainter and fainter; and in farther justification of Mr. Darcy, she could not but allow that Mr. Bingley, when questioned by Jane, had long ago asserted his blamelessness in the affair; that proud and repulsive as were his manners, she had never, in the whole course of their acquaintance— an acquaintance which had latterly brought them much together, and given her a sort of intimacy with his ways—seen anything that betrayed him to be unprincipled or unjust—anything that spoke him of irreligious or immoral habits; that among his own connections he was esteemed and valued—that even Wickham had allowed him merit as a brother, and that she had often heard him speak so affectionately of his sister as to prove him capable of *some* amiable feeling; that had his actions been what Mr. Wickham represented them, so gross a violation of everything right could hardly have been concealed from the world; and that friendship between a person capable of it, and such an amiable man as Mr. Bingley, was incomprehensible.

She grew absolutely ashamed of herself. Of neither Darcy nor Wickham could she think without feeling she had been blind, partial, prejudiced, absurd. From herself to Jane—from Jane to Bingley, her thoughts were in a line which soon brought to her recollection that Mr. Darcy's explanation *there* had appeared very insufficient, and she read it again. Widely different was the effect of a second perusal. How could she deny that credit to his assertions in one instance, which she had been obliged to give in the other? He declared himself to be totally unsuspicious of her sister's attachment; and she could not help remembering what Charlotte's opinion had always been. Neither could she deny the justice of his description of Jane. She felt that Jane's feelings, though fervent, were little displayed, and that there was a constant complacency in her air and manner not often united with great sensibility.

When she came to that part of the letter in which her family were mentioned in terms of such mortifying, yet merited reproach, her sense of shame was severe. The justice of the charge struck her too forcibly for denial, and the circumstances to which he particularly alluded as having passed at the Netherfield ball, and as confirming all his first disapprobation, could not have made a stronger impression on his mind than on hers.

The compliment to herself and her sister was not unfelt. It soothed, but it could not console her for the contempt which had thus been self-attracted by the rest of her family; and as she considered that Jane's disappointment had in fact been the work of her nearest relations, and reflected how materially the credit of both must be hurt by such impropriety of conduct, she felt depressed beyond anything she had ever known before.

After wandering aimlessly for a spell, she found herself two hours later at the threshold of Trenwith House. To her fortune, Mr. Singh informed her that his mistress had just returned from town.

"How despicably I have acted!" Lizzy cried after she had recounted to Abby all that had transpired in the past twenty-four hours. "I, who have prided myself on my discernment! I, who have valued myself on my abilities, who have often disdained the generous candour of my sister, and gratified my vanity in useless or blameable mistrust! How humiliating is this discovery! Yet, how just a humiliation! Had I been in love, I could not have been more wretchedly blind! But vanity, not love, has been my folly. Pleased with the preference of one, and offended by the neglect of the other, on the very beginning of our acquaintance, I have courted prepossession and ignorance, and driven reason away, where either were concerned. Till this moment I never knew myself."

Abby listened with uncharacteristic gravity, her brows knit deep in thought, but Lizzy was in too much distress to notice.

"I know of this Wickham," Abby said as she poured a cup of tea for her poor friend, "and I think you right to place your trust in Mr. Darcy's account of the matter."

Lizzy nodded, mindlessly accepted the cup but did not drink from it.

"I understand Mr. Darcy is to depart on the morrow," Abby continued.

"Fortunate timing!" Lizzy cried. "I do not think I could face him presently. I am too discomposed!"

"Who would not be? Yours has been a most eventful couple of days. I would I had been here—especially for your third lesson. I must beg your forgiveness for the actions of Nicholas."

Lizzy looked startled.

"Your instructor left me a stern and reproaching letter of my stepson's misdeeds. I have since banished him from Trenwith House. I would have done it before were it not for a part of me that is riddled with guilt that the estate was left to me and not to him. But that is no justification. I have failed in my role, and you have suffered from my error."

Wholly preoccupied by Mr. Darcy's letter, Lizzy had forgotten of *that*. She turned red in recollection.

"There was not much harm done," she said. "I did not come across Nicholas after partaking of the, er, aphrodisiac."

"Were you able to carry on, then, with your appointed lesson?"

Lizzy's flush deepened further. "Yes, and thank goodness. I had not thought a tonic could prove so potent."

Abby pressed her lips into a firm line. "I am sorry, truly sorry for what you had to endure."

Lizzy fell silent and looked down at her cup, the contents of which she had yet to imbibe. She could feel Abby's curious gaze upon her.

"Something happened," Abby contemplated. Her eyes widened. "You...but how wonderful!"

"I am now a fully compromised woman," Lizzy murmured.

"An enlightened woman. Baptized, if you will."

A chuckle escaped Lizzy. "Perhaps I should not make light of so serious a situation. I was not myself."

Abby's delight diminished a little as she considered, "Your instructor is not one to act when an intoxicant has been present. He must...ah."

Lizzy thought she understood the epiphany. "I *was* quite insistent."

"Of course." A new concern made Abby furrow her brow, but she cast it quickly aside, replacing it with a bright smile. "Well, I promise you would not have come across anyone better to provide you an introduction into that facet of womanhood."

"I was present enough to note the pain but also the rapture that followed." Lizzy took a deep breath. Still tossed in a storm of thoughts and feelings, she knew not where she ought to land. "I think I shall not sleep tonight."

"Drink your tea. It is a jasmine blend from China and will help calm your nerves."

The two women drank their tea in silence. Lizzy took her leave soon thereafter. Abby had been strangely pensive during their parting, but Lizzy paid it little attention, assuming her hostess to be weary from travel and no less stunned by the turn of events. It was not until Lizzy nearly reached the Parsonage that she realized Abby had never fully described the nature of her acquaintance with Mr. Darcy.

CHAPTER TWENTY-FIVE

After more than sufficient time had passed for Miss Elizabeth to have read his letter, Darcy called at the Parsonage to find Miss Elizabeth had not returned. It was not necessary that he should know her reaction to what he had written. There was the possibility she would disregard its truth, her antipathy toward the author being too great, and maintain the innocence of Wickham. Thus, Darcy took his leave after only a few minutes. He had never before divulged the full extent of Wickham's offenses to anyone but could not suffer the misapprehension that put him at such a disadvantage to the other. Her good opinion mattered more than he expected. If he could right, even a little, the tilt of her estimation, his efforts would not have been worthless.

His cousin stayed at the Parsonage for an hour but returned without having seen Miss Elizabeth. They prepared to depart the following morning and spent the whole of the evening with Anne and Catherine, who was determined to make the most of their last hours together by planning every detail of their next visit to Rosings.

"Of course, the autumn season brings with it the opportunity for the sport outdoors you men are partial to, but the weather is best in summer for travelling," Catherine said as they sat in the drawing-room after supper. "Do you not agree summer should be preferable to fall?"

The appearance of the groom delayed any answer, to her ladyship's displeasure, and she looked upon the offending letter he carried with a pointed frown.

Darcy took the letter presented to him. His heart stalled at the possibility the letter came from Miss Elizabeth. But the handwriting of the address he recognized to belong to Abby.

Catherine did not scruple to ask, "And who, I wonder, sends a correspondence at this hour?"

Without word, Darcy slipped the letter into his coat. No doubt it was a response to the letter he had left her regarding her stepson.

"Well, Darcy?" Catherine prodded when she realized she was not to receive an answer. "Do you intend to keep us in suspense? The contents must be of an urgent nature for it to be delivered at such a time."

Darcy frowned. It was unfortunate the letter had been delivered in her company, but his aunt had a point.

"If you will pardon me," he said, rising.

Catherine raised her brows and offered, "We will not take offense if you were to open it in our presence."

"Even were I not to require privacy, madam, I will not make any assumption on the desires of the author."

"Go and read it, Darcy," Colonel Fitzwilliam urged, "for, as our aunt has said, it may be of an urgent nature."

Darcy took his leave and ensconced himself in the privacy of the library. The note was brief and only asked if he might call upon her at Trenwith House. He returned the letter to his coat and dutifully went back to the drawing-room.

"Well?" Catherine inquired.

"The letter contained no pressing matter," he answered.

"Then who in Hunsford should have desired your attention?"

Both his cousins shifted in their seats at her intrusiveness, which must certainly lead only to displeasure if answered honestly.

"I should like a word with this person on the appropriateness of sending a letter at this late hour and rousing us all to worry," Catherine continued.

"I doubt that to have been her intention," Darcy replied.

"*Her*?"

"Mrs. Trenwith."

Having relented, he took his seat next to the Colonel. He doubted his aunt would pursue the matter further with Anne present.

"That woman knows no decency. I hope you will not deign to answer."

"That would make me the greater offender."

"You need not worry where *she* is concerned. As she does not appreciate the niceties of polite society, she should not expect to merit them in return."

Darcy flushed. "I have never had occasion to think ill of her."

His aunt turned many colours before settling on a hue that did no favours for her complexion.

Colonel Fitzwilliam attempted to dispel the tension. "It is rather amazing that I have never encountered Mrs. Trenwith in all my time at Rosings."

The party fell into silence.

"Anne!" he cried. "I heard you attempt the 'Goldberg Variations' by Bach earlier to-day. Will you not play a little?"

Anne obliged and the subject of the letter was attended to no more for the remainder of the evening. After everyone had retired to their chambers, Darcy penned a response to Abby, sending his regrets that he would be unable to meet with her before his departure.

BOOK TWO

CHAPTER TWENTY-SIX

A t length the chaise arrived, the trunks were fastened on, the parcels placed within, and it was pronounced to be ready. After an affectionate parting between the friends, Lizzy was attended to the carriage by Mr. Collins, and as they walked down the garden he was commissioning her with his best respects to all her family, not forgetting his thanks for the kindness he had received at Longbourn in the winter, and his compliments to Mr. and Mrs. Gardiner, though unknown. He then handed her in, Maria followed, and the door was on the point of being closed, when he suddenly reminded them, with some consternation, that they had hitherto forgotten to leave any message for the ladies at Rosings.

"But," he added, "you will of course wish to have your humble respects delivered to them, with your grateful thanks for their kindness to you while you have been here."

Lizzy made no objection; the door was then allowed to be shut, and the carriage drove off, headed to London, where they were to stop before heading home to Hertfordshire.

"Good gracious!" cried Maria, after a few minutes' silence. "It seems but a day or two since we first came, and yet how many things have happened!"

"A great many indeed," said her companion with a sigh.

"We have dined nine times at Rosings, besides drinking tea there twice! How much I shall have to tell!"

Lizzy added privately, "And how much I shall have to conceal!"

Their journey was performed without much conversation, allowing Lizzy the opportunity to reflect once more upon the events of the past few days. The matter with Mr. Darcy had eclipsed that *other* matter related to Trenwith House, but now regret reared its head over the latter. The loss of her virtue did not concern her as much as the possible effect of being with child. No one would be the wiser with

198

the former, but the latter was no easy matter to hide. The consequences upon her and her family would be disastrous. No behaviour on the part of any in her family could have doomed Jane more than her own folly. Perhaps she should have accepted Mr. Darcy's offer of marriage and saved her family from disgrace! But, no, she could not see herself married to a man she did not love. She had every aversion to the sort of union she witnessed between her mother and father. If matrimony was to hold any value for her, the companionship must have elements of respect, admiration, and affection.

And passion.

She would not marry out of convenience. She would sooner marry her instructor, for there at least was a passion of the flesh. It were possible such passion could not be sustained without the presence of higher sentiments, but for the moment, her attraction to him was vivid and powerful. That he had resisted signified character, and she did not fault him so much for succumbing as she did exalt in her own prowess to seduce a man of experience. He *must* have desired her.

Oh, but she ought not have seduced him! She ought to have heeded his initial word of warning and stayed away from Nicholas Trenwith. Regardless, the die had been cast. Fretting over what she could not undo served no purpose. She wished she had had the opportunity to speak once more with Abby before departing Hunsford and determined that she would write to her upon reaching London, where they were to remain a few days with her aunt and uncle.

Jane looked well, and Lizzy had little opportunity of studying her spirits amidst the various engagements which the kindness of her aunt had reserved for them. But Jane was to go home with her, and at Longbourn there would be leisure enough for observation.

It was not without an effort, meanwhile, that she could wait even for Longbourn, before she told her sister of Mr. Darcy's proposals. To know that she had the power of revealing what would so exceedingly astonish Jane, and must, at the same time, so highly gratify whatever of her own vanity she had not yet been able to reason away, was such a temptation to openness as nothing could have conquered but the state of indecision in which she remained as to the extent of what she should communicate; and her fear, if she once entered on the subject, of being hurried into repeating something of Bingley which might only grieve her sister further.

On the subject of her education at Trenwith House, Lizzy had no compelling reason to burden Jane with its disclosure, which, if coupled with the shock of Mr. Darcy's proposal, might place even the healthiest young person into a precarious state. It was not all concern for the welfare of Jane that silenced her, but fear that she might lose the esteem in which her sister had always regarded her. The bonds of sisterly love, though not broken—for Jane was too kind and caring to hold anyone, let alone her sister and dearest friend, in contempt— might yet lose its lustre. Or Jane might hold others culpable and look upon her sister as the victim of misfortune. Of all sentiments, Lizzy liked pity the least.

* * * * *

Lizzy finished her letter to Abby on the second day of her stay in London, but before she put it in the post, the intended recipient appeared in person herself. The Gardiners received their guest graciously. From the quality of her transportation, modish attire, and impeccable manners, they deemed she must be a person of stature, though they would not have been any less civil if otherwise. Awed by her beauty and radiance, Maria forgot Lady Catherine had warned against this person.

"What brings you to London?" Mr. Gardiner asked of Mrs. Trenwith.

"I am part of a committee that intends to submit a petition to members of Parliament to abolish slavery throughout the empire," Abby replied with as much aplomb as if she had been remarking upon the weather. "Ending the trade of slaves is insufficient. The dreadful institution thrives in our colonies, which have simply turned to other nations, our enemies included, for supply."

Lizzy glanced around at her family for their reaction. Maria had none as she knew little of the topic. Mr. Gardiner had been partaking of a biscuit and coughed upon its crumbs. Mrs. Gardiner and Jane were little surprised and, having formed no opinions on the subject, said nothing.

"I should have warned you there are no innocuous questions with me. Ask me to comment on the mundane, and I fear I should still as like provide a provocative answer."

"It is commendable that you should take a concern in the welfare of our nation," Jane replied.

"That is very considerate of you!" She turned to the Gardiners. "How fortunate you are to have two lovely nieces."

The remainder of their conversation consisted of more ordinary matters—the duration of Mrs. Trenwith's stay, the house she kept in Berkeley Square, an invitation to take in a performance at the theater—and no politics. Lizzy, excited to see her friend and wanting to be alone with her, could hardly sit still. She had a premonition that Abby's appearance was not simply a social call and was relieved when Abby requested Lizzy's company for a ride about Hyde Park in her curricle.

"Are you truly here for but a sennight?" Lizzy asked as Abby snapped the ribbons at two regal greys pulling the vehicle.

"My dear, are you accusing me of fibbing?" Abby replied.

"Not at all! It was merely an attempt, a poor one, admittedly, to lament the shortness of your stay."

"It was not long after you left Hunsford that I began to miss your company as well. We had not spoken much of your last lesson at Trenwith House, and I did not understand the full weight of Nicholas' misdeed till recently."

Lizzy raised her brows.

"I was informed of the details in a letter from your mentor. He confessed to having thrown caution to the wind and, if he thought his indiscretion to merit forgiveness, would beg it of you."

Abby spoke sternly, her frown enlarged by the infrequency of its place upon her face.

"Do not be too harsh with him," Lizzy said. "He endeavoured to do right, but I fear I was an ill-behaved student."

"Not by your own doing. Nonetheless, your charms are apparently quite potent, Miss Elizabeth Bennet, for he has, till now, been an instructor who could do no wrong and was the epitome of prudence and responsibility."

"I doubt my charms to have been the deciding influence. Is his sex not particularly susceptible to weakness of the flesh?"

"They are. For many, they more often think with their *other* head. Still, I would have eagerly bet upon his ability to resist the greatest of temptations. But I am not here to flatter you. Because of his lapse in judgment, you have been placed at risk."

Lizzy looked down at her hands.

"We—he and I—are gravely concerned for your welfare. If you should have conceived through your congress, you *must* appeal to me. Under no circumstance should you face such a situation alone. I think my apology to you when last we met was insufficient for the wrong that has been done."

"You cannot assume such blame."

"I absolutely can! I had promised you a safe harbor and instead placed you in peril."

"I knew the pursuit of education to hold many a risk."

"But you could not have foreseen this one."

"Nor you!"

"You are kind, but I cannot pardon myself. I have always suspected but never had proof of Nicholas' capacity for mischief."

The greyness of London matched their mood. Though she was glad to be with family, Lizzy missed the fresher air at Hunsford. They rode in silence for a moment to the rhythmic clipping of hooves against cobbles.

"Am I the true purpose of your travel to London?"

"Your instructor insisted I speak with you as soon as possible. I think he will suffer much anguish till he is assured of your well-being. Have you...given much thought to Darcy's proposal?"

"It shocks me still, but I can receive it as a compliment better than before."

"Are you more inclined to entertain his affections?"

Lizzy shook her head. "We should be a poor match."

"Knowing *your* opinion of him, I had not spoken much of *mine* as it regards Mr. Darcy, but he has much to recommend him. I trust you know I speak not of his wealth or status."

"You said nothing of this before."

"I saw no reason before to disavow you of your assessment—many reasonable people have held him in contempt—but in hindsight, I was a poor friend not to have risen to his defense immediately."

"I do not doubt but my adamancy led you to believe I could not be persuaded otherwise and would be suspicious of any good that could be spoken of him."

"Obdurateness has not stopped me before, but I am loath to advise people what opinions they should adopt."

Lizzy smiled, for certain they thought of one such lady who had no such compulsions.

"I think you and Darcy would not be so incompatible. You are both of you intelligent and articulate."

"I think the extent of our similarities end there."

"You would not wish a perfect replica of yourself for a partner."

"True, but there must exist enough common qualities and common values or the union would be unbalanced."

"I do not disagree, though I find it quaint that people who have not been in a relationship before to have such formed conceptions of what is required for marital bliss."

Lizzy flushed a little at her own presumption, but she would not be persuaded. Abby herself might be biased by her desire to see her friend safely married and protected against disgrace. "I doubt he would wish to wed a compromised woman."

"You may be surprised. Love alters many presumptions."

"He *claims* to love me, but it has not been tested. The strength of it would surely waiver if he knew my true situation."

Abby pressed her lips into a line. Lizzy took it as indication supportive of her own view.

"My temperament differs too much from his. We should always be at odds. He is far too dispassionate for my taste."

"It is unfortunate you think so."

"Granted, accepting his proposal would be exceedingly *convenient*, especially if the worst were to happen, but I had always thought I would rather remain a spinster than marry a man whom I did not love."

"Then there is nothing more to be said."

They soon arrived at the gates of the park. Lizzy was a little curious as to the nature of Abby's acquaintance with Mr. Darcy, but her own feelings toward the man had not yet completely settled, and she refrained from confusing herself more. Instead, she inquired into the petition and if it was expected that Mr. Wilberforce would introduce a bill in the House of Commons that year? Abby wondered when and how they might be able to enjoy each other's company once more after they quitted London. Lizzy mentioned that she was to go on a tour with her aunt and uncle in late spring, and it was resolved that Abby, having never been to Hertfordshire, would attempt to pay Lizzy a visit in the summer.

CHAPTER TWENTY-SEVEN

Darcy lay in his bed and stared at the canopy as if it could provide him relief. It was late in the night and even the crickets had gone to rest. Insomnia had plagued him since that fateful day at the Temple of Bastet. The upheaval occasioned by his proposal to Miss Elizabeth and her subsequent rejection had delayed his communicating everything to Abby, as he should have done as quickly as possible. He ought to have called upon her before he had left Rosings, but he had been too upset by the course of events to want even her company. His pride and his heart wounded, he had fixed his attentions to repairing the much damaged estimation in which Miss Elizabeth held him. He simply could not suffer her to malign him with distorted truths and fiction.

His anger, however, dissipated in the ensuing days, replaced with grave concern for Miss Elizabeth should the worst come to pass. Without doubt, he would renew the offer of his hand and prayed that, under new circumstances, she would accept him, preserving her honour and saving him from an eternity of remorse. Not knowing how she had received his letter, he did not rule out the possibility that she would refuse him still. Her abhorrence of a union between them had been plain. In his letter to Abby, he had confessed his wrong and his failure to have taken all the necessary precautions to ensure the well-being of the student. In his mind, there was not to be a third lesson; thus, the use of a sheath would not have been required.

The force of his desire for her took him by surprise, certainly, but in the past, his mind had always prevailed over any corporal urges.

Rising, Darcy went to the basin upon his sideboard and splashed the water over his face. He could not think back on what happened in the Temple without arousal. No amount of shame seemed able to dampen his lust. Memories of being inside her, enveloped by her heated wetness, cradled by the tight yet supple walls of her womanhood… His hand went to his cock. It did not take long for him to spend, but the relief could not compare to the grandeur of being with her, plunging into her, making her moan in delight, feeling her writhe against him, seeing the burst of pleasure in her face as she reached her climax.

Morning brought little solace until the post came with a letter from Abby. He had stepped out to meet a gentleman on business at the local coffeehouse but stopped upon the threshold to tear open the letter. He scanned the letter. Relief washed over him as he read that she had stayed in London long enough to confirm Miss Elizabeth had received her flux and could not be pregnant. She added that his letter to Miss Elizabeth before his departure from Rosings had been well received, and that the young lady believed truth to incline toward him over Wickham. His heart swelled that his confidence had not been in vain. It had been no easy matter to revisit that most painful past, though it pleased him somehow to have shared it with her.

"But, my dear Fitzwilliam," Abby continued, "I wish I could conclude that her opinion of you, while vastly improved, is sufficient for her to entertain any renewal of your previous offer. You have chosen to fall in love with a most independent young woman. As with you, her standards are high, and, as she is young still, she will not relinquish her ideals for anything less. And yet, I will not scruple to say that I think she would suit you quite well.

"On the other matter in your letter to me, I am not ready to entertain your resignation. You must not reproach yourself too much and, instead, appreciate the power of passion. No man is infallible. No man is impervious from fault. You do humankind an injustice to hold it before a mirror of perfection. Your integrity is not lessened by a single misstep. We may all take blame in the matter—you, myself, Nicholas—but we ought not allow the past to stifle us from what good will yet come our way in the future.

"If I were years younger and desirous of a husband, I do not think my friendship with Miss Elizabeth would stay me from competing for your affections. She is a fortunate young lady.

Yours, in friendship and love,
ABIGAIL TRENWITH"

* * * * *

It was the second week in May in which Lizzy, Jane and Maria set out together from Gracechurch Street for Hertfordshire; and, as they drew near the appointed inn where Mr. Bennet's carriage was to meet them, they quickly perceived, in token of the coachman's punctuality, both Kitty and Lydia looking out of a dining-room up stairs. These two girls had been above an hour in the place, happily employed in visiting an opposite milliner, watching the sentinel on guard, and dressing a salad and cucumber.

After welcoming their sisters, they triumphantly displayed a table set out with such cold meat as an inn larder usually affords, exclaiming, "Is not this nice? Is not this an agreeable surprise?"

"And we mean to treat you all," added Lydia, "but you must lend us the money, for we have just spent ours at the shop out there." Then, showing her purchases, "Look here, I have bought this bonnet. I do not think it is very pretty, but I thought I might as well buy it as not. I shall pull it to pieces as soon as I get home, and see if I can make it up any better."

And when her sisters abused it as ugly, she added, with perfect unconcern, "Oh! but there were two or three much uglier in the shop; and when I have bought some prettier-coloured satin to trim it with fresh, I think it will be very tolerable. Besides, it will not much signify what one wears this summer, after the regiment has left Meryton, and they are going in a fortnight."

"Are they indeed!" cried Lizzy, with the greatest satisfaction.

"They are going to be encamped near Brighton; and I do so want papa to take us all there for the summer! It would be such a delicious scheme; and I dare say would hardly cost anything at all. Mamma would like to go too of all things! Only think what a miserable summer else we shall have!"

"Yes," thought Lizzy, "*that* would be a delightful scheme indeed, and completely do for us at once. Good Heaven! Brighton, and a whole campful of soldiers, to us, who have been overset already by one poor regiment of militia, and the monthly balls of Meryton!"

"Now I have got some news for you," said Lydia, as they sat down at table. "What do you think? It is excellent news—capital news—and about a certain person we all like!"

Jane and Lizzy looked at each other, and the waiter was told he need not stay. Lydia laughed, and said:

"Aye, that is just like your formality and discretion. You thought the waiter must not hear, as if he cared! I dare say he often hears worse things said than I am going to say. But he is an ugly fellow! I am glad he is gone. I never saw such a long chin in my life. Well, but now for my news; it is about dear Wickham; too good for the waiter, is it not? There is no danger of Wickham's marrying Mary King. There's for you! She is gone down to her uncle at Liverpool: gone to stay. Wickham is safe."

"And Mary King is safe!" added Lizzy. "Safe from a connection imprudent as to fortune."

"She is a great fool for going away, if she liked him."

"But I hope there is no strong attachment on either side," said Jane.

"I am sure there is not on *his*. I will answer for it, he never cared three straws about her—who could about such a nasty little freckled thing?"

Lizzy was shocked to think that, however incapable of such coarseness of *expression* herself, the coarseness of the *sentiment* was little other than her own breast had harboured and fancied liberal!

As soon as all had ate, and the elder ones paid, the carriage was ordered; and after some contrivance, the whole party, with all their boxes, work-bags, and parcels, and the unwelcome addition of Kitty's and Lydia's purchases, were seated in it.

"How nicely we are all crammed in," cried Lydia. "I am glad I bought my bonnet, if it is only for the fun of having another bandbox! Well, now let us be quite comfortable and snug, and talk and laugh all the way home. And in the first place, let us hear what has happened to you all since you went away. Have you seen any pleasant men? Have you had any flirting? I was in great hopes that one of you would have got a husband before you came back. Jane will be quite an old maid soon, I declare. She is almost three-and-twenty! Lord, how ashamed I should be of not being married before three-and-twenty! My aunt Phillips wants you so to get husbands, you can't think. She says Lizzy had better have taken Mr. Collins, but *I* do not think there would have been any fun in it. Lord! how I should like to be married before any of you; and then I would chaperon you about to all the balls. Dear me! we had such a good piece of fun the other day at Colonel Forster's. Kitty and me were to spend the day there, and Mrs. Forster promised to have a little dance in the evening; (by the bye, Mrs.

Forster and me are *such* friends!) and so she asked the two Harringtons to come, but Harriet was ill, and so Pen was forced to come by herself; and then, what do you think we did? We dressed up Chamberlayne in woman's clothes on purpose to pass for a lady, only think what fun! Not a soul knew of it, but Colonel and Mrs. Forster, and Kitty and me, except my aunt, for we were forced to borrow one of her gowns; and you cannot imagine how well he looked! When Denny, and Wickham, and Pratt, and two or three more of the men came in, they did not know him in the least. Lord! How I laughed! And so did Mrs. Forster. I thought I should have died. And *that* made the men suspect something, and then they soon found out what was the matter."

With such kinds of histories of their parties and good jokes, did Lydia, assisted by Kitty's hints and additions, endeavour to amuse her companions all the way to Longbourn. Lizzy listened as little as she could, but there was no escaping the frequent mention of Wickham's name.

Their reception at home was most kind. Mrs. Bennet rejoiced to see Jane in undiminished beauty; and more than once during dinner did Mr. Bennet say voluntarily to Lizzy:

"I am glad you are come back, Lizzy."

Their party in the dining-room was large, for almost all the Lucases came to meet Maria and hear the news; and various were the subjects that occupied them: Lady Lucas was inquiring of Maria, after the welfare and poultry of her eldest daughter; Mrs. Bennet was doubly engaged, on one hand collecting an account of the present fashions from Jane, who sat some way below her, and, on the other, retailing them all to the younger Lucases; and Lydia, in a voice rather louder than any other person's, was enumerating the various pleasures of the morning to anybody who would hear her.

"Oh! Mary," said she, "I wish you had gone with us, for we had such fun! As we went along, Kitty and I drew up the blinds, and pretended there was nobody in the coach; and I should have gone so all the way, if Kitty had not been sick; and when we got to the George, I do think we behaved very handsomely, for we treated the other three with the nicest cold luncheon in the world, and if you would have gone, we would have treated you too. And then when we came away it was such fun! I thought we never should have got into the coach. I was ready to die of laughter. And then we were so merry all the way home! We talked and laughed so loud, that anybody might have heard us ten miles off!"

To this Mary very gravely replied, "Far be it from me, my dear sister, to depreciate such pleasures! They would doubtless be congenial with the generality of female minds. But I confess they would have no charms for *me*—I should infinitely prefer a book."

But of this answer Lydia heard not a word. She seldom listened to anybody for more than half a minute, and never attended to Mary at all.

In the afternoon Lydia was urgent with the rest of the girls to walk to Meryton, and to see how everybody went on; but Lizzy steadily opposed the scheme. It should not be said that the Miss Bennets could not be at home half a day before they were in pursuit of the officers. There was another reason too for her opposition. She dreaded seeing Mr. Wickham again, and was resolved to avoid it as long as possible. The comfort to *her* of the regiment's approaching removal was indeed beyond expression. In a fortnight they were to go—and once gone, she hoped there could be nothing more to plague her on his account.

She had not been many hours at home before she found that the Brighton scheme, of which Lydia had given them a hint at the inn, was under frequent discussion between her parents. Lizzy saw directly that her father had not the smallest intention of yielding; but his answers were at the same time so vague and equivocal, that her mother, though often disheartened, had never yet despaired of succeeding at last.

CHAPTER TWENTY-EIGHT

Lizzy's impatience to acquaint Jane with what had happened could no longer be overcome; and at length, resolving to suppress every particular in which her sister was concerned, and preparing her to be surprised, she related to her the next morning the chief of the scene between Mr. Darcy and herself.

Miss Bennet's astonishment was soon lessened by the strong sisterly partiality which made any admiration of Lizzy appear perfectly natural; and all surprise was shortly lost in other feelings. She was sorry that Mr. Darcy should have delivered his sentiments in a manner so little suited to recommend them; but still more was she grieved for the unhappiness which her sister's refusal must have given him.

"His being so sure of succeeding was wrong," said she, "and certainly ought not to have appeared, but consider how much it must increase his disappointment!"

"Indeed," replied Lizzy, "I am heartily sorry for him; but he has other feelings, which will probably soon drive away his regard for me. You do not blame me, however, for refusing him?"

"Blame you! Oh, no."

"But you blame me for having spoken so warmly of Wickham?"

"No—I do not know that you were wrong in saying what you did."

"But you *will* know it, when I tell you what happened the very next day."

She then spoke of the letter, repeating the whole of its contents as far as they concerned George Wickham. What a stroke was this for poor Jane! Who would willingly have gone through the world without believing that so much wickedness existed in the whole race of mankind, as was here collected in one individual. Nor was Darcy's vindication, though grateful to her feelings, capable of consoling her for such discovery. Most earnestly did she labour to prove the probability of error, and seek to clear the one without involving the other.

"This will not do," said Lizzy; "you never will be able to make both of them good for anything. Take your choice, but you must be satisfied with only one. There is but such a quantity of merit between them; just enough to make one good sort of man; and of late it has been shifting about pretty much. For my part, I am inclined to believe it all Darcy's; but you shall do as you choose."

It was some time, however, before a smile could be extorted from Jane. "I do not know when I have been more shocked," said she. "Wickham so very bad! It is almost past belief. And poor Mr. Darcy! Dear Lizzy, only consider what he must have suffered. Such a disappointment! and with the knowledge of your ill opinion, too! and having to relate such a thing of his sister! It is really too distressing. I am sure you must feel it so."

"Oh! No, my regret and compassion are all done away by seeing you so full of both. I know you will do him such ample justice, that I am growing every moment more unconcerned and indifferent. If you lament over him much longer, my heart will be as light as a feather."

"Poor Wickham! there is such an expression of goodness in his countenance! Such an openness and gentleness in his manner!"

"There certainly was some great mismanagement in the education of those two young men. One has got all the goodness, and the other all the appearance of it."

"I never thought Mr. Darcy so deficient in the *appearance* of it as you used to do."

"And yet I meant to be uncommonly clever in taking so decided a dislike to him, without any reason. It is such a spur to one's genius, such an opening for wit, to have a dislike of that kind. One may be continually abusive without saying anything just; but one cannot always be laughing at a man without now and then stumbling on something witty."

"Lizzy, when you first read that letter, I am sure you could not treat the matter as you do now."

"Indeed, I could not. I was uncomfortable enough, I may say unhappy. And with no one to speak to about what I felt, no Jane to comfort me and say that I had not been so very weak and vain and nonsensical as I knew I had! Oh! How I wanted you!"

"How unfortunate that you should have used such very strong

expressions in speaking of Wickham to Mr. Darcy, for now they *do* appear wholly undeserved."

"Certainly. But the misfortune of speaking with bitterness is a most natural consequence of the prejudices I had been encouraging. There is one point on which I want your advice. I want to be told whether I ought, or ought not, to make our acquaintances in general understand Wickham's character."

Miss Bennet paused a little, and then replied, "Surely there can be no occasion for exposing him so dreadfully. What is your opinion?"

"That it ought not to be attempted. Mr. Darcy has not authorised me to make his communication public. On the contrary, every particular relative to his sister was meant to be kept as much as possible to myself; and if I endeavour to undeceive people as to the rest of his conduct, who will believe me? The general prejudice against Mr. Darcy is so violent, that it would be the death of half the good people in Meryton to attempt to place him in an amiable light. I am not equal to it. Wickham will soon be gone; and therefore it will not signify to anyone here what he really is. Some time hence it will be all found out, and then we may laugh at their stupidity in not knowing it before. At present I will say nothing about it."

"You are quite right. To have his errors made public might ruin him forever. He is now, perhaps, sorry for what he has done, and anxious to re-establish a character. We must not make him desperate."

The tumult of Lizzy's mind was allayed by this conversation. She had got rid of two of the secrets which had weighed on her for a fortnight, and was certain of a willing listener in Jane, whenever she might wish to talk again of either. But there was still something lurking behind, of which prudence forbade the disclosure. She dared not relate the other half of Mr. Darcy's letter, nor explain to her sister how sincerely she had been valued by her friend. Here was knowledge in which no one could partake, and she was sensible that nothing less than a perfect understanding between the parties could justify her in throwing off this last encumbrance of mystery. "And then," said she, "if that very improbable event should ever take place, I shall merely be able to tell what Bingley may tell in a much more agreeable manner himself. The liberty of communication cannot be mine till it has lost all its value!"

She was now, on being settled at home, at leisure to observe the real state of her sister's spirits. Jane was not happy. She still cherished a very tender affection for Bingley. Having never even fancied herself in love before, her regard had all the warmth of first attachment, and, from her age and disposition, greater steadiness than most first attachments often boast; and so fervently did she value his remembrance, and prefer him to every other man, that all her good sense, and all her attention to the feelings of her friends, were requisite to check the indulgence of those regrets which must have been injurious to her own health and their tranquillity.

"Well, Lizzy," said Mrs. Bennet one day, "what is your opinion *now* of this sad business of Jane's? For my part, I am determined never to speak of it again to anybody. I told my sister Phillips so the other day. But I cannot find out that Jane saw anything of him in London. Well, he is a very undeserving young man—and I do not suppose there's the least chance in the world of her ever getting him now. There is no talk of his coming to Netherfield again in the summer; and I have inquired of everybody, too, who is likely to know."

"I do not believe he will ever live at Netherfield any more."

"Oh well! It is just as he chooses. Nobody wants him to come. Though I shall always say he used my daughter extremely ill; and if I was her, I would not have put up with it. Well, my comfort is, I am sure Jane will die of a broken heart; and then he will be sorry for what he has done."

But as Lizzy could not receive comfort from any such expectation, she made no answer.

"Well, Lizzy," continued her mother, soon afterwards, "and so the Collinses live very comfortable, do they? Well, well, I only hope it will last. And what sort of table do they keep? Charlotte is an excellent manager, I dare say. If she is half as sharp as her mother, she is saving enough. There is nothing extravagant in *their* housekeeping, I dare say."

"No, nothing at all."

"A great deal of good management, depend upon it. Yes, yes. *They* will take care not to outrun their income. *They* will never be distressed for money. Well, much good may it do them! And so, I suppose, they often talk of having Longbourn when your father is dead. They look upon it as quite their own, I dare say, whenever that happens."

"It was a subject which they could not mention before me."

"No, it would have been strange if they had; but I make no doubt they often talk of it between themselves. Well, if they can be easy with an estate that is not lawfully their own, so much the better. I should be ashamed of having one that was only entailed on me."

CHAPTER TWENTY-NINE

In the quiet of her bedchamber, Lizzy, in her mind, travelled often to Trenwith House, reliving her 'lessons,' though such recollections often incited an itch that rattled her sleep and made her restless. She could ease the worst of it with her own ministrations, but at other times, they relieved the edges only to prolong and incite the crux of her desire. She longed for *his* touch, and to her great surprise, she longed for his *presence*. As strange a man as he was, and though she knew him but little—they could not have spent much beyond a whole of ten hours in each other's company—she felt a bond with him. She found herself wondering what he might be doing at the moment and if he had taken another student? What sort of man was he by day? She had not forgotten Abby's warning that the attachment resulting from intimate physical contact and from the nature of the relationship between mentor and student should not be construed as true affection. Rather than insist her situation was unique, Lizzy was inclined to chagrin that she so easily satisfied Abby's sage prediction.

How she missed her friendship with Mrs. Trenwith, and with great delight, received a letter from her mentor inquiring into her health, asking after her family, and reiterating that she would always be welcome at Trenwith House. The letter alluded to the shame, regret, or even horror that time might afford the reflection of her 'education' at Trenwith House and once more owned all blame for whatever sorrow the final lesson may have occasioned. Lizzy quickly penned a response that she would not cry over spilt milk and, insisting that she cherished her lessons as a rare gift, acquitted Abby of any blame. Lizzy almost considered inquiring if Abby had heard from Mr. Darcy but ended her letter with anticipation of their being reunited in the summer.

The quality of her conversations with Abby could not be replicated at Longbourn, but the first week home passed quickly enough. The second began. It was the last of the regiment's stay in Meryton, and all the young ladies in the neighbourhood were drooping apace. The dejection was almost universal. The elder Miss Bennets alone were still able to eat, drink, and sleep, and pursue the usual course of their employments. Very frequently were they reproached for this insensibility by Kitty and Lydia, whose own misery was extreme, and who could not comprehend such hard-heartedness in any of the family.

"Good Heaven! what is to become of us? What are we to do?" would they often exclaim in the bitterness of woe. "How can you be smiling so, Lizzy?"

Their affectionate mother shared all their grief; she remembered what she had herself endured on a similar occasion, five-and-twenty years ago.

"I am sure," said she, "I cried for two days together when Colonel Miller's regiment went away. I thought I should have broken my heart."

"I am sure I shall break *mine*," said Lydia.

"If one could but go to Brighton!" observed Mrs. Bennet.

"Oh, yes!—if one could but go to Brighton! But papa is so disagreeable."

"A little sea-bathing would set me up forever."

"And my aunt Phillips is sure it would do *me* a great deal of good," added Kitty.

Such were the kind of lamentations resounding perpetually through Longbourn House. Lizzy tried to be diverted by them; but all sense of pleasure was lost in shame. She felt anew the justice of Mr. Darcy's objections; and never had she been so much disposed to pardon his interference in the views of his friend.

But the gloom of Lydia's prospect was shortly cleared away; for she received an invitation from Mrs. Forster, the wife of the colonel of the regiment, to accompany her to Brighton. This invaluable friend was a very young woman, and very lately married. A resemblance in good humour and good spirits had recommended her and Lydia to each other, and out of their *three* months' acquaintance they had been intimate *two*.

The rapture of Lydia on this occasion, her adoration of Mrs. Forster, the delight of Mrs. Bennet, and the mortification of Kitty, are scarcely to be described. Wholly inattentive to her sister's feelings, Lydia flew about the house in restless ecstasy, calling for everyone's congratulations, and laughing and talking with more violence than ever; whilst the luckless Kitty continued in the parlour repined at her fate in terms as unreasonable as her accent was peevish.

"I cannot see why Mrs. Forster should not ask *me* as well as Lydia," said she, "Though I am *not* her particular friend. I have just as much right to be asked as she has, and more too, for I am two years older."

In vain did Lizzy attempt to make her reasonable, and Jane to make her resigned. As for Lizzy herself, this invitation was so far from exciting in her the same feelings as in her mother and Lydia, that she considered it as the death warrant of all possibility of common sense for the latter; and detestable as such a step must make her were it known, she could not help secretly advising her father not to let her go. She represented to him all the improprieties of Lydia's general behaviour, the little advantage she could derive from the friendship of such a woman as Mrs. Forster, and the probability of her being yet more imprudent with such a companion at Brighton, where the temptations must be greater than at home. He heard her attentively, and then said:

"Lydia will never be easy until she has exposed herself in some public place or other, and we can never expect her to do it with so little expense or inconvenience to her family as under the present circumstances."

"If you were aware," said Lizzy, "of the very great disadvantage to us all which must arise from the public notice of Lydia's unguarded and imprudent manner—nay, which has already arisen from it, I am sure you would judge differently in the affair."

"Already arisen?" repeated Mr. Bennet. "What, has she frightened away some of your lovers? Poor little Lizzy! But do not be cast down. Such squeamish youths as cannot bear to be connected with a little absurdity are not worth a regret. Come, let me see the list of pitiful fellows who have been kept aloof by Lydia's folly."

"Indeed you are mistaken. I have no such injuries to resent. It is not of particular, but of general evils, which I am now complaining. Our importance, our respectability in the world must be affected by the wild volatility, the assurance and disdain of all restraint which mark Lydia's character. Excuse me, for I must speak plainly. If you, my dear father, will not take the trouble of checking her exuberant spirits, and of teaching her that her present pursuits are not to be the business of her life, she will soon be beyond the reach of amendment. Her character will be fixed, and she will, at sixteen, be the most determined flirt that ever made herself or her family ridiculous; a flirt, too, in the worst and meanest degree of flirtation; without any attraction beyond youth and a tolerable person; and, from the ignorance and emptiness of her mind, wholly unable to ward off any portion of that universal contempt which her rage for admiration will excite. In this danger Kitty also is comprehended. She will follow wherever Lydia leads. Vain, ignorant, idle, and absolutely uncontrolled! Oh! My dear father, can you suppose it possible that they will not be censured and despised wherever they are known, and that their sisters will not be often involved in the disgrace?"

Mr. Bennet saw that her whole heart was in the subject, and affectionately taking her hand said in reply:

"Do not make yourself uneasy, my love. Wherever you and Jane are known you must be respected and valued; and you will not appear to less advantage for having a couple of—or I may say, three—very silly sisters. We shall have no peace at Longbourn if Lydia does not go to Brighton. Let her go, then. Colonel Forster is a sensible man, and will keep her out of any real mischief; and she is luckily too poor to be an object of prey to anybody. At Brighton she will be of less importance even as a common flirt than she has been here. The officers will find women better worth their notice. Let us hope, therefore, that her being there may teach her her own insignificance. At any rate, she cannot grow many degrees worse, without authorising us to lock her up for the rest of her life."

With this answer Lizzy was forced to be content. She was not unaware that her strong words regarding her sister might make her the hypocrite. Who, after all, had committed the greater travesty? And was it simply the consciousness of the elder to hide her sin while the younger would flaunt hers that allowed the former to judge? Yes, Lizzy replied to herself, for she possessed a regard for others that Lydia might never have and a hope that, if her truth remained concealed, no one should come to harm. Thus, her own opinion on the matter of Lydia continued the same, and she left her father disappointed and sorry. It was not in her nature, however, to increase her vexations by dwelling on them. She was confident of having performed her duty, and to fret over unavoidable evils, or augment them by anxiety, was no part of her disposition.

Had Lydia and her mother known the substance of her conference with her father, their indignation would hardly have found expression in their united volubility. In Lydia's imagination, a visit to Brighton comprised every possibility of earthly happiness. She saw, with the creative eye of fancy, the streets of that gay bathing-place covered with officers. She saw herself the object of attention, to tens and to scores of them at present unknown. She saw all the glories of the camp—its tents stretched forth in beauteous uniformity of lines, crowded with the young and the gay, and dazzling with scarlet; and, to complete the view, she saw herself seated beneath a tent, tenderly flirting with at least six officers at once.

Had she known her sister sought to tear her from such prospects and such realities as these, what would have been her sensations? They could have been understood only by her mother, who might have felt nearly the same. Lydia's going to Brighton was all that consoled her for her melancholy conviction of her husband's never intending to go there himself.

But they were entirely ignorant of what had passed; and their raptures continued, with little intermission, to the very day of Lydia's leaving home.

Lizzy was now to see Mr. Wickham for the last time. Having been frequently in company with him since her return, agitation was pretty well over; the agitations of formal partiality entirely so. She had even learnt to detect, in the very gentleness which had first delighted her, an affectation and a sameness to disgust and weary. In his present behaviour to herself, moreover, she had a fresh source of displeasure, for the inclination he soon testified of renewing those intentions which had marked the early part of their acquaintance could only serve, after what had since passed, to provoke her. She lost all concern for him in finding herself thus selected as the object of such idle and frivolous gallantry; and while she steadily repressed it, could not but feel the reproof contained in his believing, that however long, and for whatever cause, his attentions had been withdrawn, her vanity would be gratified, and her preference secured at any time by their renewal.

On the very last day of the regiment's remaining at Meryton, he dined, with other of the officers, at Longbourn; and so little was

Lizzy disposed to part from him in good humour, that on his making some inquiry as to the manner in which her time had passed at Hunsford, she mentioned Colonel Fitzwilliam's and Mr. Darcy's having both spent three weeks at Rosings, and asked him, if he was acquainted with the former.

He looked surprised, displeased, alarmed; but with a moment's recollection and a returning smile, replied, that he had formerly seen him often; and, after observing that he was a very gentlemanlike man, asked her how she had liked him. Her answer was warmly in his favour. With an air of indifference he soon afterwards added:

"How long did you say he was at Rosings?"

"Nearly three weeks."

"And you saw him frequently?"

"Yes, almost every day."

"His manners are very different from his cousin's."

"Yes, very different. But I think Mr. Darcy improves upon acquaintance."

"Indeed!" cried Mr. Wickham with a look which did not escape her. "And pray, may I ask?—" But checking himself, he added, in a gayer tone, "Is it in address that he improves? Has he deigned to add aught of civility to his ordinary style? For I dare not hope," he continued in a lower and more serious tone, "that he is improved in essentials."

"Oh, no!" said Lizzy. "In essentials, I believe, he is very much what he ever was."

While she spoke, Wickham looked as if scarcely knowing whether to rejoice over her words, or to distrust their meaning. There was something in her countenance which made him listen with an apprehensive and anxious attention, while she added:

"When I said that he improved on acquaintance, I did not mean that his mind or his manners were in a state of improvement, but that, from knowing him better, his disposition was better understood."

Wickham's alarm now appeared in a heightened complexion and agitated look; for a few minutes he was silent, till, shaking off his embarrassment, he turned to her again, and said in the gentlest of accents:

"You, who so well know my feeling towards Mr. Darcy, will readily comprehend how sincerely I must rejoice that he is wise enough to assume even the *appearance* of what is right. His pride, in that direction, may be of service, if not to himself, to many others, for it must only deter him from such foul misconduct as I have suffered by. I only fear that the sort of cautiousness to which you, I imagine, have been alluding, is merely adopted on his visits to his aunt, of whose good opinion and judgment he stands much in awe. His fear of her has always operated, I know, when they were together; and a good deal is to be imputed to his wish of forwarding the match with Miss de Bourgh, which I am certain he has very much at heart."

Lizzy could not repress a smile at this, but she answered only by a slight inclination of the head. She saw that he wanted to engage her on the old subject of his grievances, and she was in no humour to indulge him. The rest of the evening passed with the *appearance*, on his side, of usual cheerfulness, but with no further attempt to distinguish Lizzy; and they parted at last with mutual civility, and possibly a mutual desire of never meeting again.

When the party broke up, Lydia returned with Mrs. Forster to Meryton, from whence they were to set out early the next morning. The separation between her and her family was rather noisy than pathetic. Kitty was the only one who shed tears; but she did weep from vexation and envy. Mrs. Bennet was diffuse in her good wishes for the felicity of her daughter, and impressive in her injunctions that she should not miss the opportunity of enjoying herself as much as possible—advice which there was every reason to believe would be well attended to; and in the clamorous happiness of Lydia herself in bidding farewell, the more gentle adieus of her sisters were uttered without being heard.

CHAPTER THIRTY

Had lizzy's opinion been all drawn from her own family, she could not have formed a very pleasing opinion of conjugal felicity or domestic comfort. Her father, captivated by youth and beauty, and that appearance of good humour which youth and beauty generally give, had married a woman whose weak understanding and illiberal mind had very early in their marriage put an end to all real affection for her. Respect, esteem, and confidence had vanished for ever; and all his views of domestic happiness were overthrown. But Mr. Bennet was not of a disposition to seek comfort for the disappointment which his own imprudence had brought on, in any of those pleasures which too often console the unfortunate for their folly or their vice. He was fond of the country and of books; and from these tastes had arisen his principal enjoyments. To his wife he was very little otherwise indebted, than as her ignorance and folly had contributed to his amusement. This is not the sort of happiness which a man would in general wish to owe to his wife; but where other powers of entertainment are wanting, the true philosopher will derive benefit from such as are given.

Lizzy, however, had never been blind to the impropriety of her father's behaviour as a husband. She had always seen it with pain; but respecting his abilities, and grateful for his affectionate treatment of herself, she endeavoured to forget what she could not overlook, and to banish from her thoughts that continual breach of conjugal obligation and decorum which, in exposing his wife to the contempt of her own children, was so highly reprehensible. But she had never felt so strongly as now the disadvantages which must attend the children of so unsuitable a marriage, nor ever been so fully aware of the evils arising from so ill-judged a direction of talents; talents, which, rightly used, might at least have preserved the respectability of his daughters, even if incapable of enlarging the mind of his wife.

When Lizzy had rejoiced over Wickham's departure she found little other cause for satisfaction in the loss of the regiment. Their parties abroad were less varied than before, and at home she had a mother and sister whose constant repinings at the dullness of everything around them threw a real gloom over their domestic circle; and, though Kitty might in time regain her natural degree of sense, since the disturbers of her brain were removed, her other sister, from whose disposition greater evil might be apprehended, was likely to be hardened in all her folly and assurance by a situation of such double danger as a watering-place and a camp. Upon the whole, therefore, she found, what has been sometimes found before, that an event to which she had been looking with impatient desire did not, in taking place, bring all the satisfaction she had promised herself. It was consequently necessary to name some other period for the commencement of actual felicity—to have some other point on which her wishes and hopes might be fixed, and by again enjoying the pleasure of anticipation, console herself for the present, and prepare for another disappointment. Her tour to the Lakes was now the object of her happiest thoughts; it was her best consolation for all the uncomfortable hours which the discontentedness of her mother and Kitty made inevitable; and could she have included Jane in the scheme, every part of it would have been perfect.

"But it is fortunate," thought she, "that I have something to wish for. Were the whole arrangement complete, my disappointment would be certain. But here, by carrying with me one ceaseless source of regret in my sister's absence, I may reasonably hope to have all my expectations of pleasure realised. A scheme of which every part promises delight can never be successful; and general disappointment is only warded off by the defence of some little peculiar vexation."

When Lydia went away she promised to write very often and very minutely to her mother and Kitty; but her letters were always long expected, and always very short. Those to her mother contained little else than that they were just returned from the library, where such and such officers had attended them, and where she had seen such beautiful ornaments as made her quite wild; that she had a new gown, or a new parasol, which she would have described more fully, but was obliged to leave off in a violent hurry, as Mrs. Forster called her, and they were going off to the camp; and from her correspondence with her sister, there was still less to be learnt—for her letters to

Kitty, though rather longer, were much too full of lines under the words to be made public.

After the first fortnight or three weeks of her absence, health, good humour, and cheerfulness began to reappear at Longbourn. The families who had been in town for the winter came back again, and summer finery and summer engagements arose. Mrs. Bennet was restored to her usual querulous serenity; and, by the middle of June, Kitty was so much recovered as to be able to enter Meryton without tears; an event of such happy promise as to make Lizzy hope that by the following Christmas she might be so tolerably reasonable as not to mention an officer above once a day, unless, by some cruel and malicious arrangement at the War Office, another regiment should be quartered in Meryton.

Though everything wore a happier aspect, Jane remarked to Lizzy on her frequent appearance of preoccupation, but as the pensiveness was never accompanied by melancholy and as she attributed her sister's state to concerns over Lydia and the tumult of events in Hunsford not sufficiently overcome by the passage of time, she made no further investigation.

The time fixed for the beginning of their northern tour was now fast approaching when a letter arrived from Mrs. Gardiner, which at once delayed its commencement and curtailed its extent. Mr. Gardiner would be prevented by business from setting out till a fortnight later in July, and must be in London again within a month, and as that left too short a period for them to go so far, and see so much as they had proposed, or at least to see it with the leisure and comfort they had built on, they were obliged to give up the Lakes, and substitute a more contracted tour, and, according to the present plan, were to go no farther northwards than Derbyshire. In that county there was enough to be seen to occupy the chief of their three weeks; and to Mrs. Gardiner it had a peculiarly strong attraction. The town where she had formerly passed some years of her life, and where they were now to spend a few days, was probably as great an object of her curiosity as all the celebrated beauties of Matlock, Chatsworth, Dovedale, or the Peak.

Lizzy was excessively disappointed; she had set her heart on seeing the Lakes, and still thought there might have been time enough. But it was her business to be satisfied—and certainly her temper to be happy; and all was soon right again.

The period of expectation was now doubled. Four weeks were to pass away before her uncle and aunt's arrival. In the interim, Lizzy wrote to Abby of her pending travels to Derbyshire and the ideas connected to it. She could not see the word without thinking of Pemberley and its owner. "But surely," she wrote, "I may enter his county with impunity, and rob it of a few petrified spars without his perceiving me." In a responding letter, Abby inquired into every available detail of the trip, for she herself might pass near the area and would certainly make the detour if it meant she could see her dear friend. Lizzy could not be more excited by the prospect and counted the hours till her aunt and uncle, with their four children, appeared at Longbourn. The children, two girls of six and eight years old, and two younger boys, were to be left under the particular care of their cousin Jane, who was the general favourite, and whose steady sense and sweetness of temper exactly adapted her for attending to them in every way—teaching them, playing with them, and loving them.

The Gardiners stayed only one night at Longbourn, and set off the next morning with Lizzy in pursuit of novelty and amusement. One enjoyment was certain—that of suitableness of companions; a suitableness which comprehended health and temper to bear inconveniences—cheerfulness to enhance every pleasure—and affection and intelligence, which might supply it among themselves if there were disappointments abroad.

To the little town of Lambton, the scene of Mrs. Gardiner's former residence, and where she had lately learned some acquaintance still remained, they bent their steps, after having seen all the principal wonders of the country. Within five miles of Lambton, Lizzy found from her aunt that Pemberley was situated. It was not in their direct road, nor more than a mile or two out of it. In talking over their route the evening before, Mrs. Gardiner expressed an inclination to see the place again. Mr. Gardiner declared his willingness, and Lizzy was applied to for her approbation.

"My love, should not you like to see a place of which you have heard so much?" said her aunt; "a place, too, with which so many of your acquaintances are connected. Wickham passed all his youth there, you know."

Lizzy was distressed. She felt that she had no business at Pemberley, and was obliged to assume a disinclination for seeing it. She must own that she was tired of seeing great houses; after going over so many, she really had no pleasure in fine carpets or satin curtains.

Mrs. Gardiner abused her stupidity. "If it were merely a fine house richly furnished, I should not care about it myself, but the grounds are delightful. They have some of the finest woods in the country."

Lizzy said no more, but her mind could not acquiesce. The possibility of meeting Mr. Darcy, while viewing the place, instantly occurred. It would be dreadful! She blushed at the very idea, and thought it would be better to speak openly to her aunt than to run such a risk. But against this there were objections; and she finally resolved that it could be the last resource, if her private inquiries to the absence of the family were unfavourably answered.

Accordingly, when she retired at night, she asked the chambermaid whether Pemberley were not a very fine place? what was the name of its proprietor? and, with no little alarm, whether the family were down for the summer? A most welcome negative followed the last question, and her alarms now being removed, she was at leisure to feel a great deal of curiosity to see the house herself; and when the subject was revived the next morning, and she was again applied to, could readily answer, and with a proper air of indifference, that she had not really any dislike to the scheme. To Pemberley, therefore, they were to go.

CHAPTER THIRTY-ONE

L izzy, as they drove along, watched for the first appearance of Pemberley Woods with some perturbation; and when at length they turned in at the lodge, her spirits were in a high flutter.

The park was very large, and contained great variety of ground. They entered it in one of its lowest points, and drove for some time through a beautiful wood stretching over a wide extent.

Lizzy's mind was too full for conversation, but she saw and admired every remarkable spot and point of view. They gradually ascended for half-a-mile, and then found themselves at the top of a considerable eminence, where the wood ceased, and the eye was instantly caught by Pemberley House, situated on the opposite side of a valley, into which the road with some abruptness wound. It was a large, handsome stone building, standing well on rising ground, and backed by a ridge of high woody hills; and in front, a stream of some natural importance was swelled into greater, but without any artificial appearance. Its banks were neither formal nor falsely adorned. Lizzy was delighted. She had never seen a place for which nature had done more, or where natural beauty had been so little counteracted by an awkward taste. They were all of them warm in their admiration; and at that moment she felt that to be mistress of Pemberley might be something!

They descended the hill, crossed the bridge, and drove to the door; and, while examining the nearer aspect of the house, all her apprehension of meeting its owner returned. She dreaded lest the chambermaid had been mistaken. On applying to see the place, they were admitted into the hall; and Lizzy, as they waited for the housekeeper, had leisure to wonder at her being where she was.

The housekeeper came; a respectable-looking elderly woman, much less fine, and more civil, than she had any notion of finding her. They followed her into the dining-parlour. It was a large, well proportioned room, handsomely fitted up. Lizzy, after slightly surveying it, went to a window to enjoy its prospect. The hill, crowned with wood, which they had descended, receiving increased abruptness from the distance, was a beautiful object. Every disposition of the ground was good; and she looked on the whole scene, the river, the trees scattered on its banks and the winding of the valley, as far as she could trace it, with delight. As they passed into other rooms these objects were taking different positions; but from every window there were beauties to be seen. The rooms were lofty and handsome, and their furniture suitable to the fortune of its proprietor; but Lizzy saw, with admiration of his taste, that it was neither gaudy nor uselessly fine; with less of splendour, and more real elegance, than the furniture of Rosings.

"And of this place," thought she, "I might have been mistress! With these rooms I might now have been familiarly acquainted! Instead of viewing them as a stranger, I might have rejoiced in them as my own, and welcomed to them as visitors my uncle and aunt. But no, that could never be; my uncle and aunt would have been lost to me; I should not have been allowed to invite them."

This was a lucky recollection—it saved her from something very like regret.

She longed to inquire of the housekeeper whether her master was really absent, but had not the courage for it. At length however, the question was asked by her uncle; and she turned away with alarm, while Mrs. Reynolds replied that he was, adding, "But we expect him tomorrow, with a large party of friends." How rejoiced was Lizzy that their own journey had not by any circumstance been delayed a day!

Her aunt now called her to look at a picture. She approached and saw the likeness of Mr. Wickham, suspended, amongst several other miniatures, over the mantelpiece. Her aunt asked her, smilingly, how she liked it. The housekeeper came forward, and told them it was a picture of a young gentleman, the son of her late master's steward, who had been brought up by him at his own expense. "He is now gone into the army," she added; "but I am afraid he has turned out very wild."

Mrs. Gardiner looked at her niece with a smile, but Lizzy could not return it.

"And that," said Mrs. Reynolds, pointing to another of the miniatures, "is my master—and very like him. It was drawn at the same time as the other—about eight years ago."

"I have heard much of your master's fine person," said Mrs. Gardiner, looking at the picture; "it is a handsome face. But, Lizzy, you can tell us whether it is like or not."

Mrs. Reynolds' respect for Lizzy seemed to increase on this intimation of her knowing her master. "Does that young lady know Mr. Darcy?"

Lizzy coloured, and said: "A little."

"And do not you think him a very handsome gentleman, ma'am?"

"Yes, very handsome."

"I am sure I know none so handsome; but in the gallery up stairs you will see a finer, larger picture of him than this. This room was my late master's favourite room, and these miniatures are just as they used to be then. He was very fond of them."

This accounted to Lizzy for Mr. Wickham's being among them.

Mrs. Reynolds then directed their attention to one of Miss Darcy, drawn when she was only eight years old.

"And is Miss Darcy as handsome as her brother?" said Mrs. Gardiner.

"Oh! yes—the handsomest young lady that ever was seen; and so accomplished!—She plays and sings all day long. In the next room is a new instrument just come down for her—a present from my master; she comes here tomorrow with him."

Mr. Gardiner, whose manners were very easy and pleasant, encouraged her communicativeness by his questions and remarks; Mrs. Reynolds, either by pride or attachment, had evidently great pleasure in talking of her master and his sister.

"Is your master much at Pemberley in the course of the year?"

"Not so much as I could wish, sir; but I dare say he may spend half his time here; and Miss Darcy is always down for the summer months."

"Except," thought Lizzy, "when she goes to Ramsgate."

"If your master would marry, you might see more of him."

"Yes, sir; but I do not know when *that* will be. I do not know who is good enough for him."

Mr. and Mrs. Gardiner smiled. Lizzy could not help saying, "It is very much to his credit, I am sure, that you should think so."

"I say no more than the truth, and everybody will say that knows him," replied the other. Lizzy thought this was going pretty far; and she listened with increasing astonishment as the housekeeper added, "I have never known a cross word from him in my life, and I have known him ever since he was four years old."

This was praise, of all others most extraordinary, most opposite to her ideas. That he was not a good-tempered man had been her firmest opinion. Her keenest attention was awakened; she longed to hear more, and was grateful to her uncle for saying:

"There are very few people of whom so much can be said. You are lucky in having such a master."

"Yes, sir, I know I am. If I were to go through the world, I could not meet with a better. But I have always observed, that they who are good-natured when children, are good-natured when they grow up; and he was always the sweetest-tempered, most generous-hearted boy in the world."

Lizzy almost stared at her. "Can this be Mr. Darcy?" thought she.

"His father was an excellent man," said Mrs. Gardiner.

"Yes, ma'am, that he was indeed; and his son will be just like him—just as affable to the poor."

Lizzy listened, wondered, doubted, and was impatient for more. Mrs. Reynolds could interest her on no other point. She related the subjects of the pictures, the dimensions of the rooms, and the price of the furniture, in vain. Mr. Gardiner, highly amused by the kind of family prejudice to which he attributed her excessive commendation of her master, soon led again to the subject; and she dwelt with energy on his many merits as they proceeded together up the great staircase.

"He is the best landlord, and the best master," said she, "that ever lived; not like the wild young men nowadays, who think of nothing but themselves. There is not one of his tenants or servants but will give him a good name. Some people call him proud; but I am sure I never saw anything of it. To my fancy, it is only because he does not rattle away like other young men."

"In what an amiable light does this place him!" thought Lizzy.

"This fine account of him," whispered her aunt as they walked, "is not quite consistent with his behaviour to our poor friend."

"Perhaps we might be deceived."

"That is not very likely; our authority was too good."

On reaching the spacious lobby above they were shown into a very pretty sitting-room, lately fitted up with greater elegance and lightness than the apartments below; and were informed that it was but just done to give pleasure to Miss Darcy, who had taken a liking to the room when last at Pemberley.

"He is certainly a good brother," said Lizzy, as she walked towards one of the windows.

Mrs. Reynolds anticipated Miss Darcy's delight, when she should enter the room. "And this is always the way with him," she added. "Whatever can give his sister any pleasure is sure to be done in a moment. There is nothing he would not do for her."

The picture-gallery, and two or three of the principal bedrooms, were all that remained to be shown. In the former were many good paintings; but Lizzy knew nothing of the art; and from such as had been already visible below, she had willingly turned to look at some drawings of Miss Darcy's, in crayons, whose subjects were usually more interesting, and also more intelligible.

In the gallery there were many family portraits, but they could have little to fix the attention of a stranger. Lizzy walked in quest of the only face whose features would be known to her. At last it arrested her—and she beheld a striking resemblance to Mr. Darcy, with such a smile over the face as she remembered to have sometimes seen when he looked at her. She stood several minutes before the picture, in earnest contemplation, and returned to it again before they quitted the gallery. Mrs. Reynolds informed them that it had been taken in his father's lifetime.

There was certainly at this moment, in Lizzy's mind, a more gentle sensation towards the original than she had ever felt at the height of their acquaintance. The commendation bestowed on him by Mrs. Reynolds was of no trifling nature. What praise is more valuable than the praise of an intelligent servant? As a brother, a landlord, a master, she considered how many people's happiness were in his guardianship!—how much of pleasure or pain was it in his power to bestow!—how much of good or evil must be done by him! Every idea that had been brought forward by the housekeeper was favourable to his character, and as she stood before the canvas on which he was represented, and fixed his eyes upon herself, she thought of his regard with a deeper sentiment of gratitude than it had ever raised before; she remembered its warmth, and softened its impropriety of expression.

When all of the house that was open to general inspection had been seen, they returned downstairs, and, taking leave of the housekeeper, were consigned over to the gardener, who met them at the hall-door.

As they walked across the hall towards the river, Lizzy turned back to look again; her uncle and aunt stopped also, and while the former was conjecturing as to the date of the building, the owner of it himself suddenly came forward from the road, which led behind it to the stables.

They were within twenty yards of each other, and so abrupt was his appearance, that it was impossible to avoid his sight. Their eyes instantly met, and the cheeks of both were overspread with the deepest blush. He absolutely started, and for a moment seemed immovable from surprise; but shortly recovering himself, advanced towards the party,

CHAPTER THIRTY-TWO

Darcy could not have suffered a greater blow had his steed, which he led by the reigns, kicked him square in the bollocks than was delivered by the sight of Miss Elizabeth. At first he questioned the appearance of Miss Elizabeth as an illusion wrought by his decision to relieve his horse and walk the final miles on foot. That she should be at Pemberley of all places was a coincidence too fortuitous to believe. It was as if his constant thoughts of her the past months had called her to his presence. His heart threatened to scramble from his chest.

She turned away as he approached, and for a moment he thought his letter to her had done nothing to dispel her ill opinion of him, but Abby had written him of her conversation with Miss Elizabeth and assured him his letter had had a profound impact upon its reader. He trusted Abby and had felt a great weight lifted from him, but nothing in her letter, despite his dissection of every sentence, had suggested that Miss Elizabeth's animosity, though neutralized, had made the conversion to goodwill. The letter did conclude, however, with a gentle urging that if *his* feelings were unchanged, his prospect of satisfying his heart's desire, could only be improved. He scarcely dared to consider such a possibility. Her rejection of him had pained him far greater than the dismissal of the Duchess, for though his feelings for the latter had the potency of youth and the blush of first love, the passion and authenticity of his feelings for Miss Elizabeth cut far deeper.

Darcy heard his gardener utter an expression of surprise but attended only to Miss Elizabeth. Her manners would not allow her to ignore him and she received his compliments, which he somehow managed to convey, if not in terms of perfect composure, at least of prefect civility.

She did not meet his gaze when he inquired after her family.

Perhaps she had taken umbrage at the opinions he had expressed of her family. Perhaps she thought he resented her for the rebuff he had received at Hunsford Parsonage.

"Did you depart Longbourn some time ago? Rather, have you been in Derbyshire long? Or merely a few days?" he asked, unsettled but endeavouring the most gentle manner to assure her that he bore her no ill will.

His questions seemed to discomfit her more.

"Will your stay in Derybshire be of short duration? Or long?" he tried.

"Yes."

A long and awkward pause ensued.

"You came upon fortunate weather."

"Yes."

They stood without saying a word. He could see she had no particular wish to be in his company. Recollecting himself, he took his leave. Once inside, his heart still hammered, and he barely heard the warm welcome with which Mrs. Reynolds greeted him.

"Your chambers are ready for you, though you have startled us with your early arrival," she was saying. "We did not expect the party till tomorrow."

"Yes," he responded absently, the majority of his mind still being outside.

"I hope nothing is amiss? But where are the others?"

"The young lady outside—with Joseph, I think—what brought her here?"

"You mean the visitors? They are touring the estate. Joseph was to show them the gardens."

He wondered what the chances were that Miss Elizabeth might have purposefully sought out Pemberley?

"Did she make any inquires of me?"

Mrs. Reynolds looked perplexed. "She?"

"Yes, the young lady. The, er, pretty one."

"Ah, she acknowledged she knew you a little and agreed the miniatures to be a handsome likeness of you."

He flushed, then realizing he was still in his riding attire, made for his chambers. He dressed quickly. Though Miss Elizabeth had given no indication that she took any pleasure in seeing him, he was determined to speak to her once more before she left. Perhaps he would not sound quite the jabbering idiot after the opportunity to collect his wits. Without Abby's encouragement, he would have harbored no hope of earning the good graces of Elizabeth Bennet. Even now, he felt his prospects slim. She might not despise him as much as she had, but he doubted his letter to have had the power to overcome all her hostility toward him. After his own anger had dissipated, he saw the error of having assumed that the mere offer of his hand would have flattered her into accepting or that, being a comprised woman, she would be desperate to marry. How arrogant he must have appeared to her and how worthy of her indictment!

That she had acknowledged the truth of his letter, though it must have pained her, gratified him and elevated his estimation of her. She might have as easily dismissed its contents and insisted on her own righteousness. Courage and humility were required to admit where one was wrong. He had not thought it possible for his love to grow more than it had, and he had more than once wondered what might have happened had he revealed himself to her as her instructor. But he had promised to uphold the confidentiality of all concerns of Trenwith House. That he had feelings of a tender nature for his student did not exempt him from his contract. The truth might mortify her and make her forever too embarrassed to speak with him.

Her current demeanor certainly did not hearten him, but where a woman was concerned, if there was even the tiniest shred of hope, a man must pursue it till pain too great to bear confirms its obliteration.

* * * * *

After Darcy had left, her uncle and aunt joined her, and expressed admiration of his figure; but Lizzy heard not a word, and wholly engrossed by her own feelings, followed them in silence. She was overpowered by shame and vexation. Her coming there was the most unfortunate, the most ill-judged thing in the world! How strange it must appear to him! In what a disgraceful light might it not strike so vain a man! It might seem as if she had purposely thrown herself in his way again! Oh! why did she come? Or, why did he thus come a day before he was expected? Had they been only ten minutes sooner, they should have been beyond the reach of his discrimination; for it was plain that he was that moment arrived. She blushed again and again over the perverseness of the meeting. And his behaviour, so strikingly altered—what could it mean? That he should even speak to her was amazing, but to speak with such civility, to inquire after her family! Never in her life had she seen his manners so little dignified, never had he spoken with such gentleness as on this unexpected meeting. What a contrast did it offer to his last address in Rosings Park, when he put his letter into her hand! She knew not what to think, or how to account for it. They had now entered a beautiful walk by the side of the water, and every step was bringing forward a nobler fall of ground, or a finer reach of the woods to which they were approaching; but it was some time before Lizzy was sensible of any of it. Though she answered mechanically to the repeated appeals of her uncle and aunt and seemed to direct her eyes to such objects as they pointed out, she distinguished no part of the scene. Her thoughts were all fixed on that one spot of Pemberley House, whichever it might be, where Mr. Darcy then was. She longed to know what at the moment was passing in his mind—in what manner he thought of her, and whether, in defiance of everything, she was still dear to him. Perhaps he had been civil only because he felt himself at ease; yet there had been *that* in his voice which was not like ease. Whether he had felt more of pain or of pleasure in seeing her she could not tell, but he certainly had not seen her with composure.

At length, however, the remarks of her companions on her absence of mind aroused her, and she felt the necessity of appearing more like herself.

They entered the woods, and bidding adieu to the river for a while, ascended some of the higher grounds; when, in spots where the opening of the trees gave the eye power to wander, were many charming views of the valley, the opposite hills, with the long range of woods overspreading many, and occasionally part of the stream. Mr. Gardiner expressed a wish of going round the whole park, but feared it might be beyond a walk. With a triumphant smile they were told that it was ten miles round. It settled the matter; and they pursued the accustomed circuit; which brought them again, after some time, in a descent among hanging woods, to the edge of the water, and one of its narrowest parts. They crossed it by a simple bridge, in character with the general air of the scene; it was a spot less adorned than any they had yet visited; and the valley, here contracted into a glen, allowed room only for the stream, and a narrow walk amidst the rough coppice-wood which bordered it. Lizzy longed to explore its windings; but when they had crossed the bridge, and perceived their distance from the house, Mrs. Gardiner, who was not a great walker, could go no farther, and thought only of returning to the carriage as quickly as possible. Her niece was, therefore, obliged to submit, and they took their way towards the house on the opposite side of the river, in the nearest direction; but their progress was slow, for Mr. Gardiner, though seldom able to indulge the taste, was very fond of fishing, and was so much engaged in watching the occasional appearance of some trout in the water, and talking to the man about them, that he advanced but little. Whilst wandering on in this slow manner, they were again surprised, and Lizzy's astonishment was quite equal to what it had been at first, by the sight of Mr. Darcy approaching them, and at no great distance. The walk being here less sheltered than on the other side, allowed them to see him before they met. Lizzy, however astonished, was at least more prepared for an interview than before, and resolved to appear and to speak with calmness, if he really intended to meet them. For a few moments, indeed, she felt that he would probably strike into some other path. The idea lasted while a turning in the walk concealed him from their view; the turning past, he was immediately before them. With a glance, she saw that he had lost none of his recent civility; and, to imitate his politeness, she began, as they met, to admire the beauty of the place; but she had not got beyond the words "delightful," and "charming," when some unlucky recollections obtruded, and she fancied that praise of Pemberley from her might be mischievously construed. Her colour changed, and she said no more.

Mrs. Gardiner was standing a little behind; and on her pausing, he asked her if she would do him the honour of introducing him to her friends. This was a stroke of civility for which she was quite unprepared; and she could hardly suppress a smile at his being now seeking the acquaintance of some of those very people against whom his pride had revolted in his offer to herself. "What will be his surprise," thought she, "when he knows who they are? He takes them now for people of fashion."

The introduction, however, was immediately made; and as she named their relationship to herself, she stole a sly look at him, to see how he bore it, and was not without the expectation of his decamping as fast as he could from such disgraceful companions. That he was *surprised* by the connection was evident; he sustained it, however, with fortitude, and so far from going away, turned back with them, and entered into conversation with Mr. Gardiner. Lizzy could not but be pleased, could not but triumph. It was consoling that he should know she had some relations for whom there was no need to blush. She listened most attentively to all that passed between them, and gloried in every expression, every sentence of her uncle, which marked his intelligence, his taste, or his good manners.

The conversation soon turned upon fishing; and she heard Mr. Darcy invite him, with the greatest civility, to fish there as often as he chose while he continued in the neighbourhood, offering at the same time to supply him with fishing tackle, and pointing out those parts of the stream where there was usually most sport. Mrs. Gardiner, who was walking arm-in-arm with Lizzy, gave her a look expressive of wonder. Lizzy said nothing, but it gratified her exceedingly; the compliment must be all for herself. Her astonishment, however, was extreme, and continually was she repeating, "Why is he so altered? From what can it proceed? It cannot be for *me*—it cannot be for *my* sake that his manners are thus softened. My reproofs at Hunsford could not work such a change as this. It is impossible that he should still love me."

After walking some time in this way, the two ladies in front, the two gentlemen behind, on resuming their places, after descending to the brink of the river for the better inspection of some curious water-plant, there chanced to be a little alteration. It originated in Mrs. Gardiner, who, fatigued by the exercise of the morning, found Lizzy's arm inadequate to her support, and consequently preferred her husband's. Mr. Darcy took her place by her niece, and they walked on together. After a short silence, the lady first spoke. She wished him to know that she had been assured of his absence before she came to the place, and accordingly began by observing, that his arrival had been very unexpected—"for your housekeeper," she added, "informed us that you would certainly not be here till tomorrow; and indeed, before we left Bakewell, we understood that you were not immediately expected in the country." He acknowledged the truth of it all, and said that business with his steward had occasioned his coming forward a few hours before the rest of the party with whom he had been travelling. "They will join me early tomorrow," he continued, "and among them are some who will claim an acquaintance with you—Mr. Bingley and his sisters."

Lizzy answered only by a slight bow. Her thoughts were instantly driven back to the time when Mr. Bingley's name had been the last mentioned between them; and, if she might judge by his complexion, *his* mind was not very differently engaged.

"There is also one other person in the party," he continued after a pause, "who more particularly wishes to be known to you. Will you allow me, or do I ask too much, to introduce my sister to your acquaintance during your stay at Lambton?"

The surprise of such an application was great indeed; it was too great for her to know in what manner she acceded to it. She immediately felt that whatever desire Miss Darcy might have of being acquainted with her must be the work of her brother, and, without looking farther, it was satisfactory; it was gratifying to know that his resentment had not made him think really ill of her.

They now walked on in silence, each of them deep in thought. Lizzy was not comfortable; that was impossible; but she was flattered and pleased. His wish of introducing his sister to her was a compliment of the highest kind. They soon outstripped the others, and when they had reached the carriage, Mr. and Mrs. Gardiner were half a quarter of a mile behind.

He then asked her to walk into the house—but she declared herself not tired, and they stood together on the lawn. At such a time much might have been said, and silence was very awkward. She wanted to talk, but there seemed to be an embargo on every subject. At last she recollected that she had been travelling, and they talked of Matlock and Dove Dale with great perseverance. Yet time and her aunt moved slowly—and her patience and her ideas were nearly worn out before the *tête-à-tête* was over. On Mr. and Mrs. Gardiner's coming up they were all pressed to go into the house and take some refreshment; but this was declined, and they parted on each side with utmost politeness. Mr. Darcy handed the ladies into the carriage; and when it drove off, Lizzy saw him walking slowly towards the house.

The observations of her uncle and aunt now began; and each of them pronounced him to be infinitely superior to anything they had expected. "He is perfectly well behaved, polite, and unassuming," said her uncle.

"There *is* something a little stately in him, to be sure," replied her aunt, "but it is confined to his air, and is not unbecoming. I can now say with the housekeeper, that though some people may call him proud, I have seen nothing of it."

"I was never more surprised than by his behaviour to us. It was more than civil; it was really attentive; and there was no necessity for such attention. His acquaintance with Lizzy was very trifling."

"To be sure, Lizzy," said her aunt, "he is not so handsome as Wickham; or, rather, he has not Wickham's countenance, for his features are perfectly good. But how came you to tell me that he was so disagreeable?"

Lizzy excused herself as well as she could; said that she had liked him better when they had met in Kent than before, and that she had never seen him so pleasant as this morning.

"But perhaps he may be a little whimsical in his civilities," replied her uncle. "Your great men often are; and therefore I shall not take him at his word, as he might change his mind another day, and warn me off his grounds."

Lizzy felt that they had entirely misunderstood his character, but said nothing.

"From what we have seen of him," continued Mrs. Gardiner, "I really should not have thought that he could have behaved in so cruel ha way by anybody as he has done by poor Wickham. He has not an ill-natured look. On the contrary, there is something pleasing about his mouth when he speaks. And there is something of dignity in his countenance that would not give one an unfavourable idea of his heart. But, to be sure, the good lady who showed us his house did give him a most flaming character! I could hardly help laughing aloud sometimes. But he is a liberal master, I suppose, and *that* in the eye of a servant comprehends every virtue."

Lizzy here felt herself called on to say something in vindication of his behaviour to Wickham; and therefore gave them to understand, in as guarded a manner as she could, that by what she had heard from his relations in Kent, his actions were capable of a very different construction; and that his character was by no means so faulty, nor Wickham's so amiable, as they had been considered in Hertfordshire. In confirmation of this, she related the particulars of all the pecuniary transactions in which they had been connected, without actually naming her authority, but stating it to be such as might be relied on.

Mrs. Gardiner was surprised and concerned; but as they were now approaching the scene of her former pleasures, every idea gave way to the charm of recollection; and she was too much engaged in pointing out to her husband all the interesting spots in its environs to think of anything else. Fatigued as she had been by the morning's walk they had no sooner dined than she set off again in quest of her former acquaintance, and the evening was spent in the satisfactions of a intercourse renewed after many years' discontinuance.

The occurrences of the day were too full of interest to leave Lizzy much attention for any of these new friends; and she could do nothing but think, and think with wonder, of Mr. Darcy's civility, and, above all, of his wishing her to be acquainted with his sister.

CHAPTER THIRTY-THREE

Though miss elizabeth had been reticent upon their second meeting yesterday and Darcy did not think her artful enough to engage in that uniquely female practice of feigning disinterest in an attempt to cultivate desperation in the opposite sex, her behaviour had not diminished hope, for he did not doubt that she would have a found a way to express any animosity she still felt toward him. She had settled it that he would bring his sister to visit her the very day after her reaching Pemberley, and he could hardly wait.

Fortunately, the Gardiners and Miss Elizabeth were at the inn when he and Georgiana arrived. After making the introduction, he perceived that both young ladies appeared a touch embarrassed. He expected this of Georgiana, who had always been exceedingly shy, but Miss Elizabeth's novel demeanor intrigued him, even excited him that the change in disposition might signify a change in her feelings. He had determined yesterday that he would show her he could be civil and worthy of her esteem. Every minute in her company only renewed the desire. He had much to atone for.

"I should expect another visitor to arrive shortly to wait upon you," he informed her happily. "Bingley."

He was pleased that the news of Bingley agreed with her, and she had barely time to express her satisfaction when Bingley's quick step was heard on the stairs, and in a moment he entered the room.

"Miss Elizabeth!" Bingley greeted happily. "What a delight it is to see you!"

Darcy had always known his friend to be cordial, but there was a definite enthusiasm in Bingley's expression as he inquired in a friendly, though general way, after her family. With his customary good-humored ease, he greeted Mr. and Mrs. Gardiner.

Sitting opposite her, he was afforded an unobstructed view of her beauty. She looked in good health, and her eyes had lost none of the radiance that had captivated him some time ago. To his relief, according to Abby, she had little sorrow or horror over what had transpired in the Temple of Bastet. Though he had not absolved himself for his actions, and questioned his ability to be a proper instructor if he could not reign in his own lust, he was much relieved. His agony over what he had done, which had been greatly exacerbated by her refusal of his hand, had lowered to a simmer but remained unresolved.

"I think you torment yourself unnecessarily," Abby had written to him. "If she is satisfied with what has happened, why should you persist in anguish?"

And he had reasoned in similar vein with himself, but still he could derive no peace till he had understood as much from *her*.

Bingley, too, seemed drawn to look often at Miss Elizabeth, perhaps trying to trace a resemblance to her sister.

Darcy was engaged in conversation with the Gardiners but overheard Bingley speak, in a tone which had something of real regret, to Miss Elizabeth, "It has been a very long time since I've had the pleasure of seeing you. It is above eight months. We have not met since the 26th of November, when we were all dancing together at Netherfield. Are *all* your sisters at Longbourn presently?"

There was not much in the question, nor in the preceding remark, but there was a look and a manner which gave them meaning. Time had not snuffed the tender feelings he had for Miss Bennet, and Darcy had dwelt on his culpability in that matter as well. If he had been mistaken regarding Miss Bennet, as he was led to believe by the vehemence in which Miss Elizabeth had spoken to him at the Parsonage last, then he had done a tremendous disservice to his friend. He did not doubt that Miss Bennet could find happiness with so gentle and amiable, or so well-situated, a man as Bingley even if her feelings toward him were little more than indifferent, but would her sister have sanctioned a union in which affection was so disproportionately placed? Miss Elizabeth had clearly valued her own feelings enough not to defer to the trappings his wealth and station in life would have brought to her and her family. Given the loss of her maidenhead, she had more reason than most women to accept his hand. And still she had refused him. It had been an immense blow to his pride.

But when his wound had begun to heal, he saw her actions in a different light. Indeed, not many women would have rebuffed him. He suspected, had Delana not been so superiorly situated, she would not have cast him aside. Thus, despite Miss Elizabeth's error in judgment—for how he could blame her for siding with Wickham when there was nothing to repudiate his lies—her rejection had the effect of increasing his admiration.

The warmer weather beckoned a lighter dress, and he admired the contrast of her ivory muslin to her dark hair. Her arms were bare and her décolletage exposed. The apparel could not compare to what she had worn in the Temple of Bastet, of course, and as the image was causing the blood to course more strongly in the area of his groin, he swiftly dismissed the vision and suggested that they not overstay their impromptu visit.

He turned to Georgiana. "But I think we would all wish for Mr. and Mrs. Gardiner and Miss Bennet to join us for dinner at Pemberley before they leave the country."

Georgiana, with diffidence which marked her little in the habit of giving invitations, nodded. "That would be lovely."

Mrs. Gardiner looked to her niece, but the latter had turned away. She looked to the Darcys and replied, "We should be more than happy to accept."

"Capital!" Bingley cried. He was looking at Lizzy. "I have still many inquiries to make after all our Hertfordshire friends."

"Tomorrow perhaps?" Darcy suggested.

"Alas, we have arrangements with friends," Mrs. Gardiner said.

"Then the day after next?"

"Yes, that would work well."

The visitors then took their leave.

"How fortunate our timing at Pemberley is!" Bingley exclaimed when they were outside. "I could not believe it when you first told me, and thankfully they have time to spare for dinner. It would have been too cruel of Fate if they had to depart on the morrow."

Darcy agreed as he handed Georgiana into the curricle.

"If only they could have come to dinner sooner! But perhaps we can engage them a second time before they leave?"

His giddiness drew even a small grin from Georgiana.

"She is quite agreeable," Georgiana said when they were headed back to Pemberley. "And lovely."

"Is that your true opinion or do you speak to gratify mine?" Darcy asked.

Georgiana flushed. "Mine own. I should be pleased to have…a sister."

It was his turn to flush. He kept his focus on the ribbons and the road. "*Her* feelings are less clear."

Miss Darcy, perhaps too shocked to comprehend any woman who did not think the world of her brother, said nothing.

Upon their return to Pemberley, a footman delivered him a letter just arrived. Recognizing the Trenwith seal, Darcy excused himself and sought the privacy of his own chambers. He planted himself in his favourite chair before the window overlooking the lake and opened the letter.

My Dear Fitzwilliam,

I hope that I may call upon your able assistance as a mentor of Trenwith House,for I have a young woman in want of your services. As you know, I never divulge the identity of anyone participating in our educational process and have long held that such concealment, in order to protect the innocent, does not amount to deceit. But your unique circumstance makes me think that I should be deceitful in *not* disclosing the identity of your prospective student. I had hoped to be in Derbyshire myself to arrange matters, but, alas, my presence is required here at Trenwith House. *She* has hopes of meeting with me, and I had hoped you would mitigate her disappointment by being my replacement.

Perhaps you have guessed by now that the student I wish you to meet with is none other than Miss Elizabeth Bennet. Lest you think her destination of Derbyshire to be at my prompting, her aunt and uncle may disavow you of that notion, but I will admit, as I knew you to be headed back to Pemberley the same time, I could not help but think that the hand of destiny might be at play. If you choose to proceed, this will be your fourth and final lesson with her. Through mutual acquaintances, I have been able to make certain arrangements should you wish to proceed with the lesson, but the execution of the particulars, which I have detailed on the accompanying page, will be in your hands entirely.

With warmest affections,
ABBY

CHAPTER THIRTY-FOUR

After their visitors had left, Mr. and Mrs. Gardiner expressed their favourable opinion of Bingley.

"I can see how one can be partial to such a pleasant and engaging young man," Mrs. Gardiner remarked. "I admit I had been quite curious to meet him."

"A gentleman to be sure," Mr. Gardiner agreed.

Lizzy only nodded. In seeing Bingley, her thoughts had naturally flown to her sister; and, oh! how ardently did she long to know whether any of his had been directed in a like manner. She could not be deceived as to his behaviour to Miss Darcy, who had been set up as a rival to Jane. No look appeared on either side that spoke particular regard. Nothing had occurred between them that could justify the hopes of his sister. On this point she had been soon satisfied; and two or three little circumstances occurred ere they had parted, which, in her anxious interpretation, denoted a recollection of Jane not untinctured by tenderness, and a wish of saying more that might lead to the mention of her, had he dared. His memory had been so exact as to the last date he had seen them—or Jane, rather.

"Miss Darcy did not speak much but seemed to have every appearance of gentility. She is not as handsome as the brother, but there is sense and good humor in her face."

"I had heard her to be exceedingly proud," Lizzy said, "but I think her only exceedingly shy."

"She did speak mostly in monosyllables," Mr. Gardiner said.

"She is young still, being only six and ten," Mrs. Gardiner had said, "though her figure be formed and her appearance womanly and graceful."

Lizzy had come to the quick conclusion that there was nothing to cultivate a dislike of Miss Darcy, whose manners were perfectly unassuming and gentle. She had been astonished to find the young woman as embarrassed as her. Lizzy had expected to find in her new acquaintance as acute and unembarrassed an observer as ever Mr. Darcy had been, and had been much relieved by discerning such different feelings.

"And that Mr. Darcy," Mrs. Gardiner said with a curious eye upon Lizzy, "I am quite touched by his politeness. I am inclined to believe his housekeeper's view of him."

"She certainly would be the authority," added Mr. Gardiner, "having known him since he was four years old. Her manners indicate respectability."

"There is nothing among the intelligence of our friends in Lambton that would contradict her. They have nothing to accuse him of but pride. Pride he probably has, and if not, it would be imputed easily enough by the inhabitants of a small market-town where the family does not visit."

"However, it is acknowledged that he is a liberal man and does much good among the poor."

"He discharged the debts that Wickham had left behind here in Derbyshire. I am surprised at how low in estimation that young man is regarded here."

"I am amazed at the honour of Mr. and Miss Darcy coming to visit us so soon after her arrival. I wonder how to account for such attentions from such a quarter?"

At this, Lizzy begged pardon to return to her room and dress. She had been discomposed and perturbed enough by the visit, and the inquiring looks of her aunt and uncle made everything worse. Alone, she had opportunity to process all that happened in the last half-an-hour.

It was not often that she could turn her eyes on Mr. Darcy himself; but, whenever she had caught a glimpse, she saw an expression of general complaisance, and in all that he said she heard an accent so removed from *hauteur* or disdain of his companions, as convinced her that the improvement of manners which she had yesterday witnessed, however temporary its existence might prove, had at least outlived one day. When she saw him thus seeking the acquaintance and courting the good opinion of people with whom any intercourse a few months ago would have been a disgrace—when she saw him thus civil, not only to herself, but to the very relations whom he had openly disdained, and recollected their last lively scene in Hunsford Parsonage—the difference, the change was so great, and struck so forcibly on her mind, that she could hardly restrain her astonishment from being visible. Never, even in the company of his dear friends at Netherfield, or his dignified relations at Rosings, had she seen him so desirous to please, so free from self-consequence or unbending reserve, as now, when no importance could result from the success of his endeavours, and when even the acquaintance of those to whom his attentions were addressed would draw down the ridicule and censure of the ladies both of Netherfield and Rosings.

Lizzy's thoughts were at Pemberley this evening more than the last; and the evening, though as it passed it seemed long, was not long enough to determine her feelings towards *one* in that mansion; and she lay awake two whole hours endeavouring to make them out. She certainly did not hate him. No; hatred had vanished long ago, and she had almost as long been ashamed of ever feeling a dislike against him, that could be so called. The respect created by the conviction of his valuable qualities, though at first unwillingly admitted, had for some time ceased to be repugnant to her feeling; and it was now heightened into somewhat of a friendlier nature, by the testimony so highly in his favour, and bringing forward his disposition in so amiable a light, which yesterday had produced. But above all, above respect and esteem, there was a motive within her of goodwill which could not be overlooked. It was gratitude; gratitude, not merely for having once loved her, but for loving her still well enough to forgive all the petulance and acrimony of her manner in rejecting him, and all the unjust accusations accompanying her rejection. He who, she had been persuaded, would avoid her as his greatest enemy, seemed, on this accidental meeting, most eager to preserve the acquaintance, and without any indelicate display of regard, or any peculiarity of manner, where their two selves only were concerned, was soliciting the good opinion of her friends, and bent on making her known to his sister. Such a change in a man of so much pride exciting not only astonishment but gratitude—for to love, ardent love, it must be attributed; and as such its impression on her was of a sort to be encouraged, as by no means unpleasing, though it could not be exactly defined. She respected, she esteemed, she was grateful to him, she felt a real interest in his welfare; and she only wanted to know how far she wished that welfare to depend upon herself, and how far it would be for the happiness of both that she should employ the power, which her fancy told her she still possessed, of bringing on her the renewal of his addresses.

It had been settled in the evening between the aunt and the niece, that such a striking civility as Miss Darcy's in coming to see them on the very day of her arrival at Pemberley, for she had reached it only to a late breakfast, ought to be imitated, though it could not be equalled, by some exertion of politeness on their side; and, consequently, that it would be highly expedient to wait on her at Pemberley the following morning. They were, therefore, to go. Lizzy was pleased; though when she asked herself the reason, she had very little to say in reply.

Mr. Gardiner left them soon after breakfast. The fishing scheme had been renewed the day before, and a positive engagement made of his meeting some of the gentlemen at Pemberley before noon.

* * * * *

Convinced as Lizzy now was that Miss Bingley's dislike of her had originated in jealousy, she could not help feeling how unwelcome her appearance at Pemberley must be to her, and was curious to know with how much civility on that lady's side the acquaintance would now be renewed.

On reaching the house, they were shown through the hall into the saloon, whose northern aspect rendered it delightful for summer. Its windows opening to the ground, admitted a most refreshing view of the high woody hills behind the house, and of the beautiful oaks and Spanish chestnuts which were scattered over the intermediate lawn.

In this house they were received by Miss Darcy, who was sitting there with Mrs. Hurst and Miss Bingley, and the lady with whom she lived in London. Georgiana's reception of them was very civil, but attended with all the embarrassment which, though proceeding from shyness and the fear of doing wrong, would easily give to those who felt themselves inferior the belief of her being proud and reserved. Mrs. Gardiner and her niece, however, did her justice, and pitied her.

By Mrs. Hurst and Miss Bingley they were noticed only by a curtsey; and, on their being seated, a pause, awkward as such pauses must always be, succeeded for a few moments. It was first broken by Mrs. Annesley, a genteel, agreeable-looking woman, whose endeavour to introduce some kind of discourse proved her to be more truly well-bred than either of the others; and between her and Mrs. Gardiner, with occasional help from Lizzy, the conversation was carried on. Miss Darcy looked as if she wished for courage enough to join in it; and sometimes did venture a short sentence when there was least danger of its being heard.

Lizzy soon saw that she was herself closely watched by Miss

Bingley, and that she could not speak a word, especially to Miss Darcy, without calling her attention. This observation would not have prevented her from trying to talk to the latter, had they not been seated at an inconvenient distance; but she was not sorry to be spared the necessity of saying much. Her own thoughts were employing her. She expected every moment that some of the gentlemen would enter the room. She wished, she feared that the master of the house might be amongst them; and whether she wished or feared it most, she could scarcely determine. After sitting in this manner a quarter of an hour without hearing Miss Bingley's voice, Lizzy was roused by receiving from her a cold inquiry after the health of her family. She answered with equal indifference and brevity, and the other said no more.

The next variation which their visit afforded was produced by the entrance of servants with cold meat, cake, and a variety of all the finest fruits in season; but this did not take place till after many a significant look and smile from Mrs. Annesley to Miss Darcy had been given, to remind her of her post. There was now employment for the whole party—for though they could not all talk, they could all eat; and the beautiful pyramids of grapes, nectarines, and peaches soon collected them round the table. In the center was a vase of exquisite lilies. The pollen, however, seemed to agitate Miss Darcy, who sneezed twice and had to draw out her handkerchief.

"What a lovely piece of linen," Mrs. Gardiner remarked.

"Thank you," Miss Darcy replied.

"Such remarkable embroidery."

Lizzy looked over and felt the blood drain from her face.

"The late Mrs. Darcy had a flare with needlepoint," Mrs. Annesley supplied. "This particular handkerchief she embroidered only two, one for each of her children."

Frozen, Lizzy neglected the half-chewed grape in her mouth. As it slipped down her throat, she started to cough. She reached quickly for a drink. Mrs. Hurst and Miss Bingley frowned as if she had choked on purpose.

"My dear, are you all right?" Mrs. Gardiner cried.

Lizzy nodded, but nothing could be further from the truth. She had recognized that handkerchief. Mrs. Annesley had clearly stated only two such handkerchiefs existed. Miss Darcy had been one recipient.

And now Lizzy knew the other.

CHAPTER THIRTY-FIVE

Darcy had been some time with Mr. Gardiner, who, with two or three other gentlemen from the house, was engaged by the river, and had left him only upon learning that the ladies of the family intended a visit to Georgiana that morning. When he entered the saloon, he was alarmed to see Miss Elizabeth looking so pale. She met his eyes only briefly. In an attempt to draw her gaze, he endeavoured the warmest greeting he could but received only the eye of suspicion from Caroline. Had something transpired in his absence? he wondered. Had one of the Bingley sisters been uncivil? Their disdain of the Bennets was no secret to him.

Upon his appearance, Georgiana exerted herself to talk much more. Anxious to make Miss Elizabeth at ease and eager for the two to become better acquainted, he forwarded as much as possible every attempt at conversation on either side. Miss Elizabeth was friendly enough in her response but continued to avoid his gaze.

Caroline, however, grew increasingly attentive and took the first opportunity to say with sneering civility, "Pray, Miss Eliza, are not the militia removed from Meryton? They must be a great loss to *your* family."

His colour rose. Caroline would not dare mention Wickham's name before him. She knew nothing of Georgiana's mediated elopement or she would not have dared approach any mention of that corps. To no creature had he revealed his sister's past except to Miss Elizabeth, whom he earnestly looked upon.

Miss Elizabeth appeared distressed at first, but answered in a tolerably detached tone, "You are correct, Miss Bingley, in that the militia is no longer in Meryton."

Her collected behaviour quieted his emotion. Miss Bingley appeared more vexed than ever and Georgiana returned to her customary reticence. If Miss Elizabeth experienced a return of her previous enmity, she might have answered in a manner to anguish him. She had the wit to accomplish it, but, as he suspected, she had too much decency to betray his confidence or desire to injure his sister, an innocent party. Nonetheless, he could not help but notice her continued agitation. Even her hand shook.

"How do you like the fruit?" he asked point-blank when he could no longer stay his impatience to understand what had put her in such a fragile state. Perhaps the food did not agree with her.

"The fruit is fine," she murmured.

He had no wish to call further attention upon her if she were ill, and to his great reluctance, he allowed the visit to come to an end. He had no wish to prolong her misery if she were unwell, but her attitude toward him alone was changed from yesterday. He saw the women to their carriage and had the pleasure of handing Miss Elizabeth into the vehicle, but his touch seemed to alarm her, so much so that she tripped upon the steps. He caught her. The feel of her gave him a rush and caused his heart to pound. He held her a second longer than necessary to secure her footing. Her face turned red. A little too hastily, she retreated into the carriage. He had never seen her so flustered.

Still concerned for her welfare and perplexed by her deportment, he was in no mood for Caroline's criticisms when he returned to the saloon.

"Her dress I found extremely ordinary. *Passé*, if you will," Caroline was saying to Georgiana, "and drab. It did nothing to compliment her features. But that is nothing to her odd behaviour. I really do not know what to make of it. I would not go so far as to call it boorish, but her disposition is more wanting than our last encounter. There is an aspect to her bearing that is unrefined and almost mannish. Did you discern the same, Georgiana?"

His sister did not join in the indictment. He knew his recommendation was enough to ensure Miss Elizabeth's favour. His judgment could not err, and he had spoken in such terms as to leave Georgiana without the power of finding Miss Elizabeth otherwise than lovely and amiable.

Upon seeing him, Caroline cried, "How very ill Miss Eliza Bennet looks this morning, Mr. Darcy. I never in my life saw anyone so much altered as she is since the winter. She is grown so brown and coarse! Louisa and I were agreeing that we should not have known her again."

His jaw tightened and he replied coolly, "I perceived no alteration than her being rather tanned, no miraculous consequence of travelling in the summer."

"For my own part," she rejoined, "I must confess that I never could see any beauty in her. Her face is too thin; her complexion has no brilliancy; and her features are not at all handsome. Her nose wants character—there is nothing marked in its lines. Her teeth are tolerable, but not out of the common way; and as for her eyes, which have sometimes been called so fine, I could never see anything extraordinary in them. They have a sharp, shrewish look, which I do not like at all; and in her air altogether there is a self-sufficiency without fashion, which is intolerable."

Too tempted to say something he would later regret, he remained silent.

But Caroline seemed determine to make him speak. "I remember, when we first knew her in Hertfordshire, how amazed we all were to find that she was a reputed beauty; and I particularly recollect your saying one night, after they had been dining at Netherfield, 'She a beauty! I should as soon call her mother a wit.' But afterwards she seemed to improve on you, and I believe you thought her rather pretty at one time."

Unable to contain himself, he replied, "Yes, but *that* was only when I first saw her, for it is many months since I have considered her as one of the handsomest women of my acquaintance."

He took his leave before she could vex him further. Caroline did not have a naturally cheerful temperament and this sometimes lent itself to mean-spiritedness.

He hoped Miss Elizabeth had not taken ill and wanted nothing more than to ride to the inn to inquire after her. Later, when he had a moment alone with Georgiana as she sat down to practice at her pianoforte, he attempted to glean what light his sister might shed on Miss Elizabeth's disposition.

"She looked well," Georgiana answered him. "I noticed nothing amiss, though she coughed greatly upon a grape, I think, shortly before you joined us."

Seeing some relief come across her brother, she placed a bashful hand upon his. He gripped it warmly and let out a breath.

"She seems to possess a constitution of fortitude," Georgiana offered.

"Yes, among many other admirable qualities. Perfection she is not, but there is in her person all that I desire, all that I could ever need and want. Every fiber of my being declares that there is none better suited to me than her. Even when she aggravates me, my feelings do not waiver. Indeed, they have only grown through every tribulation."

"Then it must be love," she murmured, her eyes wide at the notion that strife could ever enhance affection.

"This encounter, this second chance with her, has been an unexpected blessing, and I will not squander it."

He planted a rare playful kiss upon her hand before departing. He wanted to be with Miss Elizabeth. Now. Alone. But he was not to see her till dinner tomorrow. He contemplated riding over to the inn, but he did not want to force his hand too soon or suffocate her with his attentions. Clearly she was not at ease in his company. She wanted time and space, and he patience.

But there was perhaps *one* way to see her before the morrow, he considered as he recalled Abby's letter. His pulse quickened. Did he dare?

* * * * *

"I have not Jane's charity and, thus, I will remark that Miss Bingley and Mrs. Hurst are not nearly as agreeable as their brother. Or Mr. Darcy," Mrs. Gardiner said.

Hearing his name made Lizzy weak.

"My dear, you appear shaken. Are you well?"

Lizzy mustered as much cheer as she could to mask the mortification she felt inside. "I think I partook too much of the fruit. Perhaps I should not have, had Miss Bingley and Mrs. Hurst been more sociable."

Hoping to avoid further mention of that name, Lizzy inquired into the history of the friends they were to have dinner with that evening. This conversation occupied some time till Mr. Gardiner was returned and regaled them of the fine waters and sizable fish the men had caught. Lizzy, on the pretense of wanting a light nap, went upstairs to her room, where the full weight of her discovery presented itself. She hobbled to her bed and fell upon it, staring at the ceiling. Had a stone wall fallen upon her, she would not have felt more crushed. Her instructor and Mr. Darcy one and the same!

It could not be!

Grasping at any sliver of doubt, she jumped out of bed and went into her portmanteau where she kept the handkerchief. She was not the sentimental sort and felt the linen to be more safe in her custody. Pulling it out, she saw with dismay that it was, with certainty, the absolute identical handkerchief to the one held by Miss Darcy. Handkerchief in hand, Lizzy sank into a chair. Oh, why had he given the article to her in the first place?

Doubtless he never suspected it to find its way into the hands of someone who actually knew him. And here, she panicked that perhaps he knew her identity as much as she knew his? She ransacked her memory, confirming the sketch of her mentor and scrutinizing every chance in which her person might have been known to him. Her instructor had a similar build and similar height, but these coincidences were not extraordinary, for many men could fit the bill. Only the lower half of his physiognomy had ever been exposed to her, and in the dimness of the rooms, she could not discern enough of its aspects to be certain of a match, but neither was there an obvious element to contradict a possible likeness. But in the Temple of Bastet, he had not worn a wig. She could not recall his hair in detail, but the colour—brown, certainly—and general shape *could* fit Mr. Darcy.

The act of reminiscing made her pace the room and pull at her fingers, but she *must* review all that she could. The supposition she faced was far too alarming not to require the most thorough dissection, no matter how appalling. Her instructor had always spoken in a whisper. Thus, she could not draw any conclusions from the sound of his voice. But what of the mannerisms? Both men had moments of similar terseness and aloofness, but her mentor spoke more easily and seemed capable of a playfulness that she would never have considered in Mr. Darcy till she had seen the extent of his recent transformation. Their postures were comparable. She would describe both as proud and serious. But how could someone of his stature, his background, his upstanding qualities, take on the mantle of instructor at Trenwith House?

"The same might be asked of me," Lizzy groaned as she sat down once more. Had not his alteration from cold and arrogant to agreeable and kind not proven to her that he had many facets? Had her experience not shown how she could misunderstand him?

Last but not least, there was his *touch*. Her legs had quaked when he had handed her into the carriage. The firm but not overpowering grasp...the perfect amount of support and pressure, the warmth, the size.

"It could all be the work of fancy," Lizzy insisted to herself. "I have not been myself. And as strange a coincidence as this may all seem, there could be a simple explanation for how my handkerchief should come to be the twin of Miss Darcy's."

Only Abby could put her mind at ease and solve the mystery once and for all. And how providential that Abby was to come to Derbyshire and they should have the opportunity to speak in person! Lizzy immediately began to consider how she would broach the subject, but as she rehearsed the options, she began to question her friend. The latter was familiar with Mr. Darcy but had never elucidated the extent of her acquaintance. If Mr. Darcy was an instructor of hers, with knowledge of how Lizzy felt of the man at that time, how could she have paired the two of them? This thought made Lizzy cross at Abby. Even if Lizzy had not expressed dislike for the man, why would Abby have taken the chance to mix oil and vinegar? Abby was no fool. This thought calmed Lizzy. But when was she to see Abby? Abby had not specified a day. She only knew the inn that Lizzy had written to her of. Would they have the occasion to speak alone? What if Abby came to call at the inn and the Gardiners should be present? Lizzy could not beg to stay at the inn by herself all day, not knowing when she might hear from Abby. Lizzy began to pace anew.

A knock at the door startled her. "Lizzy?

"I thought I heard you up and about," her aunt said after Lizzy had opened the door. She handed her a letter. "I thought this might be from Jane and you would wish to read it immediately."

Lizzy looked at the letter. The address was not in her sister's hand. If not from Jane, then it must be from Abby!

"It is not from Jane but a friend of mine who was to be in Derbyshire sometime this week," Lizzy explained. "We had hopes that a meeting might be possible. I have not seen her in some months."

As Lizzy did not open the letter before her, Mrs. Gardiner withdrew to allow her niece to read the letter in privacy.

Lizzy barely heard the door close before tearing open the seal.

What she read made her chest constrict. Abby was not to come to Derbyshire! That news was heartily disappointing. But the next part was horrendous. In her place, Abby had prepared a fourth and final lesson.

"Your mentor, should you consent to the arrangement," Abby had written, "is the same gentleman you learned from at Trenwith House. I have enclosed further instructions, but I shall not be in the least insulted or put out if you elect not to proceed with a fourth lesson at this time. Rather, I should be greatly distressed if you felt *obligated* to accept this invitation and, when we do meet, upbraid you for not holding true to your own wishes and preferences."

Lizzy had to put the letter down and circle the room a good ten times before rereading it. This she did thrice. It was too much to digest in one day! She wanted air, but in her current state, she might call too much attention upon herself. Her aunt and uncle already seemed too interested. She fanned herself with the letter. She opened the windows and felt a little better.

How could she possibly proceed with a fourth lesson knowing that her instructor might be Mr. Darcy? Such a thought could not be entertained. She would be courting disaster of some kind, surely. Her head swam to think that he, Mr. Darcy, might have had his hands upon her body already, that his lips had claimed hers, and that...*her dream*...of Mr. Darcy...

"I will not think it," she insisted, and covered her ears as if that might blot out the thoughts. "I will not think it. I will not think it."

She had prepared herself for many different scenarios concerning Trenwith House, mostly pertaining to the event of discovery and how she would respond if such a thing occurred. Never had she considered the possibility that she would know her instructor, and that he should be, of all people, Mr. Fitzwilliam Darcy.

CHAPTER THIRTY-SIX

The flutter of a bird outside made Darcy tense, for it might herald the arrival of Miss Elizabeth. He had been waiting two hours and knew she might not come at all, but if she did, it would have been worth the wait. He had identified a small cottage recently occupied by a young family, tenants of his, whom he had assisted into a larger dwelling after the birth of their second set of twins. Much of the furnishings had remained, including the bed. He had reviewed all the finishing touches himself, ensuring the bedclothes had been freshly laundered, a fire glowed in the hearth, and a table of wine and cheese set. Taking out his handkerchief, he wiped the perspiration from his brow. He was attired in his customary regalia from Trenwith House, but with the warmer weather, the wig, and even his mask, was proving exceedingly uncomfortable.

The wheels of a carriage drew his attention to the window. Through the small slit in the curtains, he observed a woman alight from the vehicle. A veil shrouded most of her countenance, but he recognized her form. His heart pounded. It was Elizabeth Bennet.

Darcy poured himself a glass of sherry. Some months had passed since their last lesson. Much could have happened to her views and sentiments since. He could not simply resume from where they had left off. He could have no expectations and would have to discern her mindset for himself and in only the most careful manner so as not to agitate or frighten her. He did not dare hope she wanted a resumption of her education. The chance to kiss her was too much to be wished for. Nonetheless, now that she had arrived, the prospect was there, and the blood churned in his loins. After waiting some twenty minutes, he heard a knock at the door and had to restrain himself from leaping across the room to open it.

She was dressed in a simple muslin, one that he had not seen her in before. She had not donned a wig, but most of her hair had been pinned and covered by a bonnet. His heart throbbed. She looked positively charming. Was there nothing she could wear that would diminish her loveliness? A cloth mask covered the upper half of her face. The lips, uncovered, became the focus.

Stepping back to allow her entry, he asked if she had eaten or desired a glass of wine?

"A glass of wine," she answered.

He pulled a chair at the table for her. She sat down, but in her movements and her air, he felt her nervousness. That was to be expected. He was not immune from nerves himself, but it was necessary for him, as the mentor, to put her at ease by foremost demonstrating his. Knowing this to be his responsibility, he was able to calm himself. As he poured the wine, he felt her scrutiny upon him. He handed her a glass. She continued to stare at him as if she meant to pierce his mask with her gaze. Did she suspect him of being someone else? Had Abby not confirmed her mentor was the same?

"This is a quaint abode," she noted.

"It is dubbed the Lilac Cottage, for the garden in back abounds with lilac bushes."

"I thought I caught its scent."

She took the glass of wine from him but did not drink it.

"It has been some time since our last lesson at Trenwith House," he reassured her. "I pray you have been in good health and spirit."

"I cannot complain," she replied.

This was not the affirmation he had expected. He asked after her family.

"Had I mentioned my family to you before?" she asked, startling him.

He combed his memory but could not recall if she had ever referenced her family at Trenwith House.

"It was a general question," he said. "I assumed—but forgive me if I touch upon a sensitive matter. What brings you to Derbyshire?"

"How do you know I am but visiting?"

What the deuce was her purpose in such questions? he wondered.

"I understood from Mrs. Trenwith that you are touring the area with family."

"Ah, yes, Abby. You must be well acquainted with her?"

He recalled her loquaciousness during the first lesson.

"You are under no obligation," he told her. "As always, the pupil must approve any progression and dictates the pace of the lesson."

She nodded. "Have you known Abby long?"

Perhaps she desired conversation to return to her former level of ease and trust. He sat down and filled his own glass.

"Nearly ten years."

His answer seemed to surprise her.

"That long? You must be…good friends?"

"I consider her a dear friend." He would have stopped there but found himself seeking a deeper rapport. "She was my mentor."

He saw this bit of information stunned her.

"I was a young and naïve fellow at the time," he explained, "and thought myself deeply in love with a Duchess, a beautiful widow of noble birth. In hindsight, it was more an infatuation than true devotion. She entertained my attentions at first, but at my first attempt to kiss her, she laughed at my awkwardness. Her remarks devastated me. She recommended me to her friend, Abigail Trenwith. I had every wish to prove myself as skilled a lover as any to be had. I was an eager student, and Abby a brilliant teacher, though I suspect any novice would have been in awe of her. My efforts made no difference to the Duchess, however. She had moved on to her next admirer.

"Do not feel sorrowful," he added at seeing her lips formed in sympathy. "My heart healed soon enough."

"Did you become an instructor after that?"

"I felt greatly indebted to Abby, but it was many years before I understood that the fair sex was in as much need of proper instruction as men. Abby applied to me to serve in the capacity of a mentor. I balked, for surely there were any number of men who would leap at the opportunity. And that was precisely the problem, she pointed out to me. She had no wish for those men, but only those whom she could trust not to take advantage of the situation and those who would honour the education as the benefit of the student, not the teacher. As you can imagine, Abby can be quite persuasive."

She agreed. "It did not take me long to adopt her philosophy."

"Have you?"

"I have my reservations still. After all, what moral, upstanding citizen would not consider what we do a sin?"

"'There is nothing good or bad, but thinking makes it so,'" he quoted of Hamlet.

"Then we would, each of us, define our own morality!"

"And some of the worst sins have been perpetrated by a majority of individuals believing the same. What is the injury we do compared to what society has done—in the name of all that is good, moral, and Christian? Our preachers might do more good to turn their tongues against an institution such as slavery than condemn what man and woman were meant to do by nature."

"Take care, sir! Your speech might be considered blasphemous." But there was a quirk in her mouth that showed she did not condemn what he said.

"'For as he thinks within himself, so he is.' Book of Proverbs. I hope you do not consider yourself less worthy, less decent for what you have done."

He sensed his words, or perhaps the tone of his voice, struck a chord within her.

"I am almost fully reconciled myself as a sinner," she said with that light humor of hers. "But if it became known what I had done, innocent parties—my family—should be injured by my actions."

"Does your au—family—know you to be here?"

"My aunt and uncle are having dinner with friends in Lambton. I had mentioned the possibility of Mrs. Trenwith. I spoke true when I said I was to meet with an old acquaintance who happened to be passing through Derbyshire, but the inference they would draw from my statement would be erroneous."

A new thought came to her. "What brings *you* to Derbyshire?"

He coloured. "I had business to attend."

"Are you spending the night here at this cottage?"

"No."

"Will you be here tomorrow?"

He paused. "Only if you desire it."

Her earlier agitation seemed to return, for she finished her wine rather hastily and rose to her feet. She looked about the room.

"Have you mentored a great many students before?"

"What do you consider 'a great many'?"

"Have you ever…known any of them—beforehand or perhaps by accident you discovered their true identity?"

His pulse quickened. "Abby would take the identity of her students to the grave."

His response seem to give her some comfort.

"The odds of any one teacher and student being acquainted are extremely small," he added.

"But the whimsy of Fate is not unheard of."

"No," he murmured. "But even if a pair were acquainted, they would not themselves know it. We have taken every precaution to ensure our anonymity, which is in the interest of both student and mentor. Are you worried of discovery?"

"Yes, of course. Are you not?"

"I accepted the risks when I agreed to become an instructor for Abby. As with you, discovery would lead to unsavoury consequences for myself and my family. I have responsibility for one member in particular. And in that light, I have been considering an end to my tenure as an instructor at Trenwith House."

He rose from his chair and went to stand opposite her. "I am convinced this will be my last and final lesson."

* * * * *

"Indeed?" she replied after clearing her throat.

"A change in circumstances have led me to the appropriateness of ending my involvement in this profession."

Her heart thumped wildly. *A change in circumstances.* Could he possibly mean his feelings for her? Might he still hold her in affection? She felt torn. She had not come with any intention of pursuing a fourth lesson but to confirm the identity of her mentor. She was more certain but lacked proof still of his being Mr. Darcy. If he was ending his stint as a Trenwith instructor, this might be her last opportunity for a lesson. Abby would no doubt find her a replacement if requested, but Lizzy had no toleration to continue with anyone else. What if Mr. Darcy, despite his altered behaviour to her, had no intention of renewing his hand? Suddenly, she desired the fourth lesson beyond anything.

"I remember the safety word," she blurted.

"Pardon?"

"Montreal."

He simply stared at her. Had he forgotten it?

"The safety word," she reminded him.

"Yes, of course."

But he remained immobile.

"I have but an hour to spare, I think," she said. "I had revealed the location of my meeting so that it should not sound too mysterious to my aunt, and she had expressed a desire to meet Mrs. Trenwith."

"Are you certain you wish to proceed?"

"No—I mean, yes. Yes."

He seemed to hesitate.

"I wish to finish my, er, education," she stated more firmly.

After another pause, he approached her. Her back was to the fire, the main source of lighting, and her countenance in shadow, but his was more illuminated. She recognized the squareness of the chin, the mature jawline. He *was* Mr. Darcy. The thought sent a rush through her body. Her nerves crackled and she worried his touch might cause them to spark like lightning.

He cupped her face with both hands, tilting it up toward him, and she had to close her eyes against the *electricity* reverberating within her.

"Montreal," he reiterated.

"Montreal," she echoed in whisper.

When she sensed no movement, she opened her eyes a little. He was studying her as if admiring a gem or other precious object. Her heart skipped a beat. Abby had taught him well.

Slowly, he lowered his head and lightly pressed his mouth to hers, as if to give her a chance to escape. Her senses were ignited. There was no turning back.

She placed her hands at his wrists. He took the indication and applied greater pressure. His mouth covered hers whole. Tenderly, he kissed her, paying homage to her lips with his. The simple caress wrought havoc upon her. Her newfound feelings cast the experience in altered light. Her affection—yes, affection *and* attraction—was fuel to her desire. She wanted to be close to him in every way possible. And something seemed to come over him as well. Perhaps it was lust, amplified by the finality of the lesson, but he moved his lips over hers with a force similar to her experience in the Temple of Bastet. She returned his kiss with equal fervor, which excited him till he seemed to devour her mouth like a starved man. The area about her lips blushed with his attentions, and her tongue could barely keep apace with his probing. Not wanting him to break away, she shifted her hands to his head. It was no easy matter to thread her fingers through the pomade in the wig. Sensing her difficulty, he tore the damn thing off his head. Greedily, her fingers entwined in his locks.

Heat and moisture had already begun to form between her legs, the pressure there growing as lips and tongues danced and dueled.

He cupped the back of her head with one hand, the other encircled her waist and crushed her to him. Desire surged in her groin, and she triumphed at feeling his cock, long and hard against her. He continued to assault her with kisses. When she required a breath, he skipped his mouth across her temple and down the side of her face before landing once more upon her mouth. She felt drunk with desire, giddy with the knowledge that she was making love to *him*. She ground her hips a little at him. The motion made him groan. He swept her off her feet and carried her to the bed. After laying her down, he covered her with kisses about her neck, her collar, and the tops of her breasts. She put her hands to his chest, wanting to feel the solidness of him. He took one hand and planted a kiss on the inside of her wrist; the tenderness of it made her heart leap into her throat. Abby's warning rang in her head. She ought not mistake the lovemaking skills of her mentor as suggestive of true affection, but, oh, how she wished it were so!

She tugged at his cravat. He helped her loosen it, then shrugged out of his coat. He leaned in to kiss her, but she stayed him.

"I think it inequitable that you have always seen me sans clothing, but I have not had a similar privilege," she said, her heart beating rapidly at her own forwardness.

He seemed surprised but acquiesced by shedding his waistcoat. "I should not wish to be unfair."

She slipped her hands under his shirt and felt the ridges of his ribs. Her heart hammered. She had her hands upon Mr. Darcy, *upon his bare skin*. His breath, too, seemed to catch in his throat. Slowly, she moved her hands up to his chest. How different a man felt—all hardness and thickness. Her hands grazed his nipples. With a groan, he lowered himself over her and took her mouth once more. Locking her fingers around the back of his neck, she did her best to reflect all that she knew of kissing from what he had shown her. His hands roamed her body, cradling the back, caressing the arms, and grasping the midsection. He grabbed her buttock and fitted her closer to him. Instinctively she wrapped a leg about his thigh and pressed herself to him. She tugged at his shirt, which he pulled overhead, rewarding her with a view of his bare chest. She inhaled sharply. She knew the look of a nude man from statues and paintings, but a *living, breathing* naked man before her was altogether different. With her hands she caressed the planes of his pectorals.

"Do you recall the safety word?" he asked, though he seemed in danger of requiring it as much as she.

"Yes."

He began to untie her stays, which, conveniently, laced in the front. The yearning between her legs throbbed at the leisurely pace. After undoing the corset, he pulled her shift down below her breasts. He cupped one, which seemed to fit perfectly in his large hand, then kissed its hardened peak. He took whole mouthfuls of the flesh and fondled the nipple. Her back arched in response. The wetness flowed from her between her legs.

"Stop," she gasped when the assault was too much.

"Not the safety word," he muttered, but he allowed her some relief by applying his attentions to the other breast.

In truth, she did not wish him to stop such delicious torture, but it had been some time since her last lesson, and she found the sensations overwhelming.

His hand slipped beneath her skirts and between her legs. She cried out as he touched her there. How long had she craved for this? He continued to tug and tease her nipple while stroking the other nub of flesh below. Already excited by his actions with the former, it was not long before she was gasping and writhing. The dual stimulations fed off each other, sending ripples up and down her body. She knew not which of his hands to arch her body into. As tension mounted within her, he increased the force and speed of his ministrations. Her body was merciless at his hands. She could feel the wave of sensations gathering, mounting, and then cresting. She screamed as it crashed down around her, roiling and tumbling her in its wake.

He kissed her on her brow when, after much shuddering, she surfaced for air. She opened her eyes to find him gazing upon her with an expression she could not place, in part because of the poor lighting and the mask covering the majority of his countenance.

"*Belle*," he said with more than customary hoarseness.

She smiled but hoped her lesson was not yet over.

CHAPTER THIRTY-SEVEN

Darcy continued to skim a knuckle along the familiar friend between her thighs. There was no instrument more beautiful nor more pleasurable to play than a woman's body. Each woman had her unique sensitivities, and he wanted nothing more than the chance to explore *all* of hers. He brushed a finger against her perineum. She shivered and moaned. It took all of him not to claim more of her, but cognizant of her limited time, he pushed himself up.

She grasped his arm. "Will you...are we finished already?"

He let out a haggard breath. "I may be a seasoned mentor, *mademoiselle,* but I am yet a man and, as proven before, not without weakness."

"Thank goodness. I should be appalled to find myself in bed with a saint."

He could not help but smile despite the gravity of his prior transgression. "I should have shown more restraint than I possessed at the Temple of Bastet. It was unforgivable, especially given the consequences."

"How chivalrous you are!"

"You are gracious, but I was quite the contrary."

Instead of being nettled, however, Miss Elizabeth seemed pleased. "You were merely fulfilling the request of a demanding student."

"And if you recall, you were not in a normal state of mind."

"I am now."

He raised his brows. In response, she reached for the buttons of his fall, but he quickly stayed her hand.

"*Pray, do not tempt me.*"

She frowned. "Why?"

He could sense she meant to challenge him.

"Is your time not limited?" he reminded her. "What if your aunt and uncle return from dinner early?"

"I'll take the risk."

It was his turn to frown. The firmness in her tone did not bode well for him.

"I am of sound and unadulterated judgment," she reassured him. "I wish to proceed with our lesson."

He felt his cock harden further. Still, he hesitated, "Perhaps another time."

"I have no desire to seek another instructor."

He looked at her sharply.

"It would seem we ought make the most of this occasion," she continued, her voice husky with promise.

"You have no regrets, then, of what happened? Of your loss?"

"And if I did? What happened cannot be undone. What purpose would repining serve? But if you were willing to satisfy me then, why should you be less inclined once the main deed has been done? Lest you find me less desirous to-day than you did before?"

He nearly choked his response. "God, no."

She leaned in toward him, her hand resting on his thigh. "Then take me. As you did. As you will."

He was lost.

Seizing her to him, he kissed her with desperate fervor. He could not prevail. Her arguments were too strong, her body too compelling. This time, however, he was better prepared, but he did not yet reach for the condom. First, he made love to every inch of her body, caressing her from head to toe with lips and hands . His favourite parts of her included the smoothness of her back, the slight swell of her belly, and the suppleness of her thighs. Gently, he removed her skirts and chemise.

"I will see you in your glory this time," she said when he was done.

Obliging, he kicked off his shoes, discarded the stockings, and pulled down his trousers. His erection stood at proud attention. She caressed his parts with her gaze, her lips parted as she studied his form. He closed her mouth with his and fitted his body to hers. The softness of her skin, of bare flesh to bare flesh, made the blood pound in his groin. The scent of her desire hung in the air, fueling his lust. It would not be long before he would want to ravish her without mercy. He groped a breast and fondled the nipple. She moaned into his touch.

He kneaded the orb and toyed with the hardened rosebud till she writhed and panted. His other hand reached for a buttock and squeezed lightly the tender flesh. She wrapped her arms about his neck and ground the seat of her desire against him. His head swam and the blood churned in his groin, but he resisted the temptation to plunge himself into her depths. Remembering how exquisite she had felt about him, he could not be assured he could withhold from spending before she arrived at her own paroxysm. Instead, he poured his lust into a kiss. He moved his hand from her derrière to cup the back of her head and claimed that delicious pair of lips. She responded in the most heady fashion. He was damned. For his appetite for this woman would never be tempered or satiated.

Only when he sensed her impatience did he reach for the thin sheath that would have made all the difference before in easing the heartache and suspense. He slipped the condom on. The pause in action allowed him to collect restraint. Parting her legs farther, he applied his mouth to her. Her head fell back as his tongue circled and stroked her. She gasped in rapture. He teased and lapped at her till she was at the brink once more. Rising to his knees, he rubbed the length of his desire against her. Her hands fisted into the bedclothes beneath. And then he entered her.

She gasped loudly, and he worried that he might have hurt her, though only the crown of his shaft had penetrated. It was possible, given the length of time that had passed, the breach was little different than the taking of her virginity. She had closed her eyes, but when she opened them, they sparkled, setting him at some relief. He did his best to rein in his urgency. His cock, pulsing at the beauty before it, wanted to indulge in the greatest of all carnal thrills.

"Why do you stop?"

She shifted her hips, and he felt her inner muscles move against him. The sensation demolished all forbearance. He sank deeper into her. She felt as glorious as ever. He had to close his eyes to the magnificence of her hot womanhood pulsing all around him. He opened his eyes to behold her reaction. She responded by wrapping her legs about him with the ease of a practiced strumpet. He buried himself more fully inside her. She groaned her approval.

If only she knew with whom she lay. If she knew who brought her this bliss and rapture, she might be more receptive to his suit.

But it was also possible she would be too shocked and rendered too awkward to want to have anything to do with him. He ought to enjoy the moment. It was likely the last he would have with her.

The weight of the realization made him take her mouth with more force than he intended. Undaunted, she returned the kiss. Without releasing her lips, he began to undulate his hips. She met his every thrust. The sensation of her soft, supple body beneath him enthralled, inciting the desire to overwhelm her with the strength and hardness of his own. Entwining his fingers in hers, he pulled her arms above head and gradually began an earnest rhythm. He could sense her climax approaching by her shallow breaths, the quickened groans, and how she crushed her pelvis to him. Withdrawing from the kiss but still holding her arms in place, he concentrated on the angle of his thrusts to push her over the edge and into the pool of ecstasy.

With a cry, she trembled beneath him, her limbs jerking with wild abandon. Witnessing her in the throes of pleasure, the tension collected in his groin gathered fast and furious. Pinning her to the bed, he shoved himself at her with desperate vigor till the pressure found release. The most magnificent pleasure erupted through him, shooting through his legs, making them quiver. His groans came from a place deep and raw. His body could know no greater glory. After a few final shudders, he allowed the weight of his lower body to settle over hers, his cock still throbbing inside of her.

"My God," he murmured as he pressed his forehead to hers.

"My God," she echoed.

He pulled back to observe the brightness of her eyes and the flush of her cheeks. The perspiration only added to the glow in her countenance and reaffirmed that she was the most beautiful creature he had ever beheld. Now that he had come down from the heavens, the very height of elation, he was cognizant that his heart ached as never before.

CHAPTER THIRTY-EIGHT

Sunlight streamed in through the window. Lizzy awoke with a surge of vivacity. The slight ache between her thighs recalled the activities of the prior evening. She embraced her pillow with the glee of a child. She wanted to scream. How strange was the hand of providence! When she thought of the shock, dismay, thrill, and euphoria she had experienced in so short a span a time, it was a wonder she could think straight. It was certain that she came as near to affection and admiration for Mr. Darcy as ever she could for a man. Add to that a powerful attraction of a corporal nature, and she could want for nothing else. No other individual had excited such intensity of feelings within her. There had not been a moment last night that she did not savour. There was no manner of kiss that she did not enjoy, did not relish. She gloried in every caress, every touch.

And to-day she was to dine at Pemberley! She could hardly wait to see him again. Would she be able to contain her giddy anxiety? She could not reveal herself as his student. Of that she was certain. While it would be most hypocritical of him to judge her for her pursuit of an education, it was possible he could take a different perspective on a prospective wife and wish for a woman of purity, an unblemished virgin. But she would not trouble herself on that, for she had first to confirm his current feelings for her.

The sound of her aunt and uncle below stairs roused her from her bed. Her spirits high, she had forgotten her disappointment at not receiving a letter from Jane. But after breakfast, the post brought two letters from Jane. One was marked that it had been missent elsewhere. Lizzy was not surprised as Jane had written the direction remarkably ill. They had just been preparing to walk as the letters came in; and her uncle and aunt, leaving her to enjoy them in quiet, set off by themselves. The one missent must first be attended to; it had been written five days ago. The beginning contained an account of all their little parties and engagements, with such news as the country afforded; but the latter half, which was dated a day later, and written in evident agitation, gave more important intelligence. It was to this effect:

"Since writing the above, dearest Lizzy, something has occurred of a most unexpected and serious nature; but I am afraid of alarming you—be assured that we are all well. What I have to say relates to poor Lydia. An express came at twelve last night, just as we were all gone to bed, from Colonel Forster, to inform us that she was gone off to Scotland with one of his officers; to own the truth, with Wickham! Imagine our surprise. To Kitty, however, it does not seem so wholly unexpected. I am very, very sorry. So imprudent a match on both sides! But I am willing to hope the best, and that his character has been misunderstood. Thoughtless and indiscreet I can easily believe him, but this step (and let us rejoice over it) marks nothing bad at heart. His choice is disinterested at least, for he must know my father can give her nothing. Our poor mother is sadly grieved. My father bears it better. How thankful am I that we never let them know what has been said against him; we must forget it ourselves. They were off Saturday night about twelve, as is conjectured, but were not missed till yesterday morning at eight. The express was sent off directly. My dear Lizzy, they must have passed within ten miles of us. Colonel Forster gives us reason to expect him here soon. Lydia left a few lines for his wife, informing her of their intention. I must conclude, for I cannot be long from my poor mother. I am afraid you will not be able to make it out, but I hardly know what I have written."

Without allowing herself time for consideration, and scarcely knowing what she felt, Lizzy on finishing this letter instantly seized the other, and opening it with the utmost impatience, read as follows: it had been written a day later than the conclusion of the first.

"By this time, my dearest sister, you have received my hurried letter; I wish this may be more intelligible, but though not confined for time, my head is so bewildered that I cannot answer for being coherent. Dearest Lizzy, I hardly know what I would write, but I have bad news for you, and it cannot be delayed. Imprudent as the marriage between Mr. Wickham and our poor Lydia would be, we are now anxious to be assured it has taken place, for there is but too much reason to fear they are not gone to Scotland. Colonel Forster came yesterday, having left Brighton the day before, not many hours after the express. Though Lydia's short letter to Mrs. F. gave them to understand that they were going to Gretna Green, something was dropped by Denny expressing his belief that W. never intended to go there, or to marry Lydia at all, which was repeated to Colonel F., who, instantly taking the alarm, set off from B. intending to trace their route. He did trace them easily to Clapham, but no further; for on entering that place, they removed into a hackney coach, and dismissed the chaise that brought them from Epsom. All that is known after this is, that they were seen to continue the London road. I know not what to think. After making every possible inquiry on that side London, Colonel F. came on into Hertfordshire, anxiously renewing them at all the turnpikes, and at the inns in Barnet and Hatfield, but without any success—no such people had been seen to pass through. With the kindest concern he came on to Longbourn, and broke his apprehensions to us in a manner most creditable to his heart. I am sincerely grieved for him and Mrs. F., but no one can throw any blame on them. Our distress, my dear Lizzy, is very great. My father and mother believe the worst, but I cannot think so ill of him. Many circumstances might make it more eligible for them to be married privately in town than to pursue their first plan; and even if *he* could form such a design against a young woman of Lydia's connections, which is not likely, can I suppose her so lost to everything? Impossible! I grieve to find, however, that Colonel F. is not disposed to depend upon their marriage; he shook his head when I expressed my hopes, and said he feared W. was not a man to be trusted. My poor mother is really ill, and keeps her room. Could she exert herself, it would be better; but this is not to be expected. And as to my father, I never in my life saw him so affected. Poor Kitty has anger for having concealed their attachment; but as it was a matter of confidence, one cannot wonder. I am truly glad, dearest Lizzy, that you have been spared something of these distressing scenes; but now, as the first shock is over, shall I own that I long for your return? I am not so selfish, however, as to press for it, if inconvenient. Adieu! I take up my pen again to do what I have just told you I would not; but circumstances are such that I cannot help earnestly begging you all to come here as soon as possible. I know my dear uncle and aunt so well, that I am not afraid of requesting it, though I have still something more to ask of the former. My father is going to London with Colonel Forster instantly, to try to discover her. What he means to do I am sure I know not; but his excessive distress will not allow him to pursue any measure in the best and safest way, and Colonel Forster is obliged to be at Brighton again tomorrow evening. In such an exigence, my uncle's advice and assistance would be everything in the world; he will immediately comprehend what I must feel, and I rely upon his goodness."

"Oh! where, where is my uncle?" cried Lizzy, darting from her seat as she finished the letter, in eagerness to follow him, without losing a moment of the time so precious; but as she reached the door it was opened by a servant, and Mr. Darcy appeared. Her pale face and impetuous manner made him start, and before he could recover himself to speak, she, in whose mind every idea was superseded by Lydia's situation, hastily exclaimed, "I beg your pardon, but I must leave you. I must find Mr. Gardiner this moment, on business that cannot be delayed; I have not an instant to lose."

"Good God! What is the matter?" cried he, with more feeling than politeness; then recollecting himself, "I will not detain you a minute; but let me, or let the servant go after Mr. and Mrs. Gardiner. You are not well enough; you cannot go yourself."

Lizzy hesitated, but her knees trembled under her and she felt how little would be gained by her attempting to pursue them. Calling back the servant, therefore, she commissioned him, though in so breathless an accent as made her almost unintelligible, to fetch his master and mistress home instantly.

On his quitting the room she sat down, unable to support herself, and looking so miserably ill, that it was impossible for Darcy to leave her, or to refrain from saying, in a tone of gentleness and commiseration, "Let me call your maid. Is there nothing you could take to give you present relief? A glass of wine; shall I get you one? You are very ill."

"No, I thank you," she replied, endeavouring to recover herself. "There is nothing the matter with me. I am quite well; I am only distressed by some dreadful news which I have just received from Longbourn."

She burst into tears as she alluded to it, and for a few minutes could not speak another word. Darcy, in wretched suspense, could only say something indistinctly of his concern, and observe her in compassionate silence. At length she spoke again. "I have just had a letter from Jane, with such dreadful news. It cannot be concealed from anyone. My younger sister has left all her friends—has eloped; has thrown herself into the power of—of Mr. Wickham. They are gone off together from Brighton. *You* know him too well to doubt the rest. She has no money, no connections, nothing that can tempt him to—she is lost for ever."

Darcy was fixed in astonishment. "When I consider," she added in a yet more agitated voice, "that I might have prevented it! I, who knew what he was. Had I but explained some part of it only—some part of what I learnt, to my own family! Had his character been known, this could not have happened. But it is all—all too late now."

"I am grieved indeed," cried Darcy; "grieved—shocked. But is it certain—absolutely certain?"

"Oh, yes! They left Brighton together on Sunday night, and were traced almost to London, but not beyond; they are certainly not gone to Scotland."

"And what has been done, what has been attempted, to recover her?"

"My father is gone to London, and Jane has written to beg my uncle's immediate assistance; and we shall be off, I hope, in half-an-hour. But nothing can be done—I know very well that nothing can be done. How is such a man to be worked on? How are they even to be discovered? I have not the smallest hope. It is every way horrible!"

Darcy shook his head in silent acquiescence.

"When *my* eyes were opened to his real character—Oh! Had I known what I ought, what I dared to do! But I knew not—I was afraid of doing too much. Wretched, wretched mistake!"

Darcy made no answer. He seemed scarcely to hear her, and was walking up and down the room in earnest meditation, his brow contracted, his air gloomy. Lizzy soon observed, and instantly understood it. Her power was sinking; everything *must* sink under such a proof of family weakness, such an assurance of the deepest disgrace. She could neither wonder nor condemn, but the belief of his self-conquest brought nothing consolatory to her bosom, afforded no palliation of her distress. It was, on the contrary, exactly calculated to make her understand her own wishes; and never had she so honestly felt that she could have loved him, as now, when all love must be vain.

But self, though it would intrude, could not engross her. Lydia—the humiliation, the misery she was bringing on them all, soon swallowed up every private care; and covering her face with her handkerchief, Lizzy was soon lost to everything else; and, after a pause of several minutes, was only recalled to a sense of her situation by the voice of her companion, who, in a manner which, though it spoke compassion, spoke likewise restraint, said, "I am afraid you have been long desiring my absence, nor have I anything to plead in excuse of my stay, but real, though unavailing concern. Would to Heaven that anything could be either said or done on my part that might offer consolation to such distress! But I will not torment you with vain wishes, which may seem purposely to ask for your thanks. This unfortunate affair will, I fear, prevent my sister's having the pleasure of seeing you at Pemberley to-day."

"Oh, yes. Be so kind as to apologise for us to Miss Darcy. Say that urgent business calls us home immediately. Conceal the unhappy truth as long as it is possible, I know it cannot be long." He readily assured her of his secrecy; again expressed his sorrow for her distress, wished it a happier conclusion than there was at present reason to hope, and leaving his compliments for her relations, with only one serious, parting look, went away. As he quitted the room, Lizzy felt how improbable it was that they should ever see each other again on such terms of cordiality as had marked their several meetings in Derbyshire; and as she threw a retrospective glance over the whole of their acquaintance, so full of contradictions and varieties, sighed at the perverseness of those feelings which would now have promoted its continuance, and would formerly have rejoiced in its termination.

She saw him go with regret, and in this early example of what Lydia's infamy must produce, found additional anguish as she reflected on the wretched business. Never, since reading Jane's second letter, had she entertained a hope of Wickham's meaning to marry her. No one but Jane, she thought, could flatter herself with such an expectation. Surprise was the least of her feelings on this development. While the contents of the first letter remained in her mind, she was all surprise—all astonishment that Wickham should marry a girl whom it was impossible he could marry for money; and how Lydia could ever have attached him had appeared incomprehensible. But now it was all too natural. For such an attachment as this she might have sufficient charms; and though she did not suppose Lydia to be deliberately engaging in an elopement without the intention of marriage, she had no difficulty in believing that neither her virtue nor her understanding would preserve her from falling an easy prey.

She had never perceived, while the regiment was in Hertfordshire, that Lydia had any partiality for him; but she was convinced that Lydia wanted only encouragement to attach herself to anybody. Sometimes one officer, sometimes another, had been her favourite, as their attentions raised them in her opinion. Her affections had continually been fluctuating but never without an object. The mischief of neglect and mistaken indulgence towards such a girl—oh! how acutely did she now feel it!

She was wild to be at home—to hear, to see, to be upon the spot to share with Jane in the cares that must now fall wholly upon her, in a family so deranged, a father absent, a mother incapable of exertion, and requiring constant attendance; and though almost persuaded that nothing could be done for Lydia, her uncle's interference seemed of the utmost importance, and till he entered the room her impatience was severe. Mr. and Mrs. Gardiner had hurried back in alarm, supposing by the servant's account that their niece was taken suddenly ill; but satisfying them instantly on that head, she eagerly communicated the cause of their summons, reading the two letters aloud, and dwelling on the postscript of the last with trembling energy, though Lydia had never been a favourite with them, Mr. and Mrs. Gardiner could not but be deeply afflicted. Not Lydia only, but all were concerned in it; and after the first exclamations of surprise and horror, Mr. Gardiner promised every assistance in his power. Lizzy, though expecting no less, thanked him with tears of gratitude; and all three being actuated by one spirit, everything relating to their journey was speedily settled. They were to be off as soon as possible. "But what is to be done about Pemberley?" cried Mrs. Gardiner. "John told us Mr. Darcy was here when you sent for us; was it so?"

"Yes; and I told him we should not be able to keep our engagement. *That* is all settled."

"What is all settled?" repeated the other, as she ran into her room to prepare. "And are they upon such terms as for her to disclose the real truth? Oh, that I knew how it was!"

But wishes were vain, or at least could only serve to amuse her in the hurry and confusion of the following hour. Had Lizzy been at leisure to be idle, she would have remained certain that all employment was impossible to one so wretched as herself; but she had her share of business as well as her aunt, and amongst the rest there were notes to be written to all their friends at Lambton, with false excuses for their sudden departure. An hour, however, saw the whole completed; and Mr. Gardiner meanwhile having settled his account at the inn, nothing remained to be done but to go; and Lizzy, after all the misery of the morning, found herself, in a shorter space of time than she could have supposed, seated in the carriage, and on the road to Longbourn.

CHAPTER THIRTY-NINE

"I have been thinking it over again, Lizzy," said her uncle, as they drove from the town; "and really, upon serious consideration, I am much more inclined than I was to judge as your eldest sister does on the matter. It appears to me so very unlikely that any young man should form such a design against a girl who is by no means unprotected or friendless, and who was actually staying in his colonel's family, that I am strongly inclined to hope the best. Could he expect that her friends would not step forward? Could he expect to be noticed again by the regiment, after such an affront to Colonel Forster? His temptation is not adequate to the risk!"

"Do you really think so?" cried Lizzy, brightening up for a moment.

"Upon my word," said Mrs. Gardiner, "I begin to be of your uncle's opinion. It is really too great a violation of decency, honour, and interest, for him to be guilty of. I cannot think so very ill of Wickham. Can you yourself, Lizzy, so wholly give him up, as to believe him capable of it?"

"Not, perhaps, of neglecting his own interest; but of every other neglect I can believe him capable. If, indeed, it should be so! But I dare not hope it. Why should they not go on to Scotland if that had been the case?"

"In the first place," replied Mr. Gardiner, "there is no absolute proof that they are not gone to Scotland."

"Oh! But their removing from the chaise into a hackney coach is such a presumption! And, besides, no traces of them were to be found on the Barnet road."

"Well, then—supposing them to be in London. They may be there, though for the purpose of concealment, for no more exceptional purpose. It is not likely that money should be very abundant on either side; and it might strike them that they could be more economically, though less expeditiously, married in London than in Scotland."

"But why all this secrecy? Why any fear of detection? Why must their marriage be private? Oh, no, no—this is not likely. His most particular friend, you see by Jane's account, was persuaded of his never intending to marry her. Wickham will never marry a woman without some money. He cannot afford it. And what claims has Lydia—what attraction has she beyond youth, health, and good humour that could make him, for her sake, forego every chance of benefiting himself by marrying well? As to what restraint the apprehensions of disgrace in the corps might throw on a dishonourable elopement with her, I am not able to judge; for I know nothing of the effects that such a step might produce. But as to your other objection, I am afraid it will hardly hold good. Lydia has no brothers to step forward; and he might imagine, from my father's behaviour, from his indolence and the little attention he has ever seemed to give to what was going forward in his family, that *he* would do as little, and think as little about it, as any father could do, in such a matter."

"But can you think that Lydia is so lost to everything but love of him as to consent to live with him on any terms other than marriage?"

"It does seem, and it is most shocking indeed," replied Lizzy, with tears in her eyes, "that a sister's sense of decency and virtue in such a point should admit of doubt. But, really, I know not what to say. Perhaps I am not doing her justice. But she is very young; she has never been taught to think on serious subjects; and for the last half-year, nay, for a twelvemonth—she has been given up to nothing but amusement and vanity. She has been allowed to dispose of her time in the most idle and frivolous manner, and to adopt any opinions that came in her way. Since the militia were first quartered in Meryton, nothing but love, flirtation, and officers have been in her head. She has been doing everything in her power by thinking and talking on the subject, to give greater—what shall I call it? Susceptibility to her feelings; which are naturally lively enough. And we all know that Wickham has every charm of person and address that can captivate a woman."

"But you see that Jane," said her aunt, "does not think so very ill of Wickham as to believe him capable of the attempt."

"Of whom does Jane ever think ill? And who is there, whatever might be their former conduct, that she would think capable of such an attempt, till it were proved against them? But Jane knows, as well as I do, what Wickham really is. We both know that he has been profligate in every sense of the word; that he has neither integrity nor honour; that he is as false and deceitful as he is insinuating."

"And do you really know all this?" cried Mrs. Gardiner, whose curiosity as to the mode of her intelligence was all alive.

"I do indeed," replied Lizzy, colouring. "I told you, the other day, of his infamous behaviour to Mr. Darcy; and you yourself, when last at Longbourn, heard in what manner he spoke of the man who had behaved with such forbearance and liberality towards him. And there are other circumstances which I am not at liberty—which it is not worth while to relate; but his lies about the whole Pemberley family are endless. From what he said of Miss Darcy I was thoroughly prepared to see a proud, reserved, disagreeable girl. Yet he knew to the contrary himself. He must know that she was as amiable and unpretending as we have found her."

"But does Lydia know nothing of this? Can she be ignorant of what you and Jane seem so well to understand?"

"Oh, yes!—that, that is the worst of all. Till I was in Kent, and saw so much both of Mr. Darcy and his relation Colonel Fitzwilliam, I was ignorant of the truth myself. And when I returned home, the regiment was to leave Meryton in a week or fortnight's time. As that was the case, neither Jane, to whom I related the whole, nor I, thought it necessary to make our knowledge public; for of what use could it apparently be to any one, that the good opinion which all the neighbourhood had of him should then be overthrown? And even when it was settled that Lydia should go with Mrs. Forster, the necessity of opening her eyes to his character never occurred to me. That *she* could be in any danger from the deception never entered my head. That such a consequence as *this* could ensue, you may easily believe, was far enough from my thoughts."

"When they all removed to Brighton, therefore, you had no reason, I suppose, to believe them fond of each other?"

"Not the slightest. I can remember no symptom of affection on either side; and had anything of the kind been perceptible, you must be aware that ours is not a family on which it could be thrown away. When first he entered the corps, she was ready enough to admire him; but so we all were. Every girl in or near Meryton was out of her senses about him for the first two months; but he never distinguished *her* by any particular attention; and, consequently, after a moderate period of extravagant and wild admiration, her fancy for him gave way, and others of the regiment, who treated her with more distinction, again became her favourites."

* * * * *

Lizzy found no interval of ease or forgetfulness during their journey home. Mixed in with her anguish and self-reproach was guilt over her own deeds. Her pursuit of an education at Trenwith House would have disgraced her family equally, if not more, than Lydia's actions, the primary difference being one sister's presence of mind to hide from the world her debauchery and the flagrant carelessness of the other. As much as Lizzy censured her sister, she knew it to be unfair not to turn the criticism upon herself. That she had been spared discovery was perhaps only the whim of luck.

They travelled as expeditiously as possible, and, sleeping one night on the road, reached Longbourn by dinner time the next day. It was a comfort to Lizzy to consider that Jane could not have been wearied by long expectations.

The little Gardiners, attracted by the sight of a chaise, were standing on the steps of the house as they entered the paddock; and, when the carriage drove up to the door, the joyful surprise that lighted up their faces, and displayed itself over their whole bodies, in a variety of capers and frisks, was the first pleasing earnest of their welcome.

Lizzy jumped out; and, after giving each of them a hasty kiss, hurried into the vestibule, where Jane, who came running down from her mother's apartment, immediately met her.

Lizzy, as she affectionately embraced her, whilst tears filled the eyes of both, lost not a moment in asking whether anything had been heard of the fugitives.

"Not yet," replied Jane. "But now that my dear uncle is come, I hope everything will be well."

"Is my father in town?"

"Yes, he went on Tuesday, as I wrote you word."

"And have you heard from him often?"

"We have heard only twice. He wrote me a few lines on Wednesday to say that he had arrived in safety, and to give me his directions, which I particularly begged him to do. He merely added that he should not write again till he had something of importance to mention."

"And my mother—how is she? How are you all?"

"My mother is tolerably well, I trust; though her spirits are greatly shaken. She is up stairs and will have great satisfaction in seeing you all. She does not yet leave her dressing-room. Mary and Kitty, thank Heaven, are quite well."

"But you—how are you?" cried Lizzy. "You look pale. How much you must have gone through!"

Her sister, however, assured her of her being perfectly well; and their conversation, which had been passing while Mr. and Mrs. Gardiner were engaged with their children, was now put an end to by the approach of the whole party. Jane ran to her uncle and aunt, and welcomed and thanked them both, with alternate smiles and tears.

When they were all in the drawing-room, the questions which Lizzy had already asked were of course repeated by the others, and they soon found that Jane had no intelligence to give. The sanguine hope of good, however, which the benevolence of her heart suggested had not yet deserted her; she still expected that it would all end well, and that every morning would bring some letter, either from Lydia or her father, to explain their proceedings, and, perhaps, announce their marriage.

Mrs. Bennet, to whose apartment they all repaired, after a few minutes' conversation together, received them exactly as might be expected; with tears and lamentations of regret, invectives against the villainous conduct of Wickham, and complaints of her own sufferings and ill-usage; blaming everybody but the person to whose ill-judging indulgence the errors of her daughter must principally be owing.

"If I had been able," said she, "to carry my point in going to Brighton, with all my family, *this* would not have happened; but poor dear Lydia had nobody to take care of her. Why did the Forsters ever let her go out of their sight? I am sure there was some great neglect or other on their side, for she is not the kind of girl to do such a thing if she had been well looked after. I always thought they were very unfit to have the charge of her; but I was overruled, as I always am. Poor dear child! And now here's Mr. Bennet gone away, and I know he will fight Wickham, wherever he meets him and then he will be killed, and what is to become of us all? The Collinses will turn us out before he is cold in his grave, and if you are not kind to us, brother, I do not know what we shall do."

They all exclaimed against such terrific ideas; and Mr. Gardiner, after general assurances of his affection for her and all her family, told her that he meant to be in London the very next day, and would assist Mr. Bennet in every endeavour for recovering Lydia.

"Do not give way to useless alarm," added he; "though it is right to be prepared for the worst, there is no occasion to look on it as certain. It is not quite a week since they left Brighton. In a few days more we may gain some news of them; and till we know that they are not married, and have no design of marrying, do not let us give the matter over as lost. As soon as I get to town I shall go to my brother, and make him come home with me to Gracechurch Street; and then we may consult together as to what is to be done."

"Oh! my dear brother," replied Mrs. Bennet, "that is exactly what I could most wish for. And now do, when you get to town, find them out, wherever they may be; and if they are not married already, *make* them marry. And as for wedding clothes, do not let them wait for that, but tell Lydia she shall have as much money as she chooses to buy them, after they are married. And, above all, keep Mr. Bennet from fighting. Tell him what a dreadful state I am in, that I am frighted out of my wits—and have such tremblings, such flutterings, all over me—such spasms in my side and pains in my head, and such beatings at heart, that I can get no rest by night nor by day. And tell my dear Lydia not to give any directions about her clothes till she has seen me, for she does not know which are the best warehouses. Oh, brother, how kind you are! I know you will contrive it all."

But Mr. Gardiner, though he assured her again of his earnest endeavours in the cause, could not avoid recommending moderation to her, as well in her hopes as her fear; and after talking with her in this manner till dinner was on the table, they all left her to vent all her feelings on the housekeeper, who attended in the absence of her daughters.

Though her brother and sister were persuaded that there was no real occasion for such a seclusion from the family, they did not attempt to oppose it, for they knew that she had not prudence enough to hold her tongue before the servants, while they waited at table, and judged it better that *one* only of the household, and the one whom they could most trust should comprehend all her fears and solicitude on the subject.

In the dining-room they were soon joined by Mary and Kitty, who had been too busily engaged in their separate apartments to make their appearance before. One came from her books, and the other from her toilette. The faces of both, however, were tolerably calm; and no change was visible in either, except that the loss of her favourite sister, or the anger which she had herself incurred in this business, had given more of fretfulness than usual to the accents of Kitty. As for Mary, she was mistress enough of herself to whisper to Lizzy, with a countenance of grave reflection, soon after they were seated at table:

"This is a most unfortunate affair, and will probably be much talked of. But we must stem the tide of malice, and pour into the wounded bosoms of each other the balm of sisterly consolation."

Then, perceiving in Lizzy no inclination of replying, she added, "Unhappy as the event must be for Lydia, we may draw from it this useful lesson: that loss of virtue in a female is irretrievable; that one false step involves her in endless ruin; that her reputation is no less brittle than it is beautiful; and that she cannot be too much guarded in her behaviour towards the undeserving of the other sex."

Lizzy lifted up her eyes in amazement, but was too much oppressed to make any reply. Mary, however, continued to console herself with such kind of moral extractions from the evil before them.

In the afternoon, the two elder Miss Bennets were able to be for half-an-hour by themselves; and Lizzy instantly availed herself of the opportunity of making any inquiries, which Jane was equally eager to satisfy. After joining in general lamentations over the dreadful sequel of this event, which Lizzy considered as all but certain, and Miss Bennet could not assert to be wholly impossible, the former continued the subject, by saying, "But tell me all and everything about it which I have not already heard. Give me further particulars. What did Colonel Forster say? Had they no apprehension of anything before the elopement took place? They must have seen them together for ever."

"Colonel Forster did own that he had often suspected some partiality, especially on Lydia's side, but nothing to give him any alarm. I am so grieved for him! His behaviour was attentive and kind to the utmost. He *was* coming to us, in order to assure us of his concern, before he had any idea of their not being gone to Scotland: when that apprehension first got abroad, it hastened his journey."

"And was Denny convinced that Wickham would not marry? Did he know of their intending to go off? Had Colonel Forster seen Denny himself?"

"Yes; but, when questioned by *him*, Denny denied knowing anything of their plans, and would not give his real opinion about it. He did not repeat his persuasion of their not marrying—and from *that*, I am inclined to hope, he might have been misunderstood before."

"And till Colonel Forster came himself, not one of you entertained a doubt, I suppose, of their being really married?"

"How was it possible that such an idea should enter our brains? I felt a little uneasy—a little fearful of my sister's happiness with him in marriage, because I knew that his conduct had not been always quite right. My father and mother knew nothing of that; they only felt how imprudent a match it must be. Kitty then owned, with a very natural triumph on knowing more than the rest of us, that in Lydia's last letter she had prepared her for such a step. She had known, it seems, of their being in love with each other, many weeks."

"But not before they went to Brighton?"

"No, I believe not."

"And did Colonel Forster appear to think well of Wickham himself? Does he know his real character?"

"I must confess that he did not speak so well of Wickham as he formerly did. He believed him to be imprudent and extravagant. And since this sad affair has taken place, it is said that he left Meryton greatly in debt; but I hope this may be false."

"Oh, Jane, had we been less secret, had we told what we knew of him, this could not have happened!"

"Perhaps it would have been better," replied her sister. "But to expose the former faults of any person without knowing what their present feelings were, seemed unjustifiable. We acted with the best intentions."

"Could Colonel Forster repeat the particulars of Lydia's note to his wife?"

"He brought it with him for us to see."

Jane then took it from her pocket-book, and gave it to Lizzy. These were the contents:

"My dear Harriet,

"You will laugh when you know where I am gone, and I cannot help laughing myself at your surprise tomorrow morning, as soon as I am missed. I am going to Gretna Green, and if you cannot guess with who, I shall think you a simpleton, for there is but one man in the world I love, and he is an angel. I should never be happy without him, so think it no harm to be off. You need not send them word at Longbourn of my going, if you do not like it, for it will make the surprise the greater, when I write to them and sign my name 'Lydia Wickham.' What a good joke it will be! I can hardly write for laughing. Pray make my excuses to Pratt for not keeping my engagement, and dancing with him to-night. Tell him I hope he will excuse me when he knows all; and tell him I will dance with him at the next ball we meet, with great pleasure. I shall send for my clothes when I get to Longbourn; but I wish you would tell Sally to mend a great slit in my worked muslin gown before they are packed up. Good-bye. Give my love to Colonel Forster. I hope you will drink to our good journey.

"Your affectionate friend,
"Lydia Bennet"

"Oh! thoughtless, thoughtless Lydia!" cried Lizzy when she had finished it. "What a letter is this, to be written at such a moment! But at least it shows that *she* was serious on the subject of their journey. Whatever he might afterwards persuade her to, it was not on her side a *scheme* of infamy. My poor father! how he must have felt it!"

"I never saw anyone so shocked. He could not speak a word for full ten minutes. My mother was taken ill immediately, and the whole house in such confusion!"

"Oh! Jane," cried Lizzy, "was there a servant belonging to it who did not know the whole story before the end of the day?"

"I do not know. I hope there was. But to be guarded at such a time is very difficult. My mother was in hysterics, and though I endeavoured to give her every assistance in my power, I am afraid I did not do so much as I might have done! But the horror of what might possibly happen almost took from me my faculties."

"Your attendance upon her has been too much for you. You do not look well. Oh that I had been with you! you have had every care and anxiety upon yourself alone."

"Mary and Kitty have been very kind, and would have shared in every fatigue, I am sure; but I did not think it right for either of them. Kitty is slight and delicate; and Mary studies so much, that her hours of repose should not be broken in on. My aunt Phillips came to Longbourn on Tuesday, after my father went away; and was so good as to stay till Thursday with me. She was of great use and comfort to us all. And Lady Lucas has been very kind; she walked here on Wednesday morning to condole with us, and offered her services, or any of her daughters', if they should be of use to us."

"She had better have stayed at home," cried Lizzy; "perhaps she *meant* well, but, under such a misfortune as this, one cannot see too little of one's neighbours. Assistance is impossible; condolence insufferable. Let them triumph over us at a distance, and be satisfied."

She then proceeded to inquire into the measures which her father had intended to pursue, while in town, for the recovery of his daughter.

"He meant I believe," replied Jane, "to go to Epsom, the place where they last changed horses, see the postilions and try if anything could be made out from them. His principal object must be to discover the number of the hackney coach which took them from Clapham. It had come with a fare from London; and as he thought that the circumstance of a gentleman and lady's removing from one carriage into another might be remarked he meant to make inquiries at Clapham. If he could anyhow discover at what house the coachman had before set down his fare, he determined to make inquiries there, and hoped it might not be impossible to find out the stand and number of the coach. I do not know of any other designs that he had formed; but he was in such a hurry to be gone, and his spirits so greatly discomposed, that I had difficulty in finding out even so much as this."

CHAPTER FORTY

The whole party were in hopes of a letter from Mr. Bennet the next morning, but the post came in without bringing a single line from him. His family knew him to be, on all common occasions, a most negligent and dilatory correspondent; but at such a time they had hoped for exertion. They were forced to conclude that he had no pleasing intelligence to send; but even of *that* they would have been glad to be certain. Mr. Gardiner had waited only for the letters before he set off.

When he was gone, they were certain at least of receiving constant information of what was going on, and their uncle promised, at parting, to prevail on Mr. Bennet to return to Longbourn, as soon as he could, to the great consolation of his sister, who considered it as the only security for her husband's not being killed in a duel.

Mrs. Gardiner and the children were to remain in Hertfordshire a few days longer, as the former thought her presence might be serviceable to her nieces. She shared in their attendance on Mrs. Bennet, and was a great comfort to them in their hours of freedom. Their other aunt also visited them frequently, and always, as she said, with the design of cheering and heartening them up—though, as she never came without reporting some fresh instance of Wickham's extravagance or irregularity, she seldom went away without leaving them more dispirited than she found them.

All Meryton seemed striving to blacken the man who, but three months before, had been almost an angel of light. He was declared to be in debt to every tradesman in the place, and his intrigues, all honoured with the title of seduction, had been extended into every tradesman's family. Everybody declared that he was the wickedest young man in the world; and everybody began to find out that they had always distrusted the appearance of his goodness. Lizzy, though she did not credit above half of what was said, believed enough to make her former assurance of her sister's ruin more certain; and even Jane, who believed still less of it, became almost hopeless, more especially as the time was now come when, if they had gone to Scotland, which she had never before entirely despaired of, they must in all probability have gained some news of them.

Mr. Gardiner left Longbourn on Sunday; on Tuesday his wife received a letter from him; it told them that, on his arrival, he had immediately found out his brother, and persuaded him to come to Gracechurch Street; that Mr. Bennet had been to Epsom and Clapham, before his arrival, but without gaining any satisfactory information; and that he was now determined to inquire at all the principal hotels in town, as Mr. Bennet thought it possible they might have gone to one of them, on their first coming to London, before they procured lodgings. Mr. Gardiner himself did not expect any success from this measure, but as his brother was eager in it, he meant to assist him in pursuing it. He added that Mr. Bennet seemed wholly disinclined at present to leave London and promised to write again very soon. There was also a postscript to this effect:

"I have written to Colonel Forster to desire him to find out, if possible, from some of the young man's intimates in the regiment, whether Wickham has any relations or connections who would be likely to know in what part of town he has now concealed himself. If there were anyone that one could apply to with a probability of gaining such a clue as that, it might be of essential consequence. At present we have nothing to guide us. Colonel Forster will, I dare say, do everything in his power to satisfy us on this head. But, on second thoughts, perhaps, Lizzy could tell us what relations he has now living, better than any other person."

Lizzy was at no loss to understand from whence this deference to her authority proceeded; but it was not in her power to give any information of so satisfactory a nature as the compliment deserved. She had never heard of his having had any relations, except a father and mother, both of whom had been dead many years. It was possible, however, that some of his companions in the ——shire might be able to give more information; and though she was not very sanguine in expecting it, the application was a something to look forward to.

Every day at Longbourn was now a day of anxiety; but the most anxious part of each was when the post was expected. The arrival of letters was the grand object of every morning's impatience. Through letters, whatever of good or bad was to be told would be communicated, and every succeeding day was expected to bring some news of importance.

But before they heard again from Mr. Gardiner, a letter arrived for their father, from a different quarter, from Mr. Collins; which, as Jane had received directions to open all that came for him in his absence, she accordingly read; and Lizzy, who knew what curiosities his letters always were, looked over her, and read it likewise. It was as follows:

"My dear sir,

"I feel myself called upon, by our relationship, and my situation in life, to condole with you on the grievous affliction you are now suffering under, of which we were yesterday informed by a letter from Hertfordshire. Be assured, my dear sir, that Mrs. Collins and myself sincerely sympathise with you and all your respectable family, in your present distress, which must be of the bitterest kind, because proceeding from a cause which no time can remove. No arguments shall be wanting on my part that can alleviate so severe a misfortune—or that may comfort you, under a circumstance that must be of all others the most afflicting to a parent's mind. The death of your daughter would have been a blessing in comparison of this. And it is the more to be lamented, because there is reason to suppose as my dear Charlotte informs me, that this licentiousness of behaviour in your daughter has proceeded from a faulty degree of indulgence; though, at the same time, for the consolation of yourself and Mrs. Bennet, I am inclined to think that her own disposition must be naturally bad, or she could not be guilty of such an enormity, at so early an age. Howsoever that may be, you are grievously to be pitied; in which opinion I am not only joined by Mrs. Collins, but likewise by Lady Catherine and her daughter, to whom I have related the affair. They agree with me in apprehending that this false step in one daughter will be injurious to the fortunes of all the others; for who, as Lady Catherine herself condescendingly says, will connect themselves with such a family? And this consideration leads me moreover to reflect, with augmented satisfaction, on a certain event of last November; for had it been otherwise, I must have been involved in all your sorrow and disgrace. Let me then advise you, dear sir, to console yourself as much as possible, to throw off your unworthy child from your affection for ever, and leave her to reap the fruits of her own heinous offense.

"I am, dear sir, etc., etc."

Mr. Gardiner did not write again till he had received an answer from Colonel Forster; and then he had nothing of a pleasant nature to send. It was not known that Wickham had a single relationship with whom he kept up any connection, and it was certain that he had no near one living. His former acquaintances had been numerous; but since he had been in the militia, it did not appear that he was on terms of particular friendship with any of them. There was no one, therefore, who could be pointed out as likely to give any news of him. And in the wretched state of his own finances, there was a very powerful motive for secrecy, in addition to his fear of discovery by Lydia's relations, for it had just transpired that he had left gaming debts behind him to a very considerable amount. Colonel Forster believed that more than a thousand pounds would be necessary to clear his expenses at Brighton. He owed a good deal in town, but his debts of honour were still more formidable. Mr. Gardiner did not attempt to conceal these particulars from the Longbourn family. Jane heard them with horror. "A gamester!" she cried. "This is wholly unexpected. I had not an idea of it."

Mr. Gardiner added in his letter, that they might expect to see their father at home on the following day, which was Saturday. Rendered spiritless by the ill-success of all their endeavours, he had yielded to his brother-in-law's entreaty that he would return to his family, and leave it to him to do whatever occasion might suggest to be advisable for continuing their pursuit. When Mrs. Bennet was told of this, she did not express so much satisfaction as her children expected, considering what her anxiety for his life had been before.

"What, is he coming home, and without poor Lydia?" she cried. "Sure he will not leave London before he has found them. Who is to fight Wickham, and make him marry her, if he comes away?"

As Mrs. Gardiner began to wish to be at home, it was settled that she and the children should go to London, at the same time that Mr. Bennet came from it. The coach, therefore, took them the first stage of their journey, and brought its master back to Longbourn.

Mrs. Gardiner went away in all the perplexity about Lizzy and her Derbyshire friend that had attended her from that part of the world. His name had never been voluntarily mentioned before them by her niece; and the kind of half-expectation which Mrs. Gardiner had formed, of their being followed by a letter from him, had ended in nothing. Lizzy had received none since her return that could come from Pemberley.

The present unhappy state of the family rendered any other excuse for the lowness of her spirits unnecessary; nothing, therefore, could be fairly conjectured from *that*, though Lizzy, who was by this time tolerably well acquainted with her own feelings, was perfectly aware that, had she known nothing of Darcy, she could have borne the dread of Lydia's infamy somewhat better. It would have spared her, she thought, one sleepless night out of two.

When Mr. Bennet arrived, he had all the appearance of his usual philosophic composure. He said as little as he had ever been in the habit of saying; made no mention of the business that had taken him away, and it was some time before his daughters had courage to speak of it.

It was not till the afternoon, when he had joined them at tea, that Lizzy ventured to introduce the subject; and then, on her briefly expressing her sorrow for what he must have endured, he replied, "Say nothing of that. Who should suffer but myself? It has been my own doing, and I ought to feel it."

"You must not be too severe upon yourself," replied Lizzy.

"You may well warn me against such an evil. Human nature is so prone to fall into it! No, Lizzy, let me once in my life feel how much I have been to blame. I am not afraid of being overpowered by the impression. It will pass away soon enough."

"Do you suppose them to be in London?"

"Yes; where else can they be so well concealed?"

"And Lydia used to want to go to London," added Kitty.

"She is happy then," said her father drily; "and her residence there will probably be of some duration."

Then after a short silence he continued:

"Lizzy, I bear you no ill-will for being justified in your advice to me last May, which, considering the event, shows some greatness of mind."

They were interrupted by Miss Bennet, who came to fetch her

mother's tea.

"This is a parade," he cried, "which does one good; it gives such an elegance to misfortune! Another day I will do the same; I will sit in my library, in my nightcap and powdering gown, and give as much trouble as I can; or, perhaps, I may defer it till Kitty runs away."

"I am not going to run away, papa," said Kitty fretfully. "If I should ever go to Brighton, I would behave better than Lydia."

"*You* go to Brighton. I would not trust you so near it as Eastbourne for fifty pounds! No, Kitty, I have at last learnt to be cautious, and you will feel the effects of it. No officer is ever to enter into my house again, nor even to pass through the village. Balls will be absolutely prohibited, unless you stand up with one of your sisters. And you are never to stir out of doors till you can prove that you have spent ten minutes of every day in a rational manner."

Kitty, who took all these threats in a serious light, began to cry.

"Well, well," said he, "do not make yourself unhappy. If you are a good girl for the next ten years, I will take you to a review at the end of them."

CHAPTER FORTY-ONE

Two days after Mr. Bennet's return, as Jane and Lizzy were walking together in the shrubbery behind the house, they saw the housekeeper coming towards them, and, concluding that she came to call them to their mother, went forward to meet her; but, instead of the expected summons, when they approached her, she said to Miss Bennet, "I beg your pardon, madam, for interrupting you, but I was in hopes you might have got some good news from town, so I took the liberty of coming to ask."

"What do you mean, Hill? We have heard nothing from town."

"Dear madam," cried Mrs. Hill, in great astonishment, "don't you know there is an express come for master from Mr. Gardiner? He has been here this half-hour, and master has had a letter."

Away ran the girls, too eager to get in to have time for speech. They ran through the vestibule into the breakfast-room; from thence to the library; their father was in neither; and they were on the point of seeking him up stairs with their mother, when they were met by the butler, who said:

"If you are looking for my master, ma'am, he is walking towards the little copse."

Upon this information, they instantly passed through the hall once more, and ran across the lawn after their father, who was deliberately pursuing his way towards a small wood on one side of the paddock.

Jane, who was not so light nor so much in the habit of running as Lizzy, soon lagged behind, while her sister, panting for breath, came up with him, and eagerly cried out:

"Oh, papa, what news—what news? Have you heard from my uncle?"

"Yes I have had a letter from him by express."

"Well, and what news does it bring—good or bad?"

"What is there of good to be expected?" said he, taking the letter from his pocket. "But perhaps you would like to read it."

Lizzy impatiently caught it from his hand. Jane now came up.

"Read it aloud," said their father, "for I hardly know myself what it is about."

"Gracechurch Street, Monday, August 2.

"MY DEAR BROTHER,

"At last I am able to send you some tidings of my niece, and such as, upon the whole, I hope it will give you satisfaction. Soon after you left me on Saturday, I was fortunate enough to find out in what part of London they were. The particulars I reserve till we meet; it is enough to know they are discovered. I have seen them both—"

"Then it is as I always hoped," cried Jane; "they are married!"

Lizzy read on, "I have seen them both. They are not married, nor can I find there was any intention of being so; but if you are willing to perform the engagements which I have ventured to make on your side, I hope it will not be long before they are. All that is required of you is, to assure to your daughter, by settlement, her equal share of the five thousand pounds secured among your children after the decease of yourself and my sister; and, moreover, to enter into an engagement of allowing her, during your life, one hundred pounds per annum. These are conditions which, considering everything, I had no hesitation in complying with, as far as I thought myself privileged, for you. I shall send this by express, that no time may be lost in bringing me your answer. You will easily comprehend, from these particulars, that Mr. Wickham's circumstances are not so hopeless as they are generally believed to be. The world has been deceived in that respect; and I am happy to say there will be some little money, even when all his debts are discharged, to settle on my niece, in addition to her own fortune. If, as I conclude will be the case, you send me full powers to act in your name throughout the whole of this business, I will immediately give directions to Haggerston for preparing a proper settlement. There will not be the smallest occasion for your coming to town again; therefore stay quiet at Longbourn, and depend on my diligence and care. Send back your answer as fast as you can, and be careful to write explicitly. We have judged it best that my niece should be married from this house, of which I hope you will approve.

She comes to us to-day. I shall write again as soon as anything more is determined on. Yours, etc.,

"EDW. GARDINER."

"Is it possible?" cried Lizzy, when she had finished. "Can it be possible that he will marry her?"

"Wickham is not so undeserving, then, as we thought him," said her sister. "My dear father, I congratulate you."

"And have you answered the letter?" cried Lizzy.

"No; but it must be done soon."

Most earnestly did she then entreaty him to lose no more time before he wrote.

"Oh! my dear father," she cried, "come back and write immediately. Consider how important every moment is in such a case."

"Let me write for you," said Jane, "if you dislike the trouble yourself."

"I dislike it very much," he replied; "but it must be done."

And so saying, he turned back with them, and walked towards the house.

"And may I ask—" said Lizzy; "but the terms, I suppose, must be complied with."

"Complied with! I am only ashamed of his asking so little."

"And they *must* marry! Yet he is *such* a man!"

"Yes, yes, they must marry. There is nothing else to be done. But there are two things that I want very much to know; one is, how much money your uncle has laid down to bring it about; and the other, how am I ever to pay him."

"Money! My uncle!" cried Jane, "what do you mean, sir?"

"I mean, that no man in his senses would marry Lydia on so slight a temptation as one hundred a year during my life, and fifty after I am gone."

"That is very true," said Lizzy; "though it had not occurred to me before. His debts to be discharged, and something still to remain! Oh! It must be my uncle's doings! Generous, good man, I am afraid he has distressed himself. A small sum could not do all this."

"No," said her father; "Wickham's a fool if he takes her with a farthing less than ten thousand pounds. I should be sorry to think so ill of him, in the very beginning of our relationship."

"Ten thousand pounds! Heaven forbid! How is half such a sum to be repaid?"

Mr. Bennet made no answer, and each of them, deep in thought, continued silent till they reached the house. Their father then went on to the library to write, and the girls walked into the breakfast-room.

"And they are really to be married!" cried Lizzy, as soon as they were by themselves. "How strange this is! And for *this* we are to be thankful. That they should marry, small as is their chance of happiness, and wretched as is his character, we are forced to rejoice. Oh, Lydia!"

"I comfort myself with thinking," replied Jane, "that he certainly would not marry Lydia if he had not a real regard for her. Though our kind uncle has done something towards clearing him, I cannot believe that ten thousand pounds, or anything like it, has been advanced. He has children of his own, and may have more. How could he spare half ten thousand pounds?"

"If he were ever able to learn what Wickham's debts have been," said Lizzy, "and how much is settled on his side on our sister, we shall exactly know what Mr. Gardiner has done for them, because Wickham has not sixpence of his own. The kindness of my uncle and aunt can never be requited. Their taking her home, and affording her their personal protection and countenance, is such a sacrifice to her advantage as years of gratitude cannot enough acknowledge. By this time she is actually with them! If such goodness does not make her miserable now, she will never deserve to be happy! What a meeting for her, when she first sees my aunt!"

"We must endeavour to forget all that has passed on either side," said Jane: "I hope and trust they will yet be happy. His consenting to marry her is a proof, I will believe, that he is come to a right way of thinking. Their mutual affection will steady them; and I flatter myself they will settle so quietly, and live in so rational a manner, as may in time make their past imprudence forgotten."

"Their conduct has been such," replied Lizzy, "as neither you, nor I, nor anybody can ever forget. It is useless to talk of it."

It now occurred to the girls that their mother was in all likelihood perfectly ignorant of what had happened. They went to the library, therefore, and asked their father whether he would not wish them to make it known to her. He was writing and, without raising his head,

PRIDE, PREJUDICE & PLEASURE

coolly replied:

"Just as you please."

"May we take my uncle's letter to read to her?"

"Take whatever you like, and get away."

Lizzy took the letter from his writing-table, and they went up stairs together. Mary and Kitty were both with Mrs. Bennet: one communication would, therefore, do for all. After a slight preparation for good news, the letter was read aloud. Mrs. Bennet could hardly contain herself. As soon as Jane had read Mr. Gardiner's hope of Lydia's being soon married, her joy burst forth, and every following sentence added to its exuberance. She was now in an irritation as violent from delight, as she had ever been fidgety from alarm and vexation. To know that her daughter would be married was enough. She was disturbed by no fear for her felicity, nor humbled by any remembrance of her misconduct.

"My dear, dear Lydia!" she cried. "This is delightful indeed! She will be married! I shall see her again! She will be married at sixteen! My good, kind brother! I knew how it would be. I knew he would manage everything! How I long to see her! And to see dear Wickham too! But the clothes, the wedding clothes! I will write to my sister Gardiner about them directly. Lizzy, my dear, run down to your father, and ask him how much he will give her. Stay, stay, I will go myself. Ring the bell, Kitty, for Hill. I will put on my things in a moment. My dear, dear Lydia! How merry we shall be together when we meet!"

Her eldest daughter endeavoured to give some relief to the violence of these transports, by leading her thoughts to the obligations which Mr. Gardiner's behaviour laid them all under.

"For we must attribute this happy conclusion," she added, "in a great measure to his kindness. We are persuaded that he has pledged himself to assist Mr. Wickham with money."

"Well," cried her mother, "it is all very right; who should do it but her own uncle? If he had not had a family of his own, I and my children must have had all his money, you know; and it is the first time we have ever had anything from him, except a few presents. Well! I am so happy! In a short time I shall have a daughter married. Mrs. Wickham! How well it sounds! And she was only sixteen last June. My dear Jane, I am in such a flutter, that I am sure I can't write; so I will dictate, and you write for me. We will settle with your father about the money afterwards; but the things should be ordered immediately."

She was then proceeding to all the particulars of calico, muslin, and cambric, and would shortly have dictated some very plentiful orders, had not Jane, though with some difficulty, persuaded her to wait till her father was at leisure to be consulted. One day's delay, she observed, would be of small importance; and her mother was too happy to be quite so obstinate as usual. Other schemes, too, came into her head.

"I will go to Meryton," said she, "as soon as I am dressed, and tell the good, good news to my sister Philips. And as I come back, I can call on Lady Lucas and Mrs. Long. Kitty, run down and order the carriage. An airing would do me a great deal of good, I am sure. Girls, can I do anything for you in Meryton? Oh! Here comes Hill! My dear Hill, have you heard the good news? Miss Lydia is going to be married; and you shall all have a bowl of punch to make merry at her wedding."

Mrs. Hill began instantly to express her joy. Lizzy received her congratulations amongst the rest, and then, sick of this folly, took refuge in her own room, that she might think with freedom.

Poor Lydia's situation must, at best, be bad enough; but that it was no worse, she had need to be thankful. She felt it so; and though, in looking forward, neither rational happiness nor worldly prosperity could be justly expected for her sister, in looking back to what they had feared, only two hours ago, she felt all the advantages of what they had gained.

CHAPTER FORTY-TWO

Mr. Bennet had very often wished before this period of his life that, instead of spending his whole income, he had laid by an annual sum for the better provision of his children, and of his wife, if she survived him. He now wished it more than ever. Had he done his duty in that respect, Lydia need not have been indebted to her uncle for whatever of honour or credit could now be purchased for her. The satisfaction of prevailing on one of the most worthless young men in Great Britain to be her husband might then have rested in its proper place.

He was seriously concerned that a cause of so little advantage to anyone should be forwarded at the sole expense of his brother-in-law, and he was determined, if possible, to find out the extent of his assistance, and to discharge the obligation as soon as he could.

When first Mr. Bennet had married, economy was held to be perfectly useless, for, of course, they were to have a son. The son was to join in cutting off the entail, as soon as he should be of age, and the widow and younger children would by that means be provided for. Five daughters successively entered the world, but yet the son was to come; and Mrs. Bennet, for many years after Lydia's birth, had been certain that he would. This event had at last been despaired of, but it was then too late to be saving. Mrs. Bennet had no turn for economy, and her husband's love of independence had alone prevented their exceeding their income.

Five thousand pounds was settled by marriage articles on Mrs. Bennet and the children. But in what proportions it should be divided amongst the latter depended on the will of the parents. This was one point, with regard to Lydia, at least, which was now to be settled, and Mr. Bennet could have no hesitation in acceding to the proposal before him. In terms of grateful acknowledgment for the kindness of his brother, though expressed most concisely, he then delivered on paper his perfect approbation of all that was done, and his willingness to fulfil the engagements that had been made for him. He had never before supposed that, could Wickham be prevailed on to marry his daughter, it would be done with so little inconvenience to himself as by the present arrangement. He would scarcely be ten pounds a year the loser by the hundred that was to be paid them; for, what with her board and pocket allowance, and the continual presents in money which passed to her through her mother's hands, Lydia's expenses had been very little within that sum.

That it would be done with such trifling exertion on his side, too, was another very welcome surprise; for his wish at present was to have as little trouble in the business as possible. When the first transports of rage which had produced his activity in seeking her were over, he naturally returned to all his former indolence. His letter was soon dispatched; for, though dilatory in undertaking business, he was quick in its execution. He begged to know further particulars of what he was indebted to his brother, but was too angry with Lydia to send any message to her.

The good news spread quickly through the house, and with proportionate speed through the neighbourhood. It was borne in the latter with decent philosophy. To be sure, it would have been more for the advantage of conversation had Miss Lydia Bennet come upon the town; or, as the happiest alternative, been secluded from the world, in some distant farmhouse. But there was much to be talked of in marrying her; and the good-natured wishes for her well-doing which had proceeded before from all the spiteful old ladies in Meryton lost but a little of their spirit in this change of circumstances, because with such an husband her misery was considered certain.

It was a fortnight since Mrs. Bennet had been downstairs; but on this happy day she again took her seat at the head of her table, and in spirits oppressively high. No sentiment of shame gave a damp to her triumph. The marriage of a daughter, which had been the first object of her wishes since Jane was sixteen, was now on the point of accomplishment, and her thoughts and her words ran wholly on those attendants of elegant nuptials, fine muslins, new carriages, and servants. She was busily searching through the neighbourhood for a proper situation for her daughter, and, without knowing or considering what their income might be, rejected many as deficient in size and importance.

"Haye Park might do," said she, "if the Gouldings could quit it—or the great house at Stoke, if the drawing-room were larger; but Ashworth is too far off! I could not bear to have her ten miles from me; and as for Pulvis Lodge, the attics are dreadful."

Her husband allowed her to talk on without interruption while the servants remained. But when they had withdrawn, he said to her: "Mrs. Bennet, before you take any or all of these houses for your son and daughter, let us come to a right understanding. Into *one* house in this neighbourhood they shall never have admittance. I will not encourage the impudence of either, by receiving them at Longbourn."

A long dispute followed this declaration; but Mr. Bennet was firm. It soon led to another; and Mrs. Bennet found, with amazement and horror, that her husband would not advance a guinea to buy clothes for his daughter. He protested that she should receive from him no mark of affection whatever on the occasion. Mrs. Bennet could hardly comprehend it. That his anger could be carried to such a point of inconceivable resentment as to refuse his daughter a privilege without which her marriage would scarcely seem valid, exceeded all she could believe possible. She was more alive to the disgrace which her want of new clothes must reflect on her daughter's nuptials, than to any sense of shame at her eloping and living with Wickham a fortnight before they took place.

Lizzy was now most heartily sorry that she had, from the distress of the moment, been led to make Mr. Darcy acquainted with their fears for her sister; for since her marriage would so shortly give the proper termination to the elopement, they might hope to conceal its unfavourable beginning from all those who were not immediately on the spot.

She had no fear of its spreading farther through his means. There were few people on whose secrecy she would have more confidently depended; but, at the same time, there was no one whose knowledge of a sister's frailty would have mortified her so much—not, however, from any fear of disadvantage from it individually to herself, for, at any rate, there seemed a gulf impassable between them. Had Lydia's marriage been concluded on the most honourable terms, it was not to be supposed that Mr. Darcy would connect himself with a family where, to every other objection, would now be added an alliance and relationship of the nearest kind with a man whom he so justly scorned.

From such a connection she could not wonder that he would shrink. The wish of procuring her regard, which she had assured herself of his feeling in Derbyshire, could not in rational expectation survive such a blow as this. She was humbled, she was grieved; she repented, though she hardly knew of what. She became jealous of his esteem, when she could no longer hope to be benefited by it. She wanted to hear of him, when there seemed the least chance of gaining intelligence. She was convinced that she could have been happy with him, when it was no longer likely they should meet.

What a triumph for him, as she often thought, could he know that the proposals which she had proudly spurned only four months ago, would now have been most gladly and gratefully received! He was as generous, she doubted not, as the most generous of his sex; but while he was mortal, there must be a triumph.

She began now to comprehend that he was exactly the man who, in disposition and talents, would most suit her. His understanding and temper, though unlike her own, would have answered all her wishes. It was an union that must have been to the advantage of both; by her ease and liveliness, his mind might have been softened, his manners improved; and from his judgment, information, and knowledge of the world, she must have received benefit of greater importance.

But no such happy marriage could now teach the admiring multitude what connubial felicity really was. An union of a different tendency, and precluding the possibility of the other, was soon to be formed in their family.

How Wickham and Lydia were to be supported in tolerable independence, she could not imagine. But how little of permanent happiness could belong to a couple who were only brought together because their passions were stronger than their virtue, she could easily conjecture.

* * * * *

Mr. Gardiner soon wrote again to his brother. To Mr. Bennet's acknowledgments he briefly replied, with assurance of his eagerness to promote the welfare of any of his family; and concluded with entreaties that the subject might never be mentioned to him again. The principal purport of his letter was to inform them that Mr. Wickham had resolved on quitting the militia.

"It was greatly my wish that he should do so," he added, "as soon as his marriage was fixed on. And I think you will agree with me, in considering the removal from that corps as highly advisable, both on his account and my niece's. It is Mr. Wickham's intention to go into the regulars; and among his former friends, there are still some who are able and willing to assist him in the army. He has the promise of an ensigncy in General Holland's regiment, now quartered in the North. It is an advantage to have it so far from this part of the kingdom. He promises fairly; and I hope among different people, where they may each have a character to preserve, they will both be more prudent. I have written to Colonel Forster, to inform him of our present arrangements, and to request that he will satisfy the various creditors of Mr. Wickham in and near Brighton, with assurances of speedy payment, for which I have pledged myself. And will you give yourself the trouble of carrying similar assurances to his creditors in Meryton, of whom I shall subjoin a list according to his information? He has given in all his debts; I hope at least he has not deceived us. Haggerston has our directions, and all will be completed in a week. They will then join his regiment, unless they are first invited to Longbourn; and I understand from Mrs. Gardiner, that my niece is very desirous of seeing you all before she leaves the South. She is well, and begs to be dutifully remembered to you and your mother. — Yours, etc.,

"E. GARDINER."

Mr. Bennet and his daughters saw all the advantages of Wickham's removal from his regiment as clearly as Mr. Gardiner could do. But Mrs. Bennet was not so well pleased with it. Lydia's being settled in the North, just when she had expected most pleasure and pride in her company, for she had by no means given up her plan of their residing in Hertfordshire, was a severe disappointment; and, besides, it was such a pity that Lydia should be taken from a regiment where she was acquainted with everybody, and had so many favourites.

"She is so fond of Mrs. Forster," said she, "it will be quite shocking to send her away! And there are several of the young men, too, that she likes very much. The officers may not be so pleasant in this regiment."

His daughter's request, for such it might be considered, of being admitted into her family again before she set off for the North, received at first an absolute negative. But Jane and Lizzy, who agreed in wishing, for the sake of their sister's feelings and consequence, that she should be noticed on her marriage by her parents, urged him so earnestly yet so rationally and so mildly, to receive her and her husband at Longbourn, as soon as they were married, that he was prevailed on to think as they thought, and act as they wished. And their mother had the satisfaction of knowing that she would be able to show her married daughter in the neighbourhood before she was banished to the North. When Mr. Bennet wrote again to his brother, therefore, he sent his permission for them to come; and it was settled, that as soon as the ceremony was over, they should proceed to Longbourn. Lizzy was surprised, however, that Wickham should consent to such a scheme, and had she consulted only her own inclination, any meeting with him would have been the last object of her wishes.

CHAPTER FORTY-THREE

Their sister's wedding day arrived; and Jane and Lizzy felt for her probably more than she felt for herself. The carriage was sent to meet them, and they were to return in it by dinner-time. Their arrival was dreaded by the elder Miss Bennets, and Jane more especially, who gave Lydia the feelings which would have attended herself, had she been the culprit, and was wretched in the thought of what her sister must endure.

They came. The family were assembled in the breakfast room to receive them. Smiles decked the face of Mrs. Bennet as the carriage drove up to the door; her husband looked impenetrably grave; her daughters, alarmed, anxious, uneasy.

Lydia's voice was heard in the vestibule; the door was thrown open, and she ran into the room. Her mother stepped forwards, embraced her, and welcomed her with rapture; gave her hand, with an affectionate smile, to Wickham, who followed his lady; and wished them both joy with an alacrity which shewed no doubt of their happiness.

Their reception from Mr. Bennet, to whom they then turned, was not quite so cordial. His countenance rather gained in austerity; and he scarcely opened his lips. The easy assurance of the young couple, indeed, was enough to provoke him. Lizzy was disgusted, and even Miss Bennet was shocked. Lydia was Lydia still; untamed, unabashed, wild, noisy, and fearless. She turned from sister to sister, demanding their congratulations; and when at length they all sat down, looked eagerly round the room, took notice of some little alteration in it, and observed, with a laugh, that it was a great while since she had been there.

Wickham was not at all more distressed than herself, but his manners were always so pleasing, that had his character and his marriage been exactly what they ought, his smiles and his easy address, while he claimed their relationship, would have delighted them all. Lizzy had not before believed him quite equal to such assurance; but she sat down, resolving within herself to draw no limits in future to the impudence of an impudent man. She blushed, and Jane blushed; but the cheeks of the two who caused their confusion suffered no variation of colour.

There was no want of discourse. The bride and her mother could neither of them talk fast enough; and Wickham, who happened to sit near Lizzy, began inquiring after his acquaintance in that neighbourhood, with a good humoured ease which she felt very unable to equal in her replies. They seemed each of them to have the happiest memories in the world. Nothing of the past was recollected with pain; and Lydia led voluntarily to subjects which her sisters would not have alluded to for the world.

"Only think of its being three months," she cried, "since I went away; it seems but a fortnight I declare; and yet there have been things enough happened in the time. Good gracious! When I went away, I am sure I had no more idea of being married till I came back again! Though I thought it would be very good fun if I was."

Her father lifted up his eyes. Jane was distressed. Lizzy looked expressively at Lydia; but she, who never heard nor saw anything of which she chose to be insensible, gaily continued, "Oh! Mamma, do the people hereabouts know I am married to-day? I was afraid they might not; and we overtook William Goulding in his curricle, so I was determined he should know it, and so I let down the side-glass next to him, and took off my glove, and let my hand just rest upon the window frame, so that he might see the ring, and then I bowed and smiled like anything."

Lizzy could bear it no longer. She got up, and ran out of the room; and returned no more, till she heard them passing through the hall to the dining parlour. She then joined them soon enough to see Lydia, with anxious parade, walk up to her mother's right hand, and hear her say to her eldest sister, "Ah! Jane, I take your place now, and you must go lower, because I am a married woman."

It was not to be supposed that time would give Lydia that embarrassment from which she had been so wholly free at first. Her ease and good spirits increased. She longed to see Mrs. Phillips, the Lucases, and all their other neighbours, and to hear herself called "Mrs. Wickham" by each of them; and in the mean time, she went after dinner to show her ring, and boast of being married, to Mrs. Hill and the two housemaids.

"Well, mamma," said she, when they were all returned to the breakfast room, "and what do you think of my husband? Is not he a charming man? I am sure my sisters must all envy me. I only hope they may have half my good luck. They must all go to Brighton. That is the place to get husbands. What a pity it is, mamma, we did not all go."

"Very true; and if I had my will, we should. But my dear Lydia, I don't at all like your going such a way off. Must it be so?"

"Oh, lord! Yes;—there is nothing in that. I shall like it of all things. You and papa, and my sisters, must come down and see us. We shall be at Newcastle all the winter, and I dare say there will be some balls, and I will take care to get good partners for them all."

"I should like it beyond anything!" said her mother.

"And then when you go away, you may leave one or two of my sisters behind you; and I dare say I shall get husbands for them before the winter is over."

"I thank you for my share of the favour," said Lizzy; "but I do not particularly like your way of getting husbands."

Their visitors were not to remain above ten days with them. Mr. Wickham had received his commission before he left London, and he was to join his regiment at the end of a fortnight.

No one but Mrs. Bennet regretted that their stay would be so short; and she made the most of the time by visiting about with her daughter, and having very frequent parties at home. These parties were acceptable to all; to avoid a family circle was even more desirable to such as did think, than such as did not.

Wickham's affection for Lydia was just what Lizzy had expected to find it; not equal to Lydia's for him. She had scarcely needed her present observation to be satisfied, from the reason of things, that their elopement had been brought on by the strength of her love, rather than by his; and she would have wondered why, without violently caring for her, he chose to elope with her at all, had she not felt certain that his flight was rendered necessary by distress of circumstances; and if that were the case, he was not the young man to resist an opportunity of having a companion.

Lydia was exceedingly fond of him. He was her dear Wickham on every occasion; no one was to be put in competition with him. He did every thing best in the world; and she was sure he would kill more birds on the first of September, than any body else in the country.

One morning, soon after their arrival, as she was sitting with her two elder sisters, she said to Lizzy:

"Lizzy, I never gave *you* an account of my wedding, I believe. You were not by, when I told mamma and the others all about it. Are not you curious to hear how it was managed?"

"No really," replied Lizzy; "I think there cannot be too little said on the subject."

"La! You are so strange! But I must tell you how it went off. We were married, you know, at St. Clement's, because Wickham's lodgings were in that parish. And it was settled that we should all be there by eleven o'clock. My uncle and aunt and I were to go together; and the others were to meet us at the church. Well, Monday morning came, and I was in such a fuss! I was so afraid, you know, that something would happen to put it off, and then I should have gone quite distracted. And there was my aunt, all the time I was dressing, preaching and talking away just as if she was reading a sermon. However, I did not hear above one word in ten, for I was thinking, you may suppose, of my dear Wickham. I longed to know whether he would be married in his blue coat.

"Well, and so we breakfasted at ten as usual; I thought it would never be over; for, by the bye, you are to understand, that my uncle and aunt were horrid unpleasant all the time I was with them. If you'll believe me, I did not once put my foot out of doors, though I was there a fortnight. Not one party, or scheme, or anything. To be sure London was rather thin, but, however, the Little Theatre was open. Well, and so just as the carriage came to the door, my uncle was called away upon business to that horrid man Mr. Stone. And then, you know, when once they get together, there is no end of it. Well, I was so frightened I did not know what to do, for my uncle was to give me away; and if we were beyond the hour, we could not be married all day. But, luckily, he came back again in ten minutes' time, and then we all set out. However, I recollected afterwards that if he had been prevented going, the wedding need not be put off, for Mr. Darcy might have done as well."

"Mr. Darcy!" repeated Lizzy, in utter amazement.

"Oh, yes!—he was to come there with Wickham, you know. But gracious me! I quite forgot! I ought not to have said a word about it. I promised them so faithfully! What will Wickham say? It was to be such a secret!"

"If it was to be secret," said Jane, "say not another word on the subject. You may depend upon my seeking no further."

"Oh! certainly," said Lizzy, though burning with curiosity; "we will ask you no questions."

"Thank you," said Lydia, "for if you did, I should certainly tell you all, and then Wickham would be angry."

On such encouragement to ask, Lizzy was forced to put it out of her power, by running away.

But to live in ignorance on such a point was impossible; or at least it was impossible not to try for information. Mr. Darcy had been at her sister's wedding. It was exactly a scene, and exactly among people, where he had apparently least to do, and least temptation to go. Conjectures as to the meaning of it, rapid and wild, hurried into her brain; but she was satisfied with none. Those that best pleased her, as placing his conduct in the noblest light, seemed most improbable. She could not bear such suspense; and hastily seizing a sheet of paper, wrote a short letter to her aunt, to request an explanation of what Lydia had dropt, if it were compatible with the secrecy which had been intended.

"You may readily comprehend," she added, "what my curiosity must be to know how a person unconnected with any of us, and (comparatively speaking) a stranger to our family, should have been amongst you at such a time. Pray write instantly, and let me understand it—unless it is, for very cogent reasons, to remain in the secrecy which Lydia seems to think necessary; and then I must endeavour to be satisfied with ignorance.

"Not that I *shall*, though," she added to herself, as she finished the letter; "and my dear aunt, if you do not tell me in an honourable manner, I shall certainly be reduced to tricks and stratagems to find it out."

Jane's delicate sense of honour would not allow her to speak to Lizzy privately of what Lydia had let fall; Lizzy was glad of it—till it appeared whether her inquiries would receive any satisfaction, she had rather be without a confidante.

CHAPTER FORTY-FOUR

Lizzy had the satisfaction of receiving an answer to her letter as soon as she possibly could. She was no sooner in possession of it than, hurrying into the little copse, where she was least likely to be interrupted, she sat down on one of the benches and prepared to be happy; for the length of the letter convinced her that it did not contain a denial.

"Gracechurch Street, Sept. 6.

"MY DEAR NIECE,

"I have just received your letter, and shall devote this whole morning to answering it, as I foresee that a *little* writing will not comprise what I have to tell you. I must confess myself surprised by your application; I did not expect it from *you*. Don't think me angry, however, for I only mean to let you know that I had not imagined such inquiries to be necessary on *your* side. If you do not choose to understand me, forgive my impertinence. Your uncle is as much surprised as I am—and nothing but the belief of your being a party concerned would have allowed him to act as he has done. But if you are really innocent and ignorant, I must be more explicit.

"On the very day of my coming home from Longbourn, your uncle had a most unexpected visitor. Mr. Darcy called, and was shut up with him several hours. It was all over before I arrived; so my curiosity was not so dreadfully racked as *yours* seems to have been. He came to tell Mr. Gardiner that he had found out where your sister and Mr. Wickham were, and that he had seen and talked with them both; Wickham repeatedly, Lydia once. From what I can collect, he left Derbyshire only one day after ourselves, and came to town with the resolution of hunting for them. The motive professed was his conviction of its being owing to himself that Wickham's worthlessness had not been so well known as to make it impossible for any young woman of character to love or confide in him. He generously imputed the whole to his mistaken pride, and confessed that he had before thought it beneath him to lay his private actions open to the world. His character was to speak for itself. He called it, therefore, his duty to step forward, and endeavour to remedy an evil which had been brought on by himself. If he *had another* motive, I am sure it would never disgrace him. He had been some days in town, before he was able to discover them; but he had something to direct his search, which was more than *we* had; and the consciousness of this was another reason for his resolving to follow us.

"There is a lady, it seems, a Mrs. Younge, who was some time ago governess to Miss Darcy, and was dismissed from her charge on some cause of disapprobation, though he did not say what. She then took a large house in Edward-street, and has since maintained herself by letting lodgings. This Mrs. Younge was, he knew, intimately acquainted with Wickham; and he went to her for intelligence of him as soon as he got to town. But it was two or three days before he could get from her what he wanted. She would not betray her trust, I suppose, without bribery and corruption, for she really did know where her friend was to be found. Wickham indeed had gone to her on their first arrival in London, and had she been able to receive them into her house, they would have taken up their abode with her. At length, however, our kind friend procured the wished-for direction. He saw Wickham first, and afterwards insisted on seeing Lydia. His first object with her, he acknowledged, had been to persuade her to quit her present disgraceful situation, and return to her friends as soon as they could be prevailed on to receive her, offering his assistance, as far as it would go. But he found Lydia absolutely resolved on remaining where she was. She cared for none of her friends; she wanted no help of his; she would not hear of leaving Wickham. She was sure they should be married some time or other, and it did not much signify when. Since such were her feelings, it only remained, he thought, to secure and expedite a marriage, which, in his very first conversation with Wickham, he easily learnt had never been *his* design. He confessed himself obliged to leave the regiment, on account of some debts of honour, which were very pressing; and scrupled not to lay all the ill-consequences of Lydia's flight on her own folly alone. He meant to resign his commission immediately; and as to his future situation, he could conjecture very little about it. He must go somewhere, but he did not know where, and he knew he should have nothing to live on.

"Mr. Darcy asked him why he had not married your sister at once. Though Mr. Bennet was not imagined to be very rich, he would have been able to do something for him, and his situation must have been benefited by marriage. But he found, in reply to this question, that Wickham still cherished the hope of more effectually making his fortune by marriage in some other country. Under such circumstances, however, he was not likely to be proof against the temptation of immediate relief.

"They met several times, for there was much to be discussed. Wickham of course wanted more than he could get; but at length was reduced to be reasonable.

"Every thing being settled between *them*, Mr. Darcy's next step was to make your uncle acquainted with it, and he first called in Gracechurch Street the evening before I came home. But Mr. Gardiner could not be seen, and Mr. Darcy found, on further inquiry, that your father was still with him, but would quit town the next morning. He did not judge your father to be a person whom he could so properly consult as your uncle, and therefore readily postponed seeing him till after the departure of the former. He did not leave his name, and till the next day it was only known that a gentleman had called on business.

"On Saturday he came again. Your father was gone, your uncle at home, and, as I said before, they had a great deal of talk together.

"They met again on Sunday, and then *I* saw him too. It was not all settled before Monday: as soon as it was, the express was sent off to Longbourn. But our visitor was very obstinate. I fancy, Lizzy, that obstinacy is the real defect of his character, after all. He has been accused of many faults at different times, but *this* is the true one. Nothing was to be done that he did not do himself; though I am sure (and I do not speak it to be thanked, therefore say nothing about it), your uncle would most readily have settled the whole.

"They battled it together for a long time, which was more than either the gentleman or lady concerned in it deserved. But at last your uncle was forced to yield, and instead of being allowed to be of use to his niece, was forced to put up with only having the probable credit of it, which went sorely against the grain; and I really believe your letter this morning gave him great pleasure, because it required an explanation that would rob him of his borrowed feathers, and give the praise where it was due. But, Lizzy, this must go no farther than yourself, or Jane at most.

"You know pretty well, I suppose, what has been done for the young people. His debts are to be paid, amounting, I believe, to considerably more than a thousand pounds, another thousand in addition to her own settled upon *her*, and his commission purchased. The reason why all this was to be done by him alone, was such as I have given above. It was owing to him, to his reserve and want of proper consideration, that Wickham's character had been so misunderstood, and consequently that he had been received and noticed as he was. Perhaps there was some truth in *this*; though I doubt whether *his* reserve, or *anybody's* reserve, can be answerable for the event. But in spite of all this fine talking, my dear Lizzy, you may rest perfectly assured that your uncle would never have yielded, if we had not given him credit for *another interest* in the affair.

"When all this was resolved on, he returned again to his friends, who were still staying at Pemberley; but it was agreed that he should be in London once more when the wedding took place, and all money matters were then to receive the last finish.

"I believe I have now told you every thing. It is a relation which you tell me is to give you great surprise; I hope at least it will not afford you any displeasure. Lydia came to us; and Wickham had constant admission to the house. *He* was exactly what he had been, when I knew him in Hertfordshire; but I would not tell you how little I was satisfied with her behaviour while she stayed with us, if I had not perceived, by Jane's letter last Wednesday, that her conduct on coming home was exactly of a piece with it, and therefore what I now tell you can give you no fresh pain. I talked to her repeatedly in the most serious manner, representing to her all the wickedness of what she had done, and all the unhappiness she had brought on her family. If she heard me, it was by good luck, for I am sure she did not listen. I was sometimes quite provoked, but then I recollected my dear Lizzy and Jane, and for their sakes had patience with her.

"Mr. Darcy was punctual in his return, and as Lydia informed you, attended the wedding. He dined with us the next day, and was to leave town again on Wednesday or Thursday. Will you be very angry with me, my dear Lizzy, if I take this opportunity of saying (what I was never bold enough to say before) how much I like him. His behaviour to us has, in every respect, been as pleasing as when we were in Derbyshire. His understanding and opinions all please me; he wants nothing but a little more liveliness, and *that*, if he marry *prudently*, his wife may teach him. I thought him very sly; he hardly ever mentioned your name. But slyness seems the fashion.

"Pray forgive me if I have been very presuming, or at least do not punish me so far as to exclude me from P. I shall never be quite happy till I have been all round the park. A low phaeton, with a nice little pair of ponies, would be the very thing.

"But I must write no more. The children have been wanting me this half hour.

"Yours, very sincerely,

"M. GARDINER."

The contents of this letter threw Lizzy into a flutter of spirits, in which it was difficult to determine whether pleasure or pain bore the greatest share. The vague and unsettled suspicions which uncertainty had produced of what Mr. Darcy might have been doing to forward her sister's match, which she had feared to encourage as an exertion of goodness too great to be probable, and at the same time dreaded to be just, from the pain of obligation, were proved beyond their greatest extent to be true! He had followed them purposely to town, he had taken on himself all the trouble and mortification attendant on such a research; in which supplication had been necessary to a woman whom he must abominate and despise, and where he was reduced to meet, frequently meet, reason with, persuade, and finally bribe, the man whom he always most wished to avoid, and whose very name it was punishment to him to pronounce. He had done all this for a girl whom he could neither regard nor esteem. Her heart did whisper that he had done it for her. But it was a hope shortly checked by other considerations, and she soon felt that even her vanity was insufficient, when required to depend on his affection for her—for a woman who had already refused him—as able to overcome a sentiment so natural as abhorrence against relationship with Wickham. Brother-in-law of Wickham! Every kind of pride must revolt from the connection. He had, to be sure, done much. She was ashamed to think how much. But he had given a reason for his interference, which asked no extraordinary stretch of belief. It was reasonable that he should feel he had been wrong; he had liberality, and he had the means of exercising it; and though she would not place herself as his principal inducement, she could, perhaps, believe that remaining partiality for her might assist his endeavours in a cause where her peace of mind must be materially concerned. It was painful, exceedingly painful, to know that they were under obligations to a person who could never receive a return. They owed the restoration of Lydia, her character, every thing, to him. Oh! how heartily did she grieve over every ungracious sensation she had ever encouraged, every saucy speech she had ever directed towards him. For herself she was humbled; but she was proud of him. Proud that in a cause of compassion and honour, he had been able to get the better of himself. She read over her aunt's commendation of him again and again. It was hardly enough; but it pleased her. She was even sensible of some pleasure, though mixed with regret, on finding how steadfastly both she and her uncle had been persuaded that affection and confidence subsisted between Mr. Darcy and herself.

She was roused from her seat, and her reflections, by some one's approach; and before she could strike into another path, she was overtaken by Wickham.

"I am afraid I interrupt your solitary ramble, my dear sister?" said he, as he joined her.

"You certainly do," she replied with a smile; "but it does not follow that the interruption must be unwelcome."

"I should be sorry indeed, if it were. We were always good friends; and now we are better."

"True. Are the others coming out?"

"I do not know. Mrs. Bennet and Lydia are going in the carriage to Meryton. And so, my dear sister, I find, from our uncle and aunt, that you have actually seen Pemberley."

She replied in the affirmative.

"I almost envy you the pleasure, and yet I believe it would be too much for me, or else I could take it in my way to Newcastle. And you saw the old housekeeper, I suppose? Poor Reynolds, she was always very fond of me. But of course she did not mention my name to you."

"Yes, she did."

"And what did she say?"

"That you were gone into the army, and she was afraid had—not turned out well. At such a distance as *that*, you know, things are strangely misrepresented."

"Certainly," he replied, biting his lips. Lizzy hoped she had silenced him; but he soon afterwards said:

"I was surprised to see Darcy in town last month. We passed each other several times. I wonder what he can be doing there."

"Perhaps preparing for his marriage with Miss de Bourgh," said Lizzy. "It must be something particular, to take him there at this time of year."

"Undoubtedly. Did you see him while you were at Lambton? I thought I understood from the Gardiners that you had."

"Yes; he introduced us to his sister."

"And do you like her?"

"Very much."

"I have heard, indeed, that she is uncommonly improved within this year or two. When I last saw her, she was not very promising. I am very glad you liked her. I hope she will turn out well."

"I dare say she will; she has got over the most trying age."

"Did you go by the village of Kympton?"

"I do not recollect that we did."

"I mention it, because it is the living which I ought to have had. A most delightful place! Excellent Parsonage House! It would have suited me in every respect."

"How should you have liked making sermons?"

"Exceedingly well. I should have considered it as part of my duty, and the exertion would soon have been nothing. One ought not to repine; but, to be sure, it would have been such a thing for me! The quiet, the retirement of such a life would have answered all my ideas of happiness! But it was not to be. Did you ever hear Darcy mention the circumstance, when you were in Kent?"

"I have heard from authority, which I thought *as good*, that it was left you conditionally only, and at the will of the present patron."

"You have. Yes, there was something in *that*; I told you so from the first, you may remember."

"I *did* hear, too, that there was a time, when sermon-making was not so palatable to you as it seems to be at present; that you actually declared your resolution of never taking orders, and that the business had been compromised accordingly."

"You did! And it was not wholly without foundation. You may remember what I told you on that point, when first we talked of it."

They were now almost at the door of the house, for she had walked fast to get rid of him; and unwilling, for her sister's sake, to provoke him, she only said in reply, with a good-humoured smile:

"Come, Mr. Wickham, we are brother and sister, you know. Do not let us quarrel about the past. In future, I hope we shall be always of one mind."

She held out her hand; he kissed it with affectionate gallantry, though he hardly knew how to look, and they entered the house.

CHAPTER FORTY-FIVE

Mr. Wickham was so perfectly satisfied with this conversation that he never again distressed himself, or provoked his dear sister Lizzy, by introducing the subject of it; and she was pleased to find that she had said enough to keep him quiet.

The day of his and Lydia's departure soon came, and Mrs. Bennet was forced to submit to a separation, which, as her husband by no means entered into her scheme of their all going to Newcastle, was likely to continue at least a twelvemonth.

"Oh! my dear Lydia," she cried, "when shall we meet again?"

"Oh, lord! I don't know. Not these two or three years, perhaps."

"Write to me very often, my dear."

"As often as I can. But you know married women have never much time for writing. My sisters may write to *me*. They will have nothing else to do."

Mr. Wickham's adieus were much more affectionate than his wife's. He smiled, looked handsome, and said many pretty things.

"He is as fine a fellow," said Mr. Bennet, as soon as they were out of the house, "as ever I saw. He simpers, and smirks, and makes love to us all. I am prodigiously proud of him. I defy even Sir William Lucas himself to produce a more valuable son-in-law."

The loss of her daughter made Mrs. Bennet very dull for several days.

"I often think," said she, "that there is nothing so bad as parting with one's friends. One seems so forlorn without them."

"This is the consequence, you see, Madam, of marrying a daughter," said Lizzy. "It must make you better satisfied that your other four are single."

"It is no such thing. Lydia does not leave me because she is married, but only because her husband's regiment happens to be so far off. If that had been nearer, she would not have gone so soon."

But the spiritless condition which this event threw her into was shortly relieved, and her mind opened again to the agitation of hope, by an article of news which then began to be in circulation. The housekeeper at Netherfield had received orders to prepare for the arrival of her master, who was coming down in a day or two, to shoot there for several weeks. Mrs. Bennet was quite in the fidgets. She looked at Jane, and smiled and shook her head by turns.

"Well, well, and so Mr. Bingley is coming down, sister," said Mrs. Bennet to Mrs. Phillips. "Well, so much the better. Not that I care about it, though. He is nothing to us, you know, and I am sure *I* never want to see him again. But, however, he is very welcome to come to Netherfield, if he likes it. And who knows what *may* happen? But that is nothing to us. You know, sister, we agreed long ago never to mention a word about it. And so, is it quite certain he is coming?"

"You may depend on it," replied the other, "for Mrs. Nicholls was in Meryton last night; I saw her passing by, and went out myself on purpose to know the truth of it; and she told me that it was certain true. He comes down on Thursday at the latest, very likely on Wednesday. She was going to the butcher's, she told me, on purpose to order in some meat on Wednesday, and she has got three couple of ducks just fit to be killed."

Miss Bennet had not been able to hear of his coming without changing colour. It was many months since she had mentioned his name to Lizzy; but now, as soon as they were alone together, she said:

"I saw you look at me to-day, Lizzy, when my aunt told us of the present report; and I know I appeared distressed. But don't imagine it was from any silly cause. I was only confused for the moment, because I felt that I *should* be looked at. I do assure you that the news does not affect me either with pleasure or pain. I am glad of one thing, that he comes alone; because we shall see the less of him. Not that I am afraid of *myself*, but I dread other people's remarks."

Lizzy did not know what to make of it. Had she not seen him in Derbyshire, she might have supposed him capable of coming there with no other view than what was acknowledged; but she still thought him partial to Jane, and she wavered as to the greater probability of his coming there *with* his friend's permission, or being bold enough to come without it.

"Yet it is hard," she sometimes thought, "that this poor man cannot come to a house which he has legally hired, without raising all this speculation! I *will* leave him to himself."

In spite of what her sister declared, and really believed to be her feelings in the expectation of his arrival, Lizzy could easily perceive that her spirits were affected by it. They were more disturbed, more unequal, than she had often seen them.

The subject which had been so warmly canvassed between their parents, about a twelvemonth ago, was now brought forward again.

"As soon as ever Mr. Bingley comes, my dear," said Mrs. Bennet, "you will wait on him of course."

"No, no. You forced me into visiting him last year, and promised, if I went to see him, he should marry one of my daughters. But it ended in nothing, and I will not be sent on a fool's errand again."

His wife represented to him how absolutely necessary such an attention would be from all the neighbouring gentlemen, on his returning to Netherfield.

"'Tis an etiquette I despise," said he. "If he wants our society, let him seek it. He knows where we live. I will not spend my hours in running after my neighbours every time they go away and come back again."

"Well, all I know is, that it will be abominably rude if you do not wait on him. But, however, that shan't prevent my asking him to dine here, I am determined. We must have Mrs. Long and the Gouldings soon. That will make thirteen with ourselves, so there will be just room at table for him."

Consoled by this resolution, she was the better able to bear her husband's incivility; though it was very mortifying to know that her neighbours might all see Mr. Bingley, in consequence of it, before *they* did.

"I begin to be sorry that he comes at all," said Jane to her sister as the day of his arrival drew near. "It would be nothing; I could see him with perfect indifference, but I can hardly bear to hear it thus perpetually talked of. My mother means well; but she does not know, no one can know, how much I suffer from what she says. Happy shall I be, when his stay at Netherfield is over!"

"I wish I could say anything to comfort you," replied Lizzy; "but it is wholly out of my power. You must feel it; and the usual satisfaction of preaching patience to a sufferer is denied me, because you have always so much."

Mr. Bingley arrived. Mrs. Bennet, through the assistance of servants, contrived to have the earliest tidings of it, that the period of anxiety and fretfulness on her side might be as long as it could. She counted the days that must intervene before their invitation could be sent; hopeless of seeing him before. But on the third morning after his arrival in Hertfordshire, she saw him, from her dressing-room window, enter the paddock and ride towards the house.

Her daughters were eagerly called to partake of her joy. Jane resolutely kept her place at the table; but Lizzy, to satisfy her mother, went to the window—she looked—she saw Mr. Darcy with him, and sat down again by her sister.

"There is a gentleman with him, mamma," said Kitty, "who can it be?"

"Some acquaintance or other, my dear, I suppose; I am sure I do not know."

"La!" replied Kitty, "it looks just like that man that used to be with him before. Mr. what's-his-name. That tall, proud man."

"Good gracious! Mr. Darcy!—and so it does, I vow. Well, any friend of Mr. Bingley's will always be welcome here, to be sure; but else I must say that I hate the very sight of him."

Jane looked at Lizzy with surprise and concern. She knew but little of their meeting in Derbyshire, and therefore felt for the awkwardness which must attend her sister, in seeing him almost for the first time after receiving his explanatory letter. Both sisters were uncomfortable enough. Each felt for the other, and of course for themselves; and their mother talked on, of her dislike of Mr. Darcy, and her resolution to be civil to him only as Mr. Bingley's friend, without being heard by either of them. But Lizzy had sources of uneasiness which could not be suspected by Jane, to whom she had never yet had courage to show Mrs. Gardiner's letter, or to relate her own change of sentiment towards him. To Jane, he could be only a man whose proposals she had refused, and whose merit she had undervalued; but to her own more extensive information, he was the person to whom the whole family were indebted for the first of benefits, and whom she regarded herself with an interest, if not quite so tender, at least as reasonable and just as what Jane felt for Bingley. Her astonishment at his coming—at his coming to Netherfield, to Longbourn, and voluntarily seeking her again, was almost equal to what she had known on first witnessing his altered behaviour in Derbyshire.

* * * * *

Darcy could tell Bingley was anxious as they came upon Longbourn House. Though he shared his friend's disquiet, the abode before them was not one that the former would have sought to enter earlier in the year. A fortnight had yet to pass since last he saw Miss Elizabeth, but the absence might as well have lasted months. He had had every intention of assessing her sentiments when he had called upon her last at the inn and, depending upon the results, was ready to propose then and there. His love had grown and likewise his hunger for her. He wondered if the flame of desire would ever settle into a simmer. Each instance had only added fuel to the fire, quenching his thirst for the moment but tormenting him in between. He wanted dreadfully to reenact their intercourse at the cottage. There was still so much he could show her.

Bingley's eyes shined upon seeing Jane, who appeared flushed but received them with tolerable ease, and with a propriety of behaviour equally free from any symptom of resentment or any unnecessary complaisance. Miss Elizabeth said little to either gentleman and sat down again to her work. To Darcy, she appeared in good health and as lovely as ever. He was glad to see no effects of the tension that she must have suffered and was pleased that he had a hand in relieving her of further apprehensions.

Pleased and embarrassed, Bingley was received by Mrs. Bennet with a degree of civility that heightened the colour in her two daughters, especially when contrasted with the cold and ceremonious politeness of her curtsey and address to his friend. Though he had found it easy enough to be friendly in the company of the Gardiners, Darcy could not do the same at Longbourn. After inquiring after Mr. and Mrs. Gardiner, he fell into silence. Miss Elizabeth looked at him only once, and he could read nothing in her gaze. She had been less guarded in Derbyshire, and he wondered what would have occasioned her reticence when she ought to have been more at ease in the comfort of her own home? Had the recent events taken a toll upon her after all? Was she embarrassed at having shared the truth of Lydia and Wickham with him? Or had some of her prior hostility, perhaps fanned by her mother, returned?

He was not seated by her, but he had a good view of her and her sister, whom he observed almost equally. Miss Bennet shared in some of her sister's reserve, though Bingley's attentions were increasingly animated and directed toward her. After what her sister had disclosed to him, Darcy began to understand Miss Bennet more in the light of shyness than indifference. But what could explain the behaviour of Miss Elizabeth, who wanted none of timidity? He had seen her flustered in Derbyshire, and he attributed her reaction to the surprise of his appearance and there having been no closure, of sorts, to the events at Hunsford. On the natural, she should be a little embarrassed, especially if she were ashamed, as Abby had indicated, of how she had judged him previously.

They had gotten over the awkwardness of meeting while in Derbyshire, or so he'd thought. She had seemed more receptive to his company. Had time and distance cooled her openness? Was she concerned that he had encouraged him too much in Derbyshire and feared that he might renew his offer? Women were creative creatures when they wished to make their interest known to the opposite sex. They might be demure in their attempts, but if a man is alert, the indications are there. A look, a word, a smile was often all that was necessary. Only the more introverted, such as Miss Bennet, or awkward women might appear apathetic. Miss Elizabeth was neither bashful nor inarticulate. That she refrained from engaging with him must signify a detachment. Through the whole of their visit, Miss Elizabeth inquired after his sister and said no more to him.

However, he allowed it was no easy matter to edge in a word through her mother's prattle.

"It is a long time, Mr. Bingley, since you went away," said Mrs. Bennet. "I began to be afraid you would never come back again. People *did* say you meant to quit the place entirely at Michaelmas; but, however, I hope it is not true. A great many changes have happened in the neighbourhood, since you went away. Miss Lucas is married and settled. And one of my own daughters. I suppose you have heard of it; indeed, you must have seen it in the papers. It was in The Times and The Courier, I know; though it was not put in as it ought to be. It was only said, 'Lately, George Wickham, Esq. to Miss Lydia Bennet,' without there being a syllable said of her father, or the place where she lived, or anything. It was my brother Gardiner's drawing up too, and I wonder how he came to make such an awkward business of it. Did you see it?"

Bingley replied that he did, and made his congratulations.

"It is a delightful thing, to be sure, to have a daughter well married," continued Mrs. Bennet, "but at the same time, Mr. Bingley, it is very hard to have her taken such a way from me. They are gone down to Newcastle, a place quite northward, it seems, and there they are to stay I do not know how long. His regiment is there; for I suppose you have heard of his leaving the militia, and of his being gone into the regulars. Thank Heaven! he has *some* friends, though perhaps not so many as he deserves."

Miss Elizabeth looked uncomfortable and asked of Bingley whether he meant to make any stay in the country at present.

"A few weeks, I believe," Bingley replied.

"When you have killed all your own birds, Mr. Bingley," said Mrs. Bennet, "I beg you will come here, and shoot as many as you please on Mr. Bennet's manor. I am sure he will be vastly happy to oblige you, and will save all the best of the covies for you."

When the gentlemen rose to go away, Mrs. Bennet invited and engaged them to dine at Longbourn in a few days' time.

"You are quite a visit in my debt, Mr. Bingley," she added, "for when you went to town last winter, you promised to take a family dinner with us, as soon as you returned. I have not forgot, you see; and I assure you, I was very much disappointed that you did not come back and keep your engagement."

Bingley looked a little silly at this reflection, and said something of his concern at having been prevented by business.

CHAPTER FORTY-SIX

Mrs. Bennet had been strongly inclined to ask them to stay and dine there that day; but, though she always kept a very good table, she did not think anything less than two courses could be good enough for a man on whom she had such anxious designs, or satisfy the appetite and pride of one who had ten thousand a year.

Lizzy was glad to see them go and the misery of the hour come to an end. Her mother's officious attention to Bingley, contrasted to her treatment of Mr. Darcy, had been excruciating. Knowing that her mother owed to Mr. Darcy the preservation of her favourite daughter from irremediable infamy, Lizzy had felt hurt and distressed to a most painful degree by a distinction so ill applied. Were the same fair prospect to arise at present as had flattered them a year ago, every thing, she was persuaded, would be hastening to the same vexatious conclusion. At that instant, she felt that years of happiness could not make Jane or herself amends for moments of such painful confusion.

"The first wish of my heart," she had said to herself, "is never more to be in company with either of them. Their society can afford no pleasure that will atone for such wretchedness as this! Let me never see either one or the other again!"

As soon as they were gone, Lizzy walked out to recover her spirits; or in other words, to dwell without interruption on those subjects that must deaden them more. Mr. Darcy's behaviour astonished and vexed her.

"Why, if he came only to be silent, grave, and indifferent," said she, "did he come at all?"

She could settle it in no way that gave her pleasure.

"He could be still amiable, still pleasing, to my uncle and aunt, when he was in town; and why not to me? If he fears me, why come hither? If he no longer cares for me, why silent? Teasing, teasing, man! I will think no more about him."

Her resolution was for a short time involuntarily kept by the approach of her sister, who joined her with a cheerful look, which showed her better satisfied with their visitors, than Lizzy.

"Now," said she, "that this first meeting is over, I feel perfectly easy. I know my own strength, and I shall never be embarrassed again by his coming. I am glad he dines here on Tuesday. It will then be publicly seen that, on both sides, we meet only as common and indifferent acquaintances."

"Yes, very indifferent indeed," said Lizzy, laughingly. "Oh, Jane, take care."

"My dear Lizzy, you cannot think me so weak, as to be in danger now?"

"I think you are in very great danger of making him as much in love with you as ever."

The happy part of the afternoon was seeing how much the beauty of her sister re-kindled the admiration of her former lover. When first he came in, he had spoken to her but little, but every five minutes seemed to be giving her more of his attention. It was clear he found her as handsome as she had been last year; as good natured, and as unaffected, though not quite so chatty. Jane was anxious that no difference should be perceived in her at all, and was really persuaded that she talked as much as ever. But her mind was so busily engaged, that she did not always know when she was silent.

* * * * *

They did not see the gentlemen again till Tuesday. Mrs. Bennet, in the meanwhile, was giving way to all the happy schemes, which the good humour and common politeness of Bingley, in half an hour's visit, had revived.

On Tuesday there was a large party assembled at Longbourn; and the two who were most anxiously expected, to the credit of their punctuality as sportsmen, were in very good time. When they repaired to the dining-room, Lizzy eagerly watched to see whether Bingley would take the place, which, in all their former parties, had belonged to him, by her sister. Her prudent mother, occupied by the same ideas, forbore to invite him to sit by herself. On entering the room, he seemed to hesitate, but Jane happened to look round, and happened to smile: it was decided. He placed himself by her.

Lizzy, with a triumphant sensation, looked towards his friend. He bore it with noble indifference, and she would have imagined that Bingley had received his sanction to be happy, had she not seen his eyes likewise turned towards Mr. Darcy, with an expression of half-laughing alarm. His behaviour to her sister was such, during dinner time, as showed an admiration of her, which, though more guarded than formerly, persuaded Lizzy, that if left wholly to himself, Jane's happiness, and his own, would be speedily secured. Though she dared not depend upon the consequence, she yet received pleasure from observing his behaviour. It gave her all the animation that her spirits could boast; for she was in no cheerful humour. Mr. Darcy was almost as far from her as the table could divide them. He was on one side of her mother. She knew how little such a situation would give pleasure to either, or make either appear to advantage. She was not near enough to hear any of their discourse, but she could see how seldom they spoke to each other, and how formal and cold was their manner whenever they did. Her mother's ungraciousness, made the sense of what they owed him more painful to Lizzy's mind; and she would, at times, have given anything to be privileged to tell him that his kindness was neither unknown nor unfelt by the whole of the family.

She was in hopes that the evening would afford some opportunity of bringing them together, that the whole of the visit would not pass away without enabling them to enter into something more of conversation than the mere ceremonious salutation attending his entrance. Anxious and uneasy, the period which passed in the drawing-room, before the gentlemen came, was wearisome and dull to a degree that almost made her uncivil. She looked forward to their entrance as the point on which all her chance of pleasure for the evening must depend.

"If he does not come to me, *then*," said she, "I shall give him up forever."

The gentlemen came, and she thought he looked as if he would have answered her hopes. But, alas! The ladies had crowded round the table, where Miss Bennet was making tea, and Lizzy pouring out the coffee, in so close a confederacy that there was not a single vacancy near her which would admit of a chair. And on the gentlemen's approaching, one of the girls moved closer to her than ever, and said, in a whisper, "The men shan't come and part us, I am determined. We want none of them; do we?"

Darcy had walked away to another part of the room. She followed him with her eyes, envied everyone to whom he spoke, had scarcely patience enough to help anybody to coffee and then was enraged against herself for being so silly!

"A man who has once been refused! How could I ever be foolish enough to expect a renewal of his love? Is there one among the sex, who would not protest against such a weakness as a second proposal to the same woman? There is no indignity so abhorrent to their feelings!"

There was the matter, too, of her virginity. Even if he could entertain a replication of his offer, could he accept a wife less than pristine? His participation as a mentor at Trenwith House suggested he might have adopted the views championed by Abby on the matter and would not denounce her pursuit of a carnal education. Perhaps he still held himself to blame for the loss of her maidenhead, but she had no proof of his convictions. And she would wish him to know the truth. She could not deceive him, especially as her loss of innocence may yet be discovered upon the wedding night. He, of all people, deserved the truth.

How that truth was to come about was inconsequential if he no longer had any interest in marrying her. Thus, she must first ascertain the status of his affections. If optimistic, she would proceed to determine how he might perceive the lack of chastity. She did not think him capable of hypocrisy, but her anxiety made her certain of very little.

He brought back his coffee cup himself, and she seized the opportunity of saying, "Is your sister at Pemberley still?"

"Yes, she will remain there till Christmas."

"And quite alone? Have all her friends left her?"

"Mrs. Annesley is with her. The others have been gone on to Scarborough, these three weeks."

She could think of nothing more to say, but if he wished to converse with her, he might have better success. He stood by her, however, for some minutes, in silence; and, at last, on the young lady's whispering to Lizzy again, he walked away. When the tea-things were removed, and the card-tables placed, the ladies all rose, and Lizzy was then hoping to be soon joined by him, when all her views were overthrown by seeing him fall a victim to her mother's rapacity for whist players, and in a few moments after seated with the rest of the party. She now lost every expectation of pleasure. They were confined for the evening at different tables, and she had nothing to hope, but that his eyes were so often turned towards her side of the room, as to make him play as unsuccessfully as herself.

Mrs. Bennet had designed to keep the two Netherfield gentlemen to supper, but their carriage was unluckily ordered before any of the others, and she had no opportunity of detaining them.

"Well girls," said she, as soon as they were left to themselves, "What say you to the day? I think every thing has passed off uncommonly well, I assure you. The dinner was as well dressed as any I ever saw. The venison was roasted to a turn—and everybody said they never saw so fat a haunch. The soup was fifty times better than what we had at the Lucases last week; and even Mr. Darcy acknowledged, that the partridges were remarkably well done; and I suppose he has two or three French cooks at least. And, my dear Jane, I never saw you look in greater beauty. Mrs. Long said so too, for I asked her whether you did not. And what do you think she said besides? 'Ah! Mrs. Bennet, we shall have her at Netherfield at last.' She did indeed. I do think Mrs. Long is as good a creature as ever lived—and her nieces are very pretty behaved girls, and not at all handsome: I like them prodigiously."

Mrs. Bennet, in short, was in very great spirits; she had seen enough of Bingley's behaviour to Jane, to be convinced that she would get him at last; and her expectations of advantage to her family, when in a happy humour, were so far beyond reason, that she was quite disappointed at not seeing him there again the next day, to make his proposals.

"It has been a very agreeable day," said Miss Bennet to Lizzy. "The party seemed so well selected, so suitable one with the other. I hope we may often meet again."

Lizzy smiled.

"Lizzy, you must not do so. You must not suspect me. It mortifies me. I assure you that I have now learnt to enjoy his conversation as an agreeable and sensible young man, without having a wish beyond it. I am perfectly satisfied, from what his manners now are, that he never had any design of engaging my affection. It is only that he is blessed with greater sweetness of address, and a stronger desire of generally pleasing, than any other man."

"You are very cruel," said her sister, "you will not let me smile, and are provoking me to it every moment."

"How hard it is in some cases to be believed!"

"And how impossible in others!"

"But why should you wish to persuade me that I feel more than I acknowledge?"

"That is a question which I hardly know how to answer. We all love to instruct, though we can teach only what is not worth knowing. Forgive me; and if you persist in indifference, do not make me your confidante."

CHAPTER FORTY-SEVEN

A few days after this visit, Mr. Bingley called again, and alone. His friend had left him that morning for London but was to return home in ten days' time. He sat with them above an hour, and was in remarkably good spirits. Mrs. Bennet invited him to dine with them, but, with many expressions of concern, he confessed himself engaged elsewhere.

"Next time you call," said she, "I hope we shall be more lucky."

He should be particularly happy at any time, etc. etc.; and if she would give him leave, would take an early opportunity of waiting on them.

"Can you come tomorrow?"

Yes, he had no engagement at all for tomorrow; and her invitation was accepted with alacrity.

He came, and in such very good time that the ladies were none of them dressed. In ran Mrs. Bennet to her daughter's room, in her dressing gown, and with her hair half finished, crying out:

"My dear Jane, make haste and hurry down. He is come—Mr. Bingley is come. He is, indeed. Make haste, make haste. Here, Sarah, come to Miss Bennet this moment, and help her on with her gown. Never mind Miss Lizzy's hair."

"We will be down as soon as we can," said Jane; "but I dare say Kitty is forwarder than either of us, for she went up stairs half an hour ago."

"Oh! hang Kitty! what has she to do with it? Come be quick, be quick! Where is your sash, my dear?"

But when her mother was gone, Jane would not be prevailed on to go down without one of her sisters.

The same anxiety to get them by themselves was visible again in the evening. After tea, Mr. Bennet retired to the library, as was his custom, and Mary went up stairs to her instrument. Two obstacles of the five being thus removed, Mrs. Bennet sat looking and winking at Lizzy and Catherine for a considerable time, without making any impression on them. Lizzy would not observe her; and when at last Kitty did, she very innocently said, "What is the matter mamma? What do you keep winking at me for? What am I to do?"

"Nothing child, nothing. I did not wink at you." She then sat still five minutes longer; but unable to waste such a precious occasion, she suddenly got up, and saying to Kitty, "Come here, my love, I want to speak to you," took her out of the room. Jane instantly gave a look at Lizzy which spoke her distress at such premeditation, and her entreaty that *she* would not give in to it. In a few minutes, Mrs. Bennet half-opened the door and called out:

"Lizzy, my dear, I want to speak with you."

Lizzy was forced to go.

"We may as well leave them by themselves you know;" said her mother, as soon as she was in the hall. "Kitty and I are going up stairs to sit in my dressing-room."

Lizzy made no attempt to reason with her mother, but remained quietly in the hall, till she and Kitty were out of sight, then returned into the drawing-room.

Mrs. Bennet's schemes for this day were ineffectual. Bingley was every thing that was charming, except the professed lover of her daughter. His ease and cheerfulness rendered him a most agreeable addition to their evening party; and he bore with the ill-judged officiousness of the mother, and heard all her silly remarks with a forbearance and command of countenance particularly grateful to the daughter.

He scarcely needed an invitation to stay supper; and before he went away, an engagement was formed, chiefly through his own and Mrs. Bennet's means, for his coming next morning to shoot with her husband.

After this day, Jane said no more of her indifference. Not a word passed between the sisters concerning Bingley, but Lizzy went to bed in the happy belief that all must speedily be concluded, unless Mr. Darcy returned within the stated time. Seriously, however, she felt tolerably persuaded that all this must have taken place with that gentleman's concurrence.

Bingley was punctual to his appointment, and he and Mr. Bennet spent the morning together, as had been agreed on. The latter was much more agreeable than his companion expected. There was nothing of presumption or folly in Bingley that could provoke his ridicule, or disgust him into silence; and he was more communicative, and less eccentric, than the other had ever seen him. Bingley of course returned with him to dinner; and in the evening Mrs. Bennet's invention was again at work to get every body away from him and her daughter. Lizzy, who had a letter to write, went into the breakfast room for that purpose soon after tea; for as the others were all going to sit down to cards, she could not be wanted to counteract her mother's schemes.

But on returning to the drawing-room, when her letter was finished, she saw, to her infinite surprise, there was reason to fear that her mother had been too ingenious for her. On opening the door, she perceived her sister and Bingley standing together over the hearth, as if engaged in earnest conversation; and had this led to no suspicion, the faces of both, as they hastily turned round and moved away from each other, would have told it all. Their situation was awkward enough; but *hers* she thought was still worse. Not a syllable was uttered by either; and Lizzy was on the point of going away again, when Bingley, who as well as the other had sat down, suddenly rose, and whispering a few words to her sister, ran out of the room.

Jane could have no reserves from Lizzy, where confidence would give pleasure; and instantly embracing her, acknowledged, with the liveliest emotion, that she was the happiest creature in the world.

"'Tis too much!" she added, "by far too much. I do not deserve it. Oh! why is not everybody as happy?"

Lizzy's congratulations were given with a sincerity, a warmth, a delight, which words could but poorly express. Every sentence of kindness was a fresh source of happiness to Jane. But she would not allow herself to stay with her sister, or say half that remained to be said for the present.

"I must go instantly to my mother;" she cried. "I would not on any account trifle with her affectionate solicitude; or allow her to hear it from anyone but myself. He is gone to my father already. Oh! Lizzy, to know that what I have to relate will give such pleasure to all my dear family! how shall I bear so much happiness!"

She then hastened away to her mother, who had purposely broken up the card party, and was sitting up stairs with Kitty.

Lizzy, who was left by herself, now smiled at the rapidity and ease with which an affair was finally settled, that had given them so many previous months of suspense and vexation.

"And this," said she, "is the end of all his friend's anxious circumspection! of all his sister's falsehood and contrivance! the happiest, wisest, most reasonable end!"

In a few minutes she was joined by Bingley, whose conference with her father had been short and to the purpose.

"Where is your sister?" said he hastily, as he opened the door.

"With my mother up stairs. She will be down in a moment, I dare say."

He then shut the door, and, coming up to her, claimed the good wishes and affection of a sister. Lizzy honestly and heartily expressed her delight in the prospect of their relationship. They shook hands with great cordiality; and then, till her sister came down, she had to listen to all he had to say of his own happiness, and of Jane's perfections; and in spite of his being a lover, Lizzy really believed all his expectations of felicity to be rationally founded, because they had for basis the excellent understanding, and super-excellent disposition of Jane, and a general similarity of feeling and taste between her and himself.

It was an evening of no common delight to them all; the satisfaction of Miss Bennet's mind gave a glow of such sweet animation to her face, as made her look handsomer than ever. Kitty simpered and smiled, and hoped her turn was coming soon. Mrs. Bennet could not give her consent or speak her approbation in terms warm enough to satisfy her feelings, though she talked to Bingley of nothing else for half an hour; and when Mr. Bennet joined them at supper, his voice and manner plainly showed how really happy he was.

Not a word, however, passed his lips in allusion to it, till their visitor took his leave for the night; but as soon as he was gone, he turned to his daughter, and said:

"Jane, I congratulate you. You will be a very happy woman."

Jane went to him instantly, kissed him, and thanked him for his goodness.

"You are a good girl;" he replied, "and I have great pleasure in thinking you will be so happily settled. I have not a doubt of your doing very well together. Your tempers are by no means unlike. You are each of you so complying, that nothing will ever be resolved on;

so easy, that every servant will cheat you; and so generous, that you will always exceed your income."

"I hope not so. Imprudence or thoughtlessness in money matters would be unpardonable in me."

"Exceed their income! My dear Mr. Bennet," cried his wife, "what are you talking of? Why, he has four or five thousand a year, and very likely more." Then addressing her daughter, "Oh! my dear, dear Jane, I am so happy! I am sure I shan't get a wink of sleep all night. I knew how it would be. I always said it must be so, at last. I was sure you could not be so beautiful for nothing! I remember, as soon as ever I saw him, when he first came into Hertfordshire last year, I thought how likely it was that you should come together. Oh! he is the handsomest young man that ever was seen!"

Wickham, Lydia, were all forgotten. Jane was beyond competition her favourite child. At that moment, she cared for no other. Her younger sisters soon began to make interest with her for objects of happiness which she might in future be able to dispense.

Mary petitioned for the use of the library at Netherfield; and Kitty begged very hard for a few balls there every winter.

Bingley, from this time, was of course a daily visitor at Longbourn; coming frequently before breakfast, and always remaining till after supper; unless when some barbarous neighbour, who could not be enough detested, had given him an invitation to dinner which he thought himself obliged to accept.

Lizzy had now but little time for conversation with her sister; for while he was present, Jane had no attention to bestow on anyone else; but she found herself considerably useful to both of them in those hours of separation that must sometimes occur. In the absence of Jane, he always attached himself to Lizzy, for the pleasure of talking of her; and when Bingley was gone, Jane constantly sought the same means of relief.

"He has made me so happy," said she, one evening, "by telling me that he was totally ignorant of my being in town last spring! I had not believed it possible."

"I suspected as much," replied Lizzy. "But how did he account for it?"

"It must have been his sister's doing. They were certainly no friends to his acquaintance with me, which I cannot wonder at, since he might have chosen so much more advantageously in many respects. But when they see, as I trust they will, that their brother is happy with me, they will learn to be contented, and we shall be on good terms again; though we can never be what we once were to each other."

"That is the most unforgiving speech," said Lizzy, "that I ever heard you utter. Good girl! It would vex me, indeed, to see you again the dupe of Miss Bingley's pretended regard."

"Would you believe it, Lizzy, that when he went to town last November, he really loved me, and nothing but a persuasion of *my* being indifferent would have prevented his coming down again!"

"He made a little mistake to be sure; but it is to the credit of his modesty."

This naturally introduced a panegyric from Jane on his diffidence, and the little value he put on his own good qualities. Lizzy was pleased to find that he had not betrayed the interference of his friend; for, though Jane had the most generous and forgiving heart in the world, she knew it was a circumstance which must prejudice her against him.

"I am certainly the most fortunate creature that ever existed!" cried Jane. "Oh! Lizzy, why am I thus singled from my family, and blessed above them all! If I could but see *you* as happy! If there *were* but such another man for you!"

"If you were to give me forty such men, I never could be so happy as you. Till I have your disposition, your goodness, I never can have your happiness. No, no, let me shift for myself; and, perhaps, if I have very good luck, I may meet with another Mr. Collins in time."

The situation of affairs in the Longbourn family could not be long a secret. Mrs. Bennet was privileged to whisper it to Mrs. Phillips, and she ventured, without any permission, to do the same by all her neighbours in Meryton.

The Bennets were speedily pronounced to be the luckiest family in the world, though only a few weeks before, when Lydia had first run away, they had been generally proved to be marked out for misfortune.

CHAPTER FORTY-EIGHT

One morning, about a week after Bingley's engagement with Jane had been formed, as he and the females of the family were sitting together in the dining-room, their attention was suddenly drawn to the window, by the sound of a carriage; and they perceived a chaise and four driving up the lawn. It was too early in the morning for visitors, and besides, the equipage did not answer to that of any of their neighbours. The horses were post; and neither the carriage, nor the livery of the servant who preceded it, were familiar to them. As it was certain, however, that somebody was coming, Bingley instantly prevailed on Miss Bennet to avoid the confinement of such an intrusion, and walk away with him into the shrubbery. They both set off, and the conjectures of the remaining three continued, though with little satisfaction, till the door was thrown open and their visitor entered. It was Lady Catherine de Bourgh.

They were of course all intending to be surprised; but their astonishment was beyond their expectation; and on the part of Mrs. Bennet and Kitty, though she was perfectly unknown to them, even inferior to what Lizzy felt.

She entered the room with an air more than usually ungracious, made no other reply to Lizzy's salutation than a slight inclination of the head, and sat down without saying a word. Lizzy had mentioned her name to her mother on her ladyship's entrance, though no request of introduction had been made. Mrs. Bennet, all amazement, though flattered by having a guest of such high importance, received her with the utmost politeness.

After sitting for a moment in silence, Lady Catherine said very stiffly to Lizzy, "I hope you are well, Miss Bennet. That lady, I suppose, is your mother."

Lizzy replied very concisely that she was.

"And *that* I suppose is one of your sisters."

"Yes, madam," said Mrs. Bennet, delighted to speak to Lady Catherine. "She is my youngest girl but one. My youngest of all is lately married, and my eldest is somewhere about the grounds, walking with a young man who, I believe, will soon become a part of the family."

"You have a very small park here," returned Lady Catherine after a short silence.

"It is nothing in comparison of Rosings, my lady, I dare say; but I assure you it is much larger than Sir William Lucas's."

"This must be a most inconvenient sitting room for the evening, in summer; the windows are full west."

Mrs. Bennet assured her that they never sat there after dinner, and then added, "May I take the liberty of asking your ladyship whether you left Mr. and Mrs. Collins well."

"Yes, very well. I saw them the night before last."

Lizzy now expected that she would produce a letter for her from Charlotte, as it seemed the only probable motive for her calling. But no letter appeared, and she was completely puzzled.

Mrs. Bennet, with great civility, begged her ladyship to take some refreshment; but Lady Catherine very resolutely, and not very politely, declined eating anything; and then, rising up, said to Lizzy,

"Miss Bennet, there seemed to be a prettyish kind of a little wilderness on one side of your lawn. I should be glad to take a turn in it, if you will favour me with your company."

"Go, my dear," cried her mother, "and show her ladyship about the different walks. I think she will be pleased with the hermitage."

Lizzy obeyed, and running into her own room for her parasol, attended her noble guest downstairs. As they passed through the hall, Lady Catherine opened the doors into the dining-parlour and drawing-room, and pronouncing them, after a short survey, to be decent looking rooms, walked on.

Her carriage remained at the door, and Lizzy saw that her waiting-woman was in it. They proceeded in silence along the gravel walk that led to the copse; Lizzy was determined to make no effort for conversation with a woman who was now more than usually insolent and disagreeable.

"How could I ever think her like her nephew?" said she, as she looked in her face.

As soon as they entered the copse, Lady Catherine began in the following manner, "You can be at no loss, Miss Bennet, to understand the reason of my journey hither. Your own heart, your own conscience, must tell you why I come."

Lizzy looked with unaffected astonishment.

"Indeed, you are mistaken, Madam. I have not been at all able to account for the honour of seeing you here."

"Miss Bennet," replied her ladyship, in an angry tone, "you ought to know, that I am not to be trifled with. But however insincere *you* may choose to be, you shall not find *me* so. My character has ever been celebrated for its sincerity and frankness, and in a cause of such moment as this, I shall certainly not depart from it. A report of a most alarming nature reached me two days ago. I was told that not only your sister was on the point of being most advantageously married, but that you, that Miss Elizabeth Bennet, would, in all likelihood, be soon afterwards united to my nephew, my own nephew, Mr. Darcy. Though I *know* it must be a scandalous falsehood, though I would not injure him so much as to suppose the truth of it possible, I instantly resolved on setting off for this place, that I might make my sentiments known to you."

"If you believed it impossible to be true," said Lizzy, colouring with astonishment and disdain, "I wonder you took the trouble of coming so far. What could your ladyship propose by it?"

"At once to insist upon having such a report universally contradicted."

"Your coming to Longbourn, to see me and my family," said Lizzy coolly, "will be rather a confirmation of it; if, indeed, such a report is in existence."

"If! Do you then pretend to be ignorant of it? Has it not been industriously circulated by yourselves? Do you not know that such a report is spread abroad?"

"I never heard that it was."

"And can you likewise declare, that there is no foundation for it?"

"I do not pretend to possess equal frankness with your ladyship. You may ask questions which I shall not choose to answer."

"This is not to be borne. Miss Bennet, I insist on being satisfied. Has he, has my nephew, made you an offer of marriage?"

"Your ladyship has declared it to be impossible."

"It ought to be so; it must be so, while he retains the use of his reason. But your arts and allurements may, in a moment of infatuation, have made him forget what he owes to himself and to all his family. You may have drawn him in."

"If I have, I shall be the last person to confess it."

"Miss Bennet, do you know who I am? I have not been accustomed to such language as this. I am almost the nearest relation he has in the world, and am entitled to know all his dearest concerns."

"But you are not entitled to know mine; nor will such behaviour as this, ever induce me to be explicit."

"Let me be rightly understood. This match, to which you have the presumption to aspire, can never take place. No, never. Mr. Darcy is engaged to my daughter. Now what have you to say?"

"Only this; that if he is so, you can have no reason to suppose he will make an offer to me."

Lady Catherine hesitated for a moment, and then replied, "The engagement between them is of a peculiar kind. From their infancy, they have been intended for each other. It was the favourite wish of *his* mother, as well as of hers. While in their cradles, we planned the union: and now, at the moment when the wishes of both sisters would be accomplished in their marriage, to be prevented by a young woman of inferior birth, of no importance in the world, and wholly unallied to the family! Do you pay no regard to the wishes of his friends? To his tacit engagement with Miss de Bourgh? Are you lost to every feeling of propriety and delicacy? Have you not heard me say that from his earliest hours he was destined for his cousin?"

"Yes, and I had heard it before. But what is that to me? If there is no other objection to my marrying your nephew, I shall certainly not be kept from it by knowing that his mother and aunt wished him to marry Miss de Bourgh. You both did as much as you could in planning the marriage. Its completion depended on others. If Mr. Darcy is neither by honour nor inclination confined to his cousin, why is not he to make another choice? And if I am that choice, why may not I accept him?"

"Because honour, decorum, prudence, nay, interest, forbid it. Yes, Miss Bennet, interest; for do not expect to be noticed by his family or friends, if you wilfully act against the inclinations of all. You will be censured, slighted, and despised, by everyone connected with him. Your alliance will be a disgrace; your name will never even be mentioned by any of us."

"These are heavy misfortunes," replied Lizzy. "But the wife of Mr.

Darcy must have such extraordinary sources of happiness necessarily attached to her situation, that she could, upon the whole, have no cause to repine."

"Obstinate, headstrong girl! I am ashamed of you! Is this your gratitude for my attentions to you last spring? Is nothing due to me on that score? Let us sit down. You are to understand, Miss Bennet, that I came here with the determined resolution of carrying my purpose; nor will I be dissuaded from it. I have not been used to submit to any person's whims. I have not been in the habit of brooking disappointment."

"*That* will make your ladyship's situation at present more pitiable; but it will have no effect on me."

"I will not be interrupted. Hear me in silence. My daughter and my nephew are formed for each other. They are descended, on the maternal side, from the same noble line; and, on the father's, from respectable, honourable, and ancient—though untitled—families. Their fortune on both sides is splendid. They are destined for each other by the voice of every member of their respective houses; and what is to divide them? The upstart pretensions of a young woman without family, connections, or fortune. Is this to be endured! But it must not, shall not be. If you were sensible of your own good, you would not wish to quit the sphere in which you have been brought up."

"In marrying your nephew, I should not consider myself as quitting that sphere. He is a gentleman; I am a gentleman's daughter; so far we are equal."

"True. You *are* a gentleman's daughter. But who was your mother? Who are your uncles and aunts? Do not imagine me ignorant of their condition."

"Whatever my connections may be," said Lizzy, "if your nephew does not object to them, they can be nothing to *you*."

"Tell me once for all, are you engaged to him?"

Though Lizzy would not, for the mere purpose of obliging Lady Catherine, have answered this question, she could not but say, after a moment's deliberation, "I am not."

Lady Catherine seemed pleased.

"And will you promise me, never to enter into such an engagement?"

"I will make no promise of the kind."

"Miss Bennet I am shocked and astonished. I expected to find a more reasonable young woman. But do not deceive yourself into a belief that I will ever recede. I shall not go away till you have given me the assurance I require."

"And I certainly *never* shall give it. I am not to be intimidated into anything so wholly unreasonable. Your ladyship wants Mr. Darcy to marry your daughter; but would my giving you the wished-for promise make their marriage at all more probable? Supposing him to be attached to me, would my refusing to accept his hand make him wish to bestow it on his cousin? Allow me to say, Lady Catherine, that the arguments with which you have supported this extraordinary application have been as frivolous as the application was ill-judged. You have widely mistaken my character, if you think I can be worked on by such persuasions as these. How far your nephew might approve of your interference in his affairs, I cannot tell; but you have certainly no right to concern yourself in mine. I must beg, therefore, to be importuned no farther on the subject."

"Not so hasty, if you please. I have by no means done. To all the objections I have already urged, I have still another to add. I am no stranger to the particulars of your youngest sister's infamous elopement. I know it all; that the young man's marrying her was a patched-up business, at the expence of your father and uncles. And is such a girl to be my nephew's sister? Is her husband, is the son of his late father's steward, to be his brother? Heaven and earth!—of what are you thinking? Are the shades of Pemberley to be thus polluted?"

"You can now have nothing further to say," she resentfully answered. "You have insulted me in every possible method. I must beg to return to the house."

And she rose as she spoke. Lady Catherine rose also, and they turned back. Her ladyship was highly incensed.

"You have no regard, then, for the honour and credit of my nephew! Unfeeling, selfish girl! Do you not consider that a connection with you must disgrace him in the eyes of everybody?"

"Lady Catherine, I have nothing further to say. You know my sentiments."

"You are then resolved to have him?"

"I have said no such thing. I am only resolved to act in that manner, which will, in my own opinion, constitute my happiness, without reference to *you*, or to any person so wholly unconnected with me."

"It is well. You refuse, then, to oblige me. You refuse to obey the claims of duty, honour, and gratitude. You are determined to ruin him in the opinion of all his friends, and make him the contempt of the world."

"Neither duty, nor honour, nor gratitude," replied Lizzy, "have any possible claim on me, in the present instance. No principle of either would be violated by my marriage with Mr. Darcy. And with regard to the resentment of his family, or the indignation of the world, if the former *were* excited by his marrying me, it would not give me one moment's concern—and the world in general would have too much sense to join in the scorn."

"And this is your real opinion! This is your final resolve! Very well. I shall now know how to act. Do not imagine, Miss Bennet, that your ambition will ever be gratified. I came to try you. I hoped to find you reasonable; but, depend upon it, I will carry my point."

In this manner Lady Catherine talked on, till they were at the door of the carriage, when, turning hastily round, she added, "I take no leave of you, Miss Bennet. I send no compliments to your mother. You deserve no such attention. I am most seriously displeased."

Lizzy made no answer; and without attempting to persuade her ladyship to return into the house, walked quietly into it herself. She heard the carriage drive away as she proceeded up stairs. Her mother impatiently met her at the door of the dressing-room, to ask why Lady Catherine would not come in again and rest herself.

"She did not choose it," said her daughter, "she would go."

"She is a very fine-looking woman! and her calling here was prodigiously civil! for she only came, I suppose, to tell us the Collinses were well. She is on her road somewhere, I dare say, and so, passing through Meryton, thought she might as well call on you. I suppose she had nothing particular to say to you, Lizzy?"

Lizzy was forced to give into a little falsehood here; for to acknowledge the substance of their conversation was impossible.

CHAPTER FORTY-NINE

The discomposure of spirits which this extraordinary visit threw Lizzy into, could not be easily overcome; nor could she, for many hours, learn to think of it less than incessantly. Lady Catherine, it appeared, had actually taken the trouble of this journey from Rosings, for the sole purpose of breaking off her supposed engagement with Mr. Darcy. It was a rational scheme, to be sure! but from what the report of their engagement could originate, Lizzy was at a loss to imagine; till she recollected that *his* being the intimate friend of Bingley, and *her* being the sister of Jane, was enough, at a time when the expectation of one wedding made everybody eager for another, to supply the idea. She had not herself forgotten to feel that the marriage of her sister must bring them more frequently together. And her neighbours at Lucas Lodge, therefore (for through their communication with the Collinses, the report, she concluded, had reached Lady Catherine), had only set that down as almost certain and immediate, which she had looked forward to as possible at some future time.

In revolving Lady Catherine's expressions, however, she could not help feeling some uneasiness as to the possible consequence of her persisting in this interference. From what she had said of her resolution to prevent their marriage, it occurred to Lizzy that she must meditate an application to her nephew; and how *he* might take a similar representation of the evils attached to a connection with her, she dared not pronounce. She knew not the exact degree of his affection for his aunt, or his dependence on her judgment, but it was natural to suppose that he thought much higher of her ladyship than *she* could do; and it was certain that, in enumerating the miseries of a marriage with *one*, whose immediate connections were so unequal to his own, his aunt would address him on his weakest side. With his notions of dignity, he would probably feel that the arguments, which to Lizzy had appeared weak and ridiculous, contained much good sense and solid reasoning.

If he had been wavering before as to what he should do, which had often seemed likely, the advice and entreaty of so near a relation might settle every doubt, and determine him at once to be as happy as dignity unblemished could make him. In that case he would return no more. Lady Catherine might see him in her way through town; and his engagement to Bingley of coming again to Netherfield must give way.

"If, therefore, an excuse for not keeping his promise should come to his friend within a few days," she added, "I shall know how to understand it. I shall then give over every expectation, every wish of his constancy. If he is satisfied with only regretting me, when he might have obtained my affections and hand, I shall soon cease to regret him at all."

* * * * *

The surprise of the rest of the family, on hearing who their visitor had been, was very great; but they obligingly satisfied it, with the same kind of supposition which had appeased Mrs. Bennet's curiosity; and Lizzy was spared from much teasing on the subject.

The next morning, as she was going downstairs, she was met by her father, who came out of his library with a letter in his hand.

"Lizzy," said he, "I was going to look for you; come into my room."

She followed him thither; and her curiosity to know what he had to tell her was heightened by the supposition of its being in some manner connected with the letter he held. It suddenly struck her that it might be from Lady Catherine; and she anticipated with dismay all the consequent explanations.

She followed her father to the fire place, and they both sat down. He then said,

"I have received a letter this morning that has astonished me exceedingly. As it principally concerns yourself, you ought to know its contents. I did not know before, that I had two daughters on the brink of matrimony. Let me congratulate you on a very important conquest."

The colour now rushed into Lizzy's cheeks in the instantaneous conviction of its being a letter from the nephew, instead of the aunt; and she was undetermined whether most to be pleased that he explained himself at all, or offended that his letter was not rather addressed to herself; when her father continued:

"You look conscious. Young ladies have great penetration in such matters as these; but I think I may defy even *your* sagacity, to discover the name of your admirer. This letter is from Mr. Collins."

"From Mr. Collins! and what can *he* have to say?"

"Something very much to the purpose of course. He begins with congratulations on the approaching nuptials of my eldest daughter, of which, it seems, he has been told by some of the good-natured, gossiping Lucases. I shall not sport with your impatience, by reading what he says on that point. What relates to yourself, is as follows: 'Having thus offered you the sincere congratulations of Mrs. Collins and myself on this happy event, let me now add a short hint on the subject of another; of which we have been advertised by the same authority. Your daughter Lizzy, it is presumed, will not long bear the name of Bennet, after her elder sister has resigned it, and the chosen partner of her fate may be reasonably looked up to as one of the most illustrious personages in this land.'

"Can you possibly guess, Lizzy, who is meant by this?" 'This young gentleman is blessed, in a peculiar way, with every thing the heart of mortal can most desire—splendid property, noble kindred, and extensive patronage. Yet in spite of all these temptations, let me warn my cousin Lizzy, and yourself, of what evils you may incur by a precipitate closure with this gentleman's proposals, which, of course, you will be inclined to take immediate advantage of.'

"Have you any idea, Lizzy, who this gentleman is? But now it comes out:

"'My motive for cautioning you is as follows. We have reason to imagine that his aunt, Lady Catherine de Bourgh, does not look on the match with a friendly eye.'

"*Mr. Darcy*, you see, is the man! Now, Lizzy, I think I *have* surprised you. Could he, or the Lucases, have pitched on any man within the circle of our acquaintance, whose name would have given the lie more effectually to what they related? Mr. Darcy, who never looks at any woman but to see a blemish, and who probably never looked at you in his life! It is admirable!"

Lizzy tried to join in her father's pleasantry, but could only force one most reluctant smile. Never had his wit been directed in a manner so little agreeable to her.

"Are you not diverted?"

"Oh! yes. Pray read on."

"'After mentioning the likelihood of this marriage to her ladyship last night, she immediately, with her usual condescension, expressed what she felt on the occasion; when it became apparent, that on the score of some family objections on the part of my cousin, she would never give her consent to what she termed so disgraceful a match. I thought it my duty to give the speediest intelligence of this to my cousin, that she and her noble admirer may be aware of what they are about, and not run hastily into a marriage which has not been properly sanctioned.' Mr. Collins moreover adds, 'I am truly rejoiced that my cousin Lydia's sad business has been so well hushed up, and am only concerned that their living together before the marriage took place should be so generally known. I must not, however, neglect the duties of my station, or refrain from declaring my amazement at hearing that you received the young couple into your house as soon as they were married. It was an encouragement of vice; and had I been the rector of Longbourn, I should very strenuously have opposed it. You ought certainly to forgive them, as a Christian, but never to admit them in your sight, or allow their names to be mentioned in your hearing.' That is his notion of Christian forgiveness! The rest of his letter is only about his dear Charlotte's situation, and his expectation of a young olive-branch. But, Lizzy, you look as if you did not enjoy it. You are not going to be *missish*, I hope, and pretend to be affronted at an idle report. For what do we live, but to make sport for our neighbours, and laugh at them in our turn?"

"Oh!" cried Lizzy, "I am excessively diverted. But it is so strange!"

"Yes—*that* is what makes it amusing. Had they fixed on any other man it would have been nothing; but *his* perfect indifference, and *your* pointed dislike, make it so delightfully absurd! Much as I abominate writing, I would not give up Mr. Collins's correspondence for any consideration. Nay, when I read a letter of his, I cannot help giving him the preference even over Wickham, much as I value the impudence and hypocrisy of my son-in-law. And pray, Lizzy, what said Lady Catherine about this report? Did she call to refuse her consent?"

To this question his daughter replied only with a laugh; and as it had been asked without the least suspicion, she was not distressed by his repeating it. Lizzy had never been more at a loss to make her feelings appear what they were not. It was necessary to laugh, when she would rather have cried. Her father had most cruelly mortified her, by what he said of Mr. Darcy's indifference, and she could do nothing but wonder at such a want of penetration, or fear that perhaps, instead of his seeing too little, she might have fancied too much.

Perhaps she ought to have been more forward, more assertive in her attempts to engage Mr. Darcy when he had been here. Then she might put to bed all questions regarding his sentiments. Where was the boldness that had led her to accept an education at Trenwith House, the brazenness with which she had seduced her mentor? Would that Elizabeth Bennet have recognized the more recent young woman who sat timid, introvert, barely able to meet his gaze? To be fair, Longbourn was a far cry from Trenwith House, and Mr. Darcy's behaviour certainly did not encourage an affable response. Her demeanor only reflected the marked difference in *his*. And, in truth, she was a little intimidated by the largesse of his actions concerning Lydia. Add to that her shame for every ill word she had spoken to and of him, and dismay over her mother's conduct, then it was little wonder that she should be inclined to reticence.

There was, too, the strength of her own hopes, which she could not fob off, try as she might to temper them by compiling all the evidence and reasons for how and why Mr. Darcy should not wish to renew his interest in her. She could not deny that, while his presence had been trying and vexatious, his absence was the harder to bear. She missed him in all ways—and all manner of intercourse. Her body still warmed to the memories of Trenwith House and the Lilac Cottage. She longed—nay, burned—for his touch. And the prospect that she might never again receive his caresses caused a miserable knot in her abdomen.

Though she had told herself that once his indifference was confirmed, she would not dwell upon him, she had also arrived at the belief that it was unlikely she would ever again know a man who could command as much respect and incite such passion in her as Mr. Darcy.

CHAPTER FIFTY

"I am quite disappointed to hear that you will be attending my benefit for Thomas Clarkson next Thursday. Whatever are you doing here in London?" Abby admonished Darcy as she took a seat opposite his writing table.

He laid down his pen to attend to his guest. "I would simply respond 'on business,' but I detect the tone of your question is reminiscent of an accusation."

"Indeed, it is! And I will not concede that you are in London merely 'on business.'"

"Now you accuse me of lying."

"I am accusing you of a half-truth."

Darcy took in a deep breath. There was only one other woman from whom he would have accepted such abuse. And though Abby had once more proved herself one of the most discerning individuals he knew, he was unwilling at present to accommodate her. He returned his gaze to the letter he was writing to Charles informing his friend that he would be in London longer than anticipated.

"And cowardice," she added when she saw he would not budge.

He glanced up sharply. "You have arrived in London but less than a day and have made your first order of business my provocation?"

She tossed her golden hair. "As only a dear friend would!"

"You have a strange way of showing your friendship," he murmured. "My enemies would be less inciting."

"Your happiness is my motive."

"Forgive me if I fail to see how attacks upon my integrity and manhood should make me happy."

"Ah, Fitzwilliam! You abound in such noble qualities as I can only aspire to. But I know that if I felt the love that you do, I should not be hiding in London."

A muscle tensed along his jaw. "Pray, what other complaints do you wish to hurl my way? Let me receive them all at once."

"You would make a liar of me."

He looked quizzical. "Forgive me. I had not done it intentionally."

"You may yet save me from perpetrating a lie. Cease your stalling here in London and take yourself to *her*."

Ignoring her last statement, he asked, "What lie?"

Abby pursed her lips. He could not tell if she were smug or abashed.

"My curricle happened to pass the carriage of your esteemed aunt the other day," she said. "Having had news of Bingley's engagement to Miss Bennet, I was certain *yours* would be upon the heel of his. I congratulated her on the pending nuptials. I confess it was devilish on my part. I simply could not resist meeting her sneer at me with happy tidings."

He frowned. Lady Catherine would not have received such a jest in good humor.

"But you see how she will add the telling of falsehoods to her list of complaints against me."

He could not help reply, "It is of such a length that the addition of one more grievance will make no difference. And I would have more sympathy if I knew you to attend any part of what Catherine thinks."

"*Touché*. But what of your own self-interest? Have you no wish to be happy? I know your love for Miss Elizabeth has not diminished. What you did for her sister and Wickham proves it. Why are you not now in Hertfordshire making love to her?"

He rose from his chair and went to the window overlooking the square

"Because I have received no encouragement to do so," he said after a pause. "I was twice at her house. She could barely meet my gaze and spoke not four sentences to me."

Abby knit her brows. "I cannot account for her behaviour, but I think you read too much significance into it. How can her feelings not be enhanced by appreciation for what you have done for her family?"

"Because she knows nothing of it. I swore her aunt and uncle to secrecy. I have no interest in cultivating her gratitude and derive no satisfaction if she were to accept my hand because she felt *obliged* to. You had stated in your letter that, though her opinion of me had improved, her feelings had not elevated to affection."

"But that was some time ago."

"Have you received a more recent communication from her?"

"No."

"And your friendship is of a kind in which she would have confided her honest feelings to you?"

"I think so."

"Then I have no reason to think that I have any more hope of winning her heart to-day than I did before."

"You were not prevented from pursuing her in Derbyshire."

"I did my utmost to convince her that I could be a man she could respect and love. Apparently I was not successful."

"Are you despairing so easily? For shame, Fitzwilliam! The fair sex delights in the pursuit."

"I did not think Miss Elizabeth one to play the coquette or employ such arts as to keep a man in unnecessary confusion."

"I agree, but perhaps she has taken advice that the manner to strengthen a man's ardor is to deny him. It is an effective strategy with many men."

Darcy contemplated the possibility. "I would not want to grasp at false hopes."

"You cannot know till you have confronted her."

"Ironically, I think she would sooner wed her 'mentor.' But if her feelings are not decided in my favour, my revelation would be most unwelcome to her."

On this, Abby could say nothing. She tried another course. "You did not want enticements from her before proposing to her the *first* time."

"My arrogance led me to believe that she would accept my offer. Given the circumstances, she had more reason than most women to wed, and *still* she refused."

"You will not convince me, Fitzwilliam. Will she not make you happy?"

"Beyond measure!" he cried.

"Then short of her spoken refusal, that she would sooner kiss a sow than receive your touch, I will persist. If you do not make every exertion to win her hand and secure your own happiness, you will live to regret it."

He had no reply.

Abby rose. She had anticipated a short visit and still had her bonnet and gloves upon her.

"I will happily take a donation of funds on behalf of Mr. Clarkson," she said, "but I sincerely hope not to see you in attendance."

Crossing to him, she stood upon her toes and planted a kiss upon his cheek.

"Go to her," she said.

Her earnest look melted him. He could not stay angry with her for long and took her hand in his. "I have been blessed in my life to know at least two remarkable women."

She arched a brow and teased, "I hope you are not denigrating our sex, for there surely number far greater than two remarkable women."

"There are many who can command respect and affection, but there can be but one Abigail Trenwith."

"On that I will agree. And you may search the rest of your life, but I hazard to guess you will only find *one* Elizabeth Bennet."

* * * * *

Knowing that Miss Elizabeth was partial to her mentor, Darcy had at times entertained the fantasy of revealing himself to her, but if she bore him little regard, the shock would ruin whatever fondness her Trenwith education could be looked upon.

Perhaps Abby was right to accuse him of cowardice. He had no wish to have his heart broken twice by the same woman. As tempting as it was to follow Abby's urging, beneath her nonchalance for convention and quest for sensual adventure, Abby was a romantic. It did not surprise him that she would promote the conquest of love.

He had not resolved never to go to Longbourn. The marriage between Charles and Miss Bennet would put him in the way of Miss Elizabeth frequently enough. Abby would be disappointed, but he simply saw no reason to hasten back to Hertfordshire.

He had just reached this conclusion in the latter part of the day when he was surprised by yet another visitor to his townhome. As with Abby, Catherine came unannounced.

"You will forgive the unexpected call," his aunt said upon being shown into the parlor, "once you understand the nature of my concerns."

He asked if she desired a glass of wine.

"No, I have been many hours upon the road to-day and mean to retire to bed as soon as I am returned to my lodgings."

He sat down and waited for her to speak. The journey must have wearied her a great deal for he had never seen her looking so solemn, but there was vigor enough in her speech.

"You would not believe the revolting rumors that Trenwith woman is spreading," she said.

Darcy made no reply, wondering how her complaint could warrant her coming all this way to London.

"It is a display of her ill-breeding, for I had done nothing to provoke her, and she insisted on being presumptuous." Her nostrils flared. "It shows a great want of character, an intolerable mischievousness, spitefulness, and insolence."

He had little patience to listen to Catherine disparage Abby, and, deciding to pour himself a glass of wine, rose to his feet.

"She has ever proven my opinions of her," Catherine continued. "When she had opportunity to repeal her grievances, she only added to them. The woman seems to delight in being outrageous. Her true colours are obvious."

Darcy remained at the sideboard, his features no less serious. "On that alone I will agree. She has no more affinity for the deceitful character than I."

Catherine narrowed her eyes. "Fitzwilliam Darcy, are you defending this person?"

"I think Mrs. Trenwith a woman greatly misunderstood. I have had the fortune to know her better. She has many admirable qualities."

"Then she has cast a spell upon you—perhaps not unlike that awful Bennet girl. *My* Anne has not these arts, this trickery, to fool men into thinking they are better than they are. *She* is honest and does not pass herself off as a fraud. She may not be considered as sophisticated as some of these more artful women, but one shall always enjoy a sense of security and trustworthiness with her. You ought take care with Georgiana. She is not immune at Ramsgate from the folly that abounds the young women of to-day. I would offer my Anne as a better companion for her and should be happy to have her at Rosings more often."

But Darcy heard only a little of what had been said. "Bennet girl?"

"Or perhaps I should say *girls*, for there can be insufficient explanation otherwise for how Charles would wish to marry beneath him when he might have many superior to her to choose from, especially in light of the business with the youngest one. *You* must know what the family is about. I saw nothing in any of them to impress me."

He straightened. "You have met them?"

"I came from Hertfordshire. But even if I had not heard and seen them with mine own eyes, I know enough of their circumstances that they do not deserve the situation they aspire to. The sham marriage of that Bennet girl is enough to cast them all in grievous light."

"What persuaded you to seek them out?"

"That Trenwith woman dared congratulate me on your pending nuptials to Miss Elizabeth Bennet! I was aghast at such an allegation and went to *her* to confirm the nonsense."

"Her?" he echoed, agitation rising. "You saw Miss Elizabeth?"

She detected the eagerness in his tone. "You would have been mortified by her treatment of me. Such obstinacy, such insolence! I am ashamed for her mother and father. She values nothing of honour and decency. She dared consider herself your equal. I informed her of all the obvious objections to such a match, as well as the consequences of such a union, that none of your family and friends would welcome her, that she would be ostracized, and if she had any considerateness for *you*, she would not wish to bring such unhappiness upon you and your loved ones. But she is a most *selfish* creature, and the *advantages* of being attached to you are too much an enticement for her."

Darcy could barely contain an angry response to her diatribe, but her last statement perked his interest. "She said as much?"

"The insolent chit refused to assure me that she would be reasonable. She intimated that any woman, even one of her quality, should find happiness in being your wife."

His heartbeat quickened.

She continued, her anger growing with each recollection. "She cared not a fig that you are engaged already to your cousin Anne."

He raised his brows. "Am I?"

"Not in a *formal* manner, but you comprehend the prudence of such a union."

"I do not comprehend an engagement that I had no participation in."

For a rare moment, Catherine was silent before saying, "*You* must be reasonable where she is not. You were ever the nephew I could be proud of. You have always attended your *duty* to your family."

"I must also be true to my heart, or there should be no happiness for myself or any wife of mine."

She seemed to turn to stone. "*Any* wife? Do you mean to say you will not honour your engagement to your cousin?"

"Madam, there is no engagement."

"Are you partial then to this Bennet girl?"

"That is my affair."

"I am your aunt, and with only noble concern for you as my motive. I swore to my sister—your mother—that I would look after you. It would break her heart to see you married to anyone but Anne."

"I think my mother would wish for my happiness."

"And you have been tricked into thinking what constitutes true happiness. I promise you will think differently when Miss Elizabeth reveals her genuine self: a petty, pretentious, defiant—"

"Enough! I assure you I am capable of determining mine own happiness. And as the hour is late, I recommend your driver take the roads before night falls."

Catherine did not move, but the determination in her nephew's hardened countenance was incontrovertible. Reluctantly, she took her leave to do battle another day.

CHAPTER FIFTY-ONE

"I hope you will not replicate the stupid manner in which you stood at our first assembly here in Hertfordshire," remarked Charles with a sidelong glance at Darcy, as the two neared Longbourn House. "You will never win a lady's heart with such inertia."

Realizing he had absently urged his horse into a quick canter, Darcy slowed his steed and looked at his friend in some surprise. He had not confided in Charles and thought his friend too much in love to notice anything or anyone else save Miss Bennet. Till he confirmed what Charles was alluding to, Darcy kept his response general.

"Had I your affable nature, I should not hesitate to take instruction from you and favour you with my imitation," Darcy said, solemn, for there could be no inconsequential visit to Longbourn till he had received an answer from *her*.

"The art of making love to a woman has never been one of my better skills," he finished. His experience with Abby and at Trenwith House had helped his confidence, and though he was assured in the bedchamber, no endeavour had racked his nerves as much as the pursuit of Miss Elizabeth Bennet's hand.

"But you would never admit to any skill that you had not obtained near perfect mastery of," Charles objected. "If the feelings between two parties are mutual, the courtship is rather a simple matter."

Darcy said nothing at first. For Charles, the world held little complication. The situation with Miss Elizabeth, however, could hardly be more knotted. Despite the unpleasantness of Lady Catherine's visit of a few days ago, Darcy was grateful for the intelligence she had imparted regarding her conversation with Miss Elizabeth. With hopes that his aunt might reveal more, he had welcomed a repetition of her visit the following morning. After suffering through more diatribes of Miss Elizabeth, coupled with the virtues of marrying his cousin, he could glean no additional information, but he did resolve to return to Hertfordshire, and sent his regrets to Abby that he would be unable to attend her benefit after all.

"I urge you not to overthink it, my friend," Charles said.

"You have an easy way with people that makes such efforts seem natural. Any part of me to emulate you would only come across as false and affected. I must be satisfied with envying your sociability."

Charles laughed. "Come, come! You know as well as I that you envy me not a jot! Sometimes I think you relish your surliness."

Like a child testing his impishness, Charles gave Darcy a large smile, hopeful that his friend would not take offense at the ribbing.

"I only wish you could be as happy as me with a love of your own!" Charles added.

"For now, I am content to rejoice in your happiness. Miss Bennet is truly a find."

His statement had the desired effect of turning Charles's attentions to his beloved, whose qualities he enjoyed extolling.

The two men were received at Longbourn much in the same fashion as before. Mrs. Bennet was effusive in her welcome of Charles, and her joy of the pending nuptials overflowed enough to provide even Darcy a modestly amicable greeting.

Darcy's gaze went straight to Miss Elizabeth, who looked upon her mother with some dread as Mrs. Bennet remarked, "And Mr. Darcy, we had the pleasure the other day—"

"Pardon the interruption," Charles said, "but, as the weather is most glorious, shall we go for a walk?"

"I am not in the habit of walking," Mrs. Bennet replied, "but you younger folk, by all means, take a walk on this lovely day!"

She shooed them out the door and remained in the house with her third daughter, Mary, who regretted she could not spare the time.

Charles and Jane soon allowed the others to outstrip them. They lagged behind, leaving Darcy with Miss Elizabeth and Miss Kitty to entertain each other. The younger of the Bennet girls seemed too afraid to speak. Miss Elizabeth seemed deep in thought.

Darcy was desperate to speak with Miss Elizabeth. As Charles had wished, he had no intention of standing idly by upon this visit. He would know Miss Elizabeth's sentiments once and for all. If she bore him no affection, then the matter was at an end. But if she provided a more positive answer, what was he to do then? When and should he reveal his secret? How would she receive the fact that he had served as a mentor at Trenwith House? Though she herself was compromised, she had known no other man than he. Would she take exception to the fact that he had bedded other women? Would she be angry with him that he had known her identity? Would knowledge of all this destroy whatever tender feelings she had for him?

As speculation produced nothing, he resolved to take Charles's advice not to analyze overmuch. One step at a time, he told himself. His uncertainties would be irrelevant if Miss Elizabeth was not in the least partial to him.

They walked toward the Lucases' because Miss Kitty wished to call upon Miss Maria. Miss Elizabeth made no objection when her sister left them and went boldly with Darcy alone. Elated to have her to himself and determined to take advantage of the opportunity, he prepared to execute his resolution, but she spoke first.

"Mr. Darcy, I am a very selfish creature; and, for the sake of giving relief to my own feelings, care not how much I may be wounding yours," she said immediately. "I can no longer help thanking you for your unexampled kindness to my poor sister. Ever since I have known it, I have been most anxious to acknowledge to you how gratefully I feel it. Were it known to the rest of my family, I should not have merely my own gratitude to express."

He felt surprised, then his colour changed. "I am sorry, exceedingly sorry, that you have ever been informed of what may, in a mistaken light, have given you uneasiness. I did not think Mrs. Gardiner was so little to be trusted."

"You must not blame my aunt. Lydia's thoughtlessness first betrayed to me that you had been concerned in the matter, and, of course, I could not rest till I knew the particulars. Let me thank you again and again, in the name of all my family, for that generous compassion which induced you to take so much trouble, and bear so many mortifications, for the sake of discovering them."

"If you *will* thank me," he replied, "let it be for yourself alone. That the wish of giving happiness to you might add force to the other inducements which led me on, I shall not attempt to deny. But your *family* owe me nothing. Much as I respect them, I believe I thought only of *you*."

They had turned upon a gravel path, and for a moment there was only the sound of their footsteps upon the rocks. It was a sunny day, but his warmth came from another place. Miss Elizabeth appeared too embarrassed to reply. It was thus incumbent upon him to continue.

"You are too generous to trifle with me. If your feelings are still what they were last April, tell me so at once. *My* affections and wishes are unchanged, but one word from you will silence me on this subject forever."

Heart pounding, he stopped and turned to look at her, searching her countenance for indications of what she felt. He saw her blush but could assign no properties to it. She might be mortified, excited, awkward, or all of these.

"My sentiments," she began—and he clung to every word, attuned to every inflection of tone—"have undergone so material a change, since the period to which you allude, that I must receive your present assurances with *gratitude* and *pleasure*."

At this, he felt the vise about him loosen, allowing him to inhale. Never had a few seconds stretched so long! He wanted to clasp her to his bosom, for only she could diffuse the joy that threatened to burst his chest.

"Your reply has given me such happiness that I am unable to express it with any justice," he said. "It is a happiness such that I have never felt before. You may suspect me of hyperbole, but it is the truth."

"You are not a man given to exaggeration," she acknowledged.

He nodded. "I ought say as little as possible for fear of repeating any of the abhorrence of my first proposal, but I have such a need for you to know the depths of my love and admiration that it overpowers prudence."

He glanced around, and seeing no one, pulled her over to a thicket of trees.

"I only hope that, through time, I can prove myself worthy of your affections," he added, the look upon his face further evidence of his emotions.

"Prove worthy?" she cried. "If anyone must prove it, it is I!"

Her response wrenched his heart. Not caring who might come across them, he grasped her. "My love for you is not to be earned. I do give it freely, whether you accept it or not. My heart is yours, to cherish or to crush. I loved you against my own will at first, but that is only testament to the supremacy of the former. Now, I love in favour of my better judgment and with every ounce of desire. If you knew the torment that I had undergone this past fortnight, you might understand the violence of my feelings for you, how much your happiness means to me, and how much I adore you."

Her eyes glistened with moisture. The fondness in her countenance had him undone. He clasped her closer.

"Miss Elizabeth, may I—?"

She lifted her chin in response, and he met her with an ardent kiss. How glorious she felt in his arms! How sweet her lips! Passion surged through him, the experience heady and novel, as if they kissed for the first time. It *was* the first time, he reasoned. In the light of day, without masks, and as their true selves. The knowledge that she was to be his, that she returned his affections, lent the kiss significance beyond compare. He wanted to pour the profoundness of his love into the embrace but would not smother her with the force of his feelings. Indeed, only a lifetime of kisses could demonstrate his devotion.

Taking her mouth, he claimed her for his own. Their kiss deepened, and it seemed, as she pressed her lips eagerly to his, that she wanted him as much as he wanted her. Desire flared between them. He felt the heat in his groin and down his legs. Before they were tempted to do more than kiss, they parted for air. He folded her into his arms.

"Dear Lizzy, how happy you have made me!"

"And I had thought for certain you were lost to me," she said.

He pulled back to look at her. "How could you think that? My love for you has only grown since you spurned me."

She hesitated before answering, "Lady Catherine—your aunt—came to see me, to voice her objections over our potential union. I thought it more than probable that, once she had spoken to you, what attachment you might have had for me would defer to the wisdom of her arguments."

"Then you had *both* underestimated my love for you. Catherine did call upon me in London, and related to me her journey to Longbourn and the substance of her conversation with you. It was clear she wished to obtain the promise from me which you had refused to give. But the effect of her efforts were quite contrary to her wishes. It taught me to hope as I had scarcely allowed myself to hope before. I knew enough of your disposition to be certain that, had you been absolutely, irrevocably decided against me, you would have acknowledged it to Lady Catherine, frankly and openly."

She coloured and laughed as she replied, "Yes, you know enough of my frankness to believe me capable of *that*. After abusing you so abominably to your face, I could have no scruple in abusing you to all your relations."

"What did you say of me, that I did not deserve? For, though your accusations were ill-founded, formed on mistaken premises, my behaviour to you at the time had merited the severest reproof. It was unpardonable. I cannot think of it without abhorrence."

"We will not quarrel for the greater share of blame annexed to that evening. The conduct of neither, if strictly examined, will be irreproachable, but since then, we have both, I hope, improved in civility."

"I cannot be so easily reconciled to myself. The recollection of what I then said, of my conduct, my manners, my expressions during the whole of it, is now, and has been many months, inexpressibly painful to me. Your reproof, so well applied, I shall never forget: 'had you behaved in a more gentlemanlike manner.' Those were your words. You know not, you can scarcely conceive, how they have tortured me;—though it was some time, I confess, before I was reasonable enough to allow their justice."

"I was certainly very far from expecting them to make so strong an impression. I had not the smallest idea of their being ever felt in such a way."

"I can easily believe it. You thought me then devoid of every proper feeling, I am sure you did. The turn of your countenance I shall never forget, as you said that I could not have addressed you in any possible way that would induce you to accept me."

"Oh! do not repeat what I then said. These recollections will not do at all. I assure you that I have long been most heartily ashamed of it."

"My letter to you following—did it soon make you think better of me? Did you, on reading it, give any credit to its contents?"

She explained what its effect on her had been, and how gradually all her former prejudices had been removed.

"I knew," said he, "that what I wrote must give you pain, but it was necessary. I hope you have destroyed the letter. There was one part especially, the opening of it, which I should dread your having the power of reading again. I can remember some expressions which might justly make you hate me."

"The letter shall certainly be burnt, if you believe it essential to the preservation of my regard; but, though we have both reason to think my opinions not entirely unalterable, they are not, I hope, quite so easily changed as that implies."

"When I wrote that letter, I believed myself perfectly calm and cool, but I am since convinced that it was written in a dreadful bitterness of spirit."

"The letter, perhaps, began in bitterness, but it did not end so. The adieu is charity itself. But think no more of the letter. The feelings of the person who wrote, and the person who received it, are now so widely different from what they were then, that every unpleasant circumstance attending it ought to be forgotten. You must learn some of my philosophy. Think only of the past as its remembrance gives you pleasure."

"I cannot give you credit for any philosophy of the kind. Your retrospections must be so totally void of reproach, that the contentment arising from them is not of philosophy, but, what is much better, of innocence. But with me, it is not so. Painful recollections will intrude which cannot, which ought not, be repelled. I have been a selfish being all my life, in practice, though not in principle. As a child I was taught what was right, but I was not taught to correct my temper. I was given good principles, but left to follow them in pride and conceit. Unfortunately an only son, for many years an only child, I was spoilt by my parents, who, though good themselves—my father, particularly, all that was benevolent and amiable—allowed, encouraged, almost taught me to be selfish and overbearing; to care for none beyond my own family circle; to think meanly of all the rest of the world; to wish at least to think meanly of their sense and worth compared with my own. Such I was, from eight to eight and twenty; and such I might still have been but for you, dearest, loveliest Lizzy! What do I not owe you! You taught me a lesson, hard indeed at first, but most advantageous. By you, I was properly humbled. I came to you without a doubt of my reception. You showed me how insufficient were all my pretensions to please a woman worthy of being pleased."

"Had you then persuaded yourself that I should?"

"Indeed I had. What will you think of my vanity? I believed you to be wishing, expecting my addresses."

"My manners must have been in fault, but not intentionally, I assure you. I never meant to deceive you, but my spirits might often lead me wrong. How you must have hated me after *that* evening?"

"Hate you! I was angry perhaps at first, but my anger soon began to take a proper direction."

"I am almost afraid of asking what you thought of me, when we met at Pemberley. You blamed me for coming?"

"No, indeed. I felt nothing but surprise."

"Your surprise could not be greater than *mine* in being noticed by you. My conscience told me that I deserved no extraordinary politeness, and I confess that I did not expect to receive *more* than my due."

"My object then," he replied, "was to show you, by every civility in my power, that I was not so mean as to resent the past; and I hoped to obtain your forgiveness, to lessen your ill opinion, by letting you see that your reproofs had been attended to. How soon any other wishes introduced themselves I can hardly tell, but I believe in about half an hour after I had seen you."

He then told her of Georgiana's delight in her acquaintance, and of her disappointment at its sudden interruption; which naturally leading to the cause of that interruption, she soon learnt that his resolution of following her from Derbyshire in quest of her sister had been formed before he quitted the inn, and that his gravity and thoughtfulness there had arisen from no other struggles than what such a purpose must comprehend.

She expressed her gratitude again, but it was too painful a subject to each, to be dwelt on farther.

He took a deep breath and prepared to confess his involvement with Trenwith House, but she had pulled out her watch and noted it was time to be home. They sauntered back onto the path.

"What could become of Bingley and Jane?" she wondered.

"Are you quite delighted with their engagement?" he asked.

"Are *you*?"

"I am. Charles had given me the earliest information of it."

"I must ask whether you were surprised?"

"Not at all. When I went away, I felt that it would soon happen."

"That is to say, you had given your permission. I guessed as much."

"Charles does not require my permission on anything!"

"But he must have sought your counsel?"

"On the evening before my going to London, I made a confession to him, which I believe I ought to have made long ago. I told him of all that had occurred to make my former interference in his affairs absurd and impertinent. His surprise was great. He had never had the slightest suspicion. I told him, moreover, that I believed myself mistaken in supposing, as I had done, that your sister was indifferent to him; and as I could easily perceive that his attachment to her was unabated, I felt no doubt of their happiness together."

She smiled at his easy manner of directing his friend.

"Did you speak from your own observation," said she, "when you told him that my sister loved him, or merely from my information last spring?"

"From the former. I had narrowly observed her during the two visits which I had lately made here; and I was convinced of her affection."

"And your assurance of it, I suppose, carried immediate conviction to him."

"It did. Bingley is most unaffectedly modest. His diffidence had prevented his depending on his own judgment in so anxious a case, but his reliance on mine made every thing easy. I was obliged to confess one thing, which for a time, and not unjustly, offended him. I could not allow myself to conceal that your sister had been in town three months last winter, that I had known it, and purposely kept it from him. He was angry. But his anger, I am persuaded, lasted no longer than he remained in any doubt of your sister's sentiments. He has heartily forgiven me now."

The relaxed and friendly manner in which she conversed with him pleased him more than anything as they made their way back to Longbourn. He thought her beauty glowed more warmly than the sun, and but for the confidence he knew he had to reveal, their walk could not have been more satisfying until they had to part. Charles had turned toward the house with Miss Bennet earlier and awaited by his horse outside. Darcy walked Miss Elizabeth into the foyer of the house and there bid her adieu. He placed a chaste kiss upon her hand. Her ensuing blush reflected the memory of their earlier, more passionate caress, and perhaps a shared desire for something more.

CHAPTER FIFTY-TWO

Though Darcy had gone, Lizzy still felt his lips upon her hand. She shivered. There was no manner of touch, large or small, that she did not welcome from him. Her deepest hopes had been answered beyond expectation. Darcy loved her!

"My dear Lizzy, where can you have been walking to?" was a question which Lizzy received from Jane as soon as she entered their room, and from all the others when they sat down to table. She had only to say in reply, that they had wandered about, till she was beyond her own knowledge. She coloured as she spoke; but neither that, nor anything else, awakened a suspicion of the truth.

The evening passed quietly, unmarked by anything extraordinary. With Darcy gone, she felt agitated and confused, rather *knew* that she was happy than *felt* herself to be so; for, besides the immediate embarrassment, there were other evils before her. She anticipated what would be felt in the family when her situation became known; she was aware that no one liked him but Jane; and even feared that with the others it was a dislike which not all his fortune and consequence might do away.

And then there was the consideration of Trenwith House.

At night she opened her heart to Jane. Though suspicion was very far from Miss Bennet's general habits, she was absolutely incredulous here.

"You are joking, Lizzy. This cannot be! Engaged to Mr. Darcy! No, no, you shall not deceive me. I know it to be impossible."

"This is a wretched beginning indeed! My sole dependence was on you, and I am sure nobody else will believe me, if you do not. Yet, indeed, I am in earnest. I speak nothing but the truth. He still loves me, and we are engaged."

Jane looked at her doubtingly. "Oh, Lizzy! it cannot be. I know how much you dislike him."

"You know nothing of the matter. *That* is all to be forgot. Perhaps I did not always love him so well as I do now. But in such cases as these, a good memory is unpardonable. This is the last time I shall ever remember it myself."

Miss Bennet still looked all amazement. Lizzy again, and more seriously assured her of its truth.

"Good Heaven! Can it be really so! Yet now I must believe you," cried Jane. "My dear, dear Lizzy, I would—I do congratulate you—but are you certain? forgive the question—are you quite certain that you can be happy with him?"

"There can be no doubt of that. It is settled between us already, that we are to be the happiest couple in the world. But are you pleased, Jane? Shall you like to have such a brother?"

"Very, very much. Nothing could give either Bingley or myself more delight. But we considered it, we talked of it as impossible. And do you really love him quite well enough? Oh, Lizzy! do anything rather than marry without affection. Are you quite sure that you feel what you ought to do?"

"Oh, yes! You will only think I feel *more* than I ought to do, when I tell you all."

"What do you mean?"

"Why, I must confess that I love him better than I do Bingley. I am afraid you will be angry."

"My dearest sister, now *be* serious. I want to talk very seriously. Let me know every thing that I am to know, without delay. Will you tell me how long you have loved him?"

"It has been coming on so gradually, that I hardly know when it began. But I believe I must date it from my first seeing his beautiful grounds at Pemberley."

Another entreaty that she would be serious, however, produced the desired effect; and she soon satisfied Jane by her solemn assurances of attachment. When convinced on that article, Miss Bennet had nothing further to wish.

"Now I am quite happy," said she, "for you will be as happy as myself. I always had a value for him. Were it for nothing but his love of you, I must always have esteemed him, but now, as Bingley's friend and your husband, there can be only Bingley and yourself more dear to me. But Lizzy, you have been very sly, very reserved with me. How little did you tell me of what passed at Pemberley and Lambton!

I owe all that I know of it to another, not to you."

Lizzy told her the motives of her secrecy. She had been unwilling to mention Bingley; and the unsettled state of her own feelings had made her equally avoid the name of his friend. But now she would no longer conceal from her his share in Lydia's marriage. All, save the activities concerning Trenwith House, was acknowledged, and half the night spent in conversation. Only when she returned to her own chamber, spirited from reliving the best parts of her encounters with Darcy through the retelling of it to Jane, did she turn her mind to the greater difficulty.

She briefly entertained the thought of keeping Darcy in ignorance, but a lie of omission regarding a matter of such substance did not sit well with her. What if he were to discover the truth by other means? What if, on their wedding night, he recognized her body? What if he discerned she was no longer a virgin? Such a scene was to be avoided. They ought not begin their wedded life with secrets. On this, she was duly resolved.

But, goodness, how did one broach a subject of this nature? It was not a topic that fell easily between the weather and dinner. Perhaps she ought to wait for *his* confession? His involvement was no less significant than hers. *Did* he have any intention of informing her of his role at Trenwith House? Or would he presume the past to be irrelevant? It was not necessary, and perhaps unwise, for her to seek the particulars of what transpired in his life before she had known him. Though she might be curious as to how many women he had 'mentored,' she would not ask to be privileged to such information. What mattered were his actions when and after he had declared himself to her. Since then...but his first declaration of love had actually been in April...in Hunsford. Since then, he had met with another woman—at the Lilac Cottage. That woman had been none other than herself, but *he* had not known it. He was only aware that she was a nameless 'student.'

The realization dampened her elation of the day, but before she allowed to feel too sour, she reasoned that he had no commitment to honour for *she* had refused him—and in a manner that would have dashed all hope of attaining her affection. He had every right to turn his attentions elsewhere. After receiving such a harsh rejection, a lesser man would have resigned completely, gone to nurse his wounds to seek more fertile fields another day. To his credit, and proof of his devotion, Darcy had not forsaken her and, instead, increased his efforts to win her heart. She recalled fondly how amiable he had been when they were in Derbyshire.

But he had been equally agreeable at the Lilac Cottage. If he had been in earnest pursuit of her, how was it he could lay with another woman during that same time? Was his obligation to Abby Trenwith so great? Did he truly approach his responsibility completely devoid of sentiment for the student, as was asked of him in his role of mentor? But even Abby acknowledged that complete indifference was not always attainable. And he had certainly *seemed* attracted to his student. Could that have merely been affected? For a man who disdained insincerity, was he capable of such a performance?

Lizzy lay upon her bed, grasping her sheets tightly. Oh, what an unwanted epiphany was this! How quickly euphoria could be dashed!

In an effort to reclaim joy, she reasoned that she had no claim to his fidelity at that time. Perhaps he saw his actions as merely the fulfillment of a duty. She allowed he might even be a little attracted to this student and ought to triumph that her body was desirable to him. It was absurd to be jealous of herself. Surely his love for her was no less whole or pure because of a single night's event. There was too much goodness in him for her to think him guilty of perfidy—and she ought to guard against forming too early a judgment as she had done to him before. There was no evidence to suggest he had any attachment to this other woman.

Lizzy considered untangling her thoughts by speaking of them to Jane, but her sister was likely asleep by now, and her concerns would only upset Jane. Even if Jane were to overcome the shock of her sister's scandalous quest, she would only urge Lizzy to take the most positive and forgiving outlook. If only Abby were here! Lizzy decided she would postpone further thought till the morning and not allow the wayward emotions of a late hour to colour her reasoning. She closed her eyes, but a peaceful repose eluded her. A sinister doubt persisted until the light of day brought to her a means for putting an end to her concerns.

CHAPTER FIFTY-THREE

D arcy stared at the note. Without betraying his alarm, he asked of his valet, "When was this delivered?"

"It arrived by courier a half hour ago while you were out with Mr. Bingley," his valet replied.

Darcy had gone riding with Charles in the early morning when the air was crisp and the horses could be urged into full gallop without the weight of a warm day upon them. He would have liked, however, to ask the courier who had commissioned the note to him. Abby was the likely author, but the handwriting was not hers. Perhaps she had reason to ask another to pen the note. She knew he stayed at Netherfield. He examined the note once more. It was addressed to him but contained nothing more than a ten word directive:

Four Horses Posting Inn, Meryton. Noon Hour. To-day. Final Lesson.

It must have come from Abby. No one else would send him such a cryptic message and refer to a 'final lesson.' He supposed she meant a final lesson with Miss Elizabeth. Abby would not have known of his engagement. Perhaps this was her attempt at matchmaking.

As his valet assisted him from his riding coat, he considered penning a response to Abby that a final lesson would be unnecessary. With happy tidings to report, he would have a lifetime to provide Miss Elizabeth all the 'lessons' she should ever require.

But if an assignation had been set up for noon to-day, no reply would reach Abby in time. He surmised Miss Elizabeth to have received a similar note. He could send a message to her more easily, but then he would risk drawing attention to her. He had no wish to keep her waiting at this posting inn—if she intended to attend. The prospect rather rattled him. He preferred she didn't. He preferred her to want nothing more to do with the man who had served as her mentor now that she was in love with *him*. Though he could not fault her for wanting a final lesson before committing the rest of her life to a man whose skills at lovemaking she had no indications, the thought that she might be a little partial to her mentor made him stiffen.

Good God. He was jealous of his own person.

Yet it was a very real possibility. Many a student fell in love with their mentor. But the attachment was of a superficial sort and passed easily. Whatever attachment Miss Elizabeth might harbor for her mentor signified little. Still, he could not help being curious. He had resolved not to wait another day before baring all to his dear Lizzy. She seemed to return his affection beyond what he could have hoped for, but she may want nothing more to do with him when all was revealed. Though his happiness could not be complete till he had made a clean breast of his concerns, the joy he had experienced yesterday was incomparable. Theirs may prove a short-lived engagement, but he was determined to win her hand a thousand times over, if needed.

"Shall we make our way to Longbourn?" Charles proposed at breakfast.

"I think you must marry soon if you cannot last four and twenty hours without seeing your beloved," Darcy smiled, though he felt every bit as eager as his friend. "I have some business to attend in Meryton, but the afternoon would be convenient."

Satisfied, Charles bothered his friend no more till Darcy was headed out the door.

"Shall I ride with you and keep you company?" Charles asked.

"That won't be necessary," Darcy replied as he reached into the pocket of his riding coat for his gloves and, by accident, dislodged a black satin mask.

It fell to the ground. Charles picked it up. "Yours?"

Darcy took the mask and shoved it back into his pocket. "Must have been from an old masquerade."

"It was in your riding coat?" Charles then surveyed his friend's greatcoat with stacked shoulder capes. "Will you not be warm in that garrick?"

"This one is cut from linen, not wool," Darcy eschewed and took his leave before he might be forced into a fib.

Once saddled, he pulled his hat lower. He was not unknown in these parts and preferred to travel as inconspicuously as possible. Luck was with him, and he encountered no one he knew on the road to Meryton.

The Four Horses Posting Inn, situated on the outskirts of the township, was a modest structure with no neighbors. The regiment, while it was stationed in Meryton, had made much use of it, but at present, the place seemed nearly deserted. Darcy looked about for a stablehand but eventually saw to his own horse. Inside, he was met with a heavyset woman he presumed to be the innkeeper or the wife. She had on a surly countenance that improved greatly upon seeing the quality of her guest.

Seeking minimal interaction with her, he explained promptly, "I have an engagement here at noon."

She grunted. "Last room ta yer left, second floor. I can 'ave some wine sent ta yer room, shall I?"

"Privacy is all that is required at present."

She grunted again. "That'll cost ya a shillin' more."

He frowned but retrieved his purse and placed the coin in her grubby palm. Then he took himself up the stairs before she thought of something else to charge him for. At the end of the hall, he paused before the door, removed his hat, and pulled the short mask over his eyes. He had no premeditations for what ought to happen and would let *her* guide the session. Though it might pain him to ascertain her feelings for her mentor, he knew that as his only motive. Softly he rapped on the door.

"Come in," a voice from within said.

The windows of the room were shuttered but enough light peered through the cracks that he could discern the furniture and her silhouette upon the bed. She wore her mask from the Lilac Cottage and, like him, was clothed in a manner to conceal as much of her person as possible. An awkward silence ensued.

"I was unsure you would come," she remarked at last, "given your decision to quit your position with Mrs. Trenwith."

"My commitment to you was made prior to such a determination, and I will not desert my charge," he replied.

"You are here merely out of duty then?"

He did not quite know how to answer. In his role purely as mentor, the answer would be 'yes,' but given that his student was also the love of his life, obligation was not the entire account.

"In part," he replied truthfully.

She frowned.

"Did you wish for another mentor?" he asked, his groin tightening.

"Not at all."

He relaxed.

"But," she continued, "I would not have faulted you if you had resigned all obligations. Your sense of responsibility is admirable, but I absolve you of all concerns. You are free to leave."

"Do you desire my departure?" he inquired.

She seemed flustered. "I have no wish to compel you to stay if you do not desire it."

This was a strange exchange. What did she mean by such vagueness?

"The student dictates the direction," he reminded her.

"If I wished to pursue the lesson, you would oblige?"

He knew not how to answer. Did she want a lesson? He was unsure he could persist in the charade if she did.

"If I did not wish it," she rephrased, "would you...would you be disappointed?"

"Do you not wish for the lesson?" he asked, puzzled. He knew Abby to favour their unification, but she would not have set up a lesson without the consent of the student.

"I hesitate because my *circumstances* have changed."

He was glad to hear their engagement had provoked some qualms to lying with another man. They remained with the room between them, both hesitant, more aloof than strangers at their first lesson.

"I understand," he said, for he wished her no discomfort. "Your pending nuptials must make an education of this nature awkward."

She looked at him sharply. "Yes, *indeed.*"

He detected a rise in tension.

"And you would yet provide an engaged woman her final lesson?"

"I would not," he responded unequivocally.

"But you follow the dictates of the student."

"An engagement is a different matter. I do not mentor married or engaged women."

"Then why are you *here?*"

"As I could not send word to Abby in timely fashion, it would have been impolite to leave you to sit alone and in ignorance."

"You could have sent a note to the inn."

"Yes, but that would have been impersonal."

"Why did you not mention earlier that you would not continue with an engaged pupil?"

"Why did you not reveal your engagement?" he returned.

Something was amiss. He had inadvertently revealed his knowledge of her engagement, but she had hardly seemed surprised. Before he could ponder it more, however, she had risen to her feet and approached him.

"Are you *certain* you do not wish to have our final lesson?" she asked, her tone rich with suggestion.

His cock perked instantly.

"I am," he said.

She stood before him, peering up into his face. "Because it be your policy or your penchant?"

He observed her parted lips and silently groaned. Was she attempting to seduce him?

"What does it matter?" he responded as evenly as he could.

Mere inches separated them. She reached for and straightened one of the lapels of his garrick. He stared at her hand upon his chest. Desire swelled through his body. He wanted to take her. His body, clamoring to have her, would have a will of its own. But the disharmony of his emotions managed to stay him—for the moment. She *was* attempting to seduce her mentor. The realization shocked and vexed him. He took a step back.

She raised her brows. "Do I offend you now? You were never adverse to our contact before."

"For a woman *newly engaged*, you are keen to have this final lesson?"

Disheartened that he may have misjudged her devotion to him, he nearly choked on the words.

She stepped toward him. "Would your reservations cease if I were *not* engaged?"

He could not fathom the purpose of her hypothetical but suspected she intended to persuade him from his stance. While he wrestled with the proper course of action, she untied her cloak and let it fall to the ground. She wore a light summer muslin that conformed to her body most agreeably. The gown's wide neckline allowed her feminine assets to be presented with great advantage. Despite his dismay, he might yet succumb to her charms. He remembered how, all too easily, that had occurred before.

Stepping away from her once more, he replied, "Such speculation is of no consequence. *My* situation has changed as well."

She pulled one long glove off an arm, then the other, before closing the distance between them. "Indeed?"

He took another step back and came upon the door behind him. "I am in love. Madly, desperately in love. As such, I cannot continue in my capacity as mentor."

He wished she could have said the same with regards her position, but he kept this bitter thought to himself.

She stopped and now looked down upon the floor.

"I am sorry to have disappointed you," he said drily.

Her gaze flew to him. "You have *not* disappointed—not in the least! You have, as ever, proven to be a man of superior character. I only pray that *I* have not disappointed *you*."

He did not know what to make of her words and watched in bewilderment as she sank to her knees before him.

"Forgive me for having doubted your constancy," she said with moisture in her eyes.

Unable to bear seeing his love before him in such a manner, he, too, knelt.

"Forgive me for not having come forward before," she continued. "Perhaps one day we shall laugh at our comedy of errors. Oh! I hope it will be so and soon!"

She tore her mask asunder. His heart leapt upon seeing her lovely countenance, her eyes shimmering with pained relief. He wanted nothing but to clasp her to his bosom but was slightly paralyzed by his own nascent realizations.

"I have been your student all this time," she said. "I ought to have confessed it earlier, only fear of how you should then perceive me, fear of losing your love made me a coward. And then jealousy—I had never thought I could fall victim to that ugly emotion—it compelled me to fix upon this final lesson to test—oh! I am almost too ashamed to admit it—"

"This was *your* contrivance? Not Abby's?"

She nodded. "Abby played no part. The arrangement was mine, though I ought not have. I see now the foolishness of it all."

She looked down at her clasped hands. He began to understand the odd questions she had leveled at him. Carefully, he removed his hat and then his mask. When she looked up, there were no signs of shock.

"How long have you known?" he asked.

"Since Pemberley. Rather, I began to suspect and attempted to corroborate my suspicions at the Lilac Cottage."

His mind reeled with the information. He had never been discovered before.

"It was your handkerchief," she supplied. "And that of your sister's. Identical handkerchiefs, both embroidered by your mother."

He could not have predicted such a small article would lead to his unmasking, but a more important revelation commanded his attention.

"And you pursued this lesson because you thought I had an attachment to you—a student of mine?"

"Is it not silly beyond belief? I was jealous of—myself! I ought to have believed your professions of love and saved myself much pain! Only...I know not why I entertained these doubts that you might have been partial to another woman—your student—though it was me. The events of this year have certainly humbled me and made my flaws plain. I hardly know myself."

She looked once more at her hands. His relief complete, he grasped her hands between his and brought them to his lips.

"Darling Lizzy! You must never doubt my love or devotion. Ours is a comedy of errors indeed. Your jealousy is not unfounded. I was, as you suspected, partial to my student—exceedingly partial. And here you have bested me with the truth when it is I who ought to have confessed, for I have known your identity longer than you knew mine. I had every intention to make a clean breast of it all and feared you might not wish me for a husband when you knew my role. Then *I* was made an idiot by jealousy, for it seemed you were partial to the man who was your mentor."

She was stunned. "We were each of us jealous of ourselves? What delightful nonsense! And I had thought we were two of the more intelligent samples from our species!"

He did not share in her humor on the situation, but he enjoyed her smile.

"But how did you know who I was?" she asked.

"I knew shortly after our first encounter at Trenwith House. You, the student, nursed a cold that first lesson. The following day I called at Hunsford Parsonage and discovered Miss Elizabeth Bennet to possess the very same cold."

Her mouth fell open.

"I confronted Abby, but she refused to confirm my suspicions, even after she discerned I was in love with you. During our second lesson, I was convinced of my belief and resolved not to continue in the capacity of your mentor."

"That explains your cryptic note of the third lesson."

"But Nicholas Trenwith had made it impossible for me to leave you. My resolve subsequently fell to pieces at your hands."

She seemed to blush, murmuring, "Yes, well, that has been another discovery for me this year. I am quite the wanton, Mr. Darcy."

He smiled and kissed her fingers. "I would not have it otherwise."

Turning up her palm, he kissed her wrist. He could kiss this lovely wrist a hundred times without tiring. But the wrist was an insufficient recipient for the passion that overcame him. He pulled her to him and sought her lips. She quivered a little but returned his kiss with equal ardor. His earlier jealousy had aggravated him into an excited state, and he now poured this energy into the kiss. A trace of anger remained, though it was directed more at himself than at her. She should not have doubted the depths of what he felt for her. He tightened his embrace. He wanted to take her, consume her, overwhelm her with the fervor of his love and desire so that she might never doubt him again.

* * * * *

Lizzy could barely keep apace with the fury of his kiss. His lips had never been so demanding, so forceful and arousing. She felt its effects deep in her womanhood. The ache between her legs flourished as the kiss deepened. She wanted this man, wanted him more than she had ever wanted anything in her life. And she wanted to demonstrate this élan to him, body and soul. Wrapping her arms about the back of his neck, she pulled herself closer to him. He tasted divine. He smelled divine. He felt divine. No aphrodisiac would ever be required.

He swept her into his arms and carried her to the bed. Though she wanted more of him, more of his body, she was not ready to relinquish his lips yet. He was compelled to lay atop her as she pushed her tongue deep into his mouth. At times the ardency would soften into sweetness, slowing the waltz between their mouths, but desire continued to build. His erection was hard as flint against her, and she ground her pelvis at him. He took the wordless encouragement and pushed himself off her to strip his coat. She sat up to assist him with his neckcloth. Unable to be parted from her long, he reclaimed her mouth. He tore his waistcoat open, sending the buttons clattering to the floor. She pulled off the garment and, together, they made quick work of his shirt. She gazed upon his bared chest with hunger, then applied her lips to its planes, kissing and tugging a nipple, her hands roaming his flesh.

With a groan, he unpinned her bodice and slipped it down her arms and off her body. Her skirts soon followed.

"Lie back," he said, pushing her back into the pillows.

Pushing her shift up to her hips, he settled his upper body between her legs. She gasped when he flicked his tongue at the sensitive nub between her thighs. What had been a nightmare months before had turned into a dream, a beautiful erotic dream come to life. She allowed his tongue to turn her into a mass of quivering, aching desire. She moaned her satisfaction. They quickened soon into grunts and gasps as lust concentrated in her abdomen, between her legs, threatening to explode. He eased himself back and attended to his riding boots.

"Why did you stop?" she huffed. She would have preferred to be bereft of drink and food.

"One of the advanced lessons is delayed gratification," he responded.

She was not entirely disappointed, for she would have preferred his cock to his tongue, but she knew from past experience, that a woman could have both.

"Am I being punished?" she asked.

"On the contrary, though it may seem like it at first."

She eyed him suspiciously, for she believed his lust to be as great as hers. "Is this lesson for the benefit of the student or the mentor?"

"Both."

He turned her over and began unlacing her stays. She suppressed a pout as the moisture at her quim dripped down a thigh. Was he truly in such command of his own urges that he could apply this 'delayed gratification?'

"What would have happened if I attempted to seduce you?" she asked. "Would you have acquiesced to the lesson?"

"It was not my intention."

"But I could have prevailed upon you?" She enjoyed the thought of her own prowess.

He reached between her legs and stroked her, showing her that she would have easily surrendered to him. He was the maestro, her body his instrument.

"I thought you did not mentor married of engaged women?" she murmured.

"I have decided to make an exception," he answered as he kissed her between her shoulders, then trailed his mouth along her spine.

"A happy decision for me."

He pushed her chemise over her rump and kissed a buttock. She shivered. His long, lean fingers continued to fondle her, stoking the flame. It burned more intensely. She started to squirm and whine. He palmed a buttock to hold her still. Her need throbbed angrily.

"Take me...please," she said when his fingers slowed. Her body was on fire.

His grasp on her rump tightened. There was a pause, then she felt his cock sinking into her, filling her with its hardness. Victory! Her muscles flexed about his member. It was his turn to shiver. With a forced exhale, he thrust himself in and out of her. Every time his length brushed against her most sensitive spot was music to her body. At first he moved too slowly. But then he leaned himself against his forearms so that he could delve into her deeper and more forcefully, his chest bumping into her back with the motions, his pelvis pushing against her butt. The pent-up frustration from the deferred fulfilment had intensified her lust, and she found herself hurtling to her climax with a speed and strength that frightened her. She wanted to brace herself for the impact, but when he slammed his cock into her in rapid succession, she exploded against her will. She screamed as her body bucked and shook. Vaguely, she felt hot liquid filling her as he spent in unison with her. He collapsed on top of her, his body damp from perspiration, his heart pounding as furiously as hers. She felt shattered, relieved, and euphoric.

Their fingers found each other and entwined.

"My God, Lizzy," he murmured, kissing her temple.

"Lesson learned," she replied. "I think I shall like these advanced lessons."

He groaned and, rolling off of her, scooped her into his arms. They lay together until her spirits, rising to playfulness again, wanted him to account for his having ever fallen in love with her.

"You were in love with me even before our first lesson at Trenwith House?" she asked.

"I fought it, but my feelings for you prevailed. What a fool I was not to have had an inkling of how much you abhorred me!"

"Yes! You could have then saved yourself the pain of pressing your suit."

"I think I would still have been compelled to take the honourable course, given what transpired at our third lesson. It so happened I had a dual purpose for seeking your hand. Your compromised state only added insult to injury when you rejected me. Did you have no fear for the worst? Was I such an abomination to you that you would rather face ignominy than be married to me?"

"I suppose I was not thinking clearly at the time. Given my flaws, how could you begin to love me? I can comprehend your going on charmingly, when you had once made a beginning, but what could set you off in the first place?"

"I cannot fix on the hour, or the spot, or the look, or the words, which laid the foundation. It is too long ago. I was in the middle before I knew that I *had* begun."

"My beauty you had early withstood, and as for my manners—my behaviour to *you* was at least always bordering on the uncivil, and I never spoke to you without rather wishing to give you pain than not. Now be sincere; did you admire me for my impertinence?"

"For the liveliness of your mind, I did."

"You may as well call it impertinence at once. It was very little less. The fact is, that you were sick of civility, of deference, of officious attention. You were disgusted with the women who were always speaking, and looking, and thinking for *your* approbation alone. I roused, and interested you, because I was so unlike *them*. Had you not been really amiable, you would have hated me for it; but in spite of the pains you took to disguise yourself, your feelings were always noble and just; and in your heart, you thoroughly despised the persons who so assiduously courted you. There—I have saved you the trouble of accounting for it; and really, all things considered, I begin to think it perfectly reasonable. To be sure, you knew no actual good of me—but nobody thinks of *that* when they fall in love."

Her pretty little speech complete, she nestled into the crook of his arm.

"Was there no good in your affectionate behaviour to Jane while she was ill at Netherfield?" he replied, stroking the arm she draped over him.

"Dearest Jane! Who could have done less for her? But make a virtue of it by all means. My good qualities are under your protection, and you are to exaggerate them as much as possible; and, in return, it belongs to me to find occasions for teasing and quarrelling with you as often as may be; and I shall begin directly by asking you what made you so unwilling to come to the point at last. What made you so shy of me, when you first called, and afterwards dined here? Why, especially, when you called, did you look as if you did not care about me?"

She turned to look at him. He returned her gaze.

"Because you were grave and silent, and gave me no encouragement."

"But I was embarrassed."

"And so was I."

"You might have talked to me more when you came to dinner."

"A man who had felt less, might."

"How unlucky that you should have a reasonable answer to give, and that I should be so reasonable as to admit it! But I wonder how long you *would* have gone on, if you had been left to yourself. I wonder when you *would* have spoken, if I had not asked you! My resolution of thanking you for your kindness to Lydia had certainly great effect. *Too much*, I am afraid; for what becomes of the moral, if our comfort springs from a breach of promise? I ought not to have mentioned the subject. This will never do."

"You need not distress yourself. The moral will be perfectly fair. Lady Catherine's unjustifiable endeavours to separate us were the means of removing all my doubts. I am not indebted for my present happiness to your eager desire of expressing your gratitude. I was not in a humour to wait for any opening of yours. My aunt's intelligence had given me hope, and I was determined at once to know every thing."

"Lady Catherine has been of infinite use, which ought to make her happy, for she loves to be of use. But tell me, what did you come down to Netherfield for? Was it merely to ride to Longbourn and be embarrassed? Or had you intended any more serious consequence?"

"My real purpose was to see *you*, and to judge, if I could, whether I might ever hope to make you love me. My avowed one, or what I avowed to myself, was to see whether your sister were still partial to Bingley, and if she were, to make the confession to him which I have since made."

"Shall you ever have courage to announce to Lady Catherine what is to befall her?"

"I am more likely to want more time than courage, Lizzy. But it ought to be done, and if our good innkeeper will provide a sheet of paper at a fair price, it shall be done directly."

"And if I had not a letter to write myself, I might sit by you and admire the evenness of your writing, as another young lady once did. But I have an aunt, too, who must not be longer neglected."

Sitting up, Lizzy began collecting her garments till she noticed him staring intently at her.

"How much did you pay the keeper of the inn for the use of this room?" he asked.

"I paid half a crown for two hours of solitude."

"It has been but an hour."

She looked to him and did not protest when he pulled her back down to the bed.

CHAPTER FIFTY-FOUR

"Good gracious!" cried Mrs. Bennet, as she stood at the window, "if that disagreeable Mr. Darcy is not coming here again with our dear Bingley! What can he mean by being so tiresome as to be always coming here? I had no notion but he would go a-shooting, or something or other, and not disturb us with his company. What shall we do with him? Lizzy, you must walk out with him again, that he may not be in Bingley's way."

Lizzy could hardly help laughing at so convenient a proposal, yet was really vexed that her mother should be always giving him such an epithet. Though Lizzy had left him but two hours before, she welcomed his presence with as much eagerness as if she had not seen him for two fortnights.

As soon as the gentlemen entered, Bingley looked at her so expressively, and shook hands with such warmth, as left no doubt of his good information; and he soon afterwards said aloud, "Mrs. Bennet, have you no more lanes hereabouts in which Lizzy may lose her way again to-day?"

"I advise Mr. Darcy, and Lizzy, and Kitty," said Mrs. Bennet, "to walk to Oakham Mount. It is a nice long walk, and Mr. Darcy has never seen the view."

"It may do very well for the others," replied Mr. Bingley; "but I am sure it will be too much for Kitty. Won't it, Kitty?"

Kitty owned that she had rather stay at home. Darcy professed a great curiosity to see the view from the Mount, and Lizzy silently consented. As she went up stairs to get ready, Mrs. Bennet followed her, saying,

"I am quite sorry, Lizzy, that you should be forced to have that disagreeable man all to yourself. But I hope you will not mind it; it is all for Jane's sake, you know; and there is no occasion for talking to him, except just now and then. So, do not put yourself to inconvenience."

During their walk, it was resolved that Mr. Bennet's consent should be asked in the course of the evening. Lizzy reserved to herself the application for her mother's. She could not determine how her mother would take it; sometimes doubting whether all his wealth and grandeur would be enough to overcome her abhorrence of the man. But whether she were violently set against the match, or violently delighted with it, it was certain that her manner would be equally ill adapted to do credit to her sense; and she could no more bear that Mr. Darcy should hear the first raptures of her joy, than the first vehemence of her disapprobation.

* * * * *

In the evening, soon after Mr. Bennet withdrew to the library, she saw Mr. Darcy rise also and follow him, and her agitation on seeing it was extreme. She did not fear her father's opposition, but he was going to be made unhappy; and that it should be through her means—that *she*, his favourite child, should be distressing him by her choice, should be filling him with fears and regrets in disposing of her—was a wretched reflection, and she sat in misery till Mr. Darcy appeared again, when, looking at him, she was a little relieved by his smile.

In a few minutes he approached the table where she was sitting with Kitty; and, while pretending to admire her work said in a whisper, "Go to your father, he wants you in the library."

She was gone directly.

Her father was walking about the room, looking grave and anxious.

"Lizzy," said he, "what are you doing? Are you out of your senses, to be accepting this man? Have not you always hated him?"

How earnestly did she then wish that her former opinions had been more reasonable, her expressions more moderate! It would have spared her from explanations and professions which it was exceedingly awkward to give, but they were now necessary, and she assured him, with some confusion, of her attachment to Mr. Darcy.

"Or, in other words, you are determined to have him. He is rich, to be sure, and you may have more fine clothes and fine carriages than Jane. But will they make you happy?"

"Have you any other objection," said Lizzy, "than your belief of my indifference?"

"None at all. We all know him to be a proud, unpleasant sort of man, but this would be nothing if you really liked him."

"I do, I do like him," she replied, with tears in her eyes, "I love him. Indeed he has no improper pride. He is perfectly amiable. You do not know what he really is; then pray do not pain me by speaking of him in such terms."

"Lizzy," said her father, "I have given him my consent. He is the kind of man, indeed, to whom I should never dare refuse anything, which he condescended to ask. I now give it to *you*, if you are resolved on having him. But let me advise you to think better of it. I know your disposition, Lizzy. I know that you could be neither happy nor respectable, unless you truly esteemed your husband; unless you looked up to him as a superior. Your lively talents would place you in the greatest danger in an unequal marriage. You could scarcely escape discredit and misery. My child, let me not have the grief of seeing *you* unable to respect your partner in life. You know not what you are about."

Lizzy, still more affected, was earnest and solemn in her reply; and at length, by repeated assurances that Mr. Darcy was really the object of her choice, by explaining the gradual change which her estimation of him had undergone, relating her absolute certainty that his affection was not the work of a day, but had stood the test of many months' suspense, and enumerating with energy all his good qualities, she did conquer her father's incredulity, and reconcile him to the match.

"Well, my dear," said he, when she ceased speaking, "I have no more to say. If this be the case, he deserves you. I could not have parted with you, my Lizzy, to anyone less worthy."

To complete the favourable impression, she then told him what Mr. Darcy had voluntarily done for Lydia. He heard her with astonishment.

"This is an evening of wonders, indeed! And so, Darcy did every thing; made up the match, gave the money, paid the fellow's debts, and got him his commission! So much the better. It will save me a world of trouble and economy. Had it been your uncle's doing, I must and *would* have paid him; but these violent young lovers carry every thing their own way. I shall offer to pay him tomorrow; he will rant and storm about his love for you, and there will be an end of the matter."

He then recollected her embarrassment a few days before, on his reading Mr. Collins's letter; and after laughing at her some time, allowed her at last to go—saying, as she quitted the room, "If any young men come for Mary or Kitty, send them in, for I am quite at leisure."

Lizzy's mind was now relieved from a very heavy weight; and, after half an hour's quiet reflection in her own room, she was able to join the others with tolerable composure. Every thing was too recent for gaiety, but the evening passed tranquilly away; there was no longer anything material to be dreaded, and the comfort of ease and familiarity would come in time.

When her mother went up to her dressing-room at night, she followed her, and made the important communication. Its effect was most extraordinary; for on first hearing it, Mrs. Bennet sat quite still, and unable to utter a syllable. Nor was it under many, many minutes that she could comprehend what she heard; though not in general backward to credit what was for the advantage of her family, or that came in the shape of a lover to any of them. She began at length to recover, to fidget about in her chair, get up, sit down again, wonder, and bless herself.

"Good gracious! Lord bless me! only think! dear me! Mr. Darcy! Who would have thought it! And is it really true? Oh! my sweetest Lizzy! how rich and how great you will be! What pin-money, what jewels, what carriages you will have! Jane's is nothing to it—nothing at all. I am so pleased—so happy. Such a charming man!—so handsome! so tall!—Oh, my dear Lizzy! pray apologise for my having disliked him so much before. I hope he will overlook it. Dear, dear Lizzy. A house in town! Every thing that is charming! Three daughters married! Ten thousand a year! Oh, Lord! What will become of me. I shall go distracted."

This was enough to prove that her approbation need not be doubted: and Lizzy, rejoicing that such an effusion was heard only by herself, soon went away. But before she had been three minutes in her own room, her mother followed her.

"My dearest child," she cried, "I can think of nothing else! Ten thousand a year, and very likely more! 'Tis as good as a Lord! And a special licence. You must and shall be married by a special licence. But my dearest love, tell me what dish Mr. Darcy is particularly fond of, that I may have it tomorrow."

This was a sad omen of what her mother's behaviour to the gentleman himself might be; and Lizzy found that, though in the certain possession of his warmest affection, and secure of her relations' consent, there was still something to be wished for. But the morrow passed off much better than she expected; for Mrs. Bennet luckily stood in such awe of her intended son-in-law that she ventured not to speak to him, unless it was in her power to offer him any attention, or mark her deference for his opinion.

Lizzy had the satisfaction of seeing her father taking pains to get acquainted with him; and Mr. Bennet soon assured her that he was rising every hour in his esteem.

"I admire all my three sons-in-law highly," said he. "Wickham, perhaps, is my favourite; but I think I shall like *your* husband quite as well as Jane's."

CHAPTER FIFTY-FIVE

Together Lizzy and Darcy penned the news of their happy tidings to Abby. Lizzy jested that they ought be grateful to Nicholas Trenwith, to which Darcy replied, "Absolutely not."

"But think, were it not for his tomfoolery—"

"'Crime' would be a more fitting word."

"You might not have been compelled to propose to me when you did. I would not have had the chance to refuse you. Instead, I would have continued on, despising your pride and thinking the worst of your character. You would have had no incentive to correct my erroneous assumptions and improve your behaviour. We would have gone on unaware that we could fall in love with each other."

"I knew already I was in love with you," he reminded her. "Your condition, prompted by the delinquency of Mr. Trenwith, only hastened a proposal that I believe would have been forthcoming regardless."

Seeing his displeasure at having to mention Nicholas, Lizzy dropped the matter. Her husband-to-be had yet to learn to be laughed at, and it was rather too early to begin.

Abby's response was as they expected. She was beyond joyous at the news and believed they made a most perfect couple *in all the important ways*. She commended Darcy for coming to his senses and expressed her happiness at his absence from her event and that she had always had more faith than not in him. To Lizzy she offered herself as counsel for any question on married life and praised her for her choice of a life partner. She wished them happiness, fulfillment, and many nights of passion.

Lizzy's next letter was to Mrs. Gardiner. From an unwillingness to confess how much her intimacy with Mr. Darcy had been over-rated, she had never yet answered her aunt's long letter; but now, having *that* to communicate which she knew would be most welcome, she was almost ashamed to find that her uncle and aunt had already lost three days of happiness, and immediately wrote as follows:

"I would have thanked you before, my dear aunt, as I ought to have done, for your long, kind, satisfactory, detail of particulars; but to say the truth, I was too cross to write. You supposed more than really existed. But *now* suppose as much as you choose; give a loose rein to your fancy, indulge your imagination in every possible flight which the subject will afford, and unless you believe me actually married, you cannot greatly err. You must write again very soon, and praise him a great deal more than you did in your last. I thank you, again and again, for not going to the Lakes. How could I be so silly as to wish it! Your idea of the ponies is delightful. We will go round the Park every day. I am the happiest creature in the world. Perhaps other people have said so before, but not one with such justice. I am happier even than Jane; she only smiles, I laugh. Mr. Darcy sends you all the love in the world that he can spare from me. You are all to come to Pemberley at Christmas.

"Yours, etc."

Mr. Darcy's letter to Lady Catherine was in a different style, and still different from either was what Mr. Bennet sent to Mr. Collins, in reply to his last.

"DEAR SIR,
"I must trouble you once more for congratulations. Lizzy will soon be the wife of Mr. Darcy. Console Lady Catherine as well as you can. But, if I were you, I would stand by the nephew. He has more to give.
"Yours sincerely, etc."

Miss Bingley's congratulations to her brother, on his approaching marriage, were all that was affectionate and insincere. She wrote even to Jane on the occasion, to express her delight, and repeat all her former professions of regard. Jane was not deceived, but she was affected, and though feeling no reliance on her, could not help writing her a much kinder answer than she knew was deserved.

The joy which Miss Darcy expressed on receiving similar information, was as sincere as her brother's in sending it. Four sides of paper were insufficient to contain all her delight, and all her earnest desire of being loved by her sister.

Before any answer could arrive from Mr. Collins, or any congratulations to Lizzy from his wife, the Longbourn family heard that the Collinses were come themselves to Lucas Lodge. The reason of this sudden removal was soon evident. Lady Catherine had been rendered so exceedingly angry by the contents of her nephew's letter, that Charlotte, really rejoicing in the match, was anxious to get away till the storm was blown over. At such a moment, the arrival of her friend was a sincere pleasure to Lizzy, though in the course of their meetings she must sometimes think the pleasure dearly bought, when she saw Mr. Darcy exposed to all the parading and obsequious civility of her husband. He bore it, however, with admirable calmness. He could even listen to Sir William Lucas, when he complimented him on carrying away the brightest jewel of the country, and expressed his hopes of their all meeting frequently at St. James's, with very decent composure. If he did shrug his shoulders, it was not till Sir William was out of sight.

Mrs. Phillips's vulgarity was another, and perhaps a greater, tax on his forbearance; and though Mrs. Phillips, as well as her sister, stood in too much awe of him to speak with the familiarity which Bingley's good humour encouraged, yet, whenever she *did* speak, she must be vulgar. Nor was her respect for him, though it made her more quiet, at all likely to make her more elegant. Lizzy did all she could to shield him from the frequent notice of either, and was ever anxious to keep him to herself, and to those of her family with whom he might converse without mortification; and though the uncomfortable feelings arising from all this took from the season of courtship much of its pleasure, it added to the hope of the future; and she looked forward with delight to the time when they should be removed from society so little pleasing to either, to all the comfort and elegance of their family party at Pemberley.

* * * * *

Happy for all her maternal feelings was the day on which Mrs. Bennet got rid of her two most deserving daughters. With what delighted pride she afterwards visited Mrs. Bingley, and talked of Mrs. Darcy, may be guessed. However, the accomplishment of her earnest desire in the establishment of so many of her children did not produce so happy an effect as to make her a sensible, amiable, well-informed woman for the rest of her life; though perhaps it was lucky for her husband, who might not have relished domestic felicity in so unusual a form, that she still was occasionally nervous and invariably silly.

Mr. Bennet missed his second daughter exceedingly; his affection for her drew him oftener from home than anything else could do. He delighted in going to Pemberley, especially when he was least expected.

Mr. Bingley and Jane remained at Netherfield only a twelvemonth. So near a vicinity to her mother and Meryton relations was not desirable even to *his* easy temper, or *her* affectionate heart. The darling wish of his sisters was then gratified; he bought an estate in a neighbouring county to Derbyshire, and Jane and Lizzy, in addition to every other source of happiness, were within thirty miles of each other.

Kitty, to her very material advantage, spent the chief of her time with her two elder sisters. In society so superior to what she had generally known, her improvement was great. She was not of so ungovernable a temper as Lydia; and, removed from the influence of Lydia's example, she became, by proper attention and management, less irritable, less ignorant, and less insipid. From the further disadvantage of Lydia's society she was of course carefully kept, and though Mrs. Wickham frequently invited her to come and stay with her, with the promise of balls and young men, her father would never consent to her going.

Mary was the only daughter who remained at home; and she was necessarily drawn from the pursuit of accomplishments by Mrs. Bennet's being quite unable to sit alone. Mary was obliged to mix more with the world, but she could still moralize over every morning visit; and as she was no longer mortified by comparisons between her sisters' beauty and her own, it was suspected by her father that she submitted to the change without much reluctance.

As for Wickham and Lydia, their characters suffered no revolution from the marriage of her sisters. He bore with philosophy the conviction that Lizzy must now become acquainted with whatever of his ingratitude and falsehood had before been unknown to her; and in spite of every thing, was not wholly without hope that Darcy might yet be prevailed upon to make his fortune. The congratulatory letter which Lizzy received from Lydia on her marriage, explained to her that, by his wife at least, if not by himself, such a hope was cherished.

The letter was to this effect:

"MY DEAR LIZZY,

"I wish you joy. If you love Mr. Darcy half as well as I do my dear Wickham, you must be very happy. It is a great comfort to have you so rich, and when you have nothing else to do, I hope you will think of us. I am sure Wickham would like a place at court very much, and I do not think we shall have quite money enough to live upon without some help. Any place would do, of about three or four hundred a year; but however, do not speak to Mr. Darcy about it, if you had rather not.

"Yours, etc."

As it happened that Lizzy had *much* rather not, she endeavoured in her answer to put an end to every entreaty and expectation of the kind. Such relief, however, as it was in her power to afford, by the practice of what might be called economy in her own private expenses, she frequently sent them. It had always been evident to her that such an income as theirs, under the direction of two persons so extravagant in their wants, and heedless of the future, must be very insufficient to their support; and whenever they changed their quarters, either Jane or herself were sure of being applied to for some little assistance towards discharging their bills. Their manner of living, even when the restoration of peace dismissed them to a home, was unsettled in the extreme. They were always moving from place to place in quest of a cheap situation, and always spending more than they ought. His affection for her soon sunk into indifference; hers lasted a little longer; and in spite of her youth and her manners, she retained all the claims to reputation which her marriage had given her.

Though Darcy could never receive *him* at Pemberley, yet, for Lizzy's sake, he assisted him further in his profession. Lydia was occasionally a visitor there, when her husband was gone to enjoy himself in London or Bath; and with the Bingleys they both of them frequently staid so long, that even Bingley's good humour was overcome, and he proceeded so far as to talk of giving them a hint to be gone.

Miss Bingley was very deeply mortified by Darcy's marriage; but as she thought it advisable to retain the right of visiting at Pemberley, she dropt all her resentment; was fonder than ever of Georgiana, almost as attentive to Darcy as heretofore, and paid off every arrear of civility to Lizzy.

Pemberley was now Georgiana's home, and the attachment of the sisters was exactly what Darcy had hoped to see. They were able to love each other even as well as they intended. Georgiana had the highest opinion in the world of Lizzy; though at first she often listened with an astonishment bordering on alarm at her lively, sportive manner of talking to her brother. He, who had always inspired in herself a respect which almost overcame her affection, she now saw the object of open pleasantry. Her mind received knowledge which had never before fallen in her way. By Lizzy's instructions, she began to comprehend that a woman may take liberties with her husband which a brother will not always allow in a sister more than ten years younger than himself.

Lady Catherine was extremely indignant on the marriage of her nephew, and as she gave way to all the genuine frankness of her character in her reply to the letter which announced its arrangement, she sent him language so very abusive, especially of Lizzy, that for some time all intercourse was at an end. But at length, by Lizzy's persuasion, he was prevailed on to overlook the offence, and seek a reconciliation. After a little further resistance on the part of his aunt, her resentment gave way, either to her affection for him, or her curiosity to see how his wife conducted herself, and she condescended to wait on them at Pemberley, in spite of that pollution which its woods had received, not merely from the presence of such a mistress, but the visits of her uncle and aunt from the city.

With the Gardiners, they were always on the most intimate terms. Darcy, as well as Lizzy, really loved them, and they were both ever sensible of the warmest gratitude towards the persons who, by bringing her into Derbyshire, had been the means of uniting them.

Though not as frequent a guest to Pemberley as the others, Abby Trenwith provided the company they sought most often, apart from Jane and Charles. Her lively spirit remained as forceful as ever and, freed from having to conceal the one from the other, enjoyed an unsuppressed vigor. She and Mrs. Darcy happily collaborated on a number of charitable and political activities.

Trenwith House was always open to both husband and wife, who would avail themselves, from time to time, of the Red Chamber and the Temple of Bastet.

THE END

Thank you for choosing to spend your time with me! If you enjoyed this book, please consider leaving a review.

Much obliged,
Georgette

For my other books

https://windcolorpress.leadpages.co/georgette-brown-books.

Or read on for an excerpt.

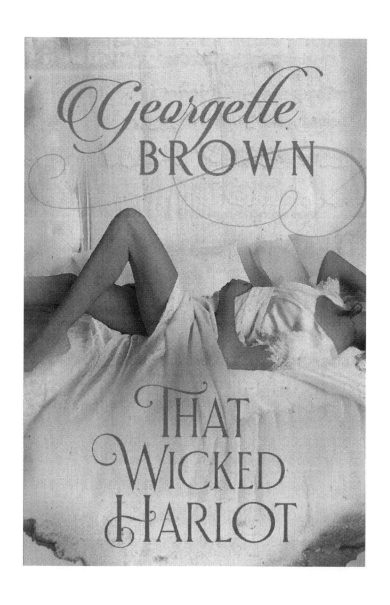

CHAPTER ONE

The beautiful woman wrapped in the arms of Radcliff M. Barrington, the fourth Baron Broadmoor, sighed into a wide smile as she nestled her body between his nakedness and the bed sheets. Gazing down at Lady Penelope Robbins, his mistress of nearly a twelvemonth, Broadmoor allowed her a moment to indulge in the afterglow of her third orgasm though he had yet to satisfy his own hardened arousal. He brushed his lips against her brow and happened to glance toward the corner of her bed chamber, where a man's waistcoat was draped over the back of a chair. He did not recognize it as his own. The fineness of the garment suggested that neither did it belong to one of her male servants.

Penelope was entertaining another lover, he concluded even as she murmured compliments regarding his skills as a lover. The realization came as no surprise to him. Indeed, he had suspected for some time. What surprised him was that he cared not overmuch. Nor had he the faintest curiosity as to who her other lover might be. He wondered, idly rather than seriously, why he continued to seek her company. Or she his. They had very little in common. He knew that from the start and yet had allowed her to seduce him into her bed.

He was possessed of enough breeding, wealth, and countenance to be able to command any number of women as his mistress. With black hair that waved above an ample brow and softened the square lines of his jaw, charcoal eyes that sparked despite the dark hue, and an impeccable posture that made him taller than most of his peers, Broadmoor presented an impressive appearance. He had no shortage of women setting their caps at him. A number of his friends kept dancers or opera singers, but he had never been partial to breaking the hearts of those young things. In contrast, Penelope was a seasoned widow and had little expectation of him, having been married once before to a wealthy but vastly older baronet, and scorning a return to that institution, preferred instead to indulge in the freedoms of widowhood.

Pulling the sheets off her, he decided it was his turn to spend. She purred her approval when he covered her slender body with his muscular one. Angling his hips, he prepared to thrust himself into her when a shrill and familiar voice pierced his ears.

"I care not that he is indisposed! If the Baron is here, I *will* speak to him!"

The voice was imperial. Haughty. Broadmoor recognized it in an instant.

Penelope's eyes flew open. "Surely that is not your aunt I hear?"

His aunt, Lady Anne Barrington, was not wont to visit him in his own home at Grosvenor Square, let alone that of his mistress. He knew Anne found him cold, heartless, and arrogant. He had a dreadful habit of refusing to encourage her histrionics, and in the role of the indulgent nephew, he was a miserable failure.

"Let us pretend we do not hear her," Penelope added, wrapping her arms about him.

It would be easier to silence a skewered pig, Broadmoor thought to himself.

A timid but anxious knock sounded at the door.

"What is it?" Penelope snapped at the maid who entered and apologized profusely for the interruption, informing them that a most insistent woman waited in the drawing room and had threatened, if she was not attended to with the utmost haste, to take herself up the stairs in search of his lordship herself.

"I fear there is no immediate escape," Broadmoor said, kissing the frown on his mistress' brow before donning his shirt and pants and wrapping a robe about himself. "But I shall return."

Before descending the stairs, he took a moment for his arousal to settle.

Whatever had compelled his aunt to come to the home of his mistress had better be of damned importance.

"Anne. To what do I owe this unexpected visit?" he asked of his uncle's wife when he strode into the room.

He discerned Anne to be in quite a state of disconcertion for she only sported two long strands of pearls—far fewer than the five or so he was accustomed to seeing upon her. Her pale pink gown did not suit her complexion and made her pallor all the more grey in his eyes.

"Radcliff! Praise the heavens I have found you!" she cried upon seeing him.

He refrained from raising an inquisitive brow. Undaunted by the lack of response from her nephew, Anne continued, "We are *undone*, Radcliff! Undone! Ruined!"

His first thought was of her daughter, Juliana, who recently had had her come-out last Season. Had the girl run off to Gretna Green with some irascible young blood? He would not hesitate to give chase, but Juliana had always impressed him as a sensible young woman with an agreeable disposition—despite whom she had for a mother.

"I can scarce breathe with the thought!" Anne bemoaned. "And you know my nerves to be fragile! Oh, the treachery of it all!"

She began to pace the room while furiously waving the fan she clutched in her hand.

"I could never show my face after this," she continued. "How fortunate your uncle is not alive to bear witness to the most disgraceful ruin ever to befall a Barrington! Though I would that he had not left me to bear the burden all alone. The strain that has been put upon me—who else, I ask, has had to suffer not only the loss of her husband and now this—this unspeakable *disgrace*? I have no wish to speak ill of your uncle, but now I think it selfish of him to have gone off to the Continent with Wellington when he *knew* he would be put in harm's way. And for what end? What end?"

Broadmoor did not reveal his suspicions that his uncle had taken himself to the Continent as much as a means to relieve himself from being hen-pecked by his wife as for military glory. Instead, he walked over to the sideboard to pour her a glass of ratafia in the hopes that it would calm the incessant fluttering of her fan.

"And what is the nature of this ruin?" he prompted.

"The *worst imaginable!*" Anne emphasized in response to his complacent tenor. "Never in my life could I have conceived such misfortune! And to think we must suffer at *her* hands. That—that unspeakable wench. That *wicked harlot*."

So it was the son and not the daughter, Broadmoor thought to himself. He should have expected it would be Edward, who was four years Juliana's senior but who possessed four fewer years to her maturity.

"You cannot conceive what torment I have endured these past days! And I have had no one, not a soul, to comfort me," Anne lamented, bypassing the ratafia as she worried the floor beneath her feet.

"The engagement to Miss Trindle has been called off?" Broadmoor guessed, slightly relieved for he did not think Edward up to the task of matrimony, even with the dowry of Miss Trindle serving as a handsome incentive. But it displeased him that Edward had not changed his ways.

"Heavens, no! Though it may well happen when the Trindles hear how we have been undone! Oh, but it is the fault of that devil-woman! My poor Edward, to have fallen victim to such a villainous lot."

Broadmoor suppressed a yawn.

"No greater ruin has *ever* befallen a Barrington," Anne added, sensing her nephew did not share her distress.

"Madam, my hostess awaits my attention," he informed her, looking towards the stairs.

Anne burned red as she remembered where she was. "As this was a calamity—yes, a calamity—of the highest order, I could not wait. If your uncle were here, there would have been no need...well, perhaps. His disquiet could often worsen my state. But your presence, Radcliff, affords me hope. I have nowhere else to turn. And you were always quite sensible. I wish that you would learn Edward your ways. You were his trustee and have fifteen more years of wisdom than he. You might take him under your wing."

He raised an eyebrow at the suggestion. "Edward came of age last year when he turned twenty-one. He is master of his own fortune and free to ruin himself as he sees fit."

"How can you speak so?"

"I have intervened once already in Edward's life and have no wish to make a practice of it," Broadmoor replied coolly.

"But..."

He placed the ratafia in her hand before she sank into the nearest sofa, bereft of words in a rare moment for Anne Barrington.

"But that *darkie* is a hundred times worse than her sister!" Anne said upon rallying herself. "Oh, are we never to rid ourselves of this cursed family and their treachery?"

Broadmoor watched in dismay as she set down her glass and began agitating her fan before her as if it alone could save her from a fainting spell. He went to pour himself a glass of brandy, his hopes of a short visit waning.

"What will become of us?" Anne moaned. "What will become of Juliana? I had hopes that she would make a match this year! Did you know that the banns might be read for Miss Helen next month and she has not nearly the countenance that Juliana has!"

"What could Edward have done to place Juliana's matrimonial prospects in jeopardy?" he asked. "Juliana has breeding and beauty and one of the most desirable assets a young woman could have: an inheritance of fifty thousand pounds."

His aunt gave an indignant gasp. Her mouth opened to utter a retort or to comment on her nephew's insensitivity but thought better of it.

"But what are we to do without Brayten?" she asked with such despondency that Broadmoor almost felt sorry for her.

"I beg your pardon?"

"The thought overwhelms me. Indeed, I can scarcely speak, the nature of it is so dreadful..."

He refrained from pointing out the irony in her statement.

"Edward has lost Brayten."

It was Broadmoor's turn to be rendered speechless, but he quickly collected himself and said in a dark voice. "Lost Brayten? Are you sure of this?"

"When I think of the care and attention I lavished upon him—and to be repaid in such a fashion! To be undone in such a manner. And by that wretched harlot. What sort of odious person would prey upon an innocent boy like Edward?"

"Edward is far from innocent," he informed her wryly, "but how is it he could have lost Brayten?"

The boy was reckless, Broadmoor knew, but Brayten was the sole source of income for Edward. The estate had been in the Barrington family for generations and boasted an impressive house in addition to its extensive lands. Surely the boy could not have been so careless as to jeopardize his livelihood.

"It is that witch, that hussy and devil-woman. They say she works magic with the cards. Witchcraft, I say!"

"Do you mean to tell me that Edward lost Brayten in a game of cards?" Broadmoor demanded.

"I had it from Mr. Thornsdale, who came to me at once after it had happened. I would that he had gone to you instead! Apparently,

Edward had to wager Brayten to win back his obligation of eighty thousand pounds."

"Eighty thousand pounds!" Broadmoor exclaimed. "He is a bigger fool than I feared."

"I wish you would not speak so harshly of your cousin."

"Madam, I shall have far harsher words when I see him!"

"It is the work of that *harlot*." Anne shook her fan as if to fend off an imaginary foe. "A sorceress, that one. The blood of pagans runs in her veins. Her kind practice the black arts. Yes, that is how she swindled my Edward. She ought to be run out of England!"

He narrowed his eyes. "Of whom do you speak?"

"*Darcy Sherwood*." Anne shuddered. "Her sister and stepmother are the most common of common, but Miss Sherwood is the worst of them all! I hear the Sherwoods are in no small way of debt. No doubt they are only too happy to put their greedy hands upon our precious estate! I wonder that the darkie, that wench, had orchestrated the entire episode to avenge herself for what Edward had done to her sister—as if a gentleman of his stature could possibly look upon such a common young woman with *any* interest."

It had been five years, but Broadmoor remembered the Sherwood name. Only it had been Priscilla Sherwood that had posed the problem then. He had not thought the young lady a suitable match for Edward, who had formed an unexpected attachment to her, and severed the relationship between the two lovebirds by removing his cousin to Paris, where Edward had promptly forgotten about Priscilla in favor of the pretty French girls with their charming accents.

But Broadmoor had only vague recollections of Miss Darcy Sherwood, the elder of the Sherwood sisters.

"Oh, wretched, wretched is our lot!" Anne continued. "To think that we could be turned out of our own home by that piece of jade."

"That will not happen," Broadmoor pronounced, setting down his glass. Perhaps Anne was right and he should have taken more of an interest in Edward's affairs.

Relief washed over Anne. "How grand you are, Radcliff! If anyone can save our family, it is you! Your father and mother, bless their souls, would have been proud of you."

His thoughts turned to the woman upstairs. Penelope would not be pleased, but he meant to have his horse saddled immediately. His first visit would be to Mr. Thornsdale, a trusted friend of the family, to confirm the facts of what Anne had relayed to him.

And if Anne had the truth, his second visit would be to Miss Darcy Sherwood.

That wicked harlot.

CHAPTER TWO

No one noticed the gentleman sitting in the dark corner of Mrs. Tillinghast's modest card-room. If they had, they would have immediately discerned him to be a man of distinction, possibly a member of the *ton*. His attire was simple but elegant, his cravat sharply tied, his black leather boots polished to perfection. On his right hand, he wore a signet bearing the seal of his title, the Baron Broadmoor.

Upon closer inspection, they would have found the edition of *The Times* that he held before him and pretended to read was over two days old. Why he should be reading the paper instead of participating in the revelry at the card tables was a mystery unto itself. No one came to Mrs. Tillinghast's gaming house to *read*. They came for three distinct reasons: the friendly tables, the surprisingly good burgundy, and a young woman named Miss Darcy Sherwood.

That wicked harlot.

Somewhere in the room a clock chimed the midnight hour, but the wine had been flowing freely for hours, making her partakers deaf to anything but the merriment immediately surrounding them. From the free manner in which the men and women interacted—one woman seemed to have her arse permanently affixed to the lap of her beaux while another boasted a décolletage so low her nipples peered above its lace trim—the Baron wondered that the gaming house might not be better deemed a brothel.

The only person to eventually take notice of Radcliff Barrington was a flaxen-haired beauty, but after providing a curt answer to her greeting without even setting down his paper, he was rewarded with an indignant snort and a return to his solitude. He rubbed his temple as he recalled how he had left the hysterics of his aunt only to be met upstairs with a tirade from his mistress about the impolitesse and hauteur of Anne Barrington to come calling at the residence of a woman she had hitherto acknowledged with the barest of civilities.

After noting that the waistcoat upon the chair had disappeared upon his return, Broadmoor had turned the full weight of his stare upon Penelope, who instantly cowered and, upon hearing that he was to take his leave, professed that naturally he must attend to the affairs of his family with due speed.

A lyrical laughter transcending the steady murmur of conversation and merrymaking broke into his reverie. It was followed by a cacophony of men exclaiming "Miss Sherwood! Miss Sherwood!" and begging of said personage to grace their gaming table of faro or piquet. Peering over his paper, Broadmoor paused. For a moment, he could not reconcile the woman he beheld to the devil incarnate his aunt had described.

Miss Darcy Sherwood had a distinct loveliness born of her mixed heritage. The gown of fashion, with its empire waist and diaphanous skirt, accentuated her curves. The pale yellow dress, which Broadmoor noted was wearing thin with wear, would have looked unexceptional on most Englishwomen, but against her caramel toned skin, it radiated like sunshine.

Her hair lacked shine or vibrancy in color, but the abundance of tight full curls framed her countenance with both softness and an alluring unruliness. However, it was her bright brown eyes, fringed with long curved lashes, and her luminous smile that struck Broadmoor the most. It was unlike the demure turn at the corners of the lips that he was accustomed to seeing.

He felt an odd desire to whisk her away from the cads and hounds that descended upon her like vultures about a kill. But this protective instinct was shortlived when he saw her choice of companions was one James Newcastle.

Miss Sherwood could not have been much more than twenty-five years of age. Newcastle was nearly twice that, and it was all but common knowledge that he buggered his female servants, most of whom were former slaves before the British court finally banned the practice from the Isles. But then, the man was worth a hefty sum, having benefitted tremendously from his business in the American slave trade.

"A song, Miss Sherwood!" cried Mr. Rutgers. "I offer twenty quid for the chance to win a song."

"Offer fifty and I shall make it a *private performance*," responded Miss Sherwood gaily as she settled at the card table.

She was no better than a common trollop, Broadmoor decided, trading her favors for money. He felt his blood race to think that the fate of his family rested in the hands of such a hussy. He could tell from the Swifterness with which she shuffled, cut, and then dealt the cards that she spent many hours at the tables. Her hands plied the cards like those of an expert pianist over the ivories. He was surprised that her hands could retain such deftness after watching her consume two glasses of wine within the hour and welcome a third. He shook his head.

Shameless.

Broadmoor felt as if he had seen enough of her unrefined behavior, but something about her compelled him to stay. Miss Sherwood, who had begun slurring her words and laughing at unwarranted moments as the night wore on, seemed to enjoy the attentions, but despite her obvious inebriation, her laughter sounded forced. There were instances when he thought he saw sadness in her eyes, but they were fleeting, like illusions taunting the fevered brain.

It was foolhardy for a woman to let down her guard in such company. She would require more than the assistance of the aging butler and scrawny page he had noticed earlier to keep these hounds at bay. Could it possibly be a sense of chivalry that obliged him to stay even as he believed that a woman of her sort deserved the fate that she was recklessly enticing? His family and friends would have been astounded to think it possible.

"My word, but Lady Luck has favored you tonight!" Rutgers exclaimed to Miss Sherwood, who had won her fourth hand in a row.

"Miss Sherwood has been in Her Company the whole week," remarked Mr. Wempole, a local banker, "since winning the deed to Brayten. I daresay you may soon pay off your debts to me."

Broadmoor ground his teeth at the mention of his late uncle's estate and barely noticed the flush that had crept up Miss Sherwood's face.

"It was quite unexpected," Miss Sherwood responded. "I rather think that I might—"

"That were no luck but pure skill!" declared Viscount Wyndham, the future Earl of Brent.

"Alas, I have lost my final pound tonight and have no hope of winning a song from Miss Sherwood," lamented Rutgers.

"I would play one final round," said Miss Sherwood as she

shuffled the deck, the cards falling from her slender fingers with a contented sigh, "but brag is best played with at least a fourth."

"Permit me," said Broadmoor, emerging from the shadows. He reasoned to himself that he very much desired to put the chit in her place, but that could only partly explain why he was drawn to her table.

She raised an eyebrow before appraising him with a gaze that swept from the top of his head to the bottom of his gleaming boots. "We welcome all manner of strangers—especially those with ample purses."

Brazen jade, Broadmoor thought to himself as he took a seat opposite her and pulled out his money.

"S'blood," the schoolboy groused immediately after the cards were dealt and reached for a bottle of burgundy to refill his glass.

Glancing up from the three cards he held, Broadmoor found Miss Sherwood staring at him with an intensity that pinned him to his chair. The corners of her mouth turned upward as her head tilted ever so slightly to the side. Looking at her sensuously full lips, Broadmoor could easily see how she had all the men here in the palm of her hand. He wondered, briefly, how those lips would feel under his.

"Our cards are known to be friendly to newcomers," she informed him. "I hope they do not fail to disappoint."

He gave only a small smile. She thought him a naïve novice if she expected him to reveal anything of the hand that he held.

Darcy turned her watchful eye to Newcastle, whose brow was furrowed in deep concentration. She leaned towards him—her breasts nearly grazing the top of the table—and playfully tapped him on the forearm. "Lady Luck can pass you by no longer for surely your patience will warrant her good graces."

Radcliff tried not to notice the two lush orbs pushed and separated above her bodice. He shifted uncomfortably in his seat for despite his inclination to find himself at odds with anything Anne said, he was beginning to believe his aunt. Miss Sherwood possessed a beauty and aura that was like the call of Sirens, luring men to their doom. His own cock stirred with a mind of its own.

His slight movement seemed to catch her eye instantly, but she responded only by reaching for her glass of wine. After taking a long drink, she slammed the glass down upon the table. "Shall we make our last round for the evening the most dramatic, my dears? I shall offer a song—and a kiss…"

A murmur of excitement mixed with hooting and hollering waved over the room.

"…worth a hundred quid," she finished.

"S'blood," the schoolboy grumbled again after opening his purse to find he did not have the requisite amount. He threw his cards onto the table with disgust and grabbed the burgundy for consolation.

Newcastle pulled at his cravat, looked at his cards several times, before finally shaking his head sadly. Miss Sherwood fixed her gaze upon Radcliff next. He returned her stare and fancied that she actually seemed unsettled for the briefest of moments.

Almond brown. Her eyes were almond brown. And despite their piercing gaze, they seemed to be filled with warmth—like the comforting flame of a hearth in winter. Broadmoor decided it must be the wine that leant such an effect to her eyes. How like the Ironies in Life that she should possess such loveliness to cover a black soul.

"Shall we put an end to the game?" Miss Sherwood asked.

"As you please," Broadmoor replied without emotion. Her Siren's call would not work on him. "I will see your cards."

He pulled out two additional hundreds, placing the money on the table with a solemn deliberation that belied his eagerness.

Smiling triumphantly, Miss Sherwood displayed an ace of hearts, a king of diamonds, and a queen of diamonds.

"Though I would have welcomed a win, the joy was in the game," Newcastle said. "I could not derive more pleasure than in losing to you, Miss Sherwood."

Miss Sherwood smiled. "Nor could I ask for a more gallant opponent."

She reached for the money in the middle of the table, but Broadmoor caught her hand.

"It is as you say, Miss Sherwood," he said and revealed a running flush of spades. "Your cards are indeed friendly to newcomers."

For the first time that evening, Broadmoor saw her frown, but she recovered quickly. "Then I presume you will hence no longer be a stranger to our tables?"

Broadmoor was quiet as he collected the money.

"Beginner's luck," the schoolboy muttered.

Newcastle turned his attention to Broadmoor for the first time. "Good sir, I congratulate you on a most remarkable win. I am James

Newcastle of Newcastle and Holmes Trading. Our offices are in Liverpool, but you may have heard of the company nonetheless. I should very much like to increase your winnings for the evening by offering you fifty pounds in exchange for Miss Sherwood's song and, er, kiss."

"I believe the song went for fifty and the kiss a hundred," Broadmoor responded.

"Er—yes. A hundred. That would make it a, er, hundred and fifty."

"I am quite content with what I have won. Indeed, I should like to delay no longer my claim to the first of my winnings."

"Very well," said Miss Sherwood cheerfully as she rose. "I but hope you will not regret that you declined the generous offer by Mr. Newcastle."

She headed towards the pianoforte in the corner of the room, but Broadmoor stopped her with his words.

"In *private*, Miss Sherwood."

In contrast to her confident manners all evening, Miss Sherwood seemed to hesitate before flashing him one of her most brilliant smiles. "Of course. But would you not care for a supper first? Or a glass of port in our dining room?"

"No."

"Very well. Then I shall escort you to our humble drawing room."

Broadmoor rose from his chair to follow her. From the corner of his eye, he saw Newcastle looking after them with both longing and consternation. As he passed out of the gaming room, he heard Rutgers mutter, "Lucky bloody bastard."

For a moment Broadmoor felt pleased with having won the game and the image of his mouth claiming hers flashed in his mind. What would her body feel like pressed to his? Those hips and breasts of hers were made to be grabbed...

But hers was a well traversed territory, he reminded himself. Based on his inquiries into Miss Sherwood, the woman changed lovers as frequently as if they were French fashion, and her skills at the card table were matched only by her skills in the bedchamber. The men spoke in almost wistful, tortured tones regarding the latter and often with an odd flush in the cheeks that Broadmoor found strange— and curious.

As with the card-room, the drawing room was modestly furnished.

Various pieces were covered with black lacquer to disguise the ordinary quality of their components. A couple giggling in the corner took their leave upon the entry of Miss Sherwood, who closed the door behind him. Sitting down on a sofa that looked as if it might have been an expensive piece at one time but that age had rendered ragged in appearance, he crossed one long leg over another and watched as she went to sit down at the spinet.

Good God, even the way she walked made him warm in the loins. The movement accentuated the flare of her hips and the curve of her rump, neither of which her gown could hide. And yet she possessed a grace on par with the most seasoned ladies at Almack's. She did not walk as much as *glide* towards the spinet.

"Do you care for Mozart?" she asked.

"As you wish," he replied.

She chose an aria from *Le Nozze di Figaro*. The opera buffa with its subject of infidelity and its satirical underpinnings regarding the aristocracy seemed a fitting choice for her. Save for her middling pronunciation of Italian, Miss Sherwood might have done well as an opera singer. She sang with force, unrestrained. The room seemed too small to hold the voice wafting above the chords of the spinet. And she sang with surprising clarity, her fingers striking the keys with precision, undisturbed by the wine he had seen her consume. Despite her earlier displays of inebriation, she now held herself well, and he could not help but wonder if the intoxication had not all been an act.

"My compliments," he said when she had finished. "Though one could have had the entire opera performed for much less than fifty pounds, I can understand why one would easily wager such an amount for this privilege."

"Thank you, but you did so without ever having heard me sing," she pointed out.

She wanted to know why, but he said simply, "I knew I would win."

Her brows rose at the challenge in his tone. The work of the devil could not always prevail. He ought bestir himself now to broach the matter that had compelled him here, but he found himself wanting to collect on the second part of his winnings: the kiss.

She rose from her bench, and his pulse pounded a faster beat. She smiled with the satisfaction of a cat that had sprung its trap on a mouse. "Would you care to test your confidence at our tables some more?"

"Are the bets here always this intriguing?" he returned.

"If you wish," she purred as she stood behind a small decorative table, a safe distance from him.

She began rearranging the flowers in a vase atop the table. "How is it you have not been here before?"

The teasing jade. If she did not kiss him soon, he would have to extract it for himself.

"I did not know its existence until today."

She studied him from above the flowers with a candor and length that no proper young woman would dare, but he did not mind her attempts to appraise him.

"You are new to London?"

Feeling restless, he stood up. He did not understand her hesitation. In the card room she had flaunted herself unabashed to any number of men, but now she chose to play coy with him?

"My preference is for Brooks's," he stated simply. "Tell me, Miss Sherwood, do your kisses always command a hundred pounds?"

Her lower lip dropped. His loins throbbed, and he found he could not tear his gaze from the maddening allure of her mouth.

"Do the stakes frighten you?" she returned.

"I find it difficult to fathom any kiss to be worth that price."

"Then why did you ante?"

"As I've said, I knew I would win."

He could tell she was disconcerted, and when he took a step towards her, she glanced around herself as if in search of an escape.

Finding little room to maneuver, she lifted her chin and smiled. "Then care to double the wager?"

"Frankly, Miss Sherwood, for a hundred pounds, you ought to be offering far more than a kiss."

As I am sure you have done, he added silently. He was standing at the table and could easily have reached across it for her.

Her eyes narrowed at him. No doubt she was more accustomed to men who became simpering puppies at her feet. Perhaps she was affronted by his tone. But he little cared. She was too close to him, her aura more inviting than the scent of the flowers that separated them. He was about to avail himself of his prize when a knock sounded at the door.

"Yes?" Miss Sherwood called with too much relief.

The page popped his head into the room. "Mistress Tillinghast requested a word with you, Miss Sherwood."

Miss Sherwood excused herself and walked past him. The room became dreary without her presence. Though at first he felt greatly agitated by the intrusion of the page, he now felt relieved. He had a purpose in coming here. And instead he was falling under her spell. Shaking off the warmth that she had engendered in his body, he forced his mind to the task at hand. Now that he had gathered his wits about him, he shook his head at himself. Was it because he had not completed bedding his mistress that he found himself so easily captivated by Miss Sherwood?

He could see how this place could retain so many patrons and ensnare those of lesser fortitude and prudence like Edward. Even Mr. Thornsdale, whom Broadmoor would have thought more at home at White's than a common gaming hall such as this, revealed that he had known of Edward's increasing losses to Miss Sherwood because he himself was an occasional patron. Mr. Thornsdale had also offered, unsolicited, that he thought Miss Sherwood to be rather charming.

But Broadmoor doubted that he would find her as charming. The fourth Baron Broadmoor had a single objective in seeking out Miss Darcy Sherwood: to wrest from the wicked harlot what rightfully belonged to his family. And he meant to do so at any cost.

Printed in Great Britain
by Amazon